ÉERIE

GIBSON MICHAELS

ARTISTIC ORIGINS

Éerie by Gibson Michaels

Published by Artistic Origins

Book cover composite by Richard Paolinelli

The fairy was obtained from bookcoverzone.com and the ship and planet images are from 123RF.com

Cover design deborahola: https://www.fiverr.com/deborahola

Interior layout by Dawn G. Ireland

ISBN 978-1-940385-40-2 (eBook)

ISBN 978-1-940385-41-9 (paperback)

Please visit Gibson Michaels Amazon page: https://www.amazon.com/Gibson-Michaels/e/B00N5G8VE8/ref=dp_byline_cont_pop_ebooks_1

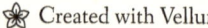 Created with Vellum

OTHER BOOKS BY GIBSON MICHAELS

The Sentience Trilogy

(A Military Space Opera)

Book 1: Storm Clouds Gathering

Book 2: Defying the Prophet

Book 3: Wrath of an Angry God

ACKNOWLEDGMENTS

Sometimes it takes a tragic event to bring out the best in people. Such events let you know who really has your back. These two really had my back when it came to the completion of *Éerie*.

Gibson was not quite finished with *Éerie* when he was taken from us way too early. I will never be able to thank Richard Paolinelli enough for stepping in and completing Gibson's last work. *Éerie* was completed and passed on to Dawn Greenfield Ireland for editing. Dawn was familiar with Gibson's writing style as she did the editing on his earlier works.

Dawn and Richard have been instrumental in getting his last story out the door. I will be indebted to them for their assistance, expert knowledge, opinions and kicking me into gear to do this, when it would have been easier and a lot less painful to let this wonderful story get dusty on the shelf.

Both are wonderful and award winning authors in their own right, it would have been easy for them to concentrate on their own works and careers, but they both were willing to put their projects on hold to help get this work completed. Please consider their work when searching for your next great read.

I would also like to thank the Houston writing community for their support during a very difficult time. Gibson loved being a part of this community.

As Gibson would say, put on a pot of coffee, put your feet up and enjoy the adventure now known as *Éerie*.

Brenda Varner Nichols

PROLOGUE

THE ISLAND OF ÉIRE IS OFTEN CALLED THE EMERALD Isle, as it is a lush, green land shrouded in mists and wonders... forever young, yet ancient beyond imagining. Beautiful beyond description, yet mystical and intriguing, the land of Éire is magical — quite literally. It was probably inevitable that the indescribable beauty of such a wondrous place has so often been spoiled by the preponderance of blood routinely spilled there. After all, even the gods fought each other to near extinction to possess the paradise that is Éire.

The island's old gods, the Tuatha Dé Danann, wielded fantastic powers, yet never mastered their own passions.

They shared all of the inherent weaknesses of character found in any race of man — perhaps worse, for what restraint is there when an infant having a tantrum can literally throw lightning bolts in his fury? But these old gods were so weakened after their titanic struggles against the Fomóraig, a fearsome race of giant, marauding sea-gods... gods of night, death and cold, they retained insufficient strength to repulse the mortal Celtae clans of the Gaels when Éire was invaded yet again.

After only two battles, the Tuatha Dé Danann were forced to divide Eire's land... Eireland, and share it with the victorious mortals. But these Celtae were cleverer than most mortals for they chose the half of the island above ground, while giving the portion below ground to the Tuatha Dé Danann. Thus, the old gods reluctantly withdrew into underground warrens and caves beneath the earth. Although the Tuatha Dé Danann were exiled from the surface, they still loved Éire, and so, vowed to utilize their magic to strengthen and maintain the lush bounty that nature had so blessed the great island with.

Those few remaining Tuatha Dé combined their strength to power their greatest magics to create the *fae*... a hybrid race of demigods having an affinity with nature. Some fae merely gave personality, intelligence and physical embodiments to the raw, elemental forces of nature itself, while others were intricate, delicate beings of high magic. Others were comparatively dull-witted, yet powerful beings having the incredible strength needed to nudge mountains and adjust the flow of rivers and streams, thus ensuring that all of nature's bounty received the blessings of life-giving water. Their work sustained the mystical qualities of a land that, from the beginning, made it so terribly desirable to all forms of life and consistently invoked killing passions of the desire of possession in both mortals and gods alike. Like all sentient creatures, the fae took on a myriad of individual personalities of their own. Some few were benevolent and kindly towards mortals, while others were hostile and fearsome. Most, however, were either ambivalent, or mischievous... delighting in pranks that mystified and mortified dull-witted mortals — mortals who, against all logic, were now masters over this wondrous land.

But while mortals might now hold sway over the surface of Éire, they knew without doubt they weren't alone there — they shared it with the races of the fae, whom the old gods had left behind as guardians, when they retreated from the mortal vale... a constant reminder that humanity's wisdom and dominion were not absolute. Although normally hidden from view, the fae can sometimes be glimpsed at certain times of the year, especially at midsummer, when the áes sidhe, (people of the hills) can sometimes be seen dancing in the moonlight... and whenever mortals and faerie interact, magical things happen.

CHAPTER ONE

If you want your children to be brilliant, read them fairy tales. If you want them to be geniuses, read them more fairy tales.
-- Albert Einstein

The Island of Éire
81 A.D.

ARYN FINNEGAN, OF THE CLAN Ó FIONNAGÁIN, focused down the length of his bronze-tipped hunting arrow and let it fly. He watched with satisfaction as his arrow buried itself in the throat of a black armored invader.

Welcome to Éire... Roman.

The Romans reacted instantly to the kill, scurrying around like disturbed ants. Orders were shouted and ranks began forming up. Two more arrows quickly dispatched as many Romans before he climbed down from the tree he was perched in, to move to a different location. When the arrow barrage paused, some nervous soldiers resumed their attempts to complete a series of three trenches across the entrance of the Drumanagh peninsula.

As he'd expected, the Romans sent a full century of armed legionaries into the forest to kill him. There was actually little danger in that, for Aryn Finnegan was the unknowing master of an art that wouldn't be fully appreciated for another two millennia. His self-made clothing was constructed from the hides of all kinds of small game — an irregularly shaped patchwork of various colors and textures that produced a mottled look that broke up his outline, making him appear to blend into the background. Instead of retreating deeper into the forest as the Romans might have expected, Aryn moved in closer, shifting around a bit to the South.

He climbed to near the top of the tallest tree at the edge of the forest, closest to the Roman camp. A robust ocean breeze caused the treetops to sway, so finding secure seating was precarious. With the top of the tree whipping back and forth, Aryn found it difficult to wedge himself into a fork where he wouldn't require a handhold. *Never a damned sylph around when you need one.* Just as he finally managed to anchor himself to where he could use both hands to draw his bow...

POP! — "What are you doing up here, Aryn?"

The unexpected appearance by the tiny pixie, who had recently taken to plaguing his life, startled him so badly that he overbalanced, almost pitching completely out of the tree. Barely catching himself with the fist of his bow hand, Aryn regained his balance and hissed, "Damn it, Rhoslyn! You scared the shite out of me."

The pixie sniffed. "No, I didn't... I smell no excrement."

Aryn sighed and shook his head. Faeries could be infuriatingly literal, not understanding human idioms at all. "Your popping in unexpectedly startled me so badly, I almost killed myself, falling out of this tree."

"*Pfft*... I wouldn't have let you fall, silly. I would have caught you."

Rhoslyn was a flower faerie of the rose family whose name meant, "Lovely Rose." Dressed in the deep green of rose leaves, she had brilliant red hair — not the orangey color called "red" in humans, but the brilliant red of the flower she was named after. Only the size of Aryn's index finger, it was difficult to see her pointed elfin ears and transparent, luminescent wings, even after she alighted on the palm of his hand.

It was easy to forget that Rhoslyn's appearance was entirely of her own choosing — a magical glamour of sorts, that she wore about her like people wear clothing. Aryn knew that her ability to fly came from her inherent magical abilities... *not* from those tiny pixie wings. She could have made herself appear the same size he was, if she'd so wished... or even as big as a house. Whether she was actually capable of catching a full-grown man falling out of the top of a tree wasn't something he wanted to test for himself.

"What are you doing here?"

"I got bored and began wondering what my friend Aryn might be up to these days. That's what I was just asking you about. Why are you so high up in this oak tree? Oak trees don't produce anything mortals consider edible. You'd be much better served climbing a walnut, beech or cherry tree."

Aryn rolled his eyes and replied, "I'm not searching for nuts or berries. I'm killing Roman invaders."

"Romans? Isn't that what Finvarra called the invaders that he prophesied were coming?"

"Yes, they're here now — so I'm killing them."

"*Humpf,* good luck with that. The way this tree is swaying in this wind, even *you* might find it difficult to hit anything from up here."

Rhoslyn somehow maintained her position, standing on Aryn's upturned palm, despite the motion of the tree and the resultant jostling of his hand. Aryn figured it must be something else he didn't understand about how faerie magic worked.

"Yes. Too bad you're not a sylph, so you could calm this wind down for me. That would be helpful."

"You *wish* that I was a sylph?" Rhoslyn sniffed — miffed. "I nurture the most beautiful flowers in all creation, and yet you wish I was an air faerie? Be careful Aryn, that's coming awfully close to an unforgivable insult to a pixie."

"I didn't say I wish that *you* were a sylph, but flowers aren't what I need right now. What I need is for this damned wind to settle down. You can't do that, can you?"

Rhoslyn's indignation morphed into a pout. "Well... no," she finally admitted sadly. "My powers cannot affect the wind, but maybe I could find you a sylph who could help you with that."

"I would appreciate it, and while you're at it, you might alert Queen Úna that the Romans have landed here, so she can pass the word on to Kyla. Can you remember this exact location... the Drumanagh peninsula?"

Rhoslyn snorted. "Are you trying to insult me again? Of course, I can remember."

The pixie disappeared with a soft pop. *Damn, she disappeared so suddenly, I never had a chance to ask her to fetch me more arrows from my cave.*

The swaying motion of the tree prevented him from focusing on a specific target, so Aryn just watched as Roman legionaries spread out and entered the forest looking for him. Only a couple at the far-right end of their line came anywhere close, and he watched them pass to either side of his lofty, swaying perch. Both carried their rectangular, rounded-edge shields close to their bodies, glancing up, as well as around, in search of their prey, but he was much too far up to be easily spotted from the ground.

Aryn watched in frustration as the sun sank lower and lower in the sky, but still that damnable wind kept up, unabated. Just as he had about decided to abandon his perch and search out another that didn't try to throw him like an unbroken horse... *POP!*

There beside him appeared a white-haired sylph he'd never seen before. She was about twice as large as Rhoslyn, dressed in a white diaphanous gown, having silvery, nearly transparent, butterfly wings with steaks of light-blue in them, and a pattern of medium blue spots. Looking closely, Aryn could just make out that her hair wasn't totally white, but also had faint streaks of light blue in it. Sylphs were air-faeries who generally inhabited the high reaches of mountainous areas and were generally what humans envisioned when thinking about the fae.

"You must be Aryn Ó *Fionnagáin*," said the sylph, as she looked him up and down, critically. "My name is Eupnea. Rhoslyn the pixie told me that I'd find you up a tree here."

"Nice to meet you, Eupnea. Can you calm this damned wind, please?"

Eupnea's facial expression changed in a flash, from mild annoyance to a thundercloud. "*Damned* wind? You dare to curse the wind to the face of an air faerie?"

"No! — Wait, don't go... please."

The sylph looked at him with the same disgust she might have shown a slug. "Rhoslyn told me that you sometimes suffered from a lack of decorum. She didn't mention that you have the manners of swine."

"My manners were quite good enough for Queen Úna," Aryn replied defensively.

"You've met, Queen Úna?"

Aryn nodded. "And her husband, Finvarra."

Eupnea looked startled at that revelation. "I'm surprised you survived an encounter with one of the old gods. They are not known for showing tolerance to discourteous mortals."

"I almost didn't... survive it, that is."

Eupnea snorted. "I don't doubt it. Perhaps you should learn some tact when dealing with faeries, before someone actually turns you into something viler than your own behavior."

"Look, I'm sorry. I've just been swinging around in the top of this tree for so long it's made me a bit grumpy."

"Rhoslyn requested that I come here to help you. I normally don't have anything to do with mortals. As an air faerie, I am a subject of King Paralda and Queen Vayu."

"Yet, are not both of them subservient to the demi-goddess, Kyla, daughter of Finvarra and Úna?"

"That is above my station. I do not concern myself with the doings of royalty or gods."

"But Rhoslyn did send you here to help me, right?"

Eupnea rolled her eyes, but finally said, "Rhoslyn will owe me a boon for this. What is it you require, human?"

"Can you calm this wind... please?"

With a mere wave of Eupnea's hand, the brisk wind died abruptly. "What else?"

Aryn sighed with relief as his unruly seat settled beneath him. "Nothing else... that's all I needed. Thank you."

"That's all? You sent Rhoslyn to fetch me all this way, just to calm the wind here? Why?"

"I need to kill Romans."

"What are Romans?"

Aryn pointed toward the Roman camp, where beached galleys continued unloading troops and horses. Tents were being erected and supplies stacked near field kitchens and mobile smithies. Legionaries were back to digging their defensive trenches across the entire mouth of the Drumanagh peninsula. Officers were shouting unintelligible orders, which the men obeyed promptly with unerring dispatch — quite unlike the chronic arguments and bickering so common within the Celtae tribes of Aryn's people.

"Those invaders coming in from the sea are Romans."

Eupnea gawked at the unusual spectacle before her. "So many..."

"Yes, now excuse me while I get back to killing some of them."

The sylph snorted audibly. "What can one man do against an entire army?"

"I can annoy them and slow their progress. Watch."

Aryn loosed a quick volley of four arrows in rapid succession, the last in flight before the first struck home. Four soldiers digging in the trench closest to Aryn's treetop perch toppled in quick progression. Their comrades dropped onto their bellies, shouting warnings and scanning the edge of the forest in search of the threat. Legionaries digging the second entrenchment also dropped to the ground, but when no further arrows were forthcoming, the centurion in charge goaded his men into resuming their task. Little further digging was accomplished after Aryn's next arrow killed a man working in the third trench.

Eupnea noticed that Aryn's quiver was now half-empty. "You have more arrows hidden nearby?"

"No, I'll have to return to my cave to get more after these run out. I figure I can keep them pinned down until dark and then go get more."

"You can navigate this forest in the dark?"

"Easily, I live here. This forest is my home."

The sylph crossed her arms and tapped one tooth in concentration, as if in deep thought. "Would a storm help to delay them, until you can return?"

"Most assuredly, but why would you volunteer to help me in this? Queen Úna will surely send Kyla to rally the fae against these invaders, but you said yourself, sylphs answer to different rulers."

"If these invaders of yours truly represent a threat to our island, King Paralda and Queen Vayu will not wish to be seen as slacking in aiding the land's defense."

"I thought you said that you didn't concern yourself with the doings of royalty," Aryn said with a grin.

"Don't be flinging my own words back into my face, mortal," Eupnea snapped. "It certainly wouldn't hurt my standing if I acted proactively on this. Besides, frustrating those other mortals sounds like fun."

"Ah, now *that* I can believe!" Aryn laughed softly.

Ignoring his amused smirk, she continued. "I'll go fetch Aral and return here."

"Who is Aral?"

"Aral is an air elemental. He is much less intelligent, but far more powerful than a sylph. Whatever small storm I can create, he can enlarge into a gale of truly monstrous proportions."

"Go then with my thanks, little sylph. I will be in your debt for any additional delay that you and Aral can impose upon these invaders, giving the clans more time to gather their war bands together."

Eupnea gave Aryn another probing look. "Aye, and it's good that you realize that. Perhaps there is hope for you after all, mortal. Farewell." And with that, she was gone in an eye blink.

Aryn continued annoying the Romans the rest of the afternoon, periodically picking them off one or two at a time while hidden amongst the trees of the forest bordering the Roman landing site. In the dwindling twilight just before full dark, he watched with satisfaction as his last arrow buried itself in the right eye of a Roman centurion. Aryn looked sadly down at his now empty quiver. He could now only watch as the Romans continued disembarking from their ships. Their largest and grandest ship hadn't come all the way to the mainland but unloaded on the isle of Reachrainn, just offshore.

That must be where their leaders are setting up camp... cowards.

Aryn felt his way down from the top of the tree he had occupied for most of the afternoon and stood silently in the semi-dark at its base, listening for any sounds that might reveal the locations of the Roman soldiers sent into the forest after him. Navigating by instinct and the meager light of a quarter-moon, he maneuvered among the trees as silently as any nocturnal predator on the prowl. Darting from tree to tree, he paused at each one to allow his faint shadow to blend in with the thousands of others all around him. Full dark eventually revealed thousands of stars over-head, glistening in all their majestic glory through holes in the forest canopy.

Nearing the blind that he had hastily built for his horse earlier, he distinctly heard the soft snap of a fallen twig, close ahead. Aryn froze against a tree, listening intently for any additional signs of whoever, or whatever was so near to him. One of the Roman legionaries hunting for the elusive archer had evidently wandered a bit too far away from his fellows... and just a little too close to where Aryn's horse was hidden. As the Roman soldier slowly crept by, oblivious to his crouching presence, Aryn easily slipped directly behind him.

Aryn's horse chose just that moment to make a slight wuffling sound, which immediately caused the Roman soldier to freeze. This afforded Aryn an opportunity to cover the man's mouth with his left hand, snapping his head back, while cutting the invader's throat with the sharp bronze dagger held in his right. Emitting only a slight gurgle, the Roman slumped as he bled out and Aryn silently lowered the man's body to the ground. He then stripped the Roman of armor, weapons and anything else that might be of value to the merchants among his people.

Aryn greeted *Frisky*, his strawberry-roan stallion, with a pat on the nose and one of the carrots he kept in a saddlebag for just that purpose. "Good boy," Aryn whispered. "You remained totally quiet until you sensed I was near... Kyla trained you well."

After allowing the horse to take the carrot and then nuzzle his hand for more, Aryn stowed the Roman armor into a large sack he had with him. He then tucked the short sword into his belt and tied the soldier's *scutum* – a rectangular rounded-edge shield designed to curve back around the soldier, over his horse's rump.

He mounted up and wondered if he would receive enough in trade for all this Roman gear to make hauling it all home worth the effort. He then negotiated the maze of twisting turns that he'd installed at the entrance to the blind. Aryn needed more arrows, and that required him to return to the hidden cave that served as his primary residence.

Aryn quickly outdistanced the Romans who were still stumbling about the forest on foot, looking for him in the dark. When he felt confident he was well away from the Romans and no longer had to remain totally vigilant, Aryn marveled at the stark beauty of the surrounding forest. His roan had an uncanny ability to retrace its steps so little guidance necessary. Frisky always seemed to know his way back to the hay and oats stored in that cave, so memories flooded back as his mind emptied. Both good and bad, they simply floated into him of their own accord.

ARYN LIVED ALONE in the forest, which provided him with almost everything he needed. He recently finished trading some of his forest bounty to merchants in the coastal village of Loughshinny, just north of the Roman landing site, when he first saw the square, striped sails of low-slung ships bearing banks of oars protruding along their sides. *Galleys. Warships.*

Traders had brought word of Roman legions subjugating the Gaelic tribes in Britannia, so everyone on the island knew what to watch for. Any other Celtae would have scurried back to sound the alarm, so the local clan warlords could gather their warriors to repel the invasion, but Aryn had merely hid his horse.

One of the few constants among the hundreds of Gaelic clans that inhabited the island of Éire was that they fought among themselves almost as much for sport, as for gain. Aryn had been the only one to see the Roman fleet as it approached the eastern shore of the island, but he felt neither obligation, nor allegiance towards any of the clans who inhabited the Emerald Isle, as most had shunned him all of his life.

Aryn wasn't quite a pariah, but even members of his own family often felt distinctively uncomfortable around him, even as a child. Not that he'd ever been mischievous or misbehaved. Quite the contrary... Aryn had always been pleasant, and extremely well behaved. Possibly a bit too well behaved, when compared to the rowdy, boisterous conduct considered a "normal" for boys among the Celtae clans.

Even his chosen weapon... a *hunting* weapon made him an object of derision among his people. Gaelic warriors invariably preferred close, hand-to-hand, and ideally, one on one, individual combat. Swords, axes, and spears were the main weapons the Celtae used. They saw killing an enemy from afar as cowardly, thus bows and other ranged weapons were primarily used only for hunting. Otherwise their use, even in wartime, was rare.

Aryn thought their refusal to kill enemies from afar was just stupid. He had always been unnaturally gifted with a bow. At the age of seven, he had taken his little half-size children's bow on his first real hunting expedition with his father, grandfather and six of his grandfather's brothers. One of his great-uncles, walking the far end of the line, scared up a quail that took flight directly away from Aryn's relatives. A few of the men got off shots that missed, but several seconds after the last arrow was fired, the madly flapping bird suddenly veered towards the ground. The men cheered heartily at the nearly impossible long-range shot, but when they reached the kill, all were stunned to see that it was an undersized child's arrow impaled in the quail's breast.

Aryn had been at the far end of the line, more than 200 yards from where the bird fell. All of the men immediately tested Aryn's little half-size bow, but none managed to launch an arrow even half that distance... even using a longer, full-length adult's arrow. Aryn had done the impossible and the adults eyed him with grave reservation, sharing fearful whispers amongst themselves all the way home. Never again was Aryn invited to accompany the men of his family on another hunting trip.

Aryn Finnegan had been unusually beautiful as a babe... notably different from the very moment of his birth. He entered the world with an incredible amount of coal-black hair that extended down to the middle of his back, with eyes the color of a bright blue sky. It was the striking contrast between the sheer blackness of his hair and brilliance of his eyes that marked him as unusual, for all of the males of his father's line for generations all shared the trait of red or blond hair.

Some had thought him a changeling, but that talk faded as Aryn continued healthy well past the age that a true changeling would have sickened and died. Others called him "an old soul," as, except for the pitch of his young voice, he had never really spoken like a child. Few were the times that he spouted nonsensical mouthing's to get attention. Aryn had rarely spoken unless prompted, but when he did, his conversation had displayed incredible wisdom and maturity, far beyond his years. Most just considered him to be *unnatural*, preferring to maintain a fair distance away from him.

Inexplicable things routinely happened around Aryn...

or didn't, as the case may be. Even as a babe Aryn hadn't cried and fussed like most newborns — contentedly cooing, gurgling and laughing for the gods only knew what reason. It wasn't surprising that folks thought the baby odd. After all, even his own mother couldn't see the pixies who danced in the air above the baby's face, and kept him continually entertained.

CHAPTER TWO

If I'm trying to sleep, the ideas won't stop. If I'm trying to write, there appears a barren nothingness.
-- Carrie Latet

The Planet Cælius
3231 A.D.

BRIAN STEELE YAWNED AND STRETCHED HIS ARMS. He'd originally taken to writing fantasy novels as a form of personal therapy — a way he could take out his job frustrations on imaginary bad guys, if not the real ones that he dealt with every day. A mere 4,300 words wasn't going to cut it, as he now still had to do the same another twenty-five times.

Notified that a publisher was interested in purchasing his "therapy" had been a godsend, or so he'd initially thought, but here he was, right back to wrestling with corporate alligators again. The editors at the publishing house wanted this changed and that changed. So many changes were demanded, he despaired of even recognizing his own work when it finally made it onto his electronic book display.

His wife Deidre had initially been overjoyed when she first heard the news, imagining mansions and a lifestyle among the idle rich. But this being his first published work, he'd only been given a minuscule advance, so now they had to wait for royalty checks, based on actual sales, to get any more money. Getting Deidre to finally come back down to earth had taken some doing, but now Brian was faced with another problem... his publishing company wanted him to write a Celtic fantasy.

This should have been cause for rejoicing, but Brian didn't have enough cash to live on while devoting all of his time to writing another novel. Writing his first book had been done at his own sedate pace... a dib here and a drab there, as he was inspired and found time. With a publishing contract now dictating his future deadlines, there would be none of that "sedate pace" stuff anymore. Brian had never attempted to write under time constraints before. God help him if he ran into a nasty case of writer's block, where his imaginary friends stopped talking to him for a while.

What to do?

Instead of reducing his stress, becoming a published author had just added to it. What he really needed to get his creative juices flowing was a lengthy space flight somewhere. It didn't really matter where. The journey itself would be enough. He just needed another long trip in the *Twilight Zone.*

Not everyone adjusted well to traveling within tachyon space. No one knew exactly what caused the strange phenomenon that many people had to endure while traveling faster than light. Some people saw nothing out of the ordinary, while others reacted so violently they had to be sedated for the entire trip. Most, however, had a personal experience that fell somewhere those two extremes.

Those blessed few who experienced nothing at all unusual were highly sought after by both the military and transportation industries, as crew personnel aboard spacecraft. Those who required sedation usually found themselves planet-bound wherever they first landed, as very few wanted to subject themselves to the terrors of space flight a second time. Besides, the transportation companies always charged for the medications, life-support and personal services required to transport someone with a known history of *freaking* during space travel.

Unfortunately, no one had yet been able to come up with any method for testing how people might react to the experience, without actually taking them into tachyon space itself. First-time interstellar space travelers were always monitored closely and the government's Department of Transportation kept detailed records on all space travelers, which fully documented their reactions to FTL space travel.

Some people believed that tachyon space was where spirits of the dead roamed and could interact with the living. Those who leaned towards that philosophy tended to call tachyon space, the "Haunted Dimension," as they believed it was inhabited by ghosts. Others claimed that idea was just a bunch of spiritualistic claptrap and the strange "visitations" people experienced were the result of *something* — call it an unknown energy field of some sort, that existed there, which stimulated portions of the human brain in strange ways, causing vivid hallucinations.

There seemed to be at least circumstantial evidence

that lent credence to that second viewpoint, as a logical explanation for what people experienced. Animals didn't usually become overly agitated during space flight, and no two people "saw" exactly the same thing... even those in close proximity within the same compartment at the time. Veteran spacers usually referred to tachyon space where they encountered all of those eerie experiences as the *Twilight Zone,* after an ancient, 2-D, pre-holovision series that told tales of bizarre and inexplicable happenings.

Brian now wondered if he were actually attempting to write a fantasy manuscript while traveling within tachyon space, would his "experiences" run parallel where his conscious thoughts were being focused? A healthy dose of hallucinations, focused along those specific lines, might be just what he needed to kick start his creativity and help him to get his next project written within the timeframe demanded by his publisher. He started thinking about how he might get himself aboard a lengthy space flight, without having to pay the exorbitant passenger fares charged by the regularly scheduled spacelines. *Hmm?*

CHAPTER THREE

A mermaid found a swimming lad
Picked him for her own,
Pressed her body to his body,
Laughed; and plunging down
Forgot in cruel happiness
That even lovers drown.
-- William Butler Yeats

Musings, along the way back to Aryn's Cave
A.D. 81

IT HAD BEEN SEVERAL YEARS SINCE ARYN LAST HAD cause to kill a man. The first time had been when High King Elim mac Conrach gathered the clans together to repel *Lochlanach* raiders... literally, "men from the land of lochs" — the Gaelic word for Norsemen —

While studying at the high king's university, Aryn finally got past his natural awkwardness around girls and became betrothed to a girl named Máire. He had fully believed her to be the great love of his life, but his education, as well as his love life, had to be put on hold to answer the high king's call for warriors. Many of his classmates were of noble birth, or from families rich enough to exempt them from mandatory service in the high king's army, but Aryn enjoyed neither of those advantages, so at 16 he found himself rudely yanked away from his life and love to march off to war.

He was spared the horrors of hacking at people with a battle-axe due to his skill as an archer, learned while hunting alone during his early years on his grandfather's land. He had first been assigned to the King's Rangers as a scout, but when the *Ovates,* the healing Druids attending the high king's army, became aware of his skills as an herbalist and apothecary, they took away his bow and stuck a mortar and pestle in his hands.

Working with the physicians, grinding medicines and making poultices for the wounded, Aryn availed himself of the opportunity to learn from them, continually asking intelligent and pointed questions. Battles often found the need for surgeons greater than the available number of qualified physicians, so eventually he was deemed skilled enough to treat the wounded and perform primitive surgeries, such as stitching wounds and performing amputations, on his own. Aryn's patients had experienced a similar mortality rate as most of the Ovate Druids, so after saving the life and leg of a noble whose horse had crushed his leg in a fall, the chief physician of the high king's army granted him a license to practice medicine as a lay physician.

Although he became skilled in the use of herbs and minor spells to cure disease in humans and livestock, Aryn had felt no desire to invest in the years of study required to learn the other half of an Ovate Druid's duties — prophecy and divination, reading omens and divining auguries, whether from the entrails of animals, the flight of birds, the shape of clouds or the weather. Nor did he truly believe in the Ovates' claims to be able to travel in time.

Then there was also his ravenous appetite for women that he had to contend with too. During his time in the high king's army, Aryn had once taken leave to get married, but sadly discovered that Máire hadn't waited for him. He was devastated to learn she had inexplicably quit the university and gone back home to Carik on Shannon, in Leitrum, where she'd gone to work for — and on — a non-Druidic lay physician there, becoming the mistress of a married man. Heartbroken, Aryn had sought solace in a mug of ale and the arms of a camp follower... if the truth be known, a lot of mugs of ale, and a *lot* of camp followers.

Aryn had always been unnaturally shy around girls, but the abuse he'd suffered from his female cousins while growing up had bruised his psyche. He was well aware that his newly awakened lust for sex actually stemmed from his need to feel loved, but Máire's betrayal had left him emotionally numb. Unfortunately, that numbness didn't extend to his physical parts. Being around women evoked an intense sexual tension that produced a notable amount of discomfort in his loins that he'd rather avoid, if at all possible. He found that he tended to act stupid around the creatures, like a dog near a bitch in heat.

So at the age of 20, and the war over for the moment, Aryn found himself discharged from the army and again walking the Haunted Forest as he contemplated what to do with the rest of his life. Marriage didn't seem on the horizon, as most of the women anywhere near his own age were married, tavern wenches, war-widows with children, or just too damned ugly for words.

What he'd really wanted was a cozy little cottage somewhere deep in the forest, well away from the distracting and disturbing influence of women, but that wasn't going to happen. Although he was already an accomplished herbalist, apothecary, physician and surgeon, Aryn had never quite gotten around to learning carpentry or stonemasonry — skills he'd needed to build a house. Nor could he delude himself that he'd ever be able to convince anyone else to build him a house in the middle of the dreaded Haunted Forest, even if he'd had the money to pay them... which he didn't.

Aryn's second choice would have been to build himself a house on a plot in the woods near to the farm he'd grown up on as a child, but even that was denied him. His grandfather had taken a bad fall, so he and Aryn's grandmother had sold their land and moved into a little cottage on the outskirts of Tallamore, where he sat idle waiting to die.

Aryn eventually took up residence in a cave hidden deep within the Haunted Forest, from where he supported himself by hunting small game and the occasional deer, for meat. He cured the hides to make his clothing and gathered valuable herbs he found growing throughout the forest. Some of these he dried for trade. Others he ground into medicinal poultices, for which there was always a considerable demand in the remote villages along the edges of the forest, or within clearings along the dirt roads that wound through it. Salt, flour and bronze arrowheads were commodities for which he commonly traded. Technically, this was all part of the high king's land too, but there was little chance of him running afoul of the king's wardens as they too tended to avoid the deep forest areas for fear of the *fae*.

As he rode, Aryn fondly remembered back on that first hunting trip that had so changed his life. He remembered hearing something — a certain something that he hadn't heard in many years... the unmistakable whine of tiny wings, and high-pitched, laughing voices.

～

The Haunted Forest
Fourteen years earlier: 67 A.D

"ARYN Ó FIONNAGÁIN!" cried the tinny, feminine voice of tiny Rhoslyn... a pixie the size of Aryn's index finger. "Tis good to be seeing you again. You be having a different look about you, I'm thinking. Have you been gone long this time?"

Time passed at a more sedate pace for the fae, and the changes in the physical appearances of humans they befriended was a constant source of mystery and delight to them.

"Hello, Rhoslyn! It's good to see you again, too," Aryn replied. "It's been over four years since I was last able to walk this forest. I was called away to war with the high king's army and have just returned."

"War," Rhoslyn *tsk'ed*. "You mortals are always hacking at each other over something, with those horrid cold iron weapons of yours. It's bad enough that you insist on chopping down trees with your axes, but must you hack on each other as well?"

"Now, now, Rhoslyn," Aryn admonished. "Do not pixies protect their territories against encroachments by the sylphs?"

Sylphs were the type of fae most representative of what

humans thought of as "faeries." Although they might appear quite similar in appearance to pixies, sylphs were air-faeries, almost 40% bigger than most pixies. As elements of the air, sylphs were classified as "social, trooping faeries," since they tend to travel freely throughout the countryside in groups, as the mood struck them. Closely related to water sprites and wood nymphs, pixies are highly territorial, regardless of their physical similarities to sylphs.

"Of course, we do," said Rhoslyn. "But sylphs don't invade our territories by the thousands like mortals do. They wander through in small groups of three or twenty, as is the custom of trooping faeries."

"What if they did?" asked Aryn. "What would pixies do if sylphs swarmed your territories in the same numbers as the Norse swarmed the southern shores of Ériu recently?"

"Now you're just being silly," Rhoslyn chided. "The sylph would never invade our territories en masse as the *Lochlanach* do. Are they not fae, as we are? Only mortals behave so irrationally," she laughed.

Aryn sighed. There appeared no way to get a faerie to envision anything hypothetically.

"So, tell me," said Aryn, changing the subject. "How are your local rose-sisters?" Aryn was cautious to say, "local," because if he'd just said "sisters," he'd have been here all month, listening to her talk about her thousands of sisters named for every type and color of flower everywhere. One had to be very careful when speaking with faeries, as they were often infuriatingly "literal" to the point of utter ridiculousness.

"Rhoswen, Rosetta, Rosina and Roxanne are well. They will be sorry to have missed you, but they will be pleased to hear that you asked of them," said Rhoslyn. "I would like to introduce you to one of my close cousins, whom I don't believe you've met before. She's very shy around humans, but as you're part *áes sídhe* yourself, perhaps I can coax her out to meet you."

Aryn was startled by Rhoslyn's passing comment. "What do you mean, I'm part áes sídhe myself?"

Now it was Rhoslyn's turn to look startled. "Didn't your grandmother ever tell you?"

"Tell me what?"

"About what she is... and is not?"

"She's my grandmother. What else is there to tell?"

Rhoslyn giggled and clapped her tiny hands, enraptured with the idea of telling him his grandmother's great secret. "She's not human, Aryn!"

"What do you mean, my grandmother isn't human?"

Now Rhoslyn laughed out loud and clapped her hands with glee. "Oh Aryn, I thought you knew! Your grandmother is one of us. She's a *mulrruhgach...* a female merrow."

Aryn was stunned. The female merrow was also called a sea-maiden (*maighdean mhara*) or simply by the generic term "mermaid" (*murúch*) used to describe females of various subspecies of Merfolk. The male and female merrows were supposedly as different as night and day. Legend had it, the rarely seen male merrows were friendly to mortals, but were hideous creatures with the upper body of a fish, eyes of a pig, a bulbous red nose, long green teeth and a lower body similar to that of a human, but with thin, scaly legs and arms like fins.

Nevertheless, seeing a male was considered good luck, as they were sometimes known to guide ships through thick fogs safely into port. No one knew exactly why these hideous creatures sometimes performed these charitable acts, but reportedly they were fond of brandy that mortals always kept aboard ship. Perhaps the expectancy of a case being tossed down to them by a grateful crew might explain it.

Some innocent souls thought these life-saving acts meant the creatures possessed an affectionate, gentle, and beneficent disposition towards humans, but it could never be safely assumed that and any member of the fae ever felt kindly, or well disposed towards mortals. Like all members of the áes sídhe or faerie races, the inhabitants of *Tir fo Thoinn* (Land Beneath the Waves) have a natural antipathy towards humans. Some legends had it that even the seemingly friendly male merrows actually captured the souls of drowned sailors, storing them in crab pots as they searched wrecked ships along the sea bottom, hunting for cases of lost brandy.

It was the females, however, who were the primary representatives of the race best known to sailors and fishermen alike... both as objects of all-consuming desire and deeply intense fear. They were reported to be the polar opposites of the males with the head and upper body of a beautiful young woman, and a lower body like the tail of a fish. It was said that *mulrruhgach* were not only incredibly beautiful, but also endowed with haunting singing voices that mortal males found irresistible.

Out on the sea, she frolics as wild as she is alluring... sometimes wearing a dark sleeveless cloak that clings about her, partially revealing the voluptuous curves of her body, teasing human males with its implied promises. But the *maighdean mhara* also wield the power to cause rain to fall and storms to stir up great waves — sometimes strong enough to break apart ships at sea or capsize smaller boats. So her presence almost always ensures a storm or other disaster at sea. She doesn't do this out of malice, because to her, this havoc is merely a delightful diversion. But to the sailors and fishermen along the shores of Éire, just seeing a *mulrruhgach* was considered an ill omen, as they are regarded as messengers of doom and death.

It was a love/hate relationship that men had with *murúch,* as it was also said that due to the hideous nature of the males of their race, the *maighdean mhara* often preferred lovers from among human males and could behave quite promiscuously towards a man she desired, becoming a subject of undying love to the man fortunate enough to attract one. So much so, that such a person will do almost anything to stay with them, to the point of death — which unfortunately it often came to.

They were known to allure mortal youths to follow her to her home beneath the waves, where they forever afterwards would live in some enchanted state — or might have, if only the mortal had only possessed a red, feathered *cohuleen druith,* or "little charmed cap," as she did. It was her enchanted *cohuleen druith* that enabled her to breath as she dove beneath the waves and descended towards her home on the sea floor. Entranced mortals attempting to follow soon found themselves drowning, as they tried to breath water.

Maighdean mhara can sometimes be found lounging upon rocks near the seashore, with the seawater glistening on her long green hair like dew, combing her it with delicate hands having soft, thin, white webbing between her fingers. But if a man not of her choosing were to come too near, she dives into the sea, laughing as she escapes. It is said the mulrruhgach must remove their enchanted cap and cloak to exit the water, so if a man can capture her enchanted red cap or cloak, she will not be able to return to the sea without it and may then be persuaded to abandon her life in the sea and marry him.

Once married to a mortal, she is an obedient, if unaffectionate wife. Although she is ever mindful of her husband and her household duties, she never fully adjusts to living on land, so a married murúch laughs rarely. Her greatest emotions simply appear as ones of a quiet caring, but the farther she is from the ocean, the more volatile her temper becomes. While living on land, the female merrow appears little different than any other woman other than the fine, almost unnoticeable webbing between her fingers and toes — and the fact that her feet are somewhat flatter than those of a mortal. Her green hair darkens into an indeterminate color and her skin may appear normal or have fine scales easily mistaken for dry skin. They are said that they have great skills in healing and herbalism — both talents that Aryn's grandmother had always displayed in abundance.

Suddenly, Aryn *knew* what that small package that his grandfather had entrusted to him contained — a package he was sworn not to speak of, to guard with his life and to give to his grandmother unopened after his grandfather's death. *It has to be her cohuleen druith.* When a mulrruhgach finds and dons her enchanted cap and cloak once again, she will recall her past life and will joyfully abandon her home, her children and her mate for the sea. And once back in the sea, she will again regain her youth and beauty that was lost while she dwelt among mortals.

My grandfather wishes me to set her free, after his death.

It was really quite ironic in a way. Aryn's mother had stored the strongbox for him while he was away at university, and still while he was with the army. His mother and his father's mother had never gotten along well, and after his parents' marriage things had gone downhill from there.

After the writ of divorcement was issued, the two were about as close to mortal enemies as he'd ever seen.

To think that my mother had the means to banish her nemesis within her hands all those years and not known it, is hilarious.

"That might actually explain a few things," mused Aryn. "Like why I have always been able to see faeries while those around me cannot."

"Why, of course you can," said Rhoslyn. "You're one of us, silly. We can all see each other so why shouldn't you be able to see us too?"

"Even if what you're telling me about my grandmother is true, that would still make me three-quarters mortal," said Aryn. "I have no fae powers, other than faerie sight, that I know of."

"You do," said Rhoslyn. "Maybe you just haven't discovered them yet."

"So, how do I go about 'discovering' these supposed faerie powers that I'm not sure whether I actually have, or not?" asked Aryn.

Rhoslyn crossed her arms and cradled her chin in one hand as she frowned in deep thought. Suddenly her face brightened and Aryn looked at her expectantly.

"I have no idea!" she exclaimed. "Perhaps one of the faerie queens could answer your question. They are ever so wise."

CHAPTER FOUR

You can't wait for inspiration. You have to go after it with a club.

-- Jack London

Aboard the SS Calypso in the Twilight Zone 3231 A.D.

BRIAN STEELE FINALLY GOT THAT LONG SPACE FLIGHT he needed when he found himself aboard a star-freighter headed out into the fringes of explored space. He'd accepted a temporary employment contract to service an elderly life-support system that he had developed maintenance training for years earlier and was one of the very few still considered fully qualified to maintain one. In addition to actually doing the initial servicing, Brian was also tasked with training the local engineers and technicians on-site at a mining facility on a rather bizarre planet on the outer fringe of explored space... a planet tentatively named *Eerie*. Time would yet tell exactly how strangely appropriate that name would eventually become.

As a paying passenger, he'd had no duties aboard the SS *Calypso*, the outbound freighter he'd booked passage on for the trip out. Interplanetary Exploration and Settlements, Inc., the company that held discovery rights for the planet, and for whom he was working, had paid his passenger fare. Unlike the crew, he had no shipboard duties and so enjoyed the luxury of bunking alone in one of the three private, if tiny, staterooms aboard the freighter. Unlike the luxurious cruise liners that catered to the very rich, the SS *Calypso* offered no shipboard entertainment, but the food was good in the crew's mess.

Unfortunately, his idea about focusing his thoughts on development of his fantasy story possibly influencing the hallucinations he experienced in tachyon space was disappointingly unsuccessful. Not a single Celtic god, fairy, Druid or sword-wielding warrior had shown up to inspire him in the slightest. Whatever it was that actually caused the phenomenon seemed to have an uncooperative mind of its own, as the visions he experienced persevered, oblivious to his desires — propelled blissfully down their own unimaginable paths for their own incomprehensible reasons.

Brian spent almost every waking moment working on his book, but he hadn't been able to finish nearly as much of it as he'd hoped. It certainly wasn't for lack of time... his inspiration just wasn't flowing. Some days he did well to just get a half decent paragraph written, after changing it fifty times. It was frustrating to be so barren of ideas while under deadline. Of course, all those decidedly non-Celtic hallucinations he *had* experienced were admittedly distracting, so he didn't beat himself up over it too badly.

When he finally arrived at Eerie, he'd be back to writing when he could — working around a killer maintenance and training schedule. He could only hope that the logjam in his inspiration would break loose pretty soon. Perhaps it would, with something else to think about besides constantly wrestling with the story. That happened sometimes, when you gave it a rest and allowed your subconscious mind a chance to chew on the problem in the background while the conscious mind was doing something else entirely.

CHAPTER FIVE

Pale Death beats equally at the poor man's gate and at the palaces of kings.

-- Horace

The Roman Command Tent — Isle of Reachrainn
Late May, 81 A.D.

"My lord, Governor."

Gnaeus Julius Agricola, governor of Roman Britannia, looked up from the scroll he had been reading to see General Servius Marius Paterculus, legate of *Legio IX Hispana,* standing at the entrance to his command tent. The legate stood stiffly with his right fist positioned over his heart, in the traditional Roman salute to a superior.

"Have you flushed out that damnable archer yet?" Agricola inquired.

"Our forces have evidently driven the assassin away, my lord. There have been no further deaths from arrows, since

Appius Salvius Varus, a centurion in the sixth cohort, took an arrow through his right eye about two hours ago."

"No further deaths from arrows, you say? How else might an archer kill, besides using arrows?"

"My lord, the body of a legionary from the fourth cohort, which we sent into the forest to flush out the archer was found about an hour ago. His throat had been cut and his body had been stripped of weapons and armor."

"So, this Hibernian not only kills our people, he insults us as well — leaving their bodies in only small clothes. How was it our man managed to get his throat cut without any of the rest of his century becoming aware of it?"

"He'd evidently wandered off by himself. Perhaps he stumbled on the archer's hiding place and the assassin saw him first."

"*Hmpf*, probably just ran out of arrows, more likely. What was the total butcher's bill?"

"We lost eighteen men, including the one with his throat cut."

Agricola frowned. "All dead?"

"All," replied the legate. "That archer is obviously a man of considerable talent with a bow. The first to die was Tribune Vibius Petronius Paterculus... my son. A throat shot, from a range we estimate must have been at least four actus ($\sim$155 yards). The last was a shot through the eye from approximately two actus ($\sim$78 yards) away."

"My condolences for the death of your son, Legate."

"Thank you, my lord. He was a soldier and he died an honorable soldier's death. There is little better he might have attained to in life than to die honorably in service to the emperor."

Agricola nodded in agreement, marveling at the legate's composure. *I'm not sure that I could remain so coldly profes-*

sional if it were my son who had been the first to die on this expedition.

"What was the distance for our furthest casualty?"

"From the nearest edge of the forest... around four and a half actus (~175 yards). A legionary digging at the third trench had removed his helmet to pour part of his water ration over his head — an arrow took him in the left temple."

"Incredible. Has anything at all been discovered besides this archer's uncanny accuracy at unbelievable ranges?"

"Just one, my lord. The arrowheads the archer used were not iron, but made of bronze."

"Bronze? No wonder that archer strived for such difficult head and throat shots. Bronze arrowheads might not have penetrated our men's armor. He might as well have been using flint arrowheads."

"Flint arrowheads would have been just as deadly with this archer's skill."

Agricola stroked his chin as he pondered. *Most of the Celtae tribes in Britannia use iron arrowheads just as we do. So do the Celtae tribes in Gaul. Why would this fellow be using ancient bronze arrowheads?*

"Bring Túathal Techtmar... that Hibernian prince, to me as soon as his galley arrives. Perhaps he can shed some light on why this fantastic archer would be using such inferior arrowheads."

~

Aryn's Cave
Early June, 81 A.D

ARYN PARTED the hanging vines that hid the entrance to his cave like a green waterfall. He led Frisky into the darkened interior and unloaded him before lighting a torch to illuminate his home. He then led the roan stallion into a makeshift stall and hung a grain sack over the horse's head. While Frisky munched oats contentedly, he unsaddled him, grabbed a horse brush and rubbed him down. He then grabbed a wooden bucket to fetch water from the stream-fed pool just outside the cave entrance, and filled a wooden trough within the stall.

Before he did the slightest thing for himself, Aryn also filled a larger wooden trough with fresh, sweet hay, and then knelt down to examine Frisky's hooves for cracks. He checked thoroughly for small rocks that sometimes lodged themselves between the hard outer rim and the soft, recessed quick. When the roan finished the oats, Aryn removed the feedbag and watched as the horse lowered his head to drink from the smaller trough. Aryn's grandfather had taught him from an early age to always care for his animals before tending to his own needs.

This cave had obviously been occupied sometime in the far, distant past, from all the residual magic still working here — probably by one of the old gods of the Tuatha Dé Danann who no longer needed it. Smoke from the torches and cooking fires that Aryn used drifted out through strategically placed holes in the high ceiling. The smoke wasn't visible from the outside, as a thick layer of ground cover vines diffused the smoke to invisibility. *I wonder why rain doesn't drip down through those holes?* Aryn could only attribute that to some kind of faerie magic.

He looked longingly towards the thick mattress filled with a double hand-span of lamb's wool and goose down that rested on an elevated stone shelf at just below waist height. The lambskin blankets Aryn used to keep himself warm during the coldest of winter nights were stored away. Only a thin sheet of linen now covered his bedding, but the two duck-down pillows sang an almost irresistible lullaby to him and he had to literally shake himself free of their spell. He had too much work to do before he could allow himself the luxury of sleeping in his own soft bed again.

He reluctantly decided to forgo another hunting trip to gather fresh game. Usually he would have taken a rabbit or a squirrel during his ride back to the cave, but he'd left all of his arrows buried in the heads of invading Romans. His mouth watered at the mere thought of fresh meat roasting and sizzling over his open cook fire, but there was no time for that. He had to settle for yet another meal of smoked, dried meat that he carried with him during his gathering and trading journeys, just like the ones he'd been eating for several days now.

That's one more thing those Romans will pay for.

He did manage to pan-bake himself fresh bread from meal mixed with a little water, but he lamented how his bronze pans didn't quite crisp the edges as well as the iron pans his mother had used during his youth... little enough to trade in exchange for the residual magic that somehow prevented his food items from spoiling. Aryn spooned a liberal portion of sweet butter onto his bread cake... butter that resolutely refused to turn rancid while inside the cave.

After finishing his meager meal, Aryn washed out the bronze pan and his wooden utensils in the pool outside the cave entrance. He then stripped down for a brisk bath in the cold, clear water. He scrubbed the sweat and grime away using clean, white sand from the bottom of the pool, and then shivered as he dried himself with a linen towel his mother had woven for him. When finally dry, he luxuriated a moment, enjoying the feel of the warmth of the sun on his skin before donning clean small clothes.

That was another wonderment of the magic within this cave — food did not spoil and soiled clothing of any kind, whether it be linen, leather, or skins was always somehow rejuvenated, free of dirt and the smell of sweat, literally overnight. *Too bad whatever cleans my clothes doesn't work on me.* Admittedly, during the winter he sometimes put off bathing a little too long, often becoming rather rank. Understandable when he had to break the ice just to get water from the pool.

Aryn sometimes wondered if a pack of *brownies* might inhabit this cave with him. Legends had it that brownies sometimes took up residence within human cottages and took care of all of the household cleaning chores in exchange for a little bread left out for them. After witnessing the miracle of freshly laundered clothes, Aryn suspected the source and began leaving not only bread, but also honey and milk, as Rhoslyn, the pixie, had told him that brownies absolutely adored honey and milk.

After donning fresh, clean hunting clothes, Aryn packed food, water, medicine, bandages and additional clothing into leather pouches that could be tied to his saddle with leather straps, and set them down next to a clean bedroll. The thought of Rhoslyn reminded him of something else that he had avoided thinking about.

No sense putting it off any longer.

Aryn kneeled down and opened a long trunk, which was here when he first took up residence in this cave. From the bottom, he withdrew a magnificent golden bow and a quiver of coal-black arrows. Just holding that bow again caused Aryn's memory to drift back to another time years ago, and into another great underground barrow.

CHAPTER SIX

The greed of gain has no time or limit to its capaciousness.
Its one object is to produce and consume. It has pity neither
for beautiful nature nor for living human beings. It is
ruthlessly ready without a moment's hesitation to crush
beauty and life out of them, molding them into money.
-- Rabindrenath Tagore

The Planet Eerie
3232 A.D.

EERIE WAS A BARREN, LIFELESS WORLD WITH FANTASTIC mineral wealth, but plagued with strange, fluctuating energy fields of a previously unknown type and undiscovered origin that played havoc with electronic equipment. In fact, all these inexplicable problems had led to the planet's given name, as *Eerie* was the only word to describe the way modern machinery and controls behaved here.

One of Brian Steele's primary on-the-job objectives was to figure out how to prevent these unusual energy fields from interfering with the operations of the life-support system he was tasked with maintaining. He wasn't overly concerned about it — he'd faced and overcome a gauntlet of electromagnetic noise and interference problems over the course of his career.

This would be his first trip to a planet having a toxic atmosphere... well, not toxic as in *poisonous* exactly, but its thin atmosphere was mostly CO_2, so he certainly couldn't breathe the stuff. Eerie was about the size of old earth, right at the outer edge of the "life-zone" from its primary star. Theoretically there should have been at least some forms of microbial life in the soil, but Interplanetary Exploration & Settlements, Inc. was more interested in extracting the plethora of rich mineral deposits they had detected from space than in studying whatever primitive life forms might have evolved here. There was money to be made in rare mineral deposits. Studying alien microbes, eh... not so much.

When he arrived inside the entry lock, Brian sighed as he undid the seals on his suit helmet. The station reeked of unwashed bodies and too much CO_2 in the air. He knew instinctively he'd not be getting any time to orient himself before having to dive immediately into repairing those air scrubbers. Sure enough, he'd hardly gotten his boots off and his suit stored in a locker that already had his name on it, just outside the lock area, when a big, hairy man with an impressive belly walked in and extended a huge hand towards him.

"You must be Steele," the big man said, as Brian hesitantly took his proffered hand. "I'm Dan Weaver, second-shift group leader over the maintenance shop.

"We've all been chomping at the bit for you to get here. I guess you can tell from all the pond scum hanging in the air, the geniuses in charge forgot to hire anyone who knew how to fix the damned life support systems before they started up this operation. Most of us maintenance-types are production equipment techs and we've been wrestling with our own alligators trying to keep those systems going, with all those weird energy fields causing all kinds of strange interference problems."

Brian shook the man's gigantic hand. Fortunately, Weaver wasn't one of those assholes that crushed his hand like a beer can, just because he could. "Nice to meet you, Dan. If I can borrow some tools and test equipment, maybe I can go ahead and get started while my gear is still being unloaded off the *Calypso*."

Weaver shot him an ear-to-ear grin. "That's exactly what I was hoping to hear! Not everyone here has their priorities straight yet, and I'm damned to glad to see you're a vet who knows what's really important out here on the hind-end of humanity."

Brian followed Weaver through the station corridors and tried to memorize the route they were taking, noting scuff marks at the intersections, as the station's location markers weren't using a system he was familiar with.

"Obviously, air comes first. What's second on my priority list... water?"

"Nope," said Weaver over his shoulder. "Temperature controls. We've got enough potable drinking water for a while, just not enough for showers. Some equipment has been overheating due to their heat exchangers not having enough temperature differential to work efficiently. You may have to switch off to working on some of the atmospherics, while trying to get the air scrubbers going again."

Brian nodded and followed. As they entered the maintenance shop, Weaver wheeled out a maintenance dolly, which was both tool chest (below) and test equipment carrier (above) in one.

"You can use my gear until yours gets unloaded. Let me introduce you to Benny over in the parts crib, so he can pull whatever you think you're gonna need before you get started."

Weaver led Brian to a fenced-off area and introduced him to a skeletal figure with a huge nose and an even larger Adams-apple. "Brian, this is Benny Lopatka. Benny, this is Brian Steele. Brian is gonna clear the air around here for us."

As Brian shook hands with Benny through the parts crib window, Weaver continued. "Benny, Brian isn't permanent staff, but everything he asks for is gonna be critical to the quality of life around here, so I'm gonna need you to look up the part numbers and fill out all the paperwork for him. Just give him whatever parts he needs and I'll sign off on the chits later."

"Well, I don't know about that, Dan," said Benny. "That's not procedure and I don't wanna get in any trouble by bending the rules."

"You want to keep on breathing all these damned black mold spores and all the other fuckin' algae floating in the air around here?" Weaver roared. "I'll take complete responsibility, so you just loosen up and shit out whatever parts Brian needs, you hear?"

"All right, all right. No need to get yer balls in an uproar. I'll do it!"

Brian recited a list of monthly, quarterly and yearly preventative maintenance replacement parts he'd need from memory — primary air scrubber filters, O_2 sensors, CO_2 sensors, fungicide scrubbers, microbial filters, and a dozen other things the system obviously needed desperately, judging by the pitiful condition of the air within the station.

"While Benny is getting all those parts pulled, let me see if we can find a set of coveralls that'll fit ya. Hate to see ya ruin your personal clothes, getting us some decent air to breath around here.

CHAPTER SEVEN

We call them faerie. We don't believe in them. Our loss.
-- Charles de Lint

Finvarra's Castle, beneath Cnoc Meadha
Fourteen years earlier: 67 A.D.

IT HAD TAKEN RHOSLYN SEVERAL DAYS OF ARGUMENT to finally convince Aryn to acquiesce to traveling clear across the great island to meet the queen of her faerie court. Rhoslyn guided him during the long journey to the home of the faerie Queen Úna, in search of his "supposed" *áes sidhe* powers. Úna's official title was *Tanya Mehta*, which literally meant "Queen of the Faeries," and Aryn was appropriately in awe of her — or inappropriately, as the case may be.

Queen Úna was full human-sized, but had double, transparent wings, very much like those of a dragonfly. Pointed, elven ears protruded through her long, snow-white hair, and her violet eyes were absolutely captivating. The faerie queen was extraordinarily beautiful, in an exotic, alluring way that Aryn had never before experienced. She wore a revealing, golden diaphanous gown, with the bodice split to her non-existent navel, exposing half of her magnificent bosom. The dress sparkled in silver flashes as she moved. Unfortunately, strategically placed slits in the sheer material also provided Aryn with fleeting glimpses of creamy white skin and voluptuous, very feminine curves — to which his intentionally neglected hormones responded instantly.

Aryn turned to the side a bit to obscure the growing bulge in his pants, but Úna's knowing smile told him that his attempt to hide his predicament hadn't been entirely successful. Aryn reddened and looked down at his feet, trying to bring his rebellious nether regions under control, but that just elicited an amused snicker from Úna. She obviously delighted in the effect her body was having on him.

"Ah, Rhoslyn, I'm so glad that you decided to pay me a visit," Úna said. "How long has it been? Two hundred years at least, if my memory still serves."

Aryn noted that Úna's voice had an odd ring to it when she spoke, like the tinkling of a crystal bell.

"Yes, your majesty. Your memory is still as good as ever," replied little Rhoslyn. "It has been 214 years since I last had the opportunity to bask in your magnificent presence."

Those numbers startled Aryn. Was it possible that Úna was truly that old? *So why am I getting aroused by a female, who isn't human, and is hundreds of years old?*

"I see you've brought a visitor with you," said Úna. "He smells of fae blood. It's thin, but he's definitely one of mine, nonetheless."

"Yes, your majesty," said Roselyn. "His paternal grandmother is a merrow. He was unaware of this fact until very recently, but he desires to know whether he might have any other fae powers — other than faerie sight, that is."

"Ah, a one-quarter blood, then. As I said... it's thin, but enough for my purposes, I think," said Úna. "Can he talk?"

Aryn reddened even further as he stammered, "Yes, um... I can talk, your majesty. Should I be kneeling or bowing in your presence? I've never been in the presence of royalty before so I don't know what protocol I should be observing. I... wouldn't want to give offense unwittingly."

Úna laughed. "We do not observe any of those silly, mortal customs of bowing and scraping here. All of the fae are my children, and so, they are family — you, are family. Besides, I don't think either bowing or kneeling would be very comfortable for you right now... not with that protruding love-muscle that's desperately trying to escape your trousers."

Aryn's face went from mere crimson to blood-red in an instant.

Úna smiled broadly. "Do you find my breasts distracting, my pet?"

Aryn looked up in the agony of humiliation. "Is there really any *safe* way for me to answer that question, your majesty?"

Úna laughed merrily. "But of course! Just be honest about your feelings. We value honesty as highly as we value loyalty here in the *faerie* kingdom. Lust is a rather strong feeling, is it not?"

"Uh... quite strong, your majesty."

"Would you like to touch them?"

Aryn blinked and swallowed nervously, not fully believing what he'd just heard. *Just how brutally honest does she really want me to be? We value honesty as highly as we value loyalty, here in the faerie kingdom... Okay then.*

"Desperately... your majesty," Aryn finally croaked out, miserably.

Queen Úna raised one eyebrow at Aryn's admission. With a sly smile, as though she might actually be considering it, Úna said mischievously, "Yes, I might enjoy that myself."

Úna again smiled wickedly. "Unfortunately, my lord husband would probably take a rather dim view of it, if I were to take you to bed. He can be such a terrible prude about those kinds of things. Still, being married to a god does have certain advantages."

In typical pixie fashion, Rhoslyn had failed to mention that Queen Úna was married to Finvarra, high king of the *Daoine Sidhe* — a smattering of the old gods of the Tuatha Dé Danann who still remained underground in Éire. The royal couple resided in Finvarra's Castle, beneath Cnoc Meadha — a hill near Tuam, in County Galway, in the province of Connacht on the island's western shore.

When Úna decided she needed to introduce Aryn to her husband, his "love-muscle" shrank in horror at the thought. Aryn was absolutely terrified at the prospect of confronting a real god. When Úna led him into Finvarra's throne room, it felt to Aryn as if his formerly unruly male member was now actively trying to hide up his butt crack in trepidation. Seated before him on a massive throne was a god fully twice the size of a mortal man.

Queen Úna rolled her eyes. "Husband, must you always don such a fearsome appearance, even when there are no others of the Daoine Sidhe here to impress? They could all appear the same, if only you allowed it."

"Who is this mortal you bring before my throne,

woman?" Finvarra's thundering voice rolled and echoed through the enormous throne room.

Aryn's eyes got as big as gold coins when Úna suddenly swelled to twice the size of her husband's impressive dimensions.

"I am no more a woman than you are a man, my husband, as you well know."

The old god reddened in anger and roared, "I told you to never, ever, appear larger than me!"

Úna immediately shrank to the size of a tiny pixie and teased, "There, does this suit your ego better?" She buzzed around her husband's head like an annoying horse-fly, and then landed on the tip of his nose.

Finvarra shook his massive head to dislodge her. She again took flight, laughing in sheer delight at her husband's discomfiture.

"You're fortunate I didn't just swat you like a pesky mosquito, wife."

"There are no mosquitoes here, my husband — nor would there be any at all, had certain gods not been quite so bitter and vindictive as to leave such a virulent pest behind them to vex their mortal conquerors."

Úna again expanded to her normal size and said, "Now, are we going to continue playing these silly '*I'm bigger than you*' games, or are you going to act sensibly and return to your normal size so we can discuss what brought me here?"

Finvarra sighed. "Very well, wife." With that, the old god's appearance shrank down significantly, yet he still remained a full head taller than Aryn.

Úna smiled. "Ah, that's much better. My husband, I am here to ask a boon of you."

The old god frowned at that. "I assume it must have something to do with this mortal. You know I am disinclined to grant boons to mortals, so why bother interceding on this one's behalf?"

"Use your nose for something other than just a place for your wife to sit, my husband. He is *fae*... one of mine."

Finvarra leaned forward and sniffed loudly. "His fae blood is thin — very thin."

"Thick enough to make him the finest archer seen on this island in generations."

Aryn was startled by Úna's claim. While his skill with a bow was considerable, he never considered it extraordinary.

"Bah, the Celtae rarely use archers in warfare," rumbled Finvarra. "Admittedly, they are magnificent brutes with axe and sword — worthy foes, indeed. If only..."

"I know, my husband. I know," Úna cut him off. "*If only* the Gaels had not come to Éire. *If only* the Tuatha Dé Danann had not already been fatally weakened by two disastrous wars against the Fir Bolg and Fomóraig."

"Aye, we prevailed — but barely. We'd already lost our most powerful combat magicians, long before the Celtae came."

"Yes, and if their Druids had not been quite so clever in thwarting your few remaining combat magicians," Úna spat heatedly, "there would have been no need for the Tuatha Dé Danann to create the fae — and you wouldn't be married to the Queen of the Faeries now!"

Finvarra's temper flared instantly, and his face reddened menacingly at Úna's temerity to talk to a god in that manner. Yet Úna stood her ground and continued to glare back at her ferocious husband. As the high king of the *Daoine Sidhe* and his queen continued to stare one another down, the moment became pregnant with menace. The tension in the gigantic room literally crackled with energy. Faint blue sparkles of lightning danced over their features, and Aryn felt his hair beginning to stand on end.

Uh, oh. This is definitely not good. If she keeps provoking him like that, he's likely to take his wrath out on the only mortal at hand — me!

But, as suddenly as his anger first appeared, Finvarra's fearsome countenance softened as he beheld his beautiful, sultry, visibly angry wife. He broke eye contact first, looked down and shook his great, golden-crowned head.

"Ah, wife," the old god sighed. "You are right. I need to let go of the past and stop allowing those painful old memories to haunt me. I must live in *what is,* and not dwell on *what might have been.*" Finvarra cracked a sly smile. "Besides, my life now does have its share of pleasures."

"I would certainly hope so," Úna snorted. "You are the most envied male amongst all the *Daoine Sidhe.*"

Aryn let out the breath he hadn't realized he'd been holding. The release of tension was almost painful in its relief.

"Ask your boon," said Finvarra. "You know I can deny you nothing."

"'Tis merely something you've had packed away since before you built this underground palace," Úna replied.

Finvarra's forehead creased in concentration, as he struggled to grasp what his wife was alluding to.

"Tell me again of these foreigners who are coming to invade Éire. The scourge that you have foretold, my husband."

"These foreign invaders who are coming are not warriors as we know them, or even understand them," Finvarra answered. "Even while peace reigns, they do not till the soil, nor harvest fields. They do not fish, nor do they hunt. They do not tend sheep, cattle or pigs. War is their only profession. They exist solely to conquer new territory, for which they receive wages, as though they produced something of real value.

"But these vermin are not satisfied with merely ruling and taxing the native peoples they conquer. No, they brutally impose their foreign culture, their foreign language and their foreign gods upon them. They literally absorb their former enemies — stripping them of their very identity by obliterating all memory of their heritage, their culture, their gods and their entire way of life.

"These coming invaders are little better than distasteful, honorless mercenaries — but their methods in making war are revolutionary, and unfortunately, highly effective. They do not fight individually nor in small groups, but in highly disciplined masses — a great beast having thousands of sword-arms but a single brain. They move and act as one."

"It sounds like the Celtae will need the combat magic of their Druids to have any hope of driving these invaders from Éire, my husband," Úna said somberly. "But, will druidic combat magic be enough to overcome them, or is there need of something more?"

"Aye, the Celtae above will need all the help they can get to rid this island of *these* invaders," Finvarra replied. "Unfortunately, there is little we of the Daoine Sidhe can do to assist them against these invaders without breaking the treaty which banished us here. Besides, our warriors have almost all passed on — either into death, or into the *Otherworld.*"

"It sounds like you need a hybrid — a mixture of both Celtae and fae blood who could champion our cause in defending Éire from these invaders."

"What is your point, wife?"

"As I told you earlier." Úna swept her arm towards

Aryn to draw her husband's attention back to him — not necessarily something that Aryn relished the thought of. "Aryn Ó Fionnagáin is the finest archer seen on this island in generations. All he lacks is something that you no longer have need of."

"My magic bow?" Finvarra asked in disbelief. "You want me to just give this... this *Celtae* my magnificent golden bow?"

The old god literally spat the word Celtae, as though it were the vilest curse imaginable.

"No, I want you to give your magic, golden bow to one of my children of the fae, so he can effectively resist this invasion from the East that you, yourself, foretold."

"What for? Fae magic does not include archery skills."

"His does," Úna replied. "His gift... um... let me think about how to say this." She took in a deep breath and let it out slowly. "Aryn perceives life-forces. He can hit a moving target at a distance, even blindfolded. Granted, he isn't much of a target shooter, but he can hit anything as long as it's alive."

Aryn started to protest, "Now wait..."

Úna and Finvarra both rounded on him. "HUSH!" they shouted in unison, cutting off his protest in mid-word.

"Úna understands fae powers instinctively," Finvarra said, speaking directly to Aryn for the first time. "If she says it is so, then it is. I trust her judgement on this matter implicitly."

Finvarra turned back to his wife. "I still don't see what good my bow would do the boy. He can't even draw that bow, nor even see his target at those ranges without a major infusion of magic."

"Have your magical powers grown so weak from disuse," Úna chided her husband, "you fear the possibility of failure if you even attempted to provide the boy with what he needs to use your bow?"

"I fear nothing!" Finvarra thundered, his face once again reddening with anger. "I know what you're trying to do by provoking me in this way."

"And? Is it working, my husband?" Úna teased.

Finvarra's mood again shifted abruptly as he laughed. "Aye, as you knew it would. But you're going to owe me a very great debt, after this boon — a very great debt."

"Ooh, good," Úna laughed. "I know exactly what kind of debt you're referring to... the kind we both enjoy when I repay my debts to you."

Now it was Aryn's turn to redden uncontrollably. Unbidden visions assaulted him... visions of a deliciously naked faerie queen providing the old god unimaginable sexual pleasure with her magically enhanced body. Shaking his head to clear it of these inappropriate thoughts, Aryn looked up to find Finvarra and Úna both grinning at him, snickering at his obvious discomfort.

He derives great pleasure from others desiring what only he can have.

Finvarra sighed audibly, shaking his great crowned head. "All right, wife. Take the human and retrieve my golden bow from our private storage room," Finvarra said at last.

"I must refresh my memory. I need to consult the grimoires in the ancient scrolls we brought with us from the frozen northern isles. You'd be angry with me if I accidentally incinerated your pet mortal by saying the wrong word during the incantation."

CHAPTER EIGHT

Most people would never admit it, but they'd been bitching since they were born. As soon as their head popped out into that bright delivery-room light, nothing had been right. Nothing had been as comfortable or felt so good. Just the effort it took to keep your stupid physical body alive, just finding food and cooking it and dishwashing, the keeping warm and bathing and sleeping, the walking and bowel movements and ingrown hairs, it was all getting to be too much work.
-- Chuck Palahniuk, Haunted

The Planet Eerie
3232 A.D.

IT TOOK BRIAN ALMOST A MONTH OF NON-STOP WORK to get the air, water and the environmentals all working — well, sort of. At least they were working a *lot* better than they had been when he arrived. It appeared there was an ungodly amount of electromagnetic radiation noise causing all kinds of false switching issues in the digital control circuits. That should have been eliminated by noise reduction circuitry connected to the earth-grounding system. (*Eerie* grounding system?) The fact it was so widespread told Brian it *had* to be a dry ground problem — something that most electrical design engineers neglected to consider, because of popular misconceptions about grounding.

"Ground" is one of the most basic concepts in all of electricity and electronics, yet it is also one of the most misunderstood. The term "ground" generally refers to a piece of equipment's zero-volt reference — the reference against which all other voltages in the system are measured. The vast majority of the time, this "zero-volt ground reference" is NOT tied directly to true earth-ground, but is a "floating ground reference" having frequency sensitive paths to earth-ground via capacitors sized to pass only a narrow bandwidth of frequencies of electromagnetic radiation noise as part of the equipment's noise reduction circuitry. The fact that the noise reduction circuitry was *not* eliminating the noise meant that either the noise was at a different frequency than the capacitors were sized to eliminate, or there was a "dry-earth" problem preventing a good connection to true earth potential.

Even most electrical engineers tend to forget that electricity flows within the soil itself between the grounding rods. Dry areas, which are resistant to electrical current flow create voltage drops that cause voltage spikes whenever current rushes into ground occur. Even when the noise reduction capacitors are sized properly, these voltage spikes cause the "zero-volt reference" for equipment's to no longer be at zero volts, which can cause false switching that can send digital circuits into electronic lockjaw. A dry-ground problem also often leads to premature capacitor failure, as they tend to overheat due to being forced into constant-duty, while designed for intermittent-duty.

Properly installed grounding grids are usually chains or other types of metallic-mesh nets buried below ground over a vast area, to maximize the metal-to-ground surface contact between them, to ensure good electrical connection to the soil. Unfortunately, the installation of a proper grounding grid is both a time consuming and expensive proposition, so many corporations cut corners by just driving metal rods into the ground at various points under and around the installation. Theoretically, that should work well enough and often does wherever the soil is of a moist, loamy type. But dry, sandy soil doesn't conduct electricity very well, and so, requires an expensive automatic watering system to ensure the ground connections.

When Brian suited up and went outside to drive his own grounding stake into the ground, he poured a generous amount of water over it and found exactly what he'd expected — over six volts difference between the station's grounding grid and his properly watered reference stake. He found similar results everywhere else he measured. Interplanetary Exploration & Settlements, Inc. was NOT going to be happy about the now documented need to install a proper grounding grid with its own watering system... *if* they really wanted all the "gremlins" in their electrical systems to go away.

But Brian also made one other rather disturbing discovery while he was outside pouring water over the stakes he had driven into the soil... tiny green shoots of what looked like grass were beginning to emerge from the barren soil, right next to his foot.

CHAPTER NINE

Using words to describe magic is like using a screwdriver to
cut roast beef.
-- Tom Robbins

Finvarra's Castle, beneath
Cnoc Meadha
Fourteen years earlier: 67 A.D.

ÚNA BECKONED ARYN WITH A CROOK OF HER DELICATE
finger. As he followed Úna down a hallway behind Finvarra's throne, Aryn hissed at the pixie riding on his right
shoulder.

"Rhoslyn," Aryn whispered. "What in perdition have
you gotten me into? I should have never let you talk me into
coming here. It's very likely going to get me killed."

"Oh, poo," Rhoslyn answered back, in a tinny voice just
slightly louder than Aryn felt truly comfortable with.
"You're in no danger here. They fuss like this all the time.

It's merely a game they enjoy playing between the two of them. Finvarra is moist clay in Úna's hands."

Aryn snorted.

"Well, maybe not her hands exactly," Rhoslyn continued. "Her cleavage is probably more influential on him than her hands."

Aryn emitted a faint, strangled cry at Rhoslyn's reminder of Úna's magnificent bosom.

Rhoslyn's brow knitted tightly, as if suddenly seeing Aryn in an entirely different light than she ever had before. "You're really enamored with Úna's breasts, aren't you?"

"*Shh...*" Aryn hissed at her. "Lower your voice. I can't help my reactions to her," Aryn whispered. "I know it's all just a glamour, but even so, the enchantment she radiates makes it damned hard for a man to resist."

Out of the corner of his eye, Aryn noticed Úna glance back over her shoulder with a satisfied smirk on her face.

"I could make mine appear just as big as hers, if that's what you really like."

Aryn made an urgent shushing motion with his hand, wiping his finger across his lips. A look of confusion crossed Rhoslyn's features, as though she didn't understand what his hand signal meant.

Fortunately, before Rhoslyn could embarrass him any further, Úna stopped at a locked door and pulled a large brass key out of her bodice. She opened the door and with a wave of her hand, two torches hanging in wall sconces suddenly lit, flooding the small stone-walled room with flickering yellow-orange light.

I don't know if I'll ever get used to beings who routinely use magic to light torches with just a wave of their hand.

Three rows of stone shelving lined the walls, as though carved purposely when the room was made. A variety of small leather trunks banded with brass adorned the shelving. Larger trunks, ceramic urns and lidded baskets made from woven reeds sat on the floor along the walls. Úna then muttered something inaudible and with another wave of her other hand, a small golden key appeared in it from within a cloud of white-silver sparkles. Úna then knelt down in front of a large trunk about seven *troighid* (six feet) long, turned the key in the lock and opened the lid.

From within, she pulled out a stunning golden bow, having reversed dragonheads engraved along the outer edges, mirroring one another, above and below the handle. Úna again reached down into the chest and extracted a quiver filled with black arrows. Handing the quiver to Aryn, she relocked the chest, and with another wave of her free hand, she sent the golden key back whence it came in another shower of silver sparkles.

Aryn followed Queen Úna back into the hallway, where with a wave of her freehand she extinguished the torches in the storage room they had just vacated. She relocked the door and dropped the brass key back down into her bodice.

Aryn looked away when he realized what she was about to do, only to see little Rhoslyn flying nearby, giving him a look of unmistakable distain. Úna turned back towards Aryn and held out her free hand to him, so he placed the quiver of coal-black arrows back into her custody.

When they returned to the throne room, Aryn saw that Finvarra was in deep discussion with two other Daoine Sidhe. Aryn hesitated to approach, but Úna wasn't intimidated by the presence of two more of the old gods, and approached the group boldly. She stopped to the side of her husband, but well within his peripheral vision. Finvarra continued in muted discussion with the two, until one of the

Daoine Sidhe across from Úna nodded in her direction to alert him she was standing there. Finvarra turned and saw his wife with the golden bow and black arrows in her hands.

"Ah, I see you found my bow." Looking sour at the quiver full of coal-black arrows in Úna's hand, Finvarra frowned. "Must I part with my never-ending arrow quiver, as well?"

Úna snorted. "You know very well that any bow is useless without arrows, my husband," she replied. "You *do* want the foreign invaders you prophesied would come to be repulsed, don't you?"

Finvarra stared at his wife for a few seconds before finally nodding. "Aye, having the Celtae living above us on the surface is bad enough, but at least they took this island from us in honorable combat — an honest test of strength between our two peoples. These foreigners coming from the East reverence no power other than their own. They take what the land provides without regard for the forces and spirits of nature, which causes it to bloom. They rape the minds of their subject peoples by stealing away all memory of their heritage. We made a vow to nurture and protect this beautiful land. It must not fall into the hands of such as these!"

"So, what will you do to fulfill that vow, my husband?"

"It is a shameful thing for we of the Daoine Sidhe to be so impotent at such a time when the land needs our strength. When the time comes, you must marshal all the forces of the fae against these invaders, wife."

"I can do that. Our daughter, Kyla, will rally the fae to the land's defense."

"Kyla?" Finvarra was startled. "You'd hazard your own daughter in combat against these invaders?"

"Did not the Tuatha Dé Danann field female warriors

against the marauding sea gods of the Fomóraig — gods of night, death and cold?"

"Aye," Finvarra admitted. "We needed all of the strength we could muster against those monsters, but those were full goddesses. Kyla is not."

"She is half *Daoine Sidhe* and half *fae* — and your daughter. You think Kyla any less capable than your Tuatha Dé Danann wenches, with all of the fae at her command?"

"Someone talking about me?"

Aryn jumped like he'd been stabbed at the unexpected voice from right behind him. He leaped to the side in a crouch, instinctively grabbing the handle of his bronze dagger as he whipped around to face... a young female even more beautiful than Úna.

"Umm, not bad reflexes — for a mortal." She gave Aryn a quick apprising look. Then, ignoring Aryn's combat stance, she looked away dismissively.

"Ah, Kyla, darling. Your timing is impeccable, as ever," said Úna. "We were just talking about you."

"What about me?"

Úna didn't answer, but merely smiled, arched one brow, and gave her husband an inquiring look. Finvarra gave his wife a hard stare, but then just shook his head, resignedly. He obviously knew he'd lost that argument before it even started.

"Even having the magic bow attuned to him," Finvarra responded grimly. "I despair of sending just one man against thousands."

Aryn gulped. *Me... alone against thousands? What kind of insanity is this?*

"He is *fae*, my husband. He will not fail me when the land needs him most."

"His fae blood is thin, wife. Very thin."

"The Tuatha Dé Danann created the entire race of the fae when your magical powers were at their weakest. Cannot your few Daoine Sidhe combine your remaining powers to augment Aryn's thin fae blood in some way?"

Finvarra glanced over at the other two Daoine Sidhe. They both looked solemn, but finally the female nodded and whispered to her male companion. He gave her a sour look, but didn't disagree with whatever she'd said. Satisfied that the male also agreed, however reluctantly, Finvarra turned to Úna and said, "It is dangerous. The boy might not survive."

Might not survive?

"See there," Aryn hissed at Rhoslyn. "I *told* you I shouldn't have come here."

"Rhoslyn," said Úna. "Expand to my size and come here."

Rhoslyn did not reply, but did exactly as her queen bade her. Aryn had never seen Rhoslyn the size of a human woman before. Her elfin features were now much more pronounced. He found himself staring, as he'd never noticed how beautiful his tiny pixie friend really was before now. Úna gave Kyla another of those crooked fingers. As she approached, Úna leaned in close to give her and Rhoslyn whispered instructions.

Kyla had coal-black hair hanging down to the middle of her back, even darker and longer than Aryn's own. In stark contrast to her mother's shimmering gown, Kyla was dressed in a puffy-sleeved cream-colored blouse, beneath a tan suede leather vest. Her legs were covered in tight fitting grass-green leggings, which disappeared into dark brown leather knee-boots. A wide brown leather belt with a large golden buckle adorned her middle, from which hung a one-handed short-sword in a decorative, but muted scabbard.

Overall, she appeared slim in figure — not at all like her mother's voluptuous curves.

Finvarra instructed Aryn to take the great golden bow and the quiver of black arrows from Úna, and stand before him. He then stepped forward and placed both of his massive hands on either side of Aryn's head and assumed a look of deep concentration. When Finvarra finally dropped his hands, the other two Daoine Sidhe grasped his outstretched hands at hip level, forming a tight circle around the mortal. Finvarra then nodded towards Úna. She, Rhoslyn and Kyla all stepped forward, placing their left hands upon each other's shoulders. Careful not to touch the Daoine Sidhe, they then extended their right arms over the clasped hands of the old gods and placed their hands on Aryn's shoulders and back.

All six closed their eyes and the Daoine Sidhe began a low chant in a language older than time. A soft, wafting mist seemed to gather about them, growing thicker as the chant continued. Aryn wondered whether he should close his eyes too, but was suddenly unable to. Without warning, his entire body abruptly stiffened — frozen, as if encased in ice.

Dark churning clouds gradually appeared above Aryn's head, having a knot of blue-white lightning cackling at their center. The clouds then expanded until they encompassed the entire throne room in a mass of rolling blackness, dark with menace. The chanting of the Daoine Sidhe changed cadence and an orange-vermillion glow slowly formed around his entire body, as if it were a personal shield of some kind. Golden sparkles became noticeable within that glow when it gained sufficient brightness. Tiny blue sparks danced over the fae hands touching Aryn's shoulders and back. The chanting increased in volume and a bright purple globe flashed into existence, enclosing all seven beings. The dark, churning clouds roiled with angry blue-white lightning bolts. The globe began rotating, changing color from purple, to scarlet, to blue to green in a cyclic pattern.

Aryn was terrified at this awesome display of magical power, but he was even more afraid that he was about to foul himself. His bladder and bowels desperately needed to evacuate, but they were apparently just as frozen as the rest of him. Just as he began to wonder if he shouldn't be feeling some kind of pain from all this, the chanting reached a crescendo and a massive lightning bolt shot down from the cloud above him, piercing the vermillion shield.

An undulating scream was torn from him. Aryn's entire existence became a roiling smear of yellow, red and orange. His eyes were flame, feeling as though they were being gouged out with red-hot pokers. The rest of his body merely suffered the agonies of being immersed in a cauldron of boiling oil. The vermillion shield flared to incandescent brightness and the pain subsided to merely unendurable. Green and blue lightning crackled within the fiery sphere that enveloped him.

Ah, gods... I can't stand this!

He silently prayed the gods would take his life to end this anguish, forgetting for the moment that it was three of those very gods who were inflicting this torture upon him. A part of him feared he was dying, yet a greater part feared he was not, and that this agony would just go on and on, forever. A deafening thunderclap rolled through his head, and his vision flared white. His agony flared even hotter and lost any reference to physical location — it just was everywhere, with Aryn embroiled in the very center of it. Then blackness began creeping into the edges of his vision as though he was entering a long tunnel, and he felt himself spiraling down into the absolute blackness of oblivion.

~

Finvarra's Castle, beneath Cnoc Meadha
67 A.D.

ÚNA APPROACHED her husband with some trepidation. She'd overheard a whispers between the two Daoine Sidhe who had assisted him during the magical incantation to enhance Aryn Ó Fionnagáin's archery skills... and what she now suspected was profoundly troubling. She found Finvarra relaxing in their personal quarters, smoking a short piece of rope. She couldn't help rolling her eyes at the idea of a god, with all of the incredible pleasures at his disposal, still chose to get high like a common sailor.

"We need to talk."

Finvarra merely gave her a blank look that told her his mind was deep into a hemp-induced haze. "So talk."

"It has come to my attention that your incantations may have altered Aryn Ó Fionnagáin in ways beyond, and unrelated to, what was absolutely necessary."

"Why would you think that?"

"Let's just say that certain visitors to this castle seem to perceive an inordinate amount of black humor in something you did to him."

"What have you heard?"

"Little," Úna confessed. "Just whispered snickering among the Daoine Sidhe involving Aryn, magic... and something hilarious."

"Soothe your fears, wife. I didn't harm the boy."

"What did you do to him?"

"Almost nothing. A mere tweak... nothing more."

"What... did... you... DO... to him?"

Finvarra sighed. "You know that nothing achieved using magic is totally free. All the more so whenever incantations involving high magic are invoked."

"Finvarra, answer me!"

"To create an ability that was not, certain other abilities had to be, umm... lessened... drawn upon so they could transform into the desired result. The power must come from somewhere!"

"You and your Daoine Sidhe could have each donated minuscule amounts of power from within your own essences, without suffering any ill effects from such a tiny drain."

"Aye, we could have. But the boy would not have survived it. The problem was not in our abilities to provide the power needed to fulfill the incantation, but in his ability to receive it safely. His fae blood was too thin. To grant him the abilities he needed without killing him, I had to tap forces already residing within his physical body."

"What forces?"

"Rather than weaken dozens of his bodily functions, which would have increased the complexity of the incantation immeasurably, I utilized a single strong one having sufficient power to provide what we needed, without incurring unnecessary risk."

"WHAT DID YOU DO TO ARYN?"

"I drained his sex drive."

"Why did you unman him?" Úna shrieked.

"I saw the way he looked at you... and you at him. I protect what is mine."

"You know I would never be unfaithful to you, no matter how much I might flirt. Your jealousy was totally uncalled for!"

"Perhaps, but I protect what is mine. Besides, Kyla will be working closely with your pet mortal when the invaders come and I didn't like the way he looked at her either."

"*Pfft*... Kyla is your daughter. Do you think she'd even consider lowering herself to rut with a mere mortal? She considers them little better than mindless cattle."

"I take no chances. At any rate, it is done now."

"Can you reverse it when all is finished?"

"I'm... not sure. Besides, why would I even want to? You are mine and Kyla is mine. As I said, I protect what is mine."

~

Aryn's Cave
67 A.D.

ARYN FLOATED IN DARKNESS, seeing nothing, hearing nothing, feeling nothing. He wouldn't have perceived that he was anything other than dead except for a faint, yet familiar smell — bacon! That recognition made his stomach roil with hunger, and he fought to swim upwards towards full consciousness. Bacon had always been one of his major weaknesses and primary motivators his entire life. He cracked open an eye and saw... more blackness. It took a moment to get past his initial confusion to notice that his sense of touch was telling him that something was wrapped around his head, covering his eyes. He attempted to raise his hand towards his eyes, but discovered that motor control of his outer extremities was sluggish and uncoordinated. His hand rose, but not to where he was attempting to guide it.

"Ah, you're waking... finally," came a feminine voice

from some distance away. "It's a good thing too, because I was really getting tired of wiping your ass and cleaning you up, every time you shit yourself."

Wiping my ass?

That voice seemed vaguely familiar somehow, but he couldn't quite place it. *I've heard that voice before, but where?* Aryn struggled to remember.

"Wh..." His throat was sand.

A strong, but gentle hand slipped beneath his head and raised it a little. "Open," said the voice. When Aryn felt something press against his lower lip, he cracked his mouth open a bit and cool water dribbled down his throat.

"Swallow."

His first attempt to swallow was ground glass, but that tiny bit lubricated his throat enough to get the rest down.

"Again."

The second sip went down more easily. The canteen was pulled away shortly thereafter, and then something different touched his lips.

"Open."

Not bacon... chicken broth... Hot!

Spoonful after spoonful of steaming broth was gently ladled down his throat. Soon, strength began returning, steadying his shaky limbs. Aryn tried to get an elbow under him.

"No! Stay down." A hand on his chest pushed him back.

"Up... want... up."

"Not yet. Our healer said it was important for you to stay prone for a few days to give your eyes a chance to heal. Sleep now."

He didn't want to sleep — he wanted answers to several questions, not the least of which involved her claim of wiping his ass. But the moment that feminine voice said, "sleep now," a fog immediately descended over his mind. His last thought before slipping back into oblivion was: *An enchantment. She cast some kind of a spell on...*

ARYN ROUSED towards wakefulness once again, as he had on and off for the gods only knew how many days now. Sometimes it was Rhoslyn's voice that awakened him. Other times it was that other feminine voice he'd still not been able to place. Usually he could tell which one was nursing him, as Rhoslyn didn't cook bacon. The chicken broth they spoon-fed him gradually thickened to include finely diced vegetables, and later, small pieces of chicken.

He always awoke from his enchanted sleeps somewhat groggy, but today he had the presence of mind to not move. He lay still in the absolute dark imposed by the bandages over his eyes and allowed his head to clear further. There was no inviting smell of bacon, nor even the usual muted smell of simmering chicken soup that he'd come to expect. He assumed it must be daylight, as the soft chirping of crickets he'd sometimes heard at night was absent. He focused his hearing as much as possible, but heard nothing.

Is anyone here?

Aryn slowly reached up and tore the aggravating bandage off his head. He tried opening his eyes, but found them all gummy from some kind of grease applied under the bandage. He tried using the bandage to wipe the grease away, but recoiled when he discovered that his eyelids were extremely tender to the touch. He tried again, more gently this time, and found he could stand the pain enough to wipe most of the grease away. He blinked several times to try to clear a thin, residual layer of grease covering the eyeball itself, revealing a soft, blurry light as if coming from around a corner.

He found sufficient strength to prop himself up on one elbow and finally, to sit up and swing his legs down toward the floor. He still didn't know where he was, so it came as a surprise when he slid off the bed and dropped about the length of his foot before reaching the floor. Still half blind, he extended his hands out in front of him and discovered rough rock walls to the side as he slowly staggered towards the light.

"Those bandages really should have stayed on another couple of days."

Aryn halted at the unexpected voice, trying not to show how badly she had startled him. It was the bacon-fryer.

"I appreciate your nursing me while I've been incapacitated. I'm not used to needing assistance from anyone."

"I'm not used to giving any," the feminine voice snorted. "Wasn't my idea... my father commanded it."

Father?

"Well, I thank you anyway. Do we know each other?"

"No, I just picked a bad time to pay a visit to my parents and got roped into all this." Her voice had an edge to it... an edge of utter distaste.

She doesn't like me. Just like my cousin Aine always hated me for no particular reason.

"I'm terribly sorry to have inconvenienced you." Aryn's voice took on an equal measure of hostility. "I can take care of myself now, so you can go back to doing whatever it is you normally do."

"Don't I just wish?"

A hand grabbed him roughly by the elbow and pulled. "Come on then. What's done is done." She evidently pulled him around the edge of whatever had been blocking the light because the blurred light immediately intensified into a few blinding white sparkles.

"Turn." The hand jerked his elbow sideways, so he had no choice but to turn or fall flat on his face. "Sit." Unsure whether there was anything under him, or if he'd fall on his backside, Aryn nonetheless did as instructed and found himself seated on a low stool. "Stay."

He rather resented being talked down to, like someone giving commands to a dog, but until he got his sight back, he had very little choice but to obey like a well-trained animal. The light source, now behind him, flared momentarily and he heard the distinct snuffle of a horse off to his right side.

A horse? "I can hear your horse nearby."

"*Pfft...* Not *my* horse any longer. He's your horse now. His name is *Frisky* and he was my best, so you'd better take very, very good care of him."

"I don't want your horse. Where is my horse?"

The girl sighed and said, "That nag you rode to Cnoc Meadha is still there."

"Where's here?"

"A cave."

The light source behind him flared again, and soon a rag, wet with cool water, began dabbing his face at the corners of his eyes. The rag was rewetted several times, evidently from a bucket close at hand. For someone who disliked him and resented being commanded to tend to his needs, she was surprisingly gentle as she wiped his eyes with the rag.

I doubt my cousin, Aine, could have restrained herself so.

"Why do you dislike me so much?"

"I don't 'dislike' you," the feminine voice snorted, as she

continued her ministrations to his eyes. "I'm just... um... ambivalent towards mortals."

"So you are fae, then?"

"Half."

"But, that gives us something in common. I am part fae as well."

The female laughed. "You think highly of yourself, archer. My mother may give weight to your tenuous fae heritage, but it cuts no fish with me. I have no mortal blood."

No mortal blood? But that would mean... Suddenly Aryn realized who it must be that was tending him. *What was her name again... Kara? Damn, I can't remember!*

RHOSLYN WAS THERE the next time Aryn awoke. She remained full human-sized while tending him, but her pained expression told him she didn't particularly care for it. She confirmed his suspicions that his other nurse was none other than the demi-goddess Kyla, daughter of High King Finvarra of the Daoine Sidhe, and Úna, Queen of the Faeries. Kyla had been extremely reticent to discuss exactly where he was, or how he had come to be here. All she would say was how she had placed her father's magic war-bow and the quiver of black arrows in a trunk near his bed, with a stern warning that they were never to be used for hunting — only for killing enemies of the land.

Rhoslyn told him he'd been brought to convalesce in a cave, hidden deep in the Haunted Forest. She not only confirmed the demi-goddess' identity, but also explained how Kyla had carried him unconscious on the back of her púca, a shape-shifter morphed into a giant eagle for the task.

Aryn shuddered at the thought. No faerie creature is more feared on the isle of Éire than the púca.

"Oh, I also brought you a present from Queen Úna," Rhoslyn said. "I told her how badly you were chafing at only being able to go out at night because your eyes can't stand the brightness of the full sun yet."

"What is it?"

"It's some kind of contraption made by the old gods — stitched leather, lamb's wool and smoked glass. She said it was something the smiths of the Daoine Sidhe wear to protect their eyes when bonding metals using a method yet unknown to mortals. You position the darkened glass parts over your eyes while I tie the leather straps around your head to hold it in place."

Aryn donned the device as Rhoslyn instructed. By feel, he discovered the glass portions were somehow encased in stiff, stitched-leather frames with virgin lamb's wool positioned around the edges as padding where the device touched his forehead, nose and cheeks. When she finished tying the straps behind his head, he was totally blind in the darkness of the cave. She grabbed his hand and guided him towards the entrance, where he noticed what had before been blinding sparkles of light filtered through the vines were now merely tolerable bright spots. When she parted the vine curtain and led him outside. He was forced to squint harshly, but his eyes quickly adjusted.

Aryn looked around and marveled. Breaking into a big grin, he said, "This is wonderful! Except for the harshness of the sun being softened and muted by the darkened glass, I can see everything quite clearly. Did Queen Úna have a name for this device?"

"Yes, she called them 'sun goggles' — whatever a *goggle* is."

CHAPTER TEN

We want a story that starts out with an earthquake and works its way up to a climax.
-- Samuel Goldwyn

The Planet Eerie
3232 A.D.

THE ENTIRE MINING COMPLEX SHOOK VIOLENTLY ONCE again, and Brian Steele staggered as the flooring beneath him undulated. The corridor lights flickered momentarily and a drizzle of dust rained down on him. Fortunately, most of the station's walls and ceilings were coated with plazsteel, which retained enough residual flexibility to withstand most of the shocks without cracking or collapsing. Electromagnetic radiation noise issues were now the least of everyone's problems ever since the planet's tectonic plates suddenly began shifting several weeks ago.

Since then, planetary quakes of varying intensities had

constantly shaken the station like a wolf with a rabbit's neck in its teeth. Mining production had come to a standstill after three miners had been killed in a cave-in on the day this geologic activity began. Two others had been badly injured, but they had both recently been upgraded off the critical list, so it appeared they would live. Since then, the dispensary had been kept busy treating a variety of injuries from broken bones, to lacerations and abrasions.

With mining operations halted, Brian had commandeered many of the production techs to help him keep up with all of the breakdowns on the station's environmental systems. Equipment used on frontier planets is usually built very rugged, but none were engineered to physically withstand the kinds of shocks and vibrations that Eerie Station was currently experiencing. The equipment on Eerie is all rather elderly and antiquated. As Brian was considered "the expert" on those old systems, he found himself literally running from place-to-place putting out fires. Often the production techs were at a complete loss and Brian had to show them how to jury-rig workarounds to bypass problems they didn't have spare parts for... at least enough to get partial functionality restored.

No one knew exactly what was causing this recent seismic activity, nor how much longer it might continue. Some had called for evacuating the station on the next supply ship, while others called for just hunkering down and watching to see what new developments might arise. Their survival wasn't immediately threatened as long as Brian could keep up with tacking the environmentals back together. They could only pray a fissure didn't open right beneath them and send the entire station spiraling down into a miles deep crevasse — and that a supply ship would arrive soon, so they'd at least have the option of evacuating.

Brian was exhausted. Several weeks of twenty-hour days were catching up with him. Not that sleep was really much of an option when his rack kept trying to throw him out of bed every time he lay down. Dust was constantly trickling down from the overheads and lay everywhere. Showers had been totally banned to conserve their supply of potable water for drinking, so he felt grungy, grimy and downright rank.

Strangely enough, it seemed that his muse had somehow returned in the midst of all this chaos and he was cranking out his Celtic fantasy book faster than ever. If he couldn't sleep, he might as well write...

~

The Roman Command Tent — Isle of Reachrainn
Early June, A.D. 81

"THE *FAE*, MY LORD," said Túathal Techtmar.

The Roman governor of Britannia, General Gnaeus Julius Agricola, studied the strapping young Hibernian prince standing before him, still dripping from the driving rain. In 55 A.D, four provincial kings had overthrown Fíacha Finnolach, high king of Hibernia, so his pregnant wife, Eithne Imgel, daughter of the king of Albion (a Caledonian tribe inhabiting the far north of Britannia) fled back to her father where she gave birth to a son, Túathal Techtmar. When Agricola advanced his legions (his own *Legio XX Valariq Victrix* and *Legio IX Hispana*) into southern Caledonia in 79 A.D., Túathal's mother came boldly into

Agricola's camp, imploring him to grant her son asylum, as he was the rightful high king of Hibernia.

Agricola immediately saw advantage in offering refuge to this exiled Hibernian prince — as well as an excuse to conquer the island and install him back onto his father's throne. Perhaps a friendly neighbor could restrain the troublesome Hibernian raiders from attacking villages along his western coastline. Agricola had encouraged the boy to raise himself an army from among the local Brigantes, (a recently conquered Celtae tribe) whose dispossessed nobility might be ready recruits for Túathal's invasion force. Besides, helping Túathal regain his father's throne appeared to also be a convenient way for Agricola to rid himself of a lot of troublesome Brigantes.

"And exactly what, in the name of all the gods, is this *fae* you're talking about?" asked Agricola.

Túathal had lived within Roman camps under Agricola's protection for the previous two years and his spoken Latin skills were already impressive... primarily because any Celtae who wished to communicate with the Romans had to do so in Latin, as Romans had little incentive to learn Gaelic.

"The *fae*... the little people — *faeries,* if you will. Surely you must have heard of them while campaigning in Britannia?"

Agricola almost choked on a sip of wine and was forced to wipe away the spillage that dribbled down his chin.

"Faeries? Bah, a bunch of superstitious nonsense. Don't tell me that *you* believe in faeries!"

"It doesn't matter what I believe, my lord," replied Túathal. "It's obvious this archer of yours believes in them. He uses bronze arrowheads to avoid offending them. Faeries cannot abide cold iron."

"And just why is it that these imaginary faeries of yours, seem so allergic to iron?"

"The fae are said to be magical creatures, my lord. It is thought that iron somehow interferes with the flow of magic at the center of their being."

"*Pfft...* Magical creatures, indeed. It would certainly go easier for us if all the Celtae on Hibernia had this same aversion to iron as that archer."

"I don't think you can count on that being the case, my lord. I'm told the Celtae clans on Éire use iron weapons very similar to those in Britannica and Germania."

"Let us hope that your Hibernian clans will employ tactics more like their cousins in Britannica, rather than those in Germania."

"Yes, let us hope. I've heard rumors that your new emperor has experienced some... um... difficulties, shall we say, in Germania. Are you quite sure the mere 10,000 men you have brought with you will be sufficient to overcome the hundreds of clans you'll encounter here, my lord?"

"Our esteemed emperor, Titus Flavius Caesar Vespasianus Augustus, has been somewhat distracted by the eruption of Mount Vesuvius burying the cities of Pompeii and Herculaneum two years ago, and then again by the massive fire within Rome itself, just last year. I have no such distractions. As long as that damned archer doesn't have 10,000 arrows at his disposal, I expect no undo difficulties in reinstating you to your father's throne. I fear that single archer more than all of the armies of Hibernia, combined."

CHAPTER ELEVEN

*Most of the time it was probably real bad being stuck down
in a dungeon. But some days, when there was a bad storm
outside, you'd look out your little window and think, "Boy,
I'm glad I'm not out in that!"*
-- Jack Handy

Aryn's Cave
Early June, 81 A.D.

BEFORE ARYN COULD HEAD BACK OUT TOWARDS THE
Drumanagh Peninsula the wind picked up, blowing
surrounding treetops around violently. Maple leaves turned
over, exposing silver undersides — both were sure signs of
an impending storm. He stepped to the cave entrance and
sniffed the wind. Sure enough, he smelled an incredible
amount of moisture in the air, even before the first drops
began pattering at his feet.

Knowing he couldn't venture out until after the storm

passed, he lit torches and set them into brass sconces fastened to the walls deep in the unused portions of the cave. If the sylph Eupnea had managed to find her air elemental friend Aral and they made good on her promise, he suspected he'd be getting an extraordinarily large number of visitors tonight.

ARYN STOOD JUST inside the entrance to his cave and watched the savage fury of the monstrous storm with awe. The wind howled a continuous, deafening crescendo. Lightning flashes revealed the trees just outside the cave were bent, shattered and uprooted everywhere. Never in his entire life had Aryn ever experienced, or even imagined, a storm like this one.

By the gods... Eupnea certainly didn't exaggerate Aral's prowess for creating storms!

The vines normally hiding the entrance to the cave had all been torn away by the wind earlier, leaving it exposed for all the world to see — not that anyone or anything having eyes was still out there to actually see it. The most ancient of all Celtic legends told of a great flood where all life was destroyed, except for a handful of people and animals packed tightly together inside a great ship. This storm reminded Aryn of that tale, as virtually every animal for miles around was nestled snugly together inside his cave — raccoons, deer, rabbits, wolves, foxes, snakes, squirrels, birds, mice and even a couple of bears, all setting aside their natural instincts and fear of one another to escape the common threat of nature at her most furious.

Strangely, even with all the unprecedented violence of the great storm, not a single drop of rain or breath of wind breached the entrance to this enchanted asylum. Neither did the flooding pool overflowing its banks right outside seek entrance. *Odd, not a single fae creature has sought sanctuary from the storm here. I suppose they are all safely tucked away in their own underground barrows.*

Aryn yawned mightily and decided to finally surrender to the siren call of his soft, warm bed. Watching the animals all curled contentedly about their mates and kits in peaceful slumber, right next to their natural enemies and prey without strife, he marveled at the sight. As he lay down and pulled the linen sheet over himself, he felt a surprising pang of discontent. He'd never really thought of his life, nor his bed, as being empty before.

~

The Roman Command Center — Isle of Reachrainn
Early June, A.D. 81

GENERAL GNAEUS JULIUS AGRICOLA, Roman governor of Britannia, gazed wearily up at the recently cleared sky and despaired at the extent of the devastation that lay before him. A minor thunderstorm had blown in the night after that damned archer had killed so many of his men had unexpectedly evolved into a gargantuan tempest of historic proportions. The broken remains of his supply galleys lay smashed against the rocks alongside what little was left of his magnificent command ship. Those poor souls who hadn't managed to make it to higher ground, had all drowned. The bloated bodies of dead horses and men of his personal guard lay strewn about the island like a child's broken and discarded toys.

Two-thirds were just missing... blown out to sea by those impossible winds, along with Agricola's command tent containing most of his field kit and personal luxuries. Only a pitifully few survivors had managed to scramble up the slopes to higher ground, near the finger of land that jutted out to sea, pointing back towards Britannia and directly away from the main island of Hibernia.

The farther from Hibernia they managed to crawl, the safer they were... a not-so-subtle message from the local Hibernian gods, perhaps?

Any other commander would have taken the hint, salvaged what he could and abandoned this campaign as ill omened. But Agricola had not achieved victory in "unconquerable" Britannia, where so many before him had suffered only failure, being timid in the face of adversity. It was difficult to be certain from here, but it appeared that his troops over on the Drumanagh peninsula of the mainland might have fared somewhat better than these poor wretches marooned here on the Isle of Reachrainn.

"Centurion!" Agricola yelled, to the highest-ranking surviving officer he'd located so far. "Have the men be on the lookout for any small boat which might still be intact, or pieces of lumber from which we might fashion one. It's imperative I get to the mainland to see what survived over there."

The bedraggled centurion stiffened to attention and placed his fist over his heart in the traditional Roman salute. "At once, my lord!"

～

The Haunted Forest
Early June, A.D. 81

THE GREAT STORM, which in much later days would be called a hurricane, raged three full days before the first animal in Aryn's cave dared to venture outside again. Once the last of them had finally scurried forth into the tangled mess of what was left of the Haunted Forest, he saddled his horse and tied his bedroll and provisions on behind with soft leather straps. He hung his sharp bronze hand axe on his belt by a loop on its handle and carefully tucked the unstrung golden dragon war bow and the quiver of black arrows snugly between the saddle blanket and saddle.

So clear was the bright blue sky on the day following that great storm, the sunlight appeared unusually intense. Aryn again donned the "sun goggles" that Úna had sent him while his eyes had still been healing after that magical incantation that Finvarra and his Daoine Sidhe had put him through. Even after he no longer needed those goggles to go outside in the sun, it had taken him several months to relearn how to focus his now magically enhanced eyes to see things clearly at various distances. Now he merely wore them as a convenient way to avoid squinting against the brightness and the inevitable headaches that followed.

He carried his regular hunting bow in his left hand as he rode. A quiver of hunting arrows hung on his back with a strap over his shoulder. He was desperately looking forward to his first hot meal after eating nothing but dried jerky for several weeks. His mouth watered at just the thought of a sizzling, succulent rabbit or squirrel, roasted over an open fire.

The Haunted Forest looked nothing like it had just hours earlier. Broken and uprooted trees lay everywhere, at impossible angles in an almost impassible snarl of debris — a snarl that only got worse as he slowly hacked his way through the rubble on his way back towards the Roman landing site on the Drumanagh peninsula. He often had to dismount in tight areas where it was difficult to cut a hole large enough for his horse to get through.

In the mid-afternoon, Aryn's stomach began growling, singing out a message that it had been empty for too long. An abrupt movement seen out of the corner of his eye drew his attention to the underbrush off to his left. There in a tiny clearing sat a fat rabbit, contentedly munching away on a leaf. Aryn slowly reached over his shoulder and pulled a hunting arrow from the quiver riding on his back. Evidently the rabbit had spotted his slow movement, as before he could get an arrow nocked and drawn the rabbit leaped behind some brush and disappeared from view.

Something Úna had said that long ago day suddenly came back to him: *Aryn perceives life forces. He can hit a moving target at distance, even blindfolded. Granted, he isn't much of a target shooter, but he can hit anything as long as it's alive.* Feeling a bit foolish, but goaded on by the intense reaction in his stomach to seeing the plumpness of that rabbit, Aryn closed his eyes. He saw nothing, but... THERE! — He *felt* it — that rabbit was definitely right there. Somehow, he just *knew* it! Without opening his eyes, Aryn loosed his arrow.

He opened his eyes quickly enough to see the tail of his arrow disappear into the thick underbrush. He also thought he'd seen something else in that split second... something impossible. He could have sworn he'd seen his arrow change direction in mid-flight, swerving at the last second as if to avoid obstacles, then enter the brush from an improbable angle. He chalked it up to a hallucination caused by his eyes still adjusting to the sudden increase in light, while trying to refocus.

It took him almost ten minutes of hacking his way through tangles of snarled underbrush to find the rabbit. The animal was still kicking feebly with Aryn's arrow sticking up from between its shoulder blades. He used his bronze dagger to finish off the animal quickly, so that it wouldn't suffer any more than it already had. He then cut a hole between the twin bones in the rear leg and inserted a small twig through the rabbit's leg, from which he hung the body from his leather belt. With his supper now dangling from his right side, Aryn continued hacking his way back toward the Roman encampment.

Near dusk, he spotted an open area near a stream and decided to call it a day. Aryn's arms and shoulders ached horribly from the abuse of swinging that undersized bronze axe, using it in ways for which it was never designed. He used his dagger to skin shavings off of twigs to get down to dry wood for kindling, and used two flints to get a small campfire going. He then skinned and gutted the rabbit, which he hung over the fire on a makeshift spit he had fashioned from green branches. As the rabbit cooked, he scraped and cleaned the hide with his dagger, and then salted and stretched it over a collapsible frame he always carried in his saddlebag for just that purpose. Living off the land for so many years had taught him to never waste anything.

He unsaddled his horse, brushed it down and hung a bag of oats over Frisky's head. He stacked his gear near the fire and laid out his bedroll next to it. When the rabbit was finally ready, Aryn burned his mouth and fingers a few times in his haste to taste that sizzling, succulent meat. As he finished off each delectable piece, he tossed the bones into the fire and watched as it flared momentarily from the burning juices still clinging to the bone. When he finally finished off the last of the rabbit, he wiped the drippings off his chin and cleaned his greasy fingers on a clean linen rag.

When Frisky finished off his oats, Aryn walked him over to the stream so he could drink from the icy cold water. As the horse drank, Aryn knelt down and splashed water onto his face and then wiped face and hands on the rag, to get rid of any remaining grease from his meal.

When the horse finally drank his fill, Aryn tied him to a nearby bush with a loose rein that would give him sufficient freedom to graze. As he lay down in his bedroll, Aryn gazed up at the stars blazing in the night sky, and smiled. Between a Roman invasion and a monstrous storm twin disasters had just struck the Emerald Isle, but at least for tonight, Aryn was content. Memories colored his dreams as he drifted off to sleep under a myriad of sparkling stars.

~

Village of Tallamore
Thirteen years earlier: 68 A.D.

SEUMAS FINNEGAN, chief of clan Ó Fionnagáin, sat in his padded chair near the fire staring out the front window, as had become his habit since giving up the farm and moving into a small cottage on the edge of the village of Tallamore. A solitary rider came into view approaching the cottage, so the white-haired old man leaned forward to see better. The dark-bearded stranger was dressed in nondescript traveling clothes of drab earth tones and a black cloak about his shoulders with the hood pulled up over his head. The stranger's horse was just as nondescript as the rest of him — a mousy brown color.

Normally Seumas would have called for his wife to come identify this stranger, as she was more than a match against any stranger with mischief on his mind, but she wasn't home. His wife of over 50 years had lost her sweet disposition when he'd moved her so far away from the coast after their marriage — away from the ocean that had always been her greatest love. She had grown notoriously loud, obnoxious and highly manipulative, but Seumas knew that was his own fault and didn't care how nasty her disposition grew. He'd been entranced from the moment he'd first laid eyes upon her haunting beauty — an outer beauty she'd lost over the many years they'd been together, along with the inner beauty of her originally sweet personality. He had never been able to pronounce his wife's birth name, so he had always called her *Clydie,* the feminine form of Clyde, meaning "heard from afar" — as fitting a name as anyone who knew her had ever heard.

When the stranger shouted and banged on the door, the old man called for him to enter. Warily, he held a sharp, bronze dagger under the blanket on his lap — just as he always did whenever his wife was away. The stranger entered and stepped closer. There was something eerily familiar about him, but Seumas couldn't quite place it.

"Can I help you, young man?" Seumas asked.

"I was told you'd lost your right foot in the accident. I'm sorry I was away with the army and unable to work the farm for you, after your injury Grandfather."

"Grandfather?" Seumas exclaimed. "ARYN? Gods be good! Is that really you?"

"It is." Aryn moved closer to the frail old man. He hadn't seen his grandfather in more than seven years, since before he'd gone off to the royal university at Deblin. He knew his appearance had changed a lot between the ages of thirteen and twenty-one, so it was no great surprise that his grandfather hadn't recognized him.

"Is Grandmother here?"

"No," replied Seumas. "Today is her market day, so she's out buying victuals for us. You will stay for supper, won't you? Your grandmother would skin me if you came by to visit and she didn't get to see you."

"No worries about that," said Aryn. "But there is something I need to discuss with you privately, while she's not here."

"Oh?"

"Grandfather, I know what she is... so I know what must be in that package that you entrusted to me the last time I saw you."

"How?" asked the startled old man. "We kept it from you after your father reacted so badly, vehemently denying his heritage."

"The faeries told me, Grandfather."

Seumas nodded knowingly. "Your father could always see them as well, but for some reason he hated the idea of being half-fae. He even took up blacksmithing... purposely working with cold iron, so they would avoid him. So, how do *you* feel about what you've discovered about yourself?"

"I have no issues with it, Grandfather. I just need to know where I'm supposed to take her when the time comes to set her free."

The old man sighed and said, "Aye, I guess it's time we

addressed that issue. She was sitting on a rock on a small island in Lough Erne, just outside the village of Pettigoe up in Donegal, when I first saw her," his grandfather mused. "When I pass on, please take her to the mouth of the River Erne, near Ballyshannon, before you give her the package. She'll easily find her way back to her people from there."

"I will."

"So, you're not disturbed by what I did to her?"

"I doubt you really had a lot of choice in the matter, Grandfather. You heard her sing, didn't you?"

"Aye, and never a sweeter sound did ever I hear. It's hard to believe she could have changed into such a shrew, but I had no choice... I had to get her away from the sea, so she wouldn't leave me."

"She couldn't have left you, even if you'd lived right next to it, Grandfather. She can't return to the sea without her *cohuleen druith*. She can't breathe under water without it, any more than you or I can."

"She never told me that!"

"You probably wouldn't have believed her, even if she had. You were under enchantment."

"Aye, but what's done is done. There's no repairing it now. Just take her there to the mouth of the River Erne, when the time comes. She won't remember a thing after she returns to the sea."

"I will, Grandfather. You were really quite fortunate that she didn't drown you, you know. My father and I almost never existed."

"I know."

"I'm a physician now, so how about you letting me take a look at that leg?"

∼

The Eerie System
3232 A.D.

"ALL HANDS! Prepare for transition... I repeat, prepare for transition into the Eerie system in five... four... three... two... one..."

Once again, the universe turned inside out, along with the digestive systems of all 27 crew members of the S.S. *Pagasus*, an independent interstellar freighter contracted to Interplanetary Exploration & Settlements, Inc. It was a profitable milk-run ferrying supplies to their mining operation on the barren but mineral-rich planet called Eerie. The station fabricated titanium containers to hold raw ore, which they then back-hauled to a foundry in orbit around the Confederation planet Cælius, so they made money in both directions. Except for an occasional systems failure it was generally considered a long but unremarkable run, offering little in the way of excitement — which was exactly the way the captain and crew liked it.

"Captain, we, uh... have a problem."

Captain Allan Johansson turned to the ship's astrogator. "A problem, Geraldo? What color problem — a yellow one or a red one? Would you care to be more specific?"

As the rest of the bridge crew softly snickered in amusement, Lieutenant Geraldo Sánchez burned with embarrassment, the latest victim of Captain Johansson's legendary savage wit. Johansson was known for running a tight ship, enforced by the constant dread of ending up on one of his verbal barbs. No one likes being ridiculed in public, but the demand for berths among the *Pegasus'* crew remained high as Johansson was also legendary for attracting highly profitable transport runs.

"Uh..." stammered a red-faced Sánchez. "I'm not sure quite how to say this, Captain. Eerie should be dead ahead of us, but it isn't."

"Astrogation error, Sánchez. How was it you somehow managed to misplace an entire planet?"

Sánchez temper flashed, but he held his tongue. Even though they were civilians, when aboard ship they operated under military style ranks because they were technically a part of the inactive military reserve, subject to being activated at any moment. That hadn't actually happened in the past 34 years, but regardless of how much he might have wanted to fling a smart-ass remark back into his captain's teeth, the penalties for insubordination aboard a starship in space were too terrible to contemplate. He took a deep, calming breath and responded with amazing civility.

"No, Captain. Star sightings have confirmed that we're exactly where we're supposed to be. It's Eerie that is somehow *not* where it's supposed to be."

"I find that highly unlikely, Lieutenant. The last I heard, the laws of physics had not been repealed, so obviously there's been an error somewhere on our end. Scan, I want a 360x360 long range scan of this entire system. Eerie is out there somewhere... FIND IT!"

"Scan, aye, Captain."

"Engineering, we have experienced some kind of astrogation error. I want full diagnostics run on all major subsystems. There's something damned funny going on here, and I want answers as to what the hell is causing it!"

CHAPTER TWELVE

---

*Once the storm is over, you won't remember how you made it
through, how you managed to survive. You won't even be
sure, in fact, whether the storm is really over. But one thing is
certain. When you come out of the storm you won't be the
same person who walked in.*
-- *Haruku Murakami*

The Roman Encampment — Drumanagh Peninsula
Mid-June, A.D. 81

LEGIO IX HISPANA OF THE ROMAN ARMY WAS HUNGRY,
desperately hungry — and Roman General Gnaeus Julius
Agricola, governor of Britannia, was frustrated. A large raft
had finally been lashed together with lumber salvaged from
the wreckage of their galleys grounded on the Isle of
Reachrainn. Agricola finally made it across to his main

encampment on the headland of the Drumanagh peninsula on the fourth day after the storm, to find the survivors there sorting out their personal effects, searching through the debris for usable items, and cataloging what remained. The numbers were dismal. Shared misery seemed to be the most abundant commodity they still had available to them.

It was vital that no one other than that damned Celtae archer who eluded them days earlier become aware of their tenuous beachhead here, so full centuries were dispatched to positions both north and south along the road, to points beyond visual range of the Roman camp. Two more centuries were dispatched about 200 yards into the forest, forming a thin skirmish line a spear-length apart in a large semi-circle, to give warning should anyone approach through the tangled forest. A makeshift stockade was fashioned to hold the trickle of Hibernian travelers captured on the road.

Fresh water was always a concern to an army in the field, but a small mountain of water casks had fortunately survived, stacked in the lee of the peak on the Isle of Reachrainn, and thus sheltered from the worst of the driving wind. That single raft made many trips back-and-forth between the island and the headland, ferrying survivors, those water casks, and a few horses.

Most of what food supplies remained had been ruined by immersion in seawater. Marching rations from the men's personal kits had to be shared with those whose kits had been lost. Even with half-rationing imposed to conserve what was left, the normal seven-day ration would be totally consumed after a mere four days. Foraging parties explored the surrounding forest for what berries and nuts might be found. Agricola ordered his archers into the forest to hunt for game, but deer were scarce and the numbers of squirrels and rabbits taken could not feed so many ravenous appetites.

Fodder for the surviving horses had been spread thinly over the ground to dry in the sun before it could mildew, but salt crystals remained behind on the sun-dried hay and the horses refused to eat it. Reluctant to see their horses suffer from hunger, Agricola ordered their surviving horses slaughtered for their meat. After one large meal of fresh, roasted meat, the rest was cut into thin strips, then smoked and dried into jerky for preservation. Until additional horses and fodder could be brought in from Britannia, his remaining cavalry troopers would have to serve as additional infantry. With the eyes and ears of Agricola's army now afoot, *Legio IX Hispana* was effectively deaf and blind.

Not only had that disastrous storm drowned over 700 Roman soldiers and blown most of their supplies into the sea, it had also blown Agricola's timetables right next to wherever his supplies had ended up. They dare not be caught here on this narrow finger of land by a major barbarian army, but without receiving a lot of replacement supplies from Britannia, they couldn't move an entire legion and their auxiliaries out into the surrounding countryside either. Bodies were stripped and burial parties employed what digging tools they had left, as they set about their grisly tasks. Completion of the triple trench defenses across the entire width of the entrance to the Drumanagh peninsula could not resume for several days after the storm passed.

Regardless of their duties, the men could often be caught stealing worried glances towards the eastern horizon for any sign of their overdue supply galleys. It wasn't until the twelfth day after the storm that the striped sail of an incoming Roman galley was finally spotted. Unfortunately, this galley arrived carrying yet more troops for Agricola's army. While reinforcements were almost always welcome, these additional mouths to feed just added to their already overstretched food supply problems. Comparing notes with the galley's commander revealed to Agricola that seventeen galleys en route to Hispania had failed to arrive. He had to presume they were swamped in the storm, with all aboard lost at sea.

Over a thousand of our people already dead, and we've not advanced so much as a spear-length, nor fought a single battle. This campaign has already become considerably more expensive than I'd anticipated.

The logistics officer for *Legio IX Hispana* dispatched the galley's commander back to Britannia with several scrolls listing the army's most urgent needs, along with handwritten orders from Agricola himself, stressing the urgency of a maximum effort to fill those needs speedily. Now all they could do was pray the gods granted this galley a safe and rapid return to Britannia with news of their plight.

CHAPTER THIRTEEN

No matter where you go, there you are.
-- Confucius

The Eerie System
3232 A.D.

"Uh, I think I may have located our wayward planet, Commander."

Lieutenant-Commander Madulla O. Gatta, executive officer of the interstellar transport SS *Pegasus,* turned to his scan operator, Lt. JG Joe Mullins and shot him an unmistakable look of disgust.

"You *think* you may have found Eerie, Lieutenant? Can you even begin to imagine what kind of response *that* statement would have elicited from Captain Johansson, had he been sitting in this chair right now? Either there is a planet of the appropriate size, orbiting approximately sixteen light-minutes out from the primary, or there isn't. How is it you're not sure?

"Because there isn't," replied Mullins. "There are no planets of *any* size or mass orbiting this star anywhere near sixteen light-minutes out."

What? Star sightings have verified that we're in the proper star system. We've visited Eerie several times before, so where is it now?

"Any indications of a debris field of any kind?" Gatta asked.

"Only a very light dust ring, Commander. But there is one anomaly we've picked up... a very large anomaly."

"Don't make me come over there and shake it out of you, Mullins," Gatta said heatedly. "Spit it out!"

"There's a very large comet headed inbound towards the primary — a very, very large comet."

Gatta shook his head wearily. "Knowing your warped sense of humor, I know I'm going to really hate myself in the morning for asking this question, but if it will get some answers out of you, okay, I'll bite... *How large is it?*"

"The size of a standard planet, but that's not really the weirdest part."

"Goddamnit, Mullins!" the XO roared in exasperation. "I'm about to come grab you by the throat and shake you until your teeth rattle. Stop with all the suspense games and tell me everything you know about this comet, right freaking NOW!"

"Well, sir. You're not going to believe this, but the comet is slowing... for no discernible reason."

"Say WHAT?"

"Our computer estimates that at the current rate of deceleration, that gigantic comet will enter into a stable orbit about the primary, approximately 8.5 light minutes out. If that thing really is our missing planet Eerie, then *something* caused it to move approximately 450 light-seconds farther into the solar system, and then decelerate again into a stable orbit — right dead center in the middle of the life-zone around this star."

Whatever Gatta might have been expecting, *this* certainly had not been it. *Oh dear God... how the hell am I ever going to explain this to Captain Johansson?*

~

The Planet Eerie
3232 A.D.

THE MAMMOTH SHIFTING of the planet's tectonic plates had subsided for a few weeks, allowing Brian Steele's maintenance crew to finally get caught up repairing all of the environmental systems — until now. Once again, the planetary crust was undulating beneath the station like waves at the seashore. Operations personnel had converted the equipment normally used to form the titanium ore containers they used to ship ore back to civilization, into manufacturing titanium columns to shore up the ceilings within the station's myriad tunnels. These were placed wherever the plazsteel coating was beginning to sag and in danger of bursting. Thus they had, so far, avoided all but one cave-in within the station proper.

The environmental systems were now experiencing a whole new round of failures. Filters were lasting less than a day before they needed replacing, so clogged filters were being recycled after being blown out with compressed air, as their stock of replacement filters had been totally depleted during the initial shocks earlier. Choking dust continued to hang in the air despite the recirculator's best efforts to clear it.

Brian's maintenance people worked around the clock just to keep the air semi-breathable. Tempers had flared on occasion, but most of that had subsided as anger required energy they no longer had. Bleary-eyed, filthy men dragged themselves from one emergency to the next, sleeping in shifts when exhaustion finally made it possible.

Cold sandwiches continued to be their meal of choice, as cooking was again suspended during this latest round of quakes. Cooks, managers, office personnel and other operations types helped by running parts from the tool crib out to the techs. One major indication of the seriousness of their situation was when Benny had finally given up trying to document all of parts he was distributing to whom, after the station manager reamed his ass for holding up the process.

It was really a shame that just trying to survive had dropped repair of the external monitors so far down on their priority list. Everyone would have really been quite amazed if only they could have seen the transformation of the surface going on all around them. Trillions of gallons of water was shooting hundreds of feet into the air from thousands of geysers as underground aquifers rushed to the surface. The sight would have been truly spectacular, if only anyone had been able to see a fresh water ocean being created all around them. Another unusual sight that went unnoticed was millions of years of evolution was occurring all around them at an incredibly accelerated rate.

CHAPTER FOURTEEN

"Yes. He saw her in his mind, exactly as she was. She bore him company with her pride, resentment, hatred, all as plain to him as her beauty; with nothing plainer to him than her hatred of him. He saw her sometimes haughty and repellent at his side, and sometimes down among his horse's feet, fallen and in the dust. But he always saw her as she was, without disguise, and watched her on the dangerous way that she was going."
-- Charles Dickens

The Haunted Forest, near the Roman
Encampment
Drumanagh Peninsula
Early July, A.D. 81

POP!

"Aryn, there is a line of Roman soldiers within the forest just ahead of you."

"Thank you for the warning, Rhoslyn," Aryn whispered back. "How far ahead are they?"

"Far enough they haven't seen you yet." Pixies weren't strong in estimating spatial distances, nor in their understanding of numbers greater than they could count on their fingers, so Aryn wasn't overly surprised she couldn't be more specific than that. He marveled that she had the presence of mind to warn him of the danger at all.

So, the Romans are still here. But where are the armies of the high king?

It had taken him over two weeks to finally hack a path back through the devastated forest — what had once been a mere three-day trip before the storm. *When they finally move, they'll have to stick to the roads, as the forest is all but impassable now.*

There was no way to approach the Roman picket line without noisily chopping his way through fallen branches, so Aryn backtracked a couple of hundred yards and began hacking another path to the Southeast, toward the Dublin Road.

"Did you warn Queen Úna and Finvarra about the Roman landing?"

"Yes. She was distressed to learn the Roman invasion Finvarra had prophesied has occurred, she was rather smug to learn it was you who first discovered it. Her husband was chagrined at her gloating about it."

Aryn groaned at the thought of his still being caught between the queen of the faeries and the chieftain of the old gods.

"She said to tell you she would instruct Kyla to rally the fae to the land's defense."

Pfft... Whatever that is supposed to mean.

Rhoslyn complained endlessly as she flew along beside him as he hacked a new path toward the Dublin Road. "You can't imagine how much work I have ahead of me, putting things to right," she whined. "Fortunately rose stems are fairly flexible, so the damage looks worse than it is. I just have to wait until the wood nymphs do something about all those fallen trees and limbs that are lying on my roses. With all this devastation, I certainly don't envy them their task."

Rhoslyn eventually quit complaining, but then started telling him all the gossip among the fae. Her endless chatter wore on Aryn's nerves. He wasn't used to being around others, but felt he had to endure it. She had warned him about the Roman sentries before he blundered into them, so he held his peace as he continued hacking at the tangled underbrush with his rapidly dulling hand axe.

The haphazard snarl of limbs and underbrush didn't seem to hamper little Rhoslyn at all, as she flitted through it as easily as a minnow darting among reeds in a stream. It was near dark by the time Aryn finally hacked himself a path to the road. Looking skyward at the gathering darkness, he decided to wait until morning before probing the Roman defenses.

"Rhoslyn, it's getting too dark to do anything constructive today, so I'm going to call it a night. Thank you for bringing me warning of those Roman sentries standing guard inside the forest."

"You're welcome."

Instead of disappearing as she usually did, Rhoslyn continued flying nearby as he pulled loose branches across the entrance to the path he'd just hacked, obscuring it from sight by anyone traveling along the road. She continued her monologue, sharing all sorts of inane drivel as only pixies can, as he backtracked towards a small stream they had crossed about a thousand yards back. Aryn continued to endure her chatter in silence, as he didn't want to offend her. Her help in scouting the Roman lines would be invaluable on the morrow, as they couldn't see her at all.

Forgoing a fire this close to the Romans, he set up a cold camp on the bank of the stream. After seeing to Frisky's needs, he tied the horse's reins to a branch, spread out his bedroll and chewed on a piece of jerky and a biscuit from his saddlebag. As most faeries don't eat meat, Rhoslyn eschewed the jerky, but she did accept a morsel of his biscuit. After finishing his meager meal, Aryn washed up in the icy stream and grabbed a whetstone from his saddlebag. He sat back down on the edge of his blanket in the deepening darkness and began stroking the whetstone along the length of his much-abused hand axe blade.

~

The Roman Encampment — Drumanagh Peninsula
Mid-July, 81 A.D.

GOVERNOR GNAEUS JULIUS AGRICOLA dispatched the Hibernian prince, Túathal Techtmar, along with an honor guard of five Celtae warriors, mostly younger sons of various Brigantes chieftains, into the storm ravaged wilderness of the island's interior. He had instructed the prince to seek out potential allies from among the Hibernian tribes who had once backed his father, Fíacha Finnolach, when he had reined as high king of Hibernia.

Agricola presumed that many of those chieftains' fortunes had fallen on hard times after Finnolach was overthrown, but they might see reason to hope for regaining their former status if they now fought alongside the son.

Agricola secretly wished he could have sent all 827 of the Brigantes that Techtmar had recruited from Britannia, as that would have meant a lot fewer mouths to feed from his meager stores. But that many men traveling together was sure to attract a lot of unwelcome notice by the locals, who wouldn't hesitate to rouse the entire countryside against what they would assume was a hostile army. Six men could conceivably move about the countryside with relative ease, without attracting undue attention.

Some supplies had finally arrived by supply galleys from Britannia, but until their losses in stores and equipment could be made good, Agricola's legion was vulnerable if a major Hibernian army caught them here on this exposed peninsula. The spiked entrenchments had finally been completed without further interference from that damned archer —whom Agricola privately hoped had been picked up by that hellacious storm and blown clear to Hispania.

Some few local travelers had been captured by his sentries posted to the North and south along the road that followed the eastern coast of the great island of Hibernia, well beyond his main encampment. Fortunately there was little road traffic, as most of the locals struggled to repair the damage to their homes and fields caused by the massive storm. A couple of wandering tinkers and four traveling merchants sat morosely within makeshift wooden cages near the center of the Roman camp, bemoaning their fate and the efficiency of the Roman troops who had suddenly appeared both before and behind, sweeping them into captivity like rabbits snared by a well disguised trap.

Lines formed at the various open messes where cook-fires burned and the evening ration of gruel was dipped in each soldier's personal mess tin from great iron pots. Bread, freshly baked in portable ceramic ovens, was handed out at the end of the line, and the evening water ration was dipped from their rapidly dwindling water barrels into the men's personal cups. Agricola watched with satisfaction as his troops ate their meager portions and settled into normal camp routine. Armor was sanded, straps tightened and short-swords honed — all tasks designed to keep their equipment at combat readiness and keep the men's hands and minds busy.

Secretly he rued the necessity of leaving his best troops behind to keep everything under control in Britannia, while he was stuck campaigning in Hibernia with Legio IX Hispania. Although not quite as disciplined nor as efficient as Agricola's own Legio XX, these men were obviously experienced Roman legionnaires who took great pride in being part of the finest army the world had ever seen. The incredible ferocity of that terrible storm had drowned a tragic number of their fellows and blown most of their food and much of their equipment into the sea, yet they had persevered against the elements and overcome their circumstances. Their resilience should make any commander proud. He scolded himself for not being as appreciative of their sacrifices as he should be.

~

The Haunted Forest, near the Roman Encampment on the Drumanagh Peninsula

Mid July, A.D. 81

BACON! — Aryn awakened drowsily to that unmistakable aroma. Unconsciously, he still associated that smell with the demi-goddess who had helped care for him during his convalescence after her father and a couple of other old gods almost burnt his eyes out of his head during that magical rite they'd subjected him to, several years ago.

Slowly he swam upwards towards full wakefulness, climbing towards that marvelous smell, as though it were rope, until finally his eyes opened of their own accord. Sure enough, there sat Kyla, daughter of Úna and Finvarra, lazily turning pieces of bacon frying in a bronze pan suspended above a small, but lively fire... on nothing discernible. The pan just seemed to float within the flames of its own accord. Aryn wondered if he would ever get used to being around creatures who routinely flung magic about, as second nature as breathing. Kyla noticed him waking, but said nothing, just continuing to turn the bacon she was frying with a bronze fork.

"We're close enough to those Roman sentries for them to smell that bacon you're frying," Aryn said.

"Good," Kyla replied. "Saves me the trouble of finding them, if they come to me."

"I thought the fae didn't eat meat."

"I'm not a pixie! You're part fae and you eat meat, don't you?"

Aryn nodded, conceding the point. He got up and scrounged around looking for kindling that had dried out since the storm. *Two cook fires won't be any more noticeable to the Romans than one.* What he found was damper than he'd have liked, but he dutifully worked at trying to get a spark to catch with his two flint-stones. Striking his flint against a piece of iron would have produced a larger, more usable spark, but he'd given up the use of iron implements during his time living among the fae.

Kyla watched him repeatedly fail in his efforts to get his tiny sparks to catch in the too-damp kindling. She shook her head with a rueful smile. When she noted an exasperated expression cross his features, her smile morphed into one of pure mischief. She nonchalantly waved her hand when Aryn bent low over the tinder, ready to cup the first successful smolder with his hands in preparation for blowing softly to encourage a flame.

Kyla smirked in undisguised amusement when Aryn's kindling all burst into flame at once, leaping up and singeing his eyebrows. Aryn jumped back with a startled yell and fell heavily onto his rump, and she laughed aloud at his look of righteous indignation.

The insolent sass that instantly flared in his mind was thwarted by his urgent need to feed more kindling, lest the tiny fire quickly consume its fuel and burn itself out. Aryn's temper smoldered as he quickly added twigs, sticks and small branches to the fire, but he bit his tongue to stifle an irate retort.

That would make just make me sound whiney.

After finally reining in his anger, he responded in a way that totally surprised her. "Thank you."

Kyla lifted one eyebrow at his unexpectedly controlled response, marveling that he had not lashed out in anger. "You're welcome."

"Since you're obviously better at lighting fires than I am, that can be one of your camp chores from now on."

Kyla bristled at his implication of having the authority

to assign her duties of any kind, but she stifled her own angry retort. *It wouldn't do for a mortal to display more emotional control than a demi-goddess.*

"I'm sure I am better than you are at quite a lot of things."

"You have me at an extreme disadvantage, my lady. I am only a poor mortal with hardly any fae blood at all, while you are half goddess. I could never be so bold nor foolhardy to believe myself your equal in any endeavor, your highness."

His words are those of a humble supplicant, but that mischievous twinkle in his eye... He is not cowed at all! — Is he mocking me?

When she didn't respond, Aryn scooped some water from the nearby stream into a small bronze pot that he always carried in his saddlebags, then dug out some ground meal and added it to the water. He tore jerky into strips, and then into yet smaller chunks and added them to the water, just in case Her Magnificence didn't see fit to share any of her delicious-smelling bacon. He quickly fashioned a small A-frame and positioned it on either side of his fire, hanging his porridge pot over it to simmer.

He then fed and watered his horse, occasionally returning to his fire to stir the thickening gruel. Kyla pulled bacon strips from her pan as they became crispy and laid them out onto a clean linen rag she had spread out on the ground beside her... popping the last one absent-mindedly into her mouth.

HOT!

Kyla quickly grabbed for her canteen to douse the flames in her mouth, and then shot a glance toward Aryn to see if he had noticed her act of foolishness. She reddened in embarrassment at Aryn's smirking grin, angry at herself for doing something so thoughtless and stupid in front of a mortal. Aryn turned away to save her any further embarrassment and grabbed a small ceramic jug having a cork plug in the top, that he then brought to Kyla.

"If you don't normally save your bacon grease, you can pour it in here." When Kyla looked up at him questioningly, he explained. "I sometimes debone small game like squirrel or rabbit and cut the meat into chunks. Then I dust them with flour and pan fry them in used grease... bacon grease is one of the best for that."

Kyla nodded and took the jug. She poured the leftover grease from her pan into it, and replaced the stopper. "I prefer mine roasted on a spit, over a fire."

"Oh, that's the way I usually eat mine too, especially when I'm tired, or in a hurry. Other times though, the extra work is well worth it as the breading seals the juices into the meat and takes on some of the flavor of the grease. Less drips off into the fire."

Kyla admitted to herself that the idea did sound rather intriguing, but she couldn't bring herself to admit it to Aryn. She merely sniffed, as though the idea was beneath notice. "Whatever," she said dismissively.

As expected, Kyla declined his offer to share his jerky infused porridge with a look of distain. She also seemed on the verge of declining his offer of a semi-stale travel biscuit until he cut one into halves with his dagger and slathered each half with boysenberry jam retrieved from his saddle-bag. Her eyes lit at the sight of jam, so he offered her one, careful to keep the smile he felt building inside from reaching his face. She took his extended offering and took a bite, eyes closing in near ecstasy as she chewed the jam-slathered biscuit.

"*Umm...* Do you always pack these kinds of luxuries with you when you travel?"

"When I can. It just seemed prudent to bring along as much as I could carry, as I expect this trip will last longer than usual. I can't just pop in and out from place to place, like *some* people... or goddesses."

Kyla ignored the jibe, but she did offer Aryn a couple of strips of her bacon in return for another entire biscuit with jam. They ate in silence until Rhoslyn suddenly popped in between them.

"There's a Roman soldier about to stumble into your campsite." She pointing towards the northeast. "Any second now... right about there."

Aryn scrambled to string his golden bow, but Kyla merely licked the jam from her fingers and picked up her bronze fork she'd recently been turning bacon with. Sure enough, seconds later a Roman soldier pushed his way through the brush into the small clearing of Aryn's campsite.

The Roman was startled to see them, but quickly reached to yank his gladius from its scabbard. But before the invader could pull his short-sword free, Kyla's thrown fork took him in the throat. The Roman's eyes widened in surprise, slowly glazing over as his knees buckled. He toppled forward, gurgling the remainder of his life away, unable to remove Kyla's fork which had pierced his windpipe and embedded itself between the bones of his neck.

"Another!" Rhoslyn shouted, as she pointed off the left. Kyla turned and reached for her dagger just as a second soldier entered the clearing and hoisted his pilum in preparation to throw. Before he could launch his spear, Aryn's razor-sharp bronze skinning knife buried itself his right eye. The soldier let out a blood-curdling scream, but was dead before his body hit the ground. Kyla parried the sword thrust of yet a third Roman, giving ground only after two more pushed their way through the underbrush in search of the source of that scream.

Rhoslyn waved her tiny hands frantically and appeared to be singing an incantation of some sort. Massive, fully mature rose bushes with stems thicker than a man's thumb suddenly erupted from the ground between Kyla and the last two Romans. Both soldiers were immediately entangled in the unusually long thorns. The third soldier again closed for the attack, but Kyla recognized that his thrust was merely a feint and launched a furious attack of her own.

The other two soldiers tore themselves free of the entangling thorns with a curse, skirting around the rose bushes to come after Aryn, who was still struggling to restring his great golden bow. As one ran towards him at a trot, the second reared back to throw his pilum. Just as the legionnaire loosed his spear, a 12-foot-tall Rhoslyn suddenly popped into visibility to the Romans. She swatted the thrown pilum out of the air with a gigantic hand, as the running soldier skidded to a stop right in front of her. The Roman recovered from the shock of the gigantic pixie's unexpected appearance, pausing for a moment to consider how he should go about attacking a creature over twice his height.

Aryn finally wrestled the balky bowstring into its notch and pulled three arrows from his quiver. He clenched two of them in his teeth as he drew the third. The Roman thrust his gladius upwards with the intension of disemboweling Rhoslyn, but she quickly disappeared again with another soft pop. Her sudden disappearance was almost as disconcerting as her sudden appearance had been, causing the Roman to overbalance when the gigantic target of his thrust wasn't there anymore. The Roman's large shield dipped just enough to allow Aryn to plant his first black-tipped magic arrow in the side of the man's neck.

The legionnaire sparring with Kyla was a good swordsman, but he was mortal and didn't possess the reflexes of a demi-goddess. Neither had his Roman army drill instructors taught him moves impossible for a mere mortal to accomplish, so Kyla had all the advantages — speed, stamina and strength —which she employed to good effect as she toyed with the Roman as a cat toys with a cornered mouse before killing and eating it.

After seeing his fellow legionnaire fall to Aryn's arrow, the Roman who had thrown the spear retreated back into the trees to call loudly for reinforcements from his fellows deeper in the forest. Losing sight of his second target, Aryn glanced over towards Kyla and noted that she was in no imminent danger from the hard-pressed Roman she was sparring with. He hurriedly packed up his cooking implements, rolled up his bedding and saddled his horse, preparing to make a quick escape before more Romans showed up in response to the screaming soldier's urgent cries for assistance.

"More Romans will be on their way here soon," Aryn called out. "You might consider finishing what you're doing, so we can make our exit before we end up having more guests than we can feed."

Kyla spared Aryn an annoyed glance and snorted, "Oh, all right. I guess I've played with this one long enough."

The Roman facing her was astounded when she abruptly sheathed her dagger and turned her back to him. Her thoughtless dismissal of him, right in the middle of combat, enraged the insulted Roman and he raised his gladius high, running to strike her down from behind. Aryn started to shout a warning, but broke it off in mid-syllable when Kyla spun suddenly and unleashed a crackling blue lightning bolt from the palm of her clawed left hand. That lightning enveloped her adversary, eliciting an undulating scream from the Roman as he crumpled to the ground. Wisps of smoke rose lazily from the man's smoldering corpse.

"Remind me not to make you angry in the future."

Kyla grinned at him and nonchalantly stooped down to retrieve her frying pan. She then walked to the stream to wash it out. "Oh, just a little something I inherited from my father," Kyla said.

Aryn handed her a drying rag from out of his saddlebag. "Remind me not to anger him, either."

Kyla snorted in amusement as she dried her frying pan with the rag. Aryn watched with interest to see where she put it afterward, as she had brought no discernible baggage. She finished drying the pan and then turned slightly away, shielding most of it from his view for just an instant. With a sweeping motion of her free hand, the frying pan simply disappeared, as though it had never been.

"Nice trick. Must cut down on your packing chores quite a bit, being able to magically create things whenever you need them."

"Not as much as you might think. That pan is real, made here by a mortal smith. It still exists. I just sent it... um, elsewhere."

"Elsewhere?"

Kyla gave Aryn a studied look, as if pondering whether she should even try to explain it to someone not having her innate abilities. "It's rather hard to explain to anyone not growing up using magic."

"I don't know much of anything about magic. Never needed to, as I don't have any myself."

"Oh, you do. You've just never been evaluated or trained in its use like I was."

Aryn raised an eyebrow at her unexpected comment. "Interesting. I wouldn't mind pursuing that thought further, but we don't really have the time to discuss it right now. We need to make ourselves gone from here pretty soon, unless you don't mind facing down a few dozen more of those Roman invaders."

Aryn snugged down the cinches on his horse's saddle and made sure his saddlebags were tied on properly. He then mounted and turned Frisky's head so that he was again facing Kyla, who was standing on the ground looking up at him.

"Do you need a ride, or are you planning to pop out, like Rhoslyn does?"

"I'm not a pixie!" Kyla snapped.

"Hey, how am I supposed to know what you can and cannot do?"

Aryn removed his foot from the stirrup on that side, and leaned down to offer the demi-goddess his hand. Kyla gave him a sour look, but finally nodded and stuck the toe of her boot into the stirrup and took his outstretched hand. Aryn grasped her hand firmly and yanked her up onto the horse's rump behind him. He then turned Frisky towards the path he had hacked through the devastated forest to the East Coast Road the previous evening and urged him forward at a fast walk. They hadn't gone more than a hundred yards or so when they heard voices shouting behind them.

"Sounds like they've found those bodies we left back in the clearing." Aryn looked back over his shoulder. "Maybe we need to move along a little faster."

He gave Frisky a slight nudge with his heels. The roan tossed his head and broke into a slow trot. Kyla looked around Aryn's shoulder at their path ahead with concern, but nodded, relieved to see that was clear enough to present no danger of Frisky breaking a leg at this speed.

"You don't have to unstring that war bow when you're not using it, you know," Kyla said.

"No, I didn't know that. I didn't get much instruction on its use after I was blinded by that magic... *whatever* your father and his fellow gods and goddesses worked on me."

"It's not like a bow made by mortals. It won't lose its strength if left strung between uses."

Aryn shrugged. "Good to know. As I said, I don't know much about magic."

Kyla didn't rise to his baited comment, which might have led her back to expounding further on her earlier contention that he really did possess unknown magical powers. She just glanced back behind them, as if watching for pursuing Romans.

When Frisky reached the barrier of shrubs Aryn had placed across the entrance to the path he'd cut the previous day, he nudged the horse to push through it. Before Kyla could protest, her complaint was cut short when she realized the shrubs were no longer attached to the ground and Frisky was pushing through them easily.

"There's the East Coast Road ahead. I'm going to head south towards Deblin. We need to find out why the clans are not gathering to repel these invaders."

When they reached the road, Kyla surprised him by saying, "Stop here."

Aryn pulled Frisky to a halt and Kyla pushed herself off the horse's rump and dropped deftly to the ground behind it. She walked around to the side and said, "Go, gather your Celtae."

"You want me to just leave you here? You don't strike me as the type to relish walking when you could ride."

"Oh, I don't plan on walking." Kyla waved her hands and muttered an incantation. Soon a shimmering distortion appeared in the air over her head. She emitted a sharp, warbling whistle, directed up towards the distortion. Short minutes later, a large bird appeared in the western sky, swiftly winging its way toward them. As the bird approached, Aryn marveled at its size. But when it came close enough to begin making out details, he gaped in astonishment. *That's no bird.* The creature had the head of an eagle, but the body of a lion.

A gryphon!

The gryphon settled down within six feet of Kyla and immediately began melting. *No, not melting... transforming.* Within seconds, the gryphon's features completely rearranged themselves. The beak elongated into a handsome equine muzzle. The legs and spine grew longer, the feet metamorphosed from claws into hooves. The chest and neck widened and became more massive. When the transformation was complete, the gryphon was gone and there stood one of the most beautiful horses Aryn had ever seen. Sleek, shining and midnight black, with snow-white mane and tail, and four white stockings... at least Aryn thought they were white.

It's kinda hard to tell through all those flames.

The beast's eyes were otherworldly, blood-red and glowing brightly from within. There before him stood the most fearsome of all fae creatures. *A púka!* Púkas were shape shifters, capable of taking on virtually every imaginable form, and even some unimaginable ones... forms straight out of nightmares. Their most common appearance was that of a normal horse, which was why horse thieves were rare on the island — one never knew if the horse one was trying to steal might be a púka in disguise.

Trying not to gawk, Aryn said, "I'm surprised Frisky isn't going wild, next to that thing."

Kyla grinned. "Frisky was raised from a foal around púkas. Somehow, he always seems to be able to recognize Nightmare, regardless of whatever form he is in."

"Nightmare? Is that what you call that thing? Appropriate."

Kyla laughed as she leapt aboard the púkas back, without the benefit of a saddle. "I thought it was. There wasn't enough room in that tiny clearing where we fought those Romans for Nightmare to land. That's why I doubled up behind you until we reached a more open area, so I could call him."

"Celtae peasants are simple people. Those flaming feet are likely to terrify everyone we come across. How are we to convince anyone to gather their war bands, if everyone we try to talk to runs away screaming?"

Kyla sniffed dismissively, as though she didn't much care about frightening Celtae peasants. Finally she nodded and leaned forward to whisper in the púkas ear. Nightmare snorted and jerked his head up, but slowly the flames surrounding his hooves diminished and then faded away altogether.

"Better."

"You'd better let me send that dragon bow away to where I sent my pan, lest your war chiefs become more interested in stealing it from you than in listening to your story about invading Romans."

CHAPTER FIFTEEN

*A slipping gear could let your M203 grenade launcher fire
when you least expect it. That would make you quite
unpopular in what's left of your unit.*
-- August 1993 issue of Preventive Maintenance Monthly

The Planet Eerie
3232 A.D.

BRIAN STEELE WAS DEVOTING ABOUT HALF OF HIS TIME
to training operations techs to perform preventative and
corrective maintenance on the station's ancient air purifiers.
Just keeping the filters clear was a Herculean task during
the hundreds of recent quakes.

Operations personnel had spent hundreds of man-hours
shoring up the ceilings in the vital equipment rooms, storage
areas and living spaces within the station proper. Three
more access tunnels had collapsed, killing another four
people, but those had eventually been dug out and cleared.

Crews were now in the process of digging their way towards the surface... a filthy process that raised ungodly clouds of dust that continuously wafted throughout the station.

Filters were being replaced and blown out about every two hours. In spite of Brian's best efforts, the air recyclers just could not cope with the incredible amount of dust that hung in the air like curtains. A thin layer of mud had to be skimmed off the surface of water before it could be used or consumed. Even the food tasted of rock dust. Almost everyone developed a hacking cough as their lungs tried to expel the crud they'd inhaled in spite of the rebreathers everyone wore. Every air compressor in the station had had to be overhauled at least twice, from overheating issues.

Electrical power was also becoming problematic. Power feeds from the solar arrays on the surface went dead on the fourth day after the first round of quakes began, forcing the crew to rely totally on the three nuclear reactors buried deep in the bedrock of the planet. Now, after this second round of quakes seemed to finally subside, only one reactor still survived... a situation that gave Brian nightmares.

Reactor #2 had to be shut down when the radiation containment vessel ruptured, requiring them to cement it in with several tons of silicon cement. Technicians in radiation suits were currently working to repair a leaking coolant circulator in Reactor #3.

Everyone desperately needed a decent meal and at least twelve hours of uninterrupted sleep, but they dared not. The slightest pause from their labors and that damnable dust would totally overwhelm them. Somehow, they had to reach the surface — not that there was any breathable air up there, but a supply ship was due to arrive any day now and the escape that ship represented was now their only logical hope for survival.

~

The Deblin Road
Mid-July, 81 A.D.

"YOU'VE CALLED this road by two different names — the *East Coast Road* and the *Deblin Road*. Why does the same road have two different names?"

Aryn glanced over where Kyla rode beside him on her disguised púka. "It's perfectly logical. Inbound, coming towards Deblin, we call it the Deblin Road because that's where it goes. Outbound, it runs north along the eastern coast of the island, so it's called the East Coast Road. Its name is dependent upon which direction you're traveling."

She blinked at him like he had three heads. *Is he jesting with me?* But as his expression remained serious, she merely shook her head and pondered how such an illogical people could have possibly managed to defeat her ancestors, the Tuatha Dé Danann. They continued their journey in silence, but just outside Deblin Aryn reluctantly surrendered his golden dragon war bow into her outstretched hand. With a sweep of her arm, Kyla sent it away to wherever her frying pan had disappeared to earlier.

Aryn chided himself for his reticence to give up that bow. He'd only used it once in all the years he'd had it and he'd killed a lot more Romans with his hunting bow than he had with the war bow. It wasn't out of fear that Kyla might actually refuse to return it when the time came. After all, her father had personally given it to him and Kyla was unlikely to second-guess the high king of the old gods, even if she was his daughter. But Aryn had lived alone in the forest so long that he'd grown unused to the idea of easily trusting other people.

Not that a demi-goddess is really anything anyone might consider "people," regardless of her relatively normal human appearance.

"Feeling naked without your dragon war bow?" Kyla asked, as they approached the city gate at a slow walk.

"Not really. That one Roman I killed back in the clearing was the first and only time I've ever used it. It's been stored in that trunk in my cave where you put it all those years ago. I only retrieved it after the Romans landed recently."

"Beware getting too attached to it. It has a strange power to ensorcel whoever wields it. Its beauty makes them feel invincible... they get careless, which usually gets them killed."

"Thanks for the warning. It's beautiful and all that, but it's those black arrows that I find most intriguing. I can't figure out why they're all tipped with what looks like glass. It seems they'd be so brittle they'd just shatter on impact on almost anything, but especially against armor breastplates."

"I wouldn't worry about that happening. But you're right, they're made of obsidian... black volcanic glass. The combat magicians of the Tuatha Dé Danann found that material ideal for enchanting arrowheads, giving them the magical ability to penetrate virtually any kind of armor."

"Oh?" Aryn's eyebrows rose at that revelation. "*That* kind of information might have been rather useful before your mother volunteered me as her champion in this war. What else might I have *not* been told that I really should know?"

Kyla's temper flashed at Aryn's implied criticism of her mother, but she stifled it quickly. *He's right.* She glanced upwards, closed her eyes, took in a deep breath and let it out slowly to calm herself.

"Look, you've spent a lot of time around Rhoslyn, so you know how faeries are. Unfortunately, my mother has a bit more of Rhoslyn in her than I like to admit. As much as I dearly love my mother, my father obviously didn't exactly marry her for her great intellect."

Aryn gawked at her in surprise, as he really hadn't expected to hear such a personal admission from the formidable demi-goddess.

"You're right though. My mother should have paid you a visit after your recovery and given you instructions on the use of the war bow and the inherent properties of the black arrows. She is sweet as molasses, but... um... let's just say she's easily distracted."

"Well, I guess I can understand that. Still, it would have been nice to know their capabilities, limitations and exactly what she and your father expect of me. Anything else you can tell me about them?"

"The war bow has virtually unlimited range. If you can see your target, you can hit it. Of course, from what Mother said about your ability to sense life essences blindfolded, you might even be able to hit an enemy you can't see. Even my father could never do that."

The pair rounded one final curve in the road and saw a line of people and carts waiting at the gate to the city. Small flocks of ducks, chickens and pigs were each herded by drover, accompanied by a small army of dirty children to keep the animals together. Four warriors were slowly passing people through the city gate, after routine questioning about identity, their intended business in the city and a cursory inspection of the goods loaded in the carts.

Authority amongst the Celtae tribes on Éire was highly

fragmented. The high kingship was largely a ceremonial position, as the high king (*rí ruírech*) technically held authority only over the territory immediately surrounding his royal compound at Tara. As such, the provincial kings (*rí coícede*) were pretty much free to act however they saw fit. The only time the high king could rule undisputed was during a national calamity, and even then the provincial kings were not always fully cooperative.

Deblin was something of an oddity on Éire, as the Celtae people native to the island were more of a rural, tribal folk, disinclined to clustering closely together in anything larger than a village. Originally built by invading *Ostmen* (Danish Vikings) during earlier days, Deblin evolved into the largest city on the island. With its sheltered harbor, the city quickly became the largest port and primary distribution hub for merchant goods coming in from all over the mostly Roman world. Thus, Deblin was primarily a sanctuary for "outsiders," those not originally from Éire... peopled mostly by foreign merchants, but governed by the local Celtae king.

Its proximity to the Roman landing site on the Drumanagh Peninsula made Aryn assume the city would be the invader's initial target after they regrouped their army and began their march. Thus, it was Deblin he decided that needed warning of the Roman invasion.

"Well, well... and what might your name be, beautiful?"

Aryn was startled out of his woolgathering to find a burly warrior leering up at Kyla. Like most Celtic warriors, this one wore a leather cuirass over a linen shirt, a plaid kilt over cotton leggings, leather boots and a two-handed long sword in a scabbard strapped across his back. Before Aryn could find his voice, the big warrior stepped closer and reached to run his hand suggestively up the inside of Kyla's leg. She looked down at the warrior's hand slowly creeping toward her groin... and she smiled — a smile so cold Aryn silently prayed he'd never see her look at him that way.

Emboldened when Kyla didn't squeal or try to slap his hand away, the leering warrior grinned broadly and suddenly thrust his hand directly into her crotch. The demi-goddess snap-kicked him under the chin, lifting him clear off his feet with her supernatural strength. The warrior closest to the altercation drew his long sword and yelled to his fellows after the groper went down and didn't move.

As the three converged on Kyla with swords drawn, Aryn finally found his voice, "HOLD!"

The closest guard snarled, "And who might you be, to be giving orders to the king's warriors?"

"I am Aryn Finnegan, of the clan Ó Fionnagáin. I have urgent news for the *rí dáil*. Invaders have landed at the Drumanagh peninsula."

~

The Planet Eerie
3232 A.D.

"WHAT'S A *RÍ DÁIL?*"

Brian Steele looked up to see big Dan Weaver, who had obviously been reading over his shoulder as he typed. Many of the station personnel Steele worked closely with knew he was writing some kind of fantasy story, based on an ancient people from a forgotten island on an almost equally forgotten world. Most people knew that humanity originated on Old Earth, before the Great Diaspora. Few, however, were aware of the recent resurgence of interest in Celtic fantasy among fans of the genre. Weaver was one of the few who was genuinely interested in Brian's writing.

"It's a Gaelic term denoting the title of a local king."

"What's Gaelic?"

"Gaelic is the language the ancient Celts spoke in Ireland, on Old Earth over 3,000 years ago."

"You speak this Gaelic thing?"

"No, but I have an English-Gaelic dictionary and thesaurus on my computer I consult whenever I need an authentic Gaelic word."

Big Dan scratched his head, obviously confused. "Why bother? I mean, why go to all the trouble to do all that research, just to salt your story with ancient words no one will understand anyway?"

"You just answered your own question, Dan. Salt — periodically salting the story with real Gaelic words lends it a level of authenticity it wouldn't otherwise have. Just as salt adds flavor to otherwise bland food, my use of genuine Gaelic adds a certain natural flavor to the story, providing readers with a level of enjoyment they wouldn't have necessarily achieved if I hadn't. It's subtle and highly subliminal, but a very effective technique."

"If you say so. Just one more question and then I'll leave you alone and quit bothering you."

"Shoot."

"I can't figure out why you're using an old, antiquated keyboard to type out your story. Wouldn't just dictating the story orally be faster?"

"Yes, but faster doesn't always mean better."

Weaver looked puzzled.

"Typing the story manually slows me down... lets me see what my phrasing will look like on the written page.

Being able to see the words displayed on the screen also helps me with self-editing and rearrangement of material when necessary. I searched for a long time just to find one of these old beasties that still worked. I paid through the nose for it, after I found it."

"Oh."

"How is the tunneling towards the surface progressing?"

A sour look crossed Weaver's features. "Slowly. Very slowly. We have to cut in a large spiral, as we can't risk more than a fifteen percent incline or the ore haulers won't be able to climb it. Our math gurus calculate this whole tectonic plate we've been working may have shifted several miles laterally, but they have no idea in what direction. At the rate the air is growing stale down here, it'll be a bloody miracle if we ever make it to the surface at all."

"Any progress on development of that VLF beacon?" It had been Brian's idea for the station's one remaining electronics engineer to design a Very Low Frequency transmitter, as signal wavelengths at those frequencies are so long they can easily penetrate miles of planetary crust and still be detectible at the surface.

"Our electronic brainiac seems to think he can have it finished in a couple more days, if he can get those home-made inductors of his to behave anywhere near the proper values. Then we just have to pray that incoming supply ship has equipment that can detect a signal at that low of a frequency."

~

City of Deblin
Mid-July 81 A.D.

"*PFFT...* Probably just another nuisance raiding party." The big warriors standing guard at the city gate looked doubtful at Aryn's claim.

Aryn shook his head. "No, this is the vanguard of a full-blown invasion. They've already built staked entrenchments clear across the mouth of the peninsula."

The three guards looked dubious at this. "The *Lochlanach* do not build such defensive fortifications while on a raid."

"These invaders are not Norsemen," Kyla answered. "They are Romans."

"Romans?" The remaining three guards looked genuinely alarmed at this pronouncement. "You two come with us. The king must be made aware of this."

A concerned murmur arose among the people outside the gate, as the words "invaders" and "Romans" filtered back through the crowd like wildfire.

"You there!" shouted another of the guards to one of the farmers waiting to enter the city with a cart loaded with wheat. He pointed to the unconscious guard that Kyla had kicked. "Hoist this man up on your cart and follow us to the rí dáil's castle."

"But, we're bound for the central market to sell our wheat to the breweries," the farmer complained.

"You're bound for wherever I tell you, farmer. Or, would you rather I commandeer someone else's cart, while you remain outside the city until winter, and your wheat rots?"

At that, the farmer frowned, but ordered his two big strapping sons to heft the unconscious guard atop the wheat on their cart.

"Careful," Kyla cautioned. "His jaw is probably broken."

The three guards laughed aloud at that absurd idea, but they all nonchalantly stepped a bit farther out of reach of Kyla's foot, just in case. Two of the three warriors remained at the gate to process the growing line of people and animals still waiting to gain entrance to the city, while the largest of them escorted the two mounted message bringers and the farmer's cart bearing their unconscious comrade to the king's fortress.

Deblin was designed from antiquity to function as the major trading port for the entire island of Éire. Thus, the majority of the city's inhabitants were merchants of foreign origin. Most were from the Celtic tribes of Britannia, Hispania, Gaul and Germania, but a few also originally hailed from the Norse kingdoms. As the major trading center, Deblin was a tempting target for raiders, so it was also the only one on the entire island to have a stone wall surrounding it. The *rí dáil's* fortress, also built of stone, perched ponderously atop a hill at the city center.

Deblin was ruled by Dáire Doimthech, whose prestige rivaled that of the provincial king. A grizzled warrior of over forty-five summers, his attire was not as grandiose as one might expect for a man of his rank — simple, and similar to that of his warriors at the gates except for the shining bronze breastplate covering his torso and a thin silver diadem just above his brow.

Doimthech sat atop an intricately carved dark wooden throne hearing the petition of a prominent merchant. He looked up when the burly warrior entered with a hunter wearing a peculiar patchwork of dissimilar animal skins and a raven-haired beauty dressed most curiously for a female.

The king raised his hand, causing the merchant to pause in presenting his plea.

"Lugaid, what is it you have brought me this morning?" asked the king.

"Travelers claiming that a Roman invasion force has landed on the Drumanagh Peninsula."

"Romans, here? Who claims to have seen this supposed landing?"

The hunter stepped forward. "I am Aryn Finnegan, of the clan Ó Fionnagáin... *fáithliaig,* (physician) *poitigeir* (apothecary) and *fiagaí* (hunter) — son of Chesser, the *gobaí,* (blacksmith) — son of Seumas, *rí clainne* (clan chieftain). I personally witnessed Roman galleys unloading an entire legion of regulars, with their auxiliaries and about a thousand Celtae warriors from Britannia."

The king gave Aryn a sour look, but nodded and turned his attention to the slender raven-haired beauty who accompanied him. "And you, my lady?"

"I am Kyla. I too can vouch there are Romans here."

"Kyla is my cousin," Aryn interjected, to divert any deeper questioning of her familial affiliation.

Doimthech pursed his lips in thought. "Lugaid, sound the war drums. Send out messengers to alert the *clanna* to gather their war bands, and bring them here to the city."

"At once, *rí dáil!*" Lugaid turned and sprinted from the throne room.

"Caoimhín Mac Aengus," the king bellowed, to summon his closest advisor.

At that moment, Rhoslyn suddenly materialized between Aryn and Kyla with a soft *pop* and immediately whispered into their ears. Aryn glanced towards Dáire Doimthech to see if he had somehow noted the pixie's arrival, but his attention was elsewhere.

Moments later, an elderly gray-haired warrior with facial wrinkles deep enough to resemble crevices stepped into the throne room. "Caoimhín, we are on a war footing, as of now. Send messengers to all of the freemen farmers and instruct them to deliver as much grain and as many meat animals as they have at hand to the city immediately. We must make all preparations to endure a siege."

The old man blinked in surprise at the king's pronouncement, but he didn't question who it was they might be at war with. He merely nodded and turned to go. "It shall be done as you command, *rí dáil*."

As the adviser turned to go, Aryn cried, "Wait!" He turned towards Doimthech.

"Rí Dáil, the Romans have suffered mightily from the recent storm. They won't be ready to march until their supplies can be replenished by sea. They huddle behind their defensive entrenchments on the Drumanagh Peninsula. If the war bands move quickly, we can trap them there on that peninsula and drive them into the sea."

Doimthech flicked his hand towards Mac Aengus in dismissal, waiting until the old man disappeared before speaking. "We too have suffered mightily from the recent tempest. There will be no attack. I need every warrior manning the city walls while we stockpile as many supplies as possible. If these *Ròmanach* of yours are delayed by supply problems of their own, so much the better. That will gain us more time to prepare to receive their assault, when it finally comes."

◞

The Tara Road
Late July 81 A.D.

LATE JULY 81 A.D. "*AMADÁN!*" (fool) Kyla exclaimed in utter disgust. For several miles, Aryn had been listening to her ongoing tirade against Dáire Doimthech's decision to hide behind his city walls instead of marching his war bands to confront the Romans immediately while they were still bottled up on the Drumanagh Peninsula. "*Cridhe na circe!*" (faint-hearted coward).

Aryn marveled at the sheer number of derogatory invectives she had come up with to express her utter disgust with the *rí dáil* of Deblin. With the king's reluctance to march, they had immediately set out for the *rí ruirech's* (high king's) residence at the Hill of Tara before Kyla's temper and mouth got them both locked up in Doimthech's dungeon. Their only hope now was that Elim mac Conrach could rally the provincial kings (*rí coicede*) and gather the 30,000 warriors it would take to overcome such a large number of highly disciplined Romans.

"You should have let me fry that sniveling coward with a bolt," Kyla accused.

Aryn had had to actually leap between the two, to keep Kyla from physically attacking the king, right in his own throne room.

"Oh, that would have solved everything! I doubt that even *you* could have hacked your way through the 100 warriors of Dáire Doimthech's personal bodyguard before they finally overwhelmed you... and then where would the land be?"

"I could have blasted that pathetic excuse for a king and then called Nightmare to come rescue us from the retribution of his bodyguards."

"So then we could have just ridden away on your flying púka, leaving Frisky behind — and me with a blood-price on my head?" Aryn snarled. "Fine for you! You can just disappear into one of your faerie barrows for a few hundred years, but I have to live here!"

"Have all the Celtae become so *cladhaireach* (cowardly) since your ancient ancestors drove the Tuatha Dé Danann underground?"

Aryn's temper flashed at her implied inclusion of *him* within her global accusation of widespread cowardice among his people, but he bit his tongue. He'd had a glimpse of the powers she wielded, so it didn't appear wise to get into an all-out confrontation with a demi-goddess.

"Why aren't you out gathering all your *bith os-nàdarra* (supernatural beings) in defense of the land? Do you have nothing better to do than defaming my people and complaining to me?"

"Very well, then," Kyla snapped. "I've endured quite enough of your insufferable company, anyway."

Kyla pulled her púka to a stop. *"Trom-laighe... cruth-atharrachadh gribhinneach."* Immediately her púka began melting, again reshaping itself from horse to griffin.

"Sgiath!" she yelled, after the transformation was complete. The púka leapt into the air on its great wings. Without looking back, Kyla and her púka quickly disappeared into a nearby cloud.

Aryn was so angry, it took him two full hours to realize she hadn't returned his magic golden dragon war bow to him before she left.

CHAPTER SIXTEEN

I have learned to use the word "impossible" with the greatest caution.
-- Wernher von Braun

SS Pegasus
The Eerie System
3232 A.D.

THE GIANT "COMET" STOPPED OUT-GASSING AND settled into a stable orbit about the system primary. It was now accepted they had indeed found their missing planet — mass analysis was virtually identical to that of Eerie to within four decimal places. No one had any idea how an entire planet might have somehow managed to move itself so far sunward, and then slow into a stable orbit again. The whole idea was preposterous and violated the known laws of physics. Orbiting bodies just did NOT leave their orbits, accelerate at a right angle from their previous orbital path, and then decelerate again into another stable orbit further in-system without being acted upon by a tremendous outside force of some kind — and by intentional, intelligent design. None dared venture a guess as to what, or who, could have possibly engineered such a feat. But they were forced to accept the fact that however it happened, the impossible *had* happened, and now they had to deal with the new reality of their situation.

The *Pegasus* crew performed extensive long-range scans as they slowly backtracked and caught up to their target world. When the ship finally entered into orbit, her bridge crew glanced at each other fearfully. On the planet's surface below them, in an almost perfect circle, was a landlocked sea made of real, honest-to-God, water.

Sitting almost centered within that improbable sea was a large, irregular island of ~32,000 square miles in total area. At its widest point (east-west), the island extended about 175 miles and at its longest (north-south), about 300 miles. But most astounding of all was this island was green... very, very green. Impossibly lush vegetation covered almost the entire island in great abundance.

Capt. Allan Johansson turned to the ship's scan operator, Lt. JG Joe Mullins. "May I assume your scanners are functioning properly, Mr. Mullins?"

"Yes, Captain. The system was entirely recalibrated after our initial scans returned with such questionable results. I can't explain it, any more than I can explain that isolated sea, but that island in the center of it is literally teeming with vegetation and animal life."

"Which is utterly impossible."

There was a pregnant pause. Finally the executive officer, LCDR Gatta, broke the tension when he asked,

"Other than that sea and that island, the rest of the planet is still lifeless and barren, correct?

"Not quite, Commander. There is now an oxygen-nitrogen atmosphere surrounding the entire planet," replied Mullins. "Other than that, it's just as all of Eerie used to be — excepting for *where* the planet is located now.

"Atmospheric composition?" asked Gatta.

"77 percent nitrogen, 20.8 percent oxygen, one percent argon, 0.4 percent carbon-dioxide and trace elements of neon and helium," answered Mullins. "Approximately 0.9 percent water vapor at sea level over that small sea. About 0.24 percent water vapor everywhere else."

"No methane?" asked Capt. Johansson.

"No, sir. None that my equipment can detect."

"Except for the lack of detectable methane, those atmospheric composition numbers are eerily close to Old Earth standard," observed the ship's astrogator, Lt. Geraldo Sánchez.

Capt. Johansson shot Sánchez an annoyed look for daring to make a pun during official ship discussion, but he didn't chasten him, as the observation was uncannily accurate. Humanity had colonized hundreds of planets, but rarely had any of them possessed atmospheric compositions so close to that of Old Earth.

"Methane is generally produced by decaying plants," said Mullins. "Normal methane levels take millennia to accumulate."

"We know for a fact that this planet had no plant life this time last year," said Gatta. "Any decay that might have occurred since whatever miracle caused these plants to grow in the first place would be minuscule."

"All right, I think we've pretty much exhausted all we can learn from the scan data," said the captain. "Comm, hail the mining complex. Let's see if anyone is still alive down there. If so, perhaps they can shed some light on what the hell has been going on here."

"Eerie Mining Station One, this is the interstellar transport, SS *Pegasus,* calling. Do you read? Over,"

called Ensign Pyrx Nata, communications officer and only alien member of the crew. Nata was an insectoid, whose uncanny resemblance to a four-foot mantis gave most humans the creeps. "Eerie Mining Station One, this is the SS *Pegasus*, calling. Do you read? Over."

Nata repeated her rhythmic call with no trace of an accent, as her race was renowned for their ability to learn and mimic other languages, so they were highly sought after as communications officers. She also experienced none of the self-consciousness a human would have to endure from such a continuous lack of response. "Eerie Mining Station One, this is the interstellar transport, SS *Pegasus* calling. Do you read? Over."

Nothing but soft white noise sounded in the bridge speakers, as there was no response to their hail.

"I suppose it would have been too much to ask," sighed Capt. Johansson. "We still have no idea whether anyone is still alive down there."

"Not entirely unsurprising, Captain," replied Gatta. "Tidal forces from all that deceleration we observed undoubtedly generated massive planet quakes, drastically altering the surface terrain. All their surface equipment must have been destroyed, or buried during the upheaval. No telling how deep the mining station is now."

"Any human life signs detectable?"

"No, sir. But our scanners are only calibrated for surface scans. Anyone deeper than twenty feet or so below the surface wouldn't show up."

"Captain, we're obligated under interstellar maritime law to conduct search and rescue operations," stated Ensign Nata.

Johansson shot Nata an absolutely poisonous look that would have withered any human crew-member, but the alien seemed oblivious to the captain's displeasure. "Do tell, Ensign? Seems that I might have heard that somewhere, in the over 35 years I've been spacing."

"Oh yes, sir," Nata replied innocently. "Article 37, paragraph 52 of the universal maritime regulations are most specific on that point."

Johansson shook his head in exasperation. His legendary sarcasm was apparently totally lost on the alien.

"God damn it! This shit is gonna play hell with our schedule. We've already lost over a week, just chasing this bitch down and now we've got to waste even more time digging their sorry asses out of there."

No one else spoke. The bridge crew knew better than to make themselves a convenient target for the captain's wrath, especially when he was grumbling about conditions beyond any of their abilities to address.

"All right," Johansson finally sighed. "Mr. Gatta, load up all the earthmoving equipment in the hold into the shuttles. Break out the survival gear and enough supplies for a week. Helm, put us into geosynchronous orbit directly above the planetary coordinates for the mining station. Have the shuttle pilots begin pre-calculating their course for a spiral descent down to the surface and begin scanning for any signs of them underground. The sooner we find them and start digging, the sooner we'll be done and on our way to making money again."

CHAPTER SEVENTEEN

*Man is the only animal that deals in that atrocity of atrocities
— war. He is the only one that gathers his brethren about him
and goes forth in cold blood and calm pulse to exterminate
his kind. He is the only animal that for sordid wages will
march out and help to slaughter strangers of his own species
who have done him no harm and with whom he has no
quarrel. And in the intervals between campaigns he washes
the blood off his hands and works for "the universal
brotherhood of man" ...with his mouth.*
-- Mark Twain

The Roman Encampment — Drumanagh Peninsula
Late-July, 81 A.D.

THE HIBERNIAN PRINCE, TÚATHAL TECHTMAR, ALONG
with his honor guard of five younger sons of various Brig-

antes chieftains returned to Agricola's camp, accompanied by three Celtae chieftains who had once been among his father's strongest supporters and lieutenants when he had reigned as high king on the island. The three Celtae marveled at the spectacle of thousands of Roman legionnaires and their auxiliaries with great trepidation. They had heard tales of spectacular Roman victories over their brethren in Britannia. To find themselves surrounded by so many fearsome Romans made them nervous. Their prince, however, displayed no such fears so they emulated his example, assuming an air of nonchalance.

Roman sentries had sent runners ahead to inform the governor of their immanent arrival in the camp. As they reined in their mounts at the newly arrived command tent, a man in resplendent golden ceremonial armor with a long blood-red cape thrown over his shoulder, emerged to greet them.

Techtmar held out his hand, palm outward. "Hail and well met, governor!"

Agricola slowly raised his white and gold baton of office with its golden imperial eagle pointed straight up, symbolizing the unspoken proclamation "above your head and mine" to represent the Roman emperor.

"Well met, Prince Techtmar. Have you success in recruiting allies from among your father's vassals?"

A Celtae servant who spoke Latin whispered the interpretation. The Celtic chieftains glanced towards one another, with Agricola's seeming acknowledgement of Techtmar's claims and authority.

"I have." Techtmar introduced Agricola to the three local chieftains, each nodding to the governor in turn, as his name was recognized.

Roman officers often tended to behave haughtily and condescending towards the Celtae, who were normally considered little more than dirty, lice-ridden barbarians by the civilized Romans. Agricola was more diplomatic than many in that he recognized that treating them as men, worthy of honor would gain him more cooperation than not. He invited the four into his command tent for refreshment... wine, which had only arrived by supply galley the night before.

In that short meeting, Agricola learned those three local chieftains could muster 600 warriors between them. Along with the 832 surviving Brigantes brought over from Britannia, Techtmar would be able to field a total of 1,432 warriors... not an inconsiderable force. Disappointing numbers to be sure, but sufficient to lend Techtmar an air of legitimacy in his quest to regain his father's throne. Agricola had always known it would be his legionnaires who would bear the brunt of his conquest of Hibernia.

It was quickly agreed that Agricola's legion would march on Deblin, the large port city just to the Southwest, coordinated with Techtmar's march on Tara, the traditional seat of the Hibernian high king. It was hoped that this twin threat would create confusion, division and bickering among the Hibernian war chiefs, causing them to divide their forces. It was also agreed that both would march in exactly one week.

~

The Haunted Forest, near the Roman Encampment — Drumanagh Peninsula Early August, 81 A.D.

ONCE AGAIN, Aryn Finnegan, of the clan Ó Fionnagáin found himself alone and high in a tree overlooking the Roman encampment on the Drumanagh Peninsula. His trip to Tara to warn the high king of the Roman invasion had ended in even greater disappointment than his first efforts at Deblin. It had taken him over a week just to gain an audience, only to have that aborted meeting almost immediately, interrupted by the untimely arrival of an urgent message. Over a thousand warriors were on the march, soon to arrive at Tara and Aryn had found himself, and his message dismissed out of hand by an alarmed and now totally distracted high king.

Even the Romans didn't seem to be cooperating. His suspicions were raised when he discovered the Roman picket line he and Kyla had tangled with earlier had been withdrawn. Sure enough, the Romans were gone. Only a small garrison force he estimated at about 500 men remained behind in their fortified camp.

Scrambling back down the tree, Aryn hastened to the blind where he had hidden Frisky. The Romans were on the march and he had to locate them as quickly as possible. He couldn't go down the Deblin road, as that would put him behind the Roman army. He needed to get ahead of them, so he backtracked towards the Tara road. His horse would allow him to make up time on the marching Romans, in spite of his having to travel almost twice the distance.

~

The Deblin Road
Early August, 81 A.D.

GENERAL GNAEUS JULIUS AGRICOLA, Roman governor of Britannia, glanced up at the brilliant blue sky and smiled in satisfaction. Few sights are as awe inspiring as Roman legions on the move, with marching drums setting the cadence, pylums and armor glistening in the sun. He was still astounded the Hibernians had been so accommodating during those awful weeks it took to resupply his battered army. He'd experienced several nightmares where he found himself fighting a desperate battle of survival against tens of thousands of Hibernian warriors screaming for his blood, trapped on that tiny little strip of land with their backs to the sea.

But after that disastrous storm had all but destroyed the ninth legion, the gods had finally smiled on the Roman army once again. Miraculously, the enemy had not attacked when the Romans were at their most vulnerable. They had endured near starvation for several weeks until that small trickle of supply galleys arriving from Britannia finally turned into a flood. Only fifty horses had arrived to remount a tiny portion of his cavalry, but he could wait no longer. His army was no longer totally blind, even if it had only a single eye cracked. Now that his under-strength legion was rested and resupplied, Agricola was once again confident of victory whenever and wherever the Hibernians finally chose to meet him in battle.

Riders from his single, minuscule cavalry detachment informed him of a narrow wooden bridge over a deep gorge containing a rushing stream just ahead. General Servius Marius Paterculus, legate of *Legio IX Hispana* rode beside him and uncannily addressed his inner concerns.

"That narrow wooden bridge would make a perfect

choke point. A tiny force could make it very expensive for us to cross. Perhaps we should rush our lead troops forward at a trot, to secure both ends of that bridge before the main army arrives, my lord."

"I'm sure our cavalry commander has already done just that, but you're right. It would certainly be prudent to hurry a couple of centuries at the head of the column forward, to reinforce the cavalry."

Legate Paterculus turned to the tribune riding beside him and issued the order. As the tribune spurred his horse into a gallop away to deliver the order to the lead elements, Agricola wondered how much the sight of that tribune's black-armor pained the legate. The legate's only son had worn armor just like that, and had been the first victim of this campaign... cut down in his prime by that damnable Hibernian archer on the day they first set foot on this cursed island.

∼

The Planet Eerie
3232 A.D.

LITTLE IN LIFE comes easy to a spacer. Just locating the mining facility proved to be more problematic than the crew of the SS *Pegasus* had expected. While they expected the shifting of the planetary tectonic plates had shifted to location of the complex off their original coordinates by a few miles, there was no sign of a VLF beacon during their initial search pattern. Now, additional shuttles were being added to their ever-expanding search grid.

The shuttle pilots were having difficulties focusing on their instruments, constantly distracted by the magnificent scenery of that impossible island below them... especially since they had finally received permission to spiral lower into the atmosphere to conduct their search. An atmosphere their instruments said was breathable was another thing that was blowing everyone's mind. Whatever weirdness was going on with this planet presented an entire litany of physical impossibilities they had no time to ponder. That became even more difficult when they began to spiral lower as they searched the island for signs of the mining facility. Although there was absolutely no evidence of any electromagnetic communications anywhere on this crazy planet, the shuttle pilots began reporting seeing people walking around down there.

～

The Deblin Road
Early August, 81 A.D.

YELLING, screaming and most of the other normal sounds of battle became apparent within minutes of the time the tribune had ridden forward to deliver new orders to the two centuries at the head of the column. An even louder roaring sound periodically threatened to drown out the cries of men. Paterculus and Agricola glanced at each other and simultaneously kicked their horses into a gallop by unspoken agreement.

The two leaders thundered past dozens of centuries running towards the sounds of battle at the double-time, in perfect cadence, maintaining a smooth, uniform stride so they continued to move as a cohesive group. When Agricola and Paterculus rounded a turn in the road and the wooden bridge finally came into view, they both reined in hard before their mounts could panic at the spectacle before them.

Legionaries swarmed over a gigantic gray-skinned hand reaching above the bridge-deck. The men stabbed at the hand with their gladius. Others were casting their pilums downward over the edge of the bridge, towards a monster standing in the gorge below. The beast bellowed in pain and anger whenever the Roman weapons pierced its tough skin. Both Roman generals slowly edged their mounts forward under a tight rein, to better see what was attacking their men.

The creature was vaguely humanoid, standing upright, having the proper number of arms and legs... and was fully three times the size of a man. A grossly oversized nose and relatively tiny eyes dominated the face. The mouth appeared to be an afterthought until they watched in disbelieving horror as the fiend grabbed a squirming man from off the bridge and bit him in half.

Blood exploded from between the lips as the brute began to chew, along with the sounds of bones snapping and crunching. The monstrosity discarded the man's lower extremities and then reached for another. Roman arrows began sprouting from the behemoth's body like individual spines remaining on a porcupine having the mange. While they were obviously paining the colossus, they were definitely not slowing it down much.

Agricola whipped around in his saddle, frantically in search of a trumpeter to sound retreat to his army. Trumpeters blew specific tattoos, relaying a general's orders to his troops afar off in the field. He and Paterculus had absent-mindedly left their trumpeters far behind in their haste to find out what was happening. Now they knew, but had no way to make their orders heard above the din of battle. Agricola cursed himself for a fool, for not foreseeing the need to provide horses for his trumpeters, whenever he, himself, was mounted.

Just as he had begun to despair of avoiding unnecessary deaths, the creature suddenly grabbed at its face and let out an unusually loud bellow that shrilled into a scream. A Roman pilum protruded from between the giant's fingers and it slowly began teetered on its feet. Just as a felled tree often appears to topple in slow motion, yet gains momentum as it gets further into its fall, so it was with this great beast as it slowly toppled onto its face, damming the stream.

A stunned silence immediately fell over the forest at the sudden and unexpected cessation of hostilities. That silence lasted all of two-seconds before a thousand voices raised a resounding cheer.

In the excitement of the moment, no one noticed the sour expression on the face of a stunning dark-haired beauty, riding a gigantic eagle as it circled high above the bridge. She had fully expected her troll would at least slow the Roman advance by a few hours, so its unexpectedly quick death had not brightened her mood any.

ARYN FINNEGAN WAS BEGINNING to wonder if he'd somehow been born in the top of a tree. He was now sitting near the top of an ancient oak tree, overlooking a vast open area encompassing over a square mile. Rhoslyn the pixie had told him the Roman army would soon be coming down that road, so he had a good vantage point from which to annoy them... if he didn't run out of arrows. Not for the first time, he wished that Kyla had thought to return his golden dragon war bow before she disappeared in a huff that day on the Tara Road. He still had what Finvarra had called his "never-ending arrow quiver" holding those black, obsidian tipped arrows with him, but he had no idea whether the magic that made them work was self-contained, or if it was somehow interlinked to that magic war bow that he didn't have. If the "never-ending arrow quiver" wouldn't work without being in proximity to that golden war bow, his day of fighting the Roman army was likely to be a short one.

Kyla wasn't here at the moment, but she had been... evidence of her recent activities was evident everywhere. Dozens of wood nymphs and dryads had effectively closed off the Deblin Road by causing thousands of honey locust thorn trees to sprout and grow to maturity almost overnight. The entire bodies of these formidable trees were covered in thorns ranging from three to eight inches long, often growing in clusters from the trunk all the way up to the tips of its branches.

In the early fall, the pulp inside ripe honey locust seed-pods are edible, but a person would have to be truly starving to risk those massive thorns to harvest them. Aryn, himself, had suffered the unpleasant experienced of being punctured by honey locust thorns many times... not from gathering seedpods, but from harvesting the thorns themselves. His people commonly used them for fashioning fishhooks, spearheads, nails, sewing needles and small game traps, so they held considerable trade value.

Various types of pixies had clogged the spaces between the honey locust trees with massive rosebushes, and deep snarls of blackberry and raspberry bushes, all bearing thorns of their own... completing a formidable obstruction to the Roman army advancing past this fae created barrier.

CHAPTER EIGHTEEN

If you don't know where you are going, you might wind up someplace else.
-- Yogi Berra

The Planet Eerie
3232 A.D.

ONE OF THE SHUTTLES CONDUCTING THE GRID SEARCH trying to locate the wayward mining facility experienced a calibration error in its onboard navigational equipment and ended up sweeping considerably farther to the east than it had been assigned to do.

"Shuttle-4, this is *Pegasus*... do you read? Over."

"*Pegasus*, this is Shuttle-4, we read you five-by-five. Go ahead."

"Shuttle-4, our scanners are showing you are deviating off-course from your assigned search grid parameters. Please run an on-board diagnostic on your navigational computer."

"Wilco, *Pegasus*... wait one."

Pegasus then sent the wayward shuttle a visual readout from their scanners, so the shuttle crew could compare the ship's readings to their own navigational scans.

"*Pegasus*... this is Shuttle-4. We concur that our position is off, but our on-board nav computer diagnostic is green. Suspect our nav scanner is out of calibration."

While the ship could have given the wayward shuttle voice instructions to route it back into it's assigned search area, the captain scrubbed that idea as he considered it too dangerous to have a shuttle having known navigation system problems operating in close proximity with the other shuttles. Having Shuttle-4 return to the ship for maintenance would delay the search, so Capt. Johansson wanted to try something else first.

"Shuttle-4, this is *Pegasus*. Loiter in your current location while we route Shuttle-3 to rendezvous with you. We wish you to attempt slaving your nav scanners to Shuttle-3's and then resetting your calibration settings to theirs."

"*Pegasus*, this is Shuttle-4. Wilco... beginning orbit of this location, as ordered."

The time delay between the ship and shuttle communications prevented them from recalibrating directly from the ship, but sending another shuttle to within visual range should allow for recalibration within normal parameters. While the shuttle orbited, holding position while it awaited the arrival of Shuttle-3, its VLF scanner found what they had been looking for.

"*Pegasus*, this is Shuttle-4. Be advised, our VLF scanner has picked up a weak distress beacon."

Shuttle-4 then began orbiting the area where the beacon appeared strongest, while the ship diverted all three other shuttles to the site to help gather a definitive triangulation to pin-point the location precisely.

But before diverting, once again, the shuttles cameras appeared to have captured images of real, honest-to-God, people walking around on the surface. This time though, it wasn't just dirty, prehistoric looking flock tenders they were seeing, but seemingly endless ranks of Roman legionaries on the march, bronze armor glistening in the sun. They appeared to emerge briefly from the forest at bend in a dirt road, before disappearing again after just a few steps, back under the cover of the thick forest. Rank upon rank, six abreast they strode purposefully towards some unknowable destination.

But the crew of the *Pegasus* couldn't afford to dwell on all the absurdities their instruments were showing them. They had to set their understanding of how the universe works on a shelf and just accept that a lot of totally impossible things were happening here. They had lives to save and could not afford to be distracted from their duties. They just had to accept was apparently was, and not bother thinking about how it might have happened.

∼

The Deblin Road
Early August, 81 A.D.

THE MILE-EATING pace of an army on the march is highly dependent upon maintaining rigid discipline within the ranks. That grinding monotony was broken during a slight break in the forest cover when some legionaries suddenly began pointing towards the sky. Agricola's initial flash of annoyance was stillborn when he saw for himself the phenomena that had so agitated his men. He quickly pulled his horse out of the line of march, so he could pause to study the darting lights high above.

There in the sky were four brilliant stars plainly visible against the clear blue, late morning, sky... at least they would have looked like stars, had they been stationary. But these stars were moving, zigging and zagging, displaying very odd, unstarlike behavior.

"By the gods! What in Jupiter's name are those?" General Servius Marius Paterculus, legate of *Legio IX Hispana*, had also pulled his horse off to the side and sat next to Agricola, astonished by the four day-stars zipping around in the sky with seeming minds of their own.

"I'm not really sure if I want to know, or if we'd be truly better off not to," Agricola replied. "After that damnable archer, that even more damnable storm and then that giant creature at the bridge, I highly doubt anything out of the ordinary on this cursed island will bode well for us. At any rate, unless those 'whatever-they-are' physically attack us, I want to reach the city before nightfall."

The two Roman commanders continued to watch those strange lights in the sky until, as a group, they disappeared behind a hill near the horizon. Paterculus merely shrugged and patiently waited alongside Agricola for a break between cohorts, when they both nudged their horses into a cantor and rejoined the march.

~

The Planet Eerie
3232 A.D.

FROM THE POSITION of the VLF beacon, the mining facility had shifted a bit over ninety miles east-southeast of its previous coordinates in relation to the planet's magnetic pole. No one could begin to fathom a guess as to how much oxygen, if any, remained within the station proper... or if anyone still survived down there. Earthmoving equipment was rushed down to the location, as every second was precious to those miners trapped beneath the surface. Fortunately the site was in an open area, free of obstructing forest... evidently used as a sheep pasture, if all those shaggy white critters that went, "baa" were any indication.

The first crewmen to ground utilized hand-held atmospheric analyzers to recheck the readings obtained by the ship's scanners. When those instruments confirmed the atmosphere was breathable, a grizzled old non-commissioned officer became the first to give the air the ultimate test... by cracking his helmet and actually breathing it.

"Ah... sweet as candy, lads! Now, let's get these damned pressure suits off and get to work. We've got lives to save."

Soon, dozens of *Pegasus* crewmen were swarming over the site, setting up a work camp a couple of hundred yards, or so, from where others were readying excavation equipment in preparation to begin digging. All were clothed in identical jumpsuits, just a shade or two more coral colored than a true florescent hot pink. The women in the crew generally loved the color, but the men universally hated it... excepting for a relative handful known for having rather dubious taste. Still, the unnatural, florescent color and the reflective strips did make them difficult to miss against almost any background — an important safety feature whenever so many people were afoot amongst heavy equipment on the move... which was exactly why the requirement for them had been adopted in the first place. The utter necessity for such a strange and unfashionable color did not forestall a constant barrage of bitching about it in the slightest.

～

The Deblin Road
Early August, 81 A.D.

CAVALRY SCOUTING AHEAD of the column reported an impassible thicket blocking the road, just where the forest resumed after a wide, open field over a mile deep concluded. They also reported the loss of nine of their number to hidden archers, whenever they approached. Agricola ordered his army to halt and rest, while the cavalry divided and sought a way around the obstacle. But after two hours of searching, both parties reported that only twenty to thirty yards deep into the surrounding forest on both sides, thickly placed trees bearing the same wickedly long thorns as the ones ahead, blocked any path around.

We're boxed in! We've walked into a trap. If those strange lights in the sky attack us now, while we're trapped out in the open, this entire army could be devastated.

Agricola wasn't sure what destructive capabilities those moving stars might possess, but that they could fly at all proved they were well beyond his understanding. He immediately decided to err on the side of caution and ordered his baggage train, containing their supplies, to turn off to the side of the road to make way for his rear guard to about face and lead the column back the way they had just come.

It wasn't long, however, before Agricola began receiving reports that where there had been dry road just a couple of hours earlier, his retreating legionaries were now marching through water up to their ankles... and that water was getting deeper with every step.

~

The Eerie Mining Facility, Deep Underground
3232 A.D.

SO FAR, the best thing that could be said for their efforts to dig their way back to the surface was that it had not progressed fast enough to induce decompression sickness, generally called "the bends," in anyone... a bittersweet victory of sorts. Despite the maintenance crew's best efforts, the air within the buried mining facility was becoming fouler by the minute. Calculations based on ambient air pressure gave back ambiguous results when trying to calculate their true depth. The one thing all their calculations agreed on though, was they'd all be dead long before they reached the surface.

But they were not totally without hope. They had positioned their VLF distress beacon near the point of their farthest penetration upwards, as to reduce the amount of planetary crust the signal had to travel through before reaching the surface. They had recently detected faint signs of reflected voltage waves returning back into their VLF transmitter. Their homemade transmitter was a rather crude and relatively low powered omni-directional device, but they managed to mathematically differentiate the direction from where those returning echoes were the strongest. These calculations indicated the presence of what they thought, and hoped, was a crevasse, which, if they could reach it, might provide them with a faster, if not quite shorter, route to the surface.

~

The Haunted Forest
Mid-August, 81 A.D.

POP!

Aryn startled at Rhoslyn's sudden, unexpected appearance at such close quarters, but stifled the verbal blast he'd started to throw at her when he realized that she was not only fully woman-sized, but also that she had his golden dragon war bow in her hand.

"Thank the gods! Or perhaps in this case... the demi-goddess."

Handing Aryn his bow, Rhoslyn returned to her normal tiny size and passed on a message from that very demi-goddess he'd been referring to. "Kyla said to tell you to target those Roman horsemen, before they can get too deeply hidden within those trees on the far side of the clearing."

"Why?"

"After the Roman army passed through into the clearing, Kyla ordered a few dozen water sprites to divert streams and brooks from all over this part of the island. Earth elementals have made trenches to channel all of that water to flood the road and forest behind the Roman army. She said you need to delay the Romans long enough so the water has sufficient time to flow, so the Romans will be boxed in on all four sides... whatever that means."

Aryn nodded and looked towards the edge of the forest on the far side of the clearing before him. The edge of that portion of forest appeared to be a little over a mile distant, but with his magically enhanced eyes, he had no difficulty discerning individual Roman soldiers reentering the forest on the far side. As he watched, the last of the Roman cavalry disappeared into the trees.

Oh yeah, target horsemen I can't see from over a mile away... right.

Aryn offered Rhoslyn a grim smile, but remembering that hidden rabbit he'd once killed, he again closed his eyes and focused his concentration on discerning the Roman's over such a great distance. It took him quite a bit longer to quiet his mind enough to distinguish individual life-force traces against the blackness of his closed eyelids, but... *There!* He grasped the magic bow firmly and arched back, loosing a volley of black, obsidian-tipped arrows that arched high over the clearing and quickly disappeared from sight against the bright blue sky.

Without opening his eyes, Aryn took a deep cleansing breath and steeled himself for what he was about to attempt.

～

The Deblin Road
Early August, 81 A.D.

GNAEUS JULIUS AGRICOLA, Roman governor of Britannia, watched intently as his hastily summoned cavalrymen waded their horses more deeply into the rapidly rising water within the forest. He'd called a halt to his infantry when the water reached mid-thigh level, preferring to test the water's depth with horses. When the cavalry signaled that the water was no more than waist deep, Agricola ordered his troops forward again.

Some tried spreading out to get more troops crossing at one time, but most fell over hidden entanglements left behind after the monster storm, face-first into the muck. Agricola sent word for his cavalrymen to locate and mark the edges of the road, as that appeared to be the only path free of hidden storm debris. He pushed away a rising sense of panic as he watched his troops struggling to wade through the slowly rising flood. He had to get his army through these floodwaters and back onto higher ground, before something truly catastrophic happened.

Then it did.

The centurion leading the Roman cavalry suddenly toppled from his saddle with a resounding splash, followed almost immediately by four more Romans unseated from atop their horses. Cavalrymen hurried to their fallen comrades lying face down in the water. When the bodies were physically lifted from the water, it was discovered that all five had died instantly. A coal-black arrow protruded from each of the men's helmets... arrows that had somehow pierced their helmets, coming from almost directly overhead.

A stunned pause ensued — a noticeable period when no further arrows fell. Then they started raining down from above. Men cried out as others nearby fell silently, with only a splash.

"Shields up!" cried the centurions, the order echoing throughout the ranks, calling for the men to engage in the standard Roman defense against incoming arrows. The men crouched down, holding their shields above their heads... not an easy thing to do while moving through near waist-deep water. Unfortunately these were not standard arrows.

Normal arrows would have bounced off of the shield's metallic outer surface, but these black arrows penetrated... perhaps slowed somewhat, but still thrusting completely through the Roman shields, piercing arms, legs and torsos. The unfortunate recipients of these incoming missiles screamed in anger and pain. Not all died, as had the earlier victims, but many received painful wounds that prevented them from proceeding further into the floodwaters. Those killed outright were probably the lucky ones, as those receiving crippling wounds found themselves in agony with little hope for anything other than drowning.

The arrows seemed to fall randomly, as men from every-where within the ranks were falling. But there was a pattern, Agricola knew. Two out of every five seemed to fall amongst those men at the head of his retreating column, as if to intentionally slow their escape from the rising water... and he'd seen one of these strange black arrows before — lodged in the neck of one of his men.

On a day about two weeks after the massive storm, some of his soldiers manning the picket line he'd set up in the forest were drawn to the smell of bacon cooking and stumbled upon a man and a woman camped not far away in a small clearing. When reinforcements finally arrived, they found four dead Romans, but no trace of the two Hibernians. One had taken a bronze skinning knife in the eye, while a second was felled by a bronze fork lodged in his throat. Another had been the one found with a black arrow, identical to these, in his neck, while another was found dead from an unknown cause, but with blackened burn marks on his body and faint traces of smoke still rising from the corpse.

That bronze fork and skinning knife had immediately reminded Agricola of the bronze arrowheads used by that damned Hibernian archer, who had so bedeviled them on the day they first landed on this accursed island. Agricola had initially discounted the account of a second giant female, suddenly appearing and disappearing, from the one surviving eyewitness as hysterical hallucination. Now, he wasn't so sure.

"Keep the men moving forward!" Agricola called. "Tell them to just ignore the damned arrows. There's not enough of them to worry about. Drowning is our greatest danger right now."

It's that same Hibernian archer. I know it is... I can feel it. — Damn him!

The Roman army continued to trudge through the slowly rising floodwaters for another hour, leaving dozens, if not hundreds, of their number floating face down with black arrows protruding obscenely from their bodies. *There are too many arrows falling too fast to be just a single archer, but where are they all coming from?*

Those leading the procession were now in water halfway up their torsos, and still those damned black arrows rained down upon them from the gods only knew where.

Maybe it is just that same Hibernian archer and he does have 10,000 arrows after all. Little would surprise me on this damned island anymore.

Just as Agricola finally received his first encouraging news that the leading edge of his army might actually be reaching a point where the water was beginning to get shallower, an ominous orange-yellow glow appeared in the darkening sky.

~

The Planet Eerie
3232 A.D.

THE WHINING, shrieking earthmovers soon dug out a great, yawning pit in the sheep pasture... to the great consternation and agitation of the sheep. Attracted by all the noise, a half-dozen primitive, dirty, kilted warriors of some kind had showed up a couple of hours into the process... the owners of the pasture and the sheep, no doubt. But the stun-rifles of their security detail discouraged those sufficiently to allow for completion of the portable force-field around the perimeter of their work area. The barbarians merely beat their swords on their shields after that, shaking fists and shouting what the workers assumed must be local obscenities in their direction.

Powerful work lights were set up, illuminating the work area in a brilliant blue-white glow. A field-kitchen was set up for feeding the workers, as well as a portable housing unit, to keep the work going in around-the-clock shifts. After testing the force-field... once... the barbarians merely watched morosely as the monstrously loud earthmovers removed tons of soil from the pit and dumped man-made mountains of refuse indiscriminately. The unusual and totally unnatural colors worn by the "invaders" seemed to fascinate the locals immensely and the security detail felt themselves coloring with embarrassment.

Eventually the barbarians tired of watching, gathered up their unconscious brethren and departed for wherever it was that impossible beings on an impossible island on an equally impossible planet went.

~

The Eerie Mining Facility, Deep Underground 3232 A.D.

CHANGING the direction of their dig towards what they thought might be a crevasse above them appeared to have changed their luck for the better. Almost immediately they encountered softer limestone, instead of the hard granite they had previously been drilling through. The limestone produced immeasurably more dust, but being softer, the particulate matter hanging in the air was larger and settled more quickly than the finer granite dust had. The drilling crew's rebreathers and surgical masks also trapped these larger particles more efficiently, so they required changing more often as they clogged faster. Still, their increased rate of progress gave everyone more hope they might actually reach the surface alive.

Brian Steele's maintenance crews continued with their seemingly unending rotation of blowing out filters, and rebuilding overheated compressors. A few had to be pulled to make repairs to a couple of the excavators that had broken down, but so far, they'd been extremely lucky there had not been a lot more of that than there was.

Strangely enough, after months of almost continuous writer's block, it seemed that the more physically exhausted Brian became, the more his inspiration for writing flowed. Between the dirty, gritty food, insanely long hours, chronic lack of sleep and constantly hacking his lungs up, he could only hope he survived long enough to finish his book... and that someone here survived long enough to somehow forward his manuscript to his publisher.

$\sim$

The Deblin Road
Early August, 81 A.D.

THE UPPER FOREST WAS ABLAZE, burning fiercely after multiple low passes by some kind of flying, two-legged, fire-breathing reptile. Some legionaries swore the beast carried a dark-haired woman on its shoulders, who was throwing bolts of blue, forked lightning with both hands. Although the monster swooped low enough that it barely cleared the treetops, it was still much too high for a thrown pilum to hit. Arrows lofted by archers among the remaining Roman cavalry just seemed to annoy the great beast.

Unable to fully give credence to the reports he'd been receiving, Agricola pushed his mount forward through the flood far enough that he could see for himself what his men at the front of the column were facing. He struggled with unaccustomed indecision over what exactly he should do next. Never in recorded history had any Roman commander ever been faced with such an open display of... well... call it what it obviously was — magic.

Choices... what choices did he have, really? How many of his men might make it to higher ground on the far side of the flood before the fire burned down to water level and engulfed them? *Burning or drowning?*

Agricola shuddered. Did any commander have the right to order his troops forward into such dire circumstance? Or, for that matter, would the troops even obey such an order? Agricola knew that the very moment any Roman general issued an order that his army refused to obey, his time in command was finished. He was confident that had these men been his own *Legio XX Valeria Victrix,* they would have charged the very gates of Tartarus, the Roman city of the damned, at his command. But these men were *Legio IX Hispana,* the legion of Legate Servius Marius Paterculus and their auxiliaries.

Turning to Paterculus, who had followed his commander to the front, Agricola asked him, "Well Servius, what are these Spaniards of yours made of?"

"My men will follow me anywhere, my lord."

Gesturing towards the blazing inferno, the governor questioned him further, "Even in there?"

Paterculus paled and swallowed. "If you command it, my lord."

Agricola smiled at the man and said, "Fear not, my friend. I've not taken total leave of my senses. How many do you think might make it across safely, before the fire becomes intolerable?"

Paterculus glanced again towards the fire, paused for thought, and then answered. "Perhaps a cohort, my lord."

"A full cohort? A thousand men... without getting their eyebrows singed?"

"I would have the men dunk themselves into the water periodically and pull their wet capes up over their heads, to prevent blowing embers from burning them."

Agricola raised an eyebrow, impressed with Paterculus' logic. "So be it, then. Take one cohort and get yourselves across this flood and away from these flames. Afterwards, make your way south and west as best you can, until you find the road again. Then turn back north and hack away those infernal briars from the far side. I'll have the rest of the army rendezvous with you, attacking the roadblock from this side."

ARYN WAS TRAPPED within a self-induced trance. His physical body repeated the same litany of motion — draw, nock, pull, release... draw, nock, pull, release... over and over again. His right arm whirling endlessly, like a water-driven gristmill. Exhaustion was held at bay by his magically enhanced muscles, and the fact that his mind was isolated from his body. His eyes remained closed... focused solely upon his gift to make the microscopic changes of position to the great golden dragon war bow necessary to hit living targets over a mile distant. Sweat literally poured from his body as he sucked great gasping gulps of air. Had anyone been paying attention, they would have grown greatly concerned for his well-being.

Aryn was literally killing himself, abusing his body well beyond its mortal limitations... but he was aware of none of it. Somewhere, deep in the recesses of his mind echoed the prophetic words of Úna, the voluptuous queen of the faeries:

"He is fae, my husband. He will not fail me when the land needs him most."

And he would not... even to the point of death. *This* was his ultimate purpose, his sole reason for being. Though it cost him his life, he would not... indeed, could not stop until he ran out of living Romans to kill.

CHAPTER NINETEEN

It's kind of fun to do the impossible.
-- Walt Disney

The Planet Éerie
Several months earlier

THROUGHOUT HISTORY HUMANITY HAS DISCOVERED many surprising, implausible creatures that met the functional definition of "life," yet intelligent life was rare indeed. No one could have possibly suspected, however, anything even remotely similar to what dwelled in the hellish environment of the churning, molten core of the planet Éerie.

Humans well understand, or at least think they do, the process by which solar systems evolved around baby stars during the birth of the Milky Way galaxy. Ejecta from newly formed stars began cooling and coalescing into what would eventually become planets.

Within the heart of one of those stars, an unimaginable

race of beings had evolved. This race possessed what can only be called a rudimentary awareness of their own existence. They thought of themselves simply as the *We* — primarily a simple acknowledgement of their own existence, and the subtle differences between themselves and their fiery environment. Locked forever within roiling plasma, the *We* lacked what humans understood as the sense of sight, perceiving only rudimentary sensations of touch and sound, and to a lesser degree, taste and smell. Yet they were the masters of their domain, manipulating their environment and communicated among themselves mind-to-mind, through a mental medium that puny humans might inadequately call telepathy and telekinesis.

During the early millennia of their existence their rapidly spinning home star was sloughing much of its original mass out into surrounding space. Some of the *We* wandered a bit too close to the outer reaches of their star and found themselves trapped by irresistible centrifugal forces, as the stellar mass surrounding them was ejected into the great void beyond at incredible velocities. A newly birthed planet eventually coalesced around them, as the outer surface cooled into a rocky crust — the temperature slowly dipping below those necessary to sustain the physical requirements of the *We*. Yet these trapped beings possessed sufficient awareness to migrate downwards towards the inner core, forever churning and molten from interior tidal forces.

Having a lifespan measured in millions of years, most of the *We* exist in the incredibly slow-moving timeframe of the medium they were originally forged in — glacially slow in both thought and action. The adolescents, however, those only a few tens of thousands of years old, are different... downright manic in comparison to their elders.

One young female was more peculiar than most, as she routinely irritated even the most active of her contemporaries. It was the very moment another adolescent female first took notice that she had strangely withdrawn within herself and curiously sought to determine "why," that changed the fate of their entire race forever.

What... do?

Come... perceive.

The curious adolescent linked minds with the one who'd become uncharacteristically preoccupied and immediately her mind was overwhelmed with vivid sensations of a kind her race had never experienced before. Alien images bombarded her with strange concepts, that once experienced, her kind needed no words to describe. Just experiencing these strange images induced in her another totally foreign concept... excitement!

The visitor unconsciously broadcast her agitation, attracted several other curious females to come investigate. These alien images spread quickly throughout the group, creating a sensation that drew the attention of many thousands more adolescent females. It wasn't long before virtually every adolescent female within the entire planet were mind-linked in the pursuit of this exhilarating new diversion.

These adolescent *We* understood instinctively that the mental images originated from an alien source outside, beyond the confines of their limited world. But only the original female who had initially sensed the presence of these alien thought patterns seemed capable of receiving them directly the source, and whatever she perceived was immediately shared among all of her sisters with unerring reproduction. Whatever the original source of these alien sensations truly was, the receiver could read its primitive mind with perfect clarity. Whatever the source knew, the receiver also understood to a similar depth. When these new thoughts from outside were combined with advanced theoretical physics postulated as mental exercises by their ancient ancestors eons ago, the receiver and all of her sisters achieved a new level of understanding of the physical universe unknown to even their elders.

With so many creatures possessing such incredibly advanced mental capabilities, all focusing their thoughts on the same thing at the same time, the sheer power of their common thought patterns radiated throughout their entire world. Their thoughts altered matter, rearranging it, physically recreating those alien thought patterns upon the surface of the cold, rocky world above them... including the creation of alien life forms and hurling the entire planet into a new orbit that would sustain them.

The adolescent *We*, like adolescents of any species everywhere, became totally absorbed in pursuing their new pet project, which the alien thought patterns also had a name for... entertainment.

$\sim$

The Haunted Forest
Mid-August, 81 A.D.

"ARYN!" Rhoslyn was getting frustrated by her inability to break through the strange trance her friend was in, as he continued launching arrows one after the other, oblivious to her attempts to get his attention.

"ARYN!"

Finally deciding that she needed to take a more direct approach, she swelled to Aryn's size and drew back her hand. *SMACK!*

Aryn's head whipped to the side from Rhoslyn's blow, but to her surprise, he recovered immediately and continued on with his rhythmic drawing and releasing of arrows.

"ARYN!"

Still Aryn remained oblivious to her attempts to break him out of his self-induced trance. Frustrated, Rhoslyn increased her size once more, this time to over twice Aryn's height.

SMACK!

Rhoslyn was started to see Aryn topple out of the tree, crashing through branches as he hurtled towards the ground thirty feet below. She quickly popped into a position farther down the tree where she could catch him, but failed to account for his momentum and... *Oof!*

Stunned by the unexpected impact, Rhoslyn was unable to do more than topple through tree limbs alongside her unconscious friend until they both impacted the ground with a thud.

~

The Planet Eerie
Deep in the Planetary Core

SOURCE... in distress.
What... do?

Behold!

～

The Eerie Mining Facility, Deep Underground
3232 A.D.

THEY WEREN'T GOING to make it. Despite their best efforts, the blowers just weren't able to keep up with the tremendous clouds of suffocating dust this softer limestone produced as they dug towards upwards toward the crevasse their instruments had detected. A thick coating of limestone dust clung to every surface and found its way into every crack and cranny... in the machinery and the people. The surgical masks everyone wore were so encased in dust and mud that many of the minors had already passed out from lack of oxygen.

Brian Steele was working the digger, right on top of the source of all that dust. As the digger operator, he was supposed to be wearing one of their precious chemical oxygen generator masks, but those had all given up the ghost days before. He held his breath while he banged his exterior surgical mask on the driver's cage to try to knock some of the caked dust off of it, and then broke into another coughing fit every time he donned it again. His eyes blurred from all the grit that somehow managed to find its way under his goggles, so it was hard for him to see the directional indicator located on the digger's control panel. His chest muscles hurt from the strain of trying to force air into his lungs through the multiple layers of cloth covering his nose and mouth, and he was beginning to feel a bit light-headed from the lack of oxygen in his blood.

At first, Brian thought he might be hallucinating when the surface he was digging into suddenly crumbled away, revealing a gaping tunnel. A yellowish-brown hurricane erupted all around him as the air within his underground chamber rushed outward into the tunnel, as the air pressure on both sides equalized. He became sure he was hallucinating when a creature seemingly made of stacked rocks, having arms, legs and glowing green eyes stepped through the mouth of the cavern against the cyclonic airflow. The lower portion of the creature's head fractured, revealing a mouth that opened widely inhaling virtually all of the dust that swirled by its massive body. Strangely, somewhere in the fog surrounding Brian's oxygen deprived brain, this rock creature seemed vaguely familiar.

An earth elemental?

A full dozen, bluish-white blurs streaked past him bringing fresh, dust-free air in their wake.

Sylphs?

Brian sluggishly pulled at the layers of cloth masking, trying to rip them from off his face. He knew full well that if what he was seeing was just hallucinations, he was signing his own death warrant, but he didn't care... he was simply desperate to take a badly needed a breath.

~

The Haunted Forest
Mid-August, 81 A.D.

ARYN'S first thought as he swam upwards out of the depths of unconsciousness was to wonder what that deep, rhythmic sound thundering in his ears was... his second thought was that he couldn't breathe. Something soft, warm and absolutely huge cradled his cheeks, smothering him completely.

Need to move.

He couldn't turn his head. He was puzzled by what could possibly be holding his head so immobile, yet seem so wonderfully comfortable at the same time. Eventually the need for air induced sufficient panic that he pushed off against those soft, giving pillows... and was shocked to discover that he'd been lying face down, smothered in the enormous cleavage of an unconscious twelve-foot pixie lying beneath him.

"Rhoslyn?"

Aryn tried to get his bearings, but he felt as weak as a newborn kitten. Every time he moved, his head spun with waves of dizziness. Nausea clawed at his stomach as he awkwardly tried to shift his weight off of his gigantic pixie friend, but his right shoulder screamed at him every time he tried to move it.

The last thing he remembered was sitting in the top of a tree peppering the Romans with arrows, only to now find himself on the ground suffocating in pixie boobs the size of his head.

How the hell did we get in this ridiculous position?

He grit his teeth against the pain to prop his weight on his left arm while reaching up to touch Rhoslyn's forehead with his right hand. His right shoulder screamed in pain whenever he tried to move his arm, but his physician training insisted that he suffer through it to find out what was wrong with Rhoslyn. A quick examination told him that she had a lump the size of a hen's egg just behind her right ear, and a smaller one the size of a robin's egg just over her left eye.

Aryn lurched and rolled... literally hurling his body off Rhoslyn's, inducing yet another scream of pain in his protesting shoulder.

Ugh, gods... that hurts!

With a muffled groan, he got to his knees and scooched over to where he could place the palms of both hands along either side of her gigantic head, carefully centering his thumbs on her temples. He closed his eyes and softly murmured a healing chant he'd learned from the Ovate druids during his time with the high king's army. While his conscious mind focused on the task at hand, subconsciously he wondered where the high king's army was now.

...and why aren't they here helping me kill all of those damned Romans?

Aryn continued his healing chant long past the point where he might have expected a human patient to begin coming to, and he began to worry that druidic healing spells might not be effective on magically created beings like fairies. When the pain in his abused right shoulder became too intolerable to maintain his focus on channeling healing magic into the gigantic pixie, he dropped his hands and rocked back on his heels to rest a minute.

Maybe I need to use a more direct, old-fashioned approach.

Aryn reached across his body with his left hand to unstrap the flap on the pouch attached to his belt near his right hip, containing the sheep's-bladder canteen he always carried there. He awkwardly finagled the canteen out of the leather pouch, pulled the cork stopper with his teeth and upended the canteen directly over Rhoslyn's face. Sure enough, it only took emptying half of the canteen before Rhoslyn roused, sputtering indignant fairy curses that meant little to Aryn, but very probably would have scandalized most fae.

Aryn paused in his pouring and it took a moment for her eyes to focus enough to recognize Aryn holding a canteen over her face, but when she did, she spewed a series of Celtic curses at him that he was seriously surprised that she knew. Aryn shrugged and tipped the canteen again, adding yet another splash of water onto her face.

"Damn it, Aryn... STOP POURING WATER ON ME!"

"Feeling better?"

"NO! — I've never felt anything like this before... it's terrible."

"It's called *pain* and we mortals experience it all the time."

"Ugh... then I'm glad I'm not mortal."

"I haven't had a chance to check you out for other damage. Do feel pain anywhere besides your head?"

"About everywhere, but nothing like the pains in my head."

"You've got minor cuts and abrasions all over you. I never knew faerie blood was green."

Aryn helped the giant pixie to sit up, but she immediately grabbed her head again, groaning in pain. "Ah, gods... the world is spinning."

"How did we manage to get down here on the ground, anyway? I was high in a tree launching arrows at the Roman army and the next thing I remember, I'm finding myself face-down in your breasts."

"I thought you liked big boobs."

"I like breathing even better. What happened? How'd

we end up down here on the ground, all banged up like this?"

Rhoslyn told him how she had tried to get his attention, but he seemed to be in some sort of self-induced trance, and of her increasingly violent efforts to break him out of it.

"So... you hit me hard enough to knock me plumb out of the tree? Damn, Rhoslyn... at the size you are now, you could have crushed my cheekbone, or broken my damned neck! I'm surprised I survived the fall from that height, without breaking half the bones in my body."

"I tried to catch you, but for some reason you were a lot heavier than I expected."

Aryn merely shook his head, not bothering to try to explain the relationship between mass and acceleration... she'd have never understood it anyway.

"So what was so important that you almost got us both killed trying to tell me?"

Rhoslyn dropped her hands from where she'd been holding her head with a startled look. "Oh! I almost forgot... Kyla sent me to fetch you. She said she needs you to come back to the cave you're living in... and it's urgent!"

"*Pfft...* she's a goddess. She can just conjure up whatever she needs by merely waving her hand. What would her haughty, disdainful highness need a mere mortal like me for?"

"You're a physician. Nightmare has been hurt!"

~

The Planet Eerie
3232 A.D.

CAPTAIN ALLAN JOHANSSON of the interstellar transport S.S. *Pegasus* detested having to wear those damned florescent-coral/pink coveralls required by regulations whenever ship's crew was groundside on an undeveloped world. Admittedly, they did make it a lot easier to tell a crewman from anything else, so he understood why the regulation was put in place. But unlike most of the rest of his crew, he didn't have the freedom to bitch about that God-awful color... he had to set an example.

While most of his crew were busy digging a spiraling pit towards the buried mining station, Johansson had several others of the crew groundside to taking holo-vids documenting all of the weirdness they'd discovered on this impossible planet, with all of its lush vegetation, sheep — even a few naked barbarian warriors off in the distance, their bodies painted blue... with their equally blue dicks dangling jauntily in the breeze.

Technically, the transport company they all worked for "owned" the rights to any discoveries made by their ships and crews, but that normally applied only to previously undiscovered planets and asteroids having commercially desirable traits. Eerie was not only previously discovered, it was actively being mined by Interplanetary Exploration and Settlements, Inc.

But Johansson felt confident they couldn't even begin to take credit for all of the physical "improvements" here... like moving the entire planet to within the life zone surrounding this star, the terraforming of this island, the accelerated evolution of plant and higher forms of animal life, the seemingly spontaneous development of humanoid intelligent life, nor any of the other physically impossible things they had documented were happening here. He was also confident that, handled properly, he and his crew could reap themselves an unimaginable windfall when they got back to civilization with news and evidence of this impossible world, where the laws of physics apparently don't apply.

He could see it all in his mind's eye — scientists would be flocking here to Eerie by the hundreds-of-thousands to study this incredible phenomenon. He and his crew would all became intergalactic celebrities, working the holovision talk show circuit and living the charmed life of the rich and famous. They'd been at the right place at exactly the right time to document all of this impossible shit and now, they'd never have to actually work another day in their lives... at least after they finished becoming heroes by rescuing all of those trapped miners still below.

Johansson glanced once again towards those naked, barbarian warriors, waving their spears and screaming unintelligible curses at them from beyond the range of their force-field generator.

I'll bet my balls are bluer than yours, asshole!

He'd never married, as starship crews were renowned for their incredibly high divorce rate. He'd suffered through years of strict celibacy aboard ship after achieving his captaincy, as he'd known several ship captains who had their careers prematurely aborted after using their position of authority to elicit sexual favors from members of their crews. His smile morphed into a wolfish grin when his dick twitched at the thought of all those beautiful women who would come flocking to his door, once he had possession of all of that wonderful money.

Johansson then frowned again, as his communicator began warbling. He sighed audibly when he saw the incoming message was from his communications officer, Ensign Pyrx Nata, back aboard the ship. He knew he'd been lucky that Commander Gatta had enticed the insectoid to sign on as part of the crew, but he still inwardly cringed every time he had to interact with the alien. He knew his gut reaction to her appearance was against everything he'd always thought he stood for, but...

"This is the captain, go ahead."

"Captain, we have received an update from one of the shuttles concerning the VLF signal coming from the mining station."

That's damned odd... Nata knows better than to give me an incomplete report. I wonder what it is that even the alien is hesitant to tell me?

"Well, are you going to tell me, or do you expect me to play twenty questions, until I guess what it is?"

"Oh, no sir... the original message arrived about two hours ago, but I delayed contacting you until the newest readings were verified by other shuttles."

God, give me strength!

"I'm still waiting, Ensign."

"The station's VLF beacon has changed position, Captain. It's now emanating from a point approximately 24.3 miles south-southwest of your current position. You're digging in the wrong place."

~

Deep Underground
3232 A.D.

BRYAN STEELE WAS EXPERIENCING, by far and away, the strangest dream he'd ever had. He dreamt he was drifting in and out of consciousness, rousing occasionally to find himself being carried. The dream was so real, he could swear he felt a distinct tickling in his nose. He tried to focus his eyes on what appeared to be thick, reddish hairs at extremely close range, but never quite managed it. He turned his head away from those blurry hairs to see a dark tunnel, illuminated only by the dancing yellow-orange light of flickering torches.

Stocky beings, only half his height, but having huge, muscular arms and long, bushy beards of various colors cradled the mining crew in their arms as gently is if they were mere babes. They all wore wide leather belts resembling back braces around their waists, below rough homespun shirts of drab, muted colors. Most had massive hammers strapped across their broad backs. There was something familiar about them, but what?

Dwarves?

He remembered that he'd been considering adding a chapter about dwarves to his book, so maybe that was why he was dreaming about them.

Brian recognized big Dan Weaver nearby him, obviously unconscious, who was also being carried by one of the more diminutive of these strange creatures. He initially did a double take, as only the short, stumpy legs of the dwarf carrying Dan were visible to him. The discrepancy in their relative size made it look like those legs were growing perpendicular out of the back of Dan's ass cheeks, and the absurdity of the sight elicited a sudden chuckle he couldn't stifle.

"Ah... you alive!"

Brian turned his head to look up into the grinning face of the being carrying him. A large, bulbous nose predominated the face that was half again wider then Brian's own. Across the forehead was a thick leather strap that held an ocean of red hair away from the face. The bottom of that face was mostly hidden within a forest of red beard that hung down to lay clear across Brian's chest. Even if he could only barely see the dwarf's smile peeking out from behind his braided beard and flowing mustache, Brian could recognize the being's good humor from the twinkle in his tiny blue eyes.

Wait a minute... people in dreams don't talk... at least none of mine ever has.

"Am I dead, or just dreaming?"

"Neither... all real."

"That's not possible... this has to be a dream."

The dwarf cradling him in its arms stopped a moment and raised one knee to support his backside to free up one enormous hand... which he used to yank roughly on Bryan's nose.

"OUCH!"

Shit, that hurt!

"Okay, okay... you proved your point. You're real."

The dwarf grinned down at him and then hoisted him up, as if weighed no more than a child, to get that offending hand under him again and resumed walking.

"You can put me down. I think I can walk on my own."

"Faster, if I carry."

"Where are you taking us?"

"Kleidmar... our chieftain... he say follow elemental into depths. Bring beings we find up... near surface."

"How could your chief possibly know we were down there?"

"Gods tell."

"Gods? — Do your gods speak to your people often?"

"First time."

"How is it that you speak my language?"

"All who dwell in caverns and tunnels speak same."

"Wait! — If all this is truly real, I need to go back down to retrieve my computer."

The hairy dwarf's eyebrows pinched together as his expression changed to one of puzzlement. "What is com...put...er?"

"I'm an author. My computer is a device that I use to write books."

"Many strange words... books? That something like scrolls?"

"Yes! Like scrolls... exactly."

"Ah, you a scribe, then?"

"Something like that, but we use computers to store words, instead of scrolls."

"What this thing you need, look like?"

"It looks like a thin metal rectangle, about as wide as my forearm is long."

"Inside black leather bag?"

"YES! — Have you seen it?"

"Bag hanging on hammer behind me."

"But... my computer was locked in the desk in my room down in the mining station. How did you get it?"

"Sylph bring me, while I prying you out of... um... peculiar metal contrivance. She say bring... you need."

CHAPTER TWENTY

Time is carnivorous. Urgency rips the peaceful flesh from our bones.
-- Jonathan Lockwood Huie

The Haunted Forest
Mid-August, 81 A.D.

ARYN HADN'T BEEN ABLE TO LEAVE FOR HIS CAVE immediately after Rhoslyn finally remembered to deliver Kyla's message. When he suggested that the tremendous pain in her head might be proportional to her unusual size, and might lessen if she returned to her normal, finger-length size, the gigantic 12-foot pixie agreed and was aghast when her attempt to do so failed... that great fall they took together had evidently left the battered pixie unable to return to her normal size.

Nor could she "pop" from place-to-place, or even fly, like she normally did. Aryn suspected that egg-sized lump on the back of her head was somehow interfering with her faerie powers. It took him quite a while to calm the hysterical pixie down, finally convincing her that her body would heal itself and her powers would return in time... he hoped.

It took time for him to retrieve his horse, Frisky, from the blind he'd built for him... and then another considerable amount of time trying to fashion a sling for his right arm. He knew from the inordinate amount of pain whenever he tried to move that arm, he had torn something in that shoulder joint. Rhoslyn had tried to help him tie the knot, but with fingers the size of tree branches...

The Romans were close enough they could hear them chopping away at the giant black locus trees blocking the Deblin Road... and also close enough they could distinctly hear all of the obvious Latin curses whenever a legionary ran afoul of those wicked thorns.

Rhoslyn couldn't make the long trip back to the cave with him, so they were also faced with the problem of how to hide a 12-foot grumbling, ground-bound pixie who couldn't even walk, because she'd never had to learn how. Other than occasionally landing, or laying down to sleep, Rhoslyn had always flitted from place-to-place, or just "popped" to wherever she wanted to be. She certainly didn't accept the loss of her faerie powers gracefully, especially when she'd had to ask for help from a type of pixie that rose faeries normally looked down on.

Most flower faeries, tasked with shepherding non-thorn bearing varieties, felt left out of all the excitement of combating the Roman invasion of their island, so Wilmonia, a tiny lilac faerie, squealed in delight when she'd been summoned and asked for her help, from her higher ranked cousin. Over time, the little pixie worked her magic and eventually the 12-foot Rhoslyn was completely hidden, encircled by a ring of tightly spaced, 16-foot lilac bushes. Rhoslyn's foul mood was not at all lightened by Aryn's warning that it was imperative she remain awake until that lump behind her ear receded to at least half its original size. He knew from his physician's training that mortals experiencing blows to the head such as Rhoslyn had experienced could sometimes morph into a type of sleeping sickness that could last for days, weeks, or even years before the victim finally awoke — if ever.

Eager for news of how the battle against the invaders was going, Wilmonia pestered Aryn with questions as only an inquisitive faerie can. Upon learning of Kyla's plea for him to return to the cave where he normally lived, and of the púca's injury, Wilmonia told him to wait while she fetched another fae who might be able to help him in his quest. She winked out with a soft pop, but soon returned, accompanied by an irate wood nymph named Lomar.

Lomar was an oak faerie, whose appearance was distinctly different than that of pixies or sylphs. He was about two feet tall and lacked the distinctive faerie wings. His skin looked like tree bark and he was clothed only in the rounded green leaves of a pin oak. Lomar had also been feeling similarly left out of the struggle against the Roman invaders, but his mood brightened considerably when offered an opportunity to assist Aryn in making his way back to the cave where Kyla awaited him. He nodded thoughtfully and told Aryn to wait there, feed his horse and to get himself something to eat, while he fetched additional allies from among the fae. They had a long night ahead of them.

∽

The Deblin Road
Mid-August, 81 A.D.

ROMAN GENERAL GNAEUS JULIUS AGRICOLA, governor of Britannia was weary, yet grateful. That terrible rain of deadly black arrows had mysteriously stopped some hours before, allowing his legionaries enough of a reprieve to hack away at the thorny barrier that surrounded them. The Roman army does not use axes in combat, so most had chop away with their rapidly dulling short swords, trying to fell the gigantic black locust trees blocking the road to Deblin.

We should have brought many more long-handled axes in the baggage train for just such an event, but who could have foreseen that we'd find monsters such as these, growing in right the middle of the road?

Even after felling the monstrous trees, additional time had to then be taken to scrape away the thorns on the trunks before ropes could safely be attached, allowing them to be dragged off to the sides of the road. Then came the tedious process of inspecting every inch of ground the trunks had touched, to ensure no thorns remained hidden within the leaves fallen on the road, or the ground cover of the forest. Then the stumps had to be dug out, dragged away and their holes refilled with dirt and packed down, so the wagons of the baggage train could pass over without breaking an axle. Fortunately they did have shovels with them in their baggage.

The position of the sun, sinking toward the western horizon, told them that night would fall before they could possibly link up with the cohort that Legate Servius Marius Paterculus had managed to get across that flooded inferno behind them, whom Agricola hoped were now hacking away at this same barrier from the Deblin side. He was loathe to spend the night here in this clearing at the edge of the forest, where so terribly many of his brave Romans had so recently died, but there was nothing for it. Soon, he would have to order his men to cease work on the barrier, to begin erecting field fortifications around their marching camp. They'd have to forego their usual wooden wall, digging only the standard V-shaped trench, as the only logs they had available were much too dangerous to work.

~

The Haunted Forest
Mid-August, 81 A.D.

ARYN DID EXACTLY as Lomar suggested, feeding both himself and Frisky in preparation for their long trip back to his cave. He and the grumpy 12-foot pixie, hidden behind the ring of lilac bushes, held a quiet conversation while he worked, as it helped to help keep her awake. He wasn't exactly sure whether a pixie that had taken a nasty bump on her noggin might be susceptible to the same kind of sleeping sickness that sometimes-afflicted humans, but it didn't hurt anything to take precautions.

He checked the level of water remaining in his canteens and wondered whether there was enough left for them both. Just as he determined there wasn't, and decided to give all there was to his horse, a three-foot water sprite popped into existence nearby. She was almost transparent, with the fluid features of her element. It was a bit difficult to understand her when she spoke, as her voice gurgled like the sound of a babbling book. Aryn thought she said her name was Rinkla, but he couldn't be sure. Rinkla poked a finger into the ground at her feet, and when she pulled it out again a small fountain of icy cold water shot straight up out of the hole, about as high as the length of Aryn's foot. He quickly filled Frisky's watering boot and hung it over the horse's head. Then refilled all of his canteens before kneeling down to drink directly from the magical spring. When he finished drinking his fill, he sat back on his haunches and marveled... the water wasn't spreading out over the ground, but sank immediately back into the ground, less than the length of a knuckle beyond the splash.

Lomar didn't return until near dusk, but was accompanied by a small army of other types of wood nymphs, representing almost every type of tree found anywhere on Éire. Most resembled Lomar, except for the texture of their bark-like skin and the shape of the leaves that compromised their clothing. But the strangest of all those that accompanied Lomar back to Rhoslyn's lilac ring was a creature Aryn had only heard about in legends — a dryad.

Although Aryn had never actually seen one before, there was little doubt this had to be a dryad... there was nothing else imaginable that it could possibly be. It was about four feet tall and looked to be comprised of multiple bunches of small sticks, all about the diameter of Aryn's finger, arranged into a vaguely humanoid shape. Each of those individual sticks was covered with differing kinds of bark, representing virtually every kind of tree that Aryn was familiar with. The face even had recognizable features, comprised of cleverly arranged sticks. The creature's voice, however, was even harder to understand than the water sprite's had been, as it was the soft sound of leaves rustling in the wind.

Dryads were the most powerful of all tree spirits, much

like air elementals were far more powerful than sylphs. While wood nymphs were limited to nurturing a single species of tree, it was said dryads possessed magic that could affect all species of trees, nurturing them... or destroying them completely. Unlike wood nymphs who can only nurture, a dryad can kill a terminally diseased tree before the affliction spreads to its neighbors, and then magically accelerate the natural decomposition process, rapidly turning it into rotted compost.

Aryn was ready to set off immediately, but Lomar insisted he wait... to give his fae allies a chance to get a jump on clearing the fallen and broken trees hindering his path. Knowing that trying to ride Frisky through that tangled mass at night would seriously risk him tripping and breaking a leg, he reluctantly acquiesced to their combined wisdom. Assured that other fae would be joining him to light his way when the time came for him to leave, he lay down on his bedroll to rest.

If Nightmare is really badly hurt and I can't get there damned soon... Kyla is going to kill me.

〜

Aryn's Cave
Mid-August, 81 A.D.

WHERE IS THAT DAMNED ARCHER?

Kyla knelt, fretting over her wounded púca like a mother with a fevered baby. She stroked his massive wyvern head and cooed soft reassurances to her suffering beast. She cursed herself for being so foolish as to constantly urge

Nightmare to fly lower and lower, as his fiery breath ignited the treetops. She never dreamed those puny Roman arrows could even hit him... much less hurt him in wyvern form. It had all been quite the lark to her... great fun, terrifying those insignificant mortals, watching them scurry away from the flames like so many ants, from the back of her indestructible púca.

Pfft... not nearly as indestructible as I'd thought!

One moment they were soaring just above the treetops and then Nightmare suddenly screamed and began snapping at something just out of reach on his chest. She could tell that something was terribly wrong by the way the púca began writhing in the air, undulating like a serpent slithering along the ground. Initially she'd been terrified they would both be killed as they tumbled right out of the sky, but he calmed a bit in response to her command voice, reminding him that she was still mounted just forward of his wings. All she'd known at that moment was that somehow Nightmare was badly hurt.

Although Kyla was a demi-goddess, she had never studied healing magic. She had specialized in combat magic in her attempt to replace her father's only son, killed during the ancient Fomóraig war. All of her life she'd idolized her father, but felt she was a disappointment to him for having been born female. She'd become a warrior to try to please him, giving up all vestiges of femininity and natural affections. The only emotional attachments she'd ever allowed herself were toward animals and the fae. But nothing she'd ever accomplished quite measured up to the magnificent son her father once had... and lost... long before she was even born.

Knowing nothing of healing, she'd instinctively urged her beloved púca to glide towards the ancient home of a great physician of the Tuatha Dé Danann. The cave of Dian Cécht was still known to retain a great deal of residual healing magic long after his death — the same cave where she'd brought that infuriating archer and nursed him back to health... at her father's insistence.

Thinking of that cave led to her remembering something the archer had said when they were in the throne room of that cowardly Celtae king holed up in Deblin. He'd claimed to be a *fáithliaig*... a physician. Though she was loath to ask any boon of *him*, Nightmare was hurt and desperately needed a physician. She'd originally thought to summon a sylph to send for a physician of the Tuatha Dé Danann, in hopes that one might be visiting her father from their home in one of the many Otherworld cities, such as Tír na nÓg, Mag Mell, or Tír na mBeo, but strangely, no sylphs had responded to her supernatural call.

Damned odd, that.

She couldn't imagine what could have possibly prevented them from responding.

Kyla actually had very little experience dealing with mortals... or with the Daoine Sidhe for that matter, preferring to escape the confines of her father's underground prison by spending most of her life above ground with the fae. Being a demi-goddess, daughter of the chief of the Daoine Sidhe and the queen of the faeries, all had shown her proper deference all of her life, displaying the reverence she was due.

All except for... him!

Deciding that her love for the púca was greater than her resentment of having to ask for help from that insufferable archer, she'd called for Rhoslyn the pixie to have him meet her here.

Many times along the way, Nightmare faltered...

wobbling in the air like a drunken Celtae weaving his way home from a tavern. Her heart stopped every time it happened, fearing he would die right out from under her. Eventually they managed to glide to the pool outside the cave, but the púca's landing was little better than a semi-controlled crash. Kyla went flying over the great beast's shoulder as they both tumbled ass-over-teakettle, finally sliding to a stop just inside the cave entrance.

Kyla's head banged painfully against a wooden bucket, but she ignored the pain and sprang to Nightmare's side, where she could then see an arrow protruding at an odd angle from the wyvern's chest. One of those Roman cavalry archers had somehow managed an almost impossible shot, at just the right angle for the arrowhead to slip right between two of the wyvern's overlapping breastplates. She couldn't be sure, but she feared their impact with the ground might have pushed that damned arrow even deeper into Nightmare's chest.

The púca laid panting and moaning pitifully, so Kyla grabbed the bucket that the back of her head had so recently made acquaintances with, and ran to fill it from the pool right outside. She coaxed the great beast to open his mouth and she tipped the bucket, slowly pouring water down his gullet. He drank the entire bucket greedily, so she ran back to the pool to refill it. The suffering wyvern swallowed four more buckets of water before finally turning his head away, refusing more.

Kyla scooted down next to Nightmare where he could lay his great head in her lap. The púca's labored breathing and soft whimpers of pain cut deeply into her... emotional pain such as she'd never experienced before. She was also totally unaccustomed to feeling so incredibly helpless... and worthless, just sitting there, not knowing what, if anything, she might possibly do to alleviate the wyvern's suffering. She stroked the beast's massive head and softly cooed reassurances... being careful as to exactly where she placed her arm after nearly being scalded by the steam that occasionally wafted from his nostrils.

Where is that damned archer?

Kyla was confident that if anyone knew where to find him, the pixie would. She knew Rhoslyn had found him earlier, to give him the golden dragon war bow, when hundreds of those black enchanted arrows suddenly began peppering those damned Romans like a rain of death. The teamwork between them had been exhilarating, with her and Nightmare burning the forest around them, while the archer rained death down on them with her father's bow.

Was that only this morning?

But all that changed in the early afternoon when the púca suddenly screamed in pain and indignation. Since then, she'd been consumed with worry... worry for her púca and puzzled by the birth of another odd sensation she'd never experienced before — a tiny niggling of regret for the way she'd treated that archer the last time she'd seen him.

She'd been ranting about the cowardice of that Celtae king in Deblin, hiding within his stone fortress instead of immediately marching his clans to attack those Roman invaders while they were vulnerable, trapped on the Drumanagh peninsula with their backs to the sea. She'd been angry... especially angry with him for treating her like a common tavern wench — having the audacity to bodily pick her up and throw her over his shoulder so she couldn't see that craven cur, thus preventing her from frying him with a bolt there in his own throne room. They'd argued, and admittedly she'd said some pretty nasty things, not only about that king in particular, but about the entire Celtae people in general.

He accused me of being arrogant, and haughty.

As she watched the sky darkening toward evening she now could see where he might be angry with her, having possibly taken offense at her indelicate words. She had never been in a situation before where she needed to concern herself with the feelings of lesser beings. Truth be known, she'd rarely given the slightest thought to their having actual "feelings" at all!

Nightmare's breathing became noticeably more labored and his whimpering feebler. His skin felt as though it was becoming hotter and hotter by the minute... not that it was easy to tell with a fire wyvern. But it was becoming frighteningly obvious that he was slowly losing his battle for life, and Kyla became alarmed the archer might not arrive in time... or might not obey her summons. So she continued to fret, as that had been hours ago and there was still no sign that he had received it.

Perhaps he just ignored me. If so, and Nightmare dies, Mother's champion or no... I'll kill him.

CHAPTER TWENTY-ONE

"The impossible could not have happened, therefore the impossible must be possible in spite of appearances."
-- Agatha Christie

The Haunted Forest
Mid-August, 81 A.D.

ARYN OFTEN WONDERED IF ANYONE ELSE SAW THE irony of people calling a night like this the "new moon" — because there wasn't one. It was the darkest night of the month... a very bad time to be attempting to travel through a thick, storm-shattered forest. In fact, his journey would have been all but impossible, had it not been for the small army of *will-o'-the-wisps* gathered to light his way through the surrounding gloom.

The Celtae clans on Éire rarely traveled at night, for fear of these unique fae creatures that normally inhabited the swamps and bogs of the island. Their luminescent beauty was known to lure unwary travelers to their deaths, drowning in their watery habitats. Some called them *corpse lights*, as they were also known to frequent graveyards for indiscernible reasons of their own. Either way, the Celtae clans generally feared them and therefore avoided night travel accordingly. Aryn seriously doubted the tiny, glowing creatures harbored any real malice towards people... it was all too easy to mistake them for a swarm of harmless fireflies, or even the lights from night torches of a small village, off in the distance. Still, he'd definitely felt the cold fingers of dread run up his spine when such a large group of them initially appeared all around him.

Aryn roused from his bedroll, interpreting their appearance as the signal it was finally time for him to leave. He had tried his best to rest, but the lingering ache in his damaged shoulder had made sleep impossible. Frisky startled in surprise, snuffling softly as he climbed aboard the stallion in the dark.

The narrow path before him was little wider than that necessary for a single horse to travel, but it was obvious in the soft glow of the multitude of *will-o'-the-wisps* darting before him. The forest on both sides of the cleared path remained a snarled, tangled mess from the damage caused by the great storm. Some of the largest pieces appeared to have been dragged out of the way, or simply thrown atop the pile. Aryn wondered whether the dryad might have enlisted the aid of a troll, to move the heaviest pieces out of the way.

Frisky's rolling gate had never been a problem for him before, but the swaying motion of the horse's walking pace aggravated the ache in his shoulder. Anxious to get back to his cave as quickly as possible in response to Kyla's summons, Aryn softly tapped Frisky's flanks with his heels to nudge him into a cantor, but the bouncing quickly made his shoulder pain unbearable, so he had to slow the horse back to a walk rather quickly. It was going to take him a lot longer to get back to his cave at a walk, but there was nothing for it...

~

Underground
3232 A.D.

BRYAN STEELE AWOKE DISORIENTED, chilled from lying on the ground inside the dank tunnel. The yellow-orange light from flickering torches was harsh against the darkness, so he had to wait for his eyes to adjust to it before he could see clearly. His eyes teared a bit from the thin, wispy torch smoke, but he found that could see if he squinted against the glare. Shivering, Bryan rolled to get his knees under him and stood up shakily. He'd wanted to warm his hands near one of the freestanding torches, but as soon as he became vertical again, a wracking cough gripped him as his body attempted to clear several weeks of accumulated dust from his lungs.

"Yeah, we've all been hacking like that every time we stand up."

Stooped over, Brian turned to see who had spoken. Benny Lopatka, the skinny tool-crib clerk from the mining complex sat leaning against the tunnel wall a little farther down.

"Best just to stay down. The dwarves that brought us up

out of the mine said they'd be back soon with food and water for us."

"Dwarves?"

"Don't know what else ya could possibly call 'em. Only about waist high, but twice as thick as us. Thick, hairy little critters from right out of a fairy story."

"I thought I'd dreamed that."

"Yanked me right out of the tool-crib, they did, without so much as a howdy-do... kiss my ass... ner nothin. Looked like they knew how to use them nasty-ass hammers they had strapped on their backs, so ah figured it best to just go with 'em, without makin' too much of a fuss."

"I vaguely remember thinking I was being carried by a dwarf with a bright red beard."

"Mighta been... several o'the critters like that. The one that hoisted me o're his shoulder had black hair. Ain't seen no blondes amongst 'em though."

Brian heard footsteps behind him and turned to see Dan Weaver, the big second shift maintenance group leader who'd first welcomed him to the station when he'd just arrived off of the S.S. *Calypso*, all those months ago. Dan was too tall to walk fully upright in the low tunnel, so he was walking in a stoop that had to be playing hell on his back.

"Hey, Dan!"

Weaver grinned when he saw Brian and grabbed him, in a smothering bear hug.

"Steele! Damn, was I sure glad to hear that you were among the survivors."

"Survivors? — Not everyone made it out?"

"No." Weaver shook his head. "Nineteen of the guys died before the dwarves got to them... mostly off-shift personnel. Poor bastards evidently suffocated in their sleep.

I guess they were just so exhausted, the struggle to keep breathing became too much for them."

"My, God. I'm so sorry to hear that. We all tried so damned hard to keep those air filtration systems going, but..."

"I know... I feel it too. Don't blame yourself. The company didn't start us off with new, top-of-the-line equipment to begin with. Mostly half worn-out stuff they bought used, just because it was cheaper."

Brian shook his head. "Yeah, ain't that always the way?"

Their moment of shared sorrow was interrupted by a couple of long-bearded dwarves emerging into the torchlight from farther back down the tunnel. As they turned to look, Dan Weaver's jaw dropped.

"Hey, isn't that the..."

"Yeah, it is."

The first dwarf was carrying their jury-rigged VLF beacon that had been attached to the digger that Brian had been operating when all of this weirdness started. The second, close behind him, carried a high capacity, deep-discharge battery pack that both knew weighed over 800 lbs. Three wires connecting the battery pack to the VLF beacon drooped between the two dwarves, bobbing slightly as they walked.

"That battery pack doesn't go with that VLF beacon, but it does appear to be functioning," whispered Weaver, incredulously.

"No, but it's the right voltage, so it is compatible."

"But... how the hell could they possibly know how to..."

"They couldn't."

"So how..."

Brian merely shook his head, remembering what "his"

dwarf had told him about how they knew the minors needed help: *"Gods tell."*

"Heads up," yelled Benny. "Chow's here!"

Both men turned to see a line of burly, long-bearded creatures approaching with bags hanging from long poles on their shoulders. They were marching in an offset single file, so their poles didn't interfere with one another. They both nudged closer to the tunnel wall to provide more room for the dwarves traveling deeper into the tunnel to get by.

"There is no life native to this planet, ya know," Brian whispered.

"So... what would you call *them?*"

Brian shook his head. "Impossible is what they are... but they *are* real... we wouldn't have survived without them."

Weaver settled himself into a sitting position next to the wall and nodded in agreement. "I'd just like to know where all that damned dust went, and where all this fresh air came from. There's no atmosphere on this planet."

Brian remembered, or thought he did, that incredible rock creature bursting through the mine wall, that just seemed to inhale all the dust swirling in the air around the digger he was operating. He also remembered seeing small blue-white blurs swirling by him, that brought a gale of fresh, sweet air sweeping into the mine behind them. Steele just shook his head and snorted.

"No dwarves on this planet either, but yet, here they are. Don't ask me how the dust and fresh air happened. You wouldn't believe me, if I told you."

"Try me."

Before Brian could answer, the red-bearded dwarf who had carried him out of the mine came into their section of the tunnel and handed him a bag.

"What's this?"

"Food... eat. Water... here."

Brian was desperately thirsty, so he looked to where the dwarf pointed and grabbed what appeared to be an irregularly shaped pig's bladder having a small rope carry strap, with a cork stopper in one end. He looked at it dubiously, but his thirst drove him to pulling the cork and pouring whatever came out, down his parched throat.

Damn, that's good! — Still cool... it must have been icy cold when they first filled it, for it to remain so incredibly refreshing by the time they carried it down here. Surprising that there's no aftertaste from the animal bladder they made the water bag out of, too.

Brian looked around and saw Dan Weaver, Benny Lopatka and a few others from the mining facility also gorging themselves from the water bags they'd been handed. He tipped his own back to take a second massive guzzle, but only managed another couple of swallows before one of the dwarves yelled.

"No drink much... eat first... more water later!"

Brian complied, recognizing the wisdom of the command. He re-corked his water bag and reached into the food bag he'd been brought. Inside, he found dried fruit that resembled apricots, some nuts, a wedge of cheese, a small loaf of some kind of dark bread, and wrapped inside of a thin oil-skin paper was an assortment of fresh sautéed mushrooms, with what appeared to be onions and tasted slightly of garlic.

"I've had a lot worse."

Brian turned to Weaver, who'd spoken.

"Yes, surprisingly good fare... especially for totally impossible food, brought to us by equally impossible creatures that rescued us from an impossible situation on a totally lifeless planet having no breathable atmosphere."

"Dwarves... not creatures!" growled the dwarf who'd brought Dan's meal and water to him.

"I'm sorry. I certainly didn't mean any offense by what I said."

"You like tall mortals on surface... arrogant."

"Tall mortals living on the surface?"

"Yes... we trade... they snicker... no find it funny after we break legs."

"But, that's impossible!"

"Not impossible... just rude."

"Are you saying there are people like us that live on the surface?"

"Not like... similar. Hairier."

"What do you call those people?"

"We call... savages — call self *Celtae*."

CHAPTER TWENTY-TWO

*The best doctor in the world is the veterinarian.
He can't ask his patients what is the matter — he's got to just
know.*
-- Will Rogers

Aryn's Cave
Mid-August, 81 A.D.

IT WAS WELL PAST MIDNIGHT BY THE TIME FRISKY finally stumbled to the pool outside Aryn's cave. Aryn was exhausted and groggy, but aware enough to throw his right leg over the horse's neck and slide down his flank to the ground. After so many hours on horseback, his legs immediately buckled on impact with the ground and he crumbled backward to the ground beneath Frisky's feet. His unaccustomed dismount induced the horse to side step a bit, resulting in Frisky's dangling stallion parts smacking Aryn right in the face.

Aryn's temper flared to incandescence at this unexpected indignity, but he stifled the impulse to lash out and rolled out from beneath the horse's hooves, before he got stepped on.

Sigh... It's been that kind of day.

As Frisky lowered his head to slurp water from the pool, Aryn struggled to get his knees under him, and knee-walked close enough to the pool to fall face first into the water, right next to his horse's head. After a few seconds, he pushed up on his one good arm to bring his head out of the water. He then arched his back to get his upper body vertical again, sat back on his haunches, and turned his gaze skyward. The night was absolutely black, broken only by a myriad of bright, twinkling stars overhead.

Frisky suddenly raised his head from the water and turned it towards the cave entrance with a snuffle. His ears flicked forward as if listening intently for something, before ambling towards the cave.

Favoring his damaged right shoulder that was still in a sling, Aryn groaned and got to his feet awkwardly. The interior of the cave was pitch black, but as he started to step into the entrance, Frisky warned him off with a soft nicker. Wondering what it was that his horse sensed in the absolute darkness, Aryn paused to consider his next move.

Rhoslyn told me that Kyla said to come here, so where is she?

Fortunately, *will-o'-the-wisps* are inquisitive little creatures. A few that had helped to guide Aryn on his journey home unexpectedly doubled back and darted within the cave... illuminating the interior in their soft glow, so he could see it. Right in front of Aryn's foot was the curled tail of a huge reptile.

Damn, I would have tripped right over that tail, if Frisky hadn't warned me!

Sleeping against the cave wall sat Kyla, with a gigantic wyvern head in her lap. The disguised púka cracked open one huge eyelid, revealing the fearsome creature was awake and aware of him. Aryn felt no immediate alarm in the wyvern's gaze. He'd spend most of his early childhood roaming the forests surrounding his grandfather's farmstead alone, and other than the prey animals he hunted for food, he'd grown up considering all of the denizens of the forest as friends. He was experienced in dealing with the forest's predators too. He knew exactly what actions and circumstances would likely cause one to attack...

Of course, all bets are off when one is wounded and in pain.

And Nightmare was most definitely wounded. In the soft glow of the swirling *will-o'-the-wisps* he could see a Roman cavalry arrow sticking obscenely out of the púka's chest at an odd angle.

Aryn tip-toed around the great beast until he was positioned where could gently prod Kyla's shoulder with the handle of his bronze, skinning knife. Her eyes opened after he poked her the second time.

"Wake up... I need your help if we're going to treat your púka."

Kyla's eyes immediately flicked with alarm down into her lap, where Nightmare's great head lay. His open eyes reassured her that he still lived and was awake, so she glanced back up at Aryn, who was holding out a down pillow to her.

"Put this under his head to elevate it, after you wiggle yourself out from under his head."

Kyla nodded understanding, did as he instructed, and stood up.

"We're going to need a lot more light in here. Light every torch you can find, while I search through my medicinal supplies."

"What's wrong with your arm?" asked Kyla, nodding toward his sling.

"Tore out my rotator joint, killing several hundred Romans with your father's bow. Seems that magical incantation of his gave me abilities my physical body was never designed to perform."

Kyla's temper flashed, but she bit off the scathing retort that arose from his implied criticism of her father, remembering her vow to be nicer to the archer... at least until after he saved Nightmare's life. She lit several torches from Aryn's stockpile with small snaps of blue lightning from a single fingertip, and placed them in freestanding brass sconces on all sides of the suffering wyvern.

Aryn sorted through several shelves of dried herbs and pre-made medicinal concoctions, calling for Kyla to come gather the ones he needed. Ordinarily she would have resented being ordered about by a mere mortal, but he knew how to help Nightmare, so she stifled the impulse. Admittedly, he did have only one good arm, so helping him gather what he needed meant that the púka's wound would be tended to faster.

"What took you so damned long to get here? I sent Rhoslyn to fetch you early this afternoon."

"She knocked me out of the top of a thirty-foot tree and I landed face down in the breasts of an unconscious 12-foot pixie."

Kyla snorted in amusement at that mental image.

"Rhoslyn tried to catch me, but ended up taking the

brunt of our mutual fall through the tree branches. It took me a while to get her awake, and then even longer before she remembered to give me your message. —You know how pixies are."

"So, where is Rhoslyn now"

"She's got a knot the size of a hen's egg behind her left ear, and a smaller one the size of a robin's egg above her right eye. She evidently suffered a brain bruise that is preventing her from flying, popping, or even reassuming her normal size. We were close enough to the Romans we could distinctly hear them chopping at all those black locus trees blocking the road. As she's never learned how to walk, I had to hide her by enlisting the aid of Wilmonia, a lilac pixie, to surround her with gigantic lilac bushes."

"Rhoslyn has lost her powers? I didn't know that was possible."

"I didn't either. Brain bruises are strange injuries. Nothing can be done for them, other to let them heal on their own over time, and hope everything eventually returns to normal."

Aryn lifted down his small brass measuring balance and weights in their brown leather case and set them on the wooden table where he'd previously directed Kyla to place all the ingredients for him. He then had her fetch one and one-quarter small ceramic jars of water from the pool outside, and pour them into a small brass pot hanging over his small fire pit.

"Get a fire going under that water, so it can be coming to a boil while you come help me measure out the right proportions of the ingredients we'll need."

"What is all this you're doing? — Shouldn't you be focusing on getting that arrow out of his chest, first thing?"

"I could, but he'd probably bleed to death if we don't do

things in the right order. That arrow is currently acting like a cork in the mouth of the wound. Once the arrow is out, we'll need something to stop the bleeding very quickly, before Nightmare bleeds out."

"So, you're concocting something that will stop the bleeding, after you remove the arrow?"

"No, we'll make that later... first we have to give him something to keep him from killing both of us, while you're trying to cut that arrowhead out of him."

"ME?" Kyla shrieked. "You're the physician, not me!"

"A right-handed physician, with a bad shoulder... who can't control a knife with the deftness necessary to clear the barbs on that arrowhead from the chest muscle it's imbedded in, so we don't do any more damage than necessary, getting it out."

"I can't do that!" Kyla wailed. "I could never cut on Nightmare with a knife."

"You certainly didn't have any problems embedding your fork in that Roman's throat a while back."

"That was different! That Roman was just a mor..." Kyla stopped herself before she finished blurting out what they both knew she'd started to say: *a mortal... like him.*

There was an awkward silence between them that seemed to stretch on forever, but eventually Aryn said softly, "Well, you think about it. It'll take quite a bit of time for us to put the wyvern under, anyway."

"What do you mean, 'put the wyvern under?' Under what?"

"Do you think you have enough control over that beast so that he remains absolutely still, for whatever time it takes us to get the arrow out, and the wound properly packed? — Remember, while we're cutting that arrow out of him, it's going to hurt... a lot!"

"Nightmare will do wha..." Again, she stopped herself, as she truly thought the question through. Shaking her head, Kyla finally admitted, "No... if he's really going to be in that kind of intense pain, probably not. So what can we do?"

"We're going to put him to sleep. Watch and learn."

Over the next half hour Aryn instructed her in how to measure out very exacting quantities of belladonna, poppy juice, thornapple, crushed henbane seeds and mandrake root powder on the little brass balance scale, against weights from his apothecary kit.

"What is all this stuff?"

"Poisons, mostly."

"POISONS! — You intend to give Nightmare all of these poisons?"

"They're only deadly if ingested in too great a quantity. But if specific dosages are combined in exactly the right amounts, and administered properly, they can induce a sleep so profound a surgeon can then go about the business of cutting out an arrowhead, without the patient suffering any pain at all."

"No pain? — At all?"

"None... at least until he wakes up. The wound area will still be sore for a couple of weeks, but nothing like he's suffering now."

Once all of the ingredients were measured out and the water in the pot came to a boil, Aryn told Kyla where to find his spare linens and instructed her to tear most of them into strips for bandaging the wound. He also had her tie a doubled strip of linen around both of their heads, being careful to fully cover their nose and mouths. Once that was done, he had her dump all of the pre-measured poisons into the boiling water and then raise it higher above the fire to simmer. He then sent her out into the forest to find a stick, at least half her body length long, and then use a bronze clip to attach a sponge from his storage shelves onto it.

"Now, dip the sponge into the pot to thoroughly wet it, and stir the mixture around. Shake the excess back into the pot and then hold the sponge about one hand-width in front of Nightmare's nostrils."

"Oh... I thought we were gonna have to try to entice him to drink that nasty concoction somehow."

"No, that would kill him, for sure. He just needs to inhale the vapors coming off the sponge."

"Where did you learn how to do all this?"

"I learned herbalism from my paternal grandmother... the *maighdean mhara,* from whom I inherited my fae blood. I learned to grind and mix medicines from an old man who ran an apothecary shop in the village where I spent my adolescent years. I learned to be a physician and surgeon, working with the Ovate Druids during my time in the high king's army."

Hmm... A physician, surgeon, herbalist, and apothecary, all occupations of peace and healing... and yet he's killed a lot more Roman invaders then I have.

"Celtae villages everywhere on Éire are always in need all of those skills. Why didn't you settle down in a village somewhere, get married, and raise yourself a passel of children? — Why is it you took up residence in this cave, to live like a hermit after your eyes healed?"

Aryn looked blankly at Kyla, and wondered why the haughty demi-goddess cared enough to ask.

"I was an only child. I spent my early years roaming the forest alone, outside my paternal grandfather's farmstead. I was constantly surrounded by adults and was rarely around any other children, so my social skills never really developed properly... other kids always just seemed to act so damned childish to me. I've never really had any friends, other than the animals and the fae. I understood being alone, so I just stayed in this cave after my eyes healed... I really had nowhere else to go."

The archer's story struck a chord within the demi-goddess, as it so closely paralleled her own. She too had been her parent's only child, growing up primarily alone... wandering the forest among the animals and the fae, just as he had. She'd never found acceptance among her father's people that she'd once desperately hoped for. Most of the *Daoine Sidhe* saw her only as a curiosity. And for the first time, she found herself beginning to think of him as "Aryn," instead of just "that insufferable archer."

WHILE WAITING for fumes off the sponge to work their wonders, Aryn gathered the items he'd need to stop the bleeding after the arrowhead was dug out. Kyla again assisted with the measurements and readied the bandages, so they'd be close at hand when the time came.

After three-quarters of an hour the wyvern no longer responded to light pricks from Aryn's bronze dagger, and he declared it was finally time to get that arrow out Nightmare's chest. He poured whisky over both of her hands and the blade of his skinning knife and handed it to Kyla.

"You ready to do this?"

"I'm not sure if I can."

"You have to... Nightmare will die, if you don't. Come on, where's that haughty, self-assured little demi-goddess that I've come to know and detest?"

Kyla winced inside... Aryn's flippant question stung her

more than she had thought possible, just hours ago. For reasons she did not understand, it was suddenly important that this man think well of her. Girding herself, she snatched the knife from his hand and knelt next to the unconscious wyvern.

Aryn moved two of the bronze torch holders closer and placed them to either side, so that there would be no shadows cast by her hand, as she wielded the blade.

"Why did you pour whisky over my hands and the blade first?"

"I don't really know. The Ovate Druids believe it an offering to the gods that lessens the possibility of the wound festering after surgery. Although, after meeting a few of them, I have my doubts about how much *they* really have to do with it."

Kyla's confidence about what she was doing wasn't enhanced by her failure to make much of a dent in the scale the arrow was lodged under. "This knife isn't working. Nightmare's chest scales are just too tough to cut with a bronze knife."

"Yeah... a Damascus steel blade would probably work, but I don't have any of those handy."

"Too much iron in Damascus steel. It would probably kill him if we tried using one anyway... he is a fae creature, you know."

"You wouldn't by chance have an enchanted, armor piercing blade, would you?"

"No... so what can we do?"

"Only one other thing I can think of, that might work."

With that, Aryn went over to where his gear that he'd taken off Frisky was stacked and opened his saddlebag. From it he removed half of a black arrow that had been broken in the fall he'd taken when Rhoslyn had knocked him out of that tree.

"Here, try using the tip of this broken arrow to see if you can saw through that scale with it."

Kyla looked startled, but smiled when she saw the logic of Aryn's idea.

"That just might work."

It did... the obsidian arrowhead, which was enchanted to penetrate metal armor, sliced through the wyvern's chest scale like butter. At Aryn's instruction, she then used his bronze skinning knife to cut away the soft tissue that adhered the underside of the scale to the underlying chest muscle, so she could remove the scale in two pieces. The entrance wound was now plainly visible, with the arrow body hanging at an acute angle where it had entered the chest from below.

Aryn had Kyla pour whisky over his left hand and he prodded the muscle tissues with his fingers until he located the hard iron arrowhead buried within, and felt of its contours.

"Damn..."

When Kyla looked at him questioningly, he told her to put her middle finger exactly where his was.

"You feel that hard lump, under the muscle?"

"Yes"

"That hard spot you're feeling is the center of the arrowhead body. What we need to determine now is exactly what type of arrowhead we're dealing with. Use your other fingers to probe around the muscle on all sides of where your middle finger is, but especially below, nearer to the entrance wound."

"It's hard to tell, but I think I can feel a bit of hardness, extending back on both sides, as I probe farther back toward the entrance wound."

Aryn grinned at her. "That's exactly right!"

Kyla flushed with pleasure at his unexpected praise and asked, "So what does this tell us?"

"The Romans sometimes use arrow points shaped like a beech leaf. I was hoping it might have been one of those, because we could have just backed it out with just a hard yank opposite to the line of flight, without causing too much damage to the surrounding tissue. — Are those hard areas you're feeling about a finger width apart, or are they on opposite sides of each other?"

Kyla probed again and thought for a moment before answering, "Opposite... I think."

"Very good! — Now we know exactly what kind of arrowhead we're dealing with."

"We do?"

"Yes, and that knowledge is vital if we're going to get this thing out of him with minimal damage. Had the hard areas been about a finger width apart, that would have indicated it was a three-bladed broadhead arrow, having small barbs on all three blades... which would have been bad. With the hard areas on opposite sides, as you correctly surmised, it tells us this is a double-bladed broadhead, having fewer, but larger, nastier barbs on it."

"That still doesn't sound good."

"No, but it does give us options for getting it out more easily, that we couldn't have used had there been a third barb on the underneath side we couldn't get to."

Aryn then had Kyla locate his surgical kit and separate out two sets of "muscle pullers." These were primarily heavy-duty wires, looped back on themselves and twisted for extra strength, forming a hook, with curved, wooden pieces set into twin finger loops at the opposite end.

"Okay, now comes at the hardest part. Look closely at the muscle tissue... can you see there where it has a distinct grain to it — parallel fibers, much like the grain in a piece of wood?"

"Yes."

"Just as you can split a log by driving a wedge along the grain of the wood, we're going to separate the muscle tissue by inserting the tip of the skinning knife between the muscle fibers, keeping the blade parallel to the grain of the muscle so we don't actually cut them... we just want to separate them."

Kyla inserted the knife tip between the muscle fibers and gently pushed it deeper until she came up against the hard iron arrowhead.

"Okay, I think I'm down far enough that the knife tip is up against the arrowhead... what now?"

"Now comes the awkward part. In the high king's army we always had other physicians, or surgical helpers to assist us using the muscle pullers to further separate the muscles."

Aryn pulled his right arm out of the sling, winced in pain, but grabbed the two muscle pullers, inserting his index and middle fingers into the wood covered loops.

"Twist the knife blade to further separate the muscle fibers, forming a hole in the muscle."

When Kyla complied, Aryn inserted the muscle pullers under the exposed muscles to either side of the hole and pulled to separate them, making the hole in the muscle much larger.

"Can you see the socket where the shaft mounts into the arrowhead?"

"Yes."

"Fortunately these Roman shafts aren't actually made of wood, but softer marsh reeds. Carefully use the knife to cut through the reed to detach the shaft from the iron head. Just be careful not to cut any deeper than necessary to fully get the shaft free."

Kyla positioned the knife perpendicular to the shaft and gently sawed at the reed.

"Okay, you're getting close to being all the way through."

Even with Aryn's warning, the reed parted more suddenly than she'd expected, and she jerked the knife away with a lurch... heart in her throat.

"Nice job... now pull the shaft straight out of the wound along the angle of flight. Then grab a clean linen rag and wipe your brow, before all that sweat beading on your forehead drips into your eyes."

Kyla gently pulled the arrow shaft from the wound and stood up, not realizing how badly her back muscles had tensed up. She grabbed a piece of clean linen and wiped her face as he'd instructed.

"I didn't realize it was so hot in here."

"That sweat that builds up on your forehead during surgery isn't from the heat, but the constant tension of trying to do things so slowly and carefully."

"Now what?"

Not relaxing his hold, but continuing to hold the muscle tissue open, exposing the arrowhead, he told her to locate a middling size pair of bronze tongs from his surgical kit.

"Next you need to use the knife to gently pull away any tissues clinging to the backside of the barbs. Feel free to cut anything that won't clear the barb, by just moving it."

Anguish showed on Aryn's face as he diligently held the wound open, despite the agony in his damaged shoulder.

Kyla was torn as she worked painstakingly to remove any tissue likely to hang up on the barbs when the iron arrowhead was removed. She wanted to hurry for Aryn's sake, but needed to be through for Nightmare's.

"The barbs are as clear, as I can get them."

"Okay, hold the tongs perpendicular to the barbs and shove the tips deep enough you can get a firm grip on the arrowhead with them," Aryn hissed between clenched teeth.

"Ready."

"Grip the tongs just as tightly as you can and then jerk the arrowhead out, in the opposite direction that it went in."

The tongs slipped off repetitively and it took Kyla four tries to finally get the arrowhead out.

Aryn quickly grabbed a wad of linen and shoved it down hard into the wound, to staunch the flow of blood that immediately began pooling in the hole.

"Grab that mixture we put together earlier and be prepared to throw a handful of it into the hole, when I remove this bandage."

Kyla grabbed a fist full of the green, gooey substance and shouted, "Ready!"

Aryn jerked the bandage away and Kyla deftly tossed her handful of goop deep into the wound. Aryn then grabbed a thick, pre-made linen bandage and pressed it to down over the wound, while Kyla grabbed long strips of linen and tied them completely around the wyvern's great body, to hold the bandage firmly in place.

"Are we done?"

"Yes... and you did a damned fine job of it too. — I knew you could do it!"

Kyla smiled, basking in the glow of Aryn's praise, as she tried to wipe off all of the goo still clinging to her fingers.

"What was in that goop you had me throw into the wound?"

"Honey, mixed with equal measures of powdered malachite to staunch the bleeding... and bread mold to reduce to possibility of the wound turning foul."

Kyla nodded and walked outside to wash her hands in the pool. When she returned, she saw that Aryn had put his damaged arm back into his sling, and was starting to put things away.

"What can I do to help?"

Aryn's eyebrow rose a bit at the earnestness in her voice, as she volunteered to help clean up the mess.

"You can wash the knife and tongs off in the pool, if you will."

When she returned, she placed both articles on the table and asked, "What else?"

"Got any bacon, handy?"

CHAPTER TWENTY-THREE

If you go long enough without a bath, even the fleas will leave you alone.
-- Ernie Pyle

The Deblin Road
Mid-August, 81 A.D.

GENERAL GNAEUS JULIUS AGRICOLA, ROMAN governor of Britannia, grinned mightily when the last of those monstrous black locust trees that had blocked the road, trapping his army, finally fell with a crash. General Servius Marius Paterculus, legate of *Legio IX Hispana* rode through to join him after the road had been thoroughly policed for any hidden thorn clusters that might still be lurking within the scattered leaves. Agricola asked Paterculus to join him in his command tent for wine, as they conferred over casualties and the general state of their now recombined army.

The total butcher's bill for this march was 1,412 legionaries and their auxiliaries... the combined tally of dead and seriously wounded, from burning, drowning, falling victim to that horrible rain of black arrows, or some combination thereof. Another 283 displayed painful wounds from clearing the thorn trees. Like Agricola, Paterculus had assigned men, not actively involved in attacking the trees, to digging graves and conducting burial details, so their rapid departure from this horrible entrapment not be delayed more than necessary.

Within the hour, tents were struck, smithies quenched, and the baggage train loaded with equipment, unused supplies and wounded men. Trumpets blew and what remained of the ninth legion of the Roman army formed itself into centuries, and centuries formed into their cohorts, in preparation to march away from this scene of so much horror and death.

It seemed like the very land they trod upon was setting itself against them. They'd already lost one-quarter of their army without ever seeing their first hairy Hibernian warrior. First had come that great storm, then the troll at the bridge, and most lately *the trap in the thorn trees,* where water flooded in from everywhere, a flying fire breathing reptile set the forest ablaze around them... and worst of all, those clouds of deadly black arrows raining down from the gods only knew where.

What could mere mortal men hope to accomplish, when the local Hibernian gods were so actively against them? — Most of the men secretly wished they could abandon this foolish quest to conquer Hibernia and return to Britannia, but none suggested it outwardly. Too much Roman blood had already been spilled... too many Roman lives had been lost. With a blast of trumpets, the lead elements of *Legio IX Hispana* stepped out smartly, continuing their march to the Hibernian port city of Deblin.

~

Aryn's Cave
Mid-August, 81 A.D.

KYLA'S EYES cracked open from the cozy confines of Aryn's soft, warm bed. Bright afternoon sunlight flooded the entrance to the cave and she squinted against the glare. Instinctively, her eyes sought out Nightmare, to assure herself he still lived. Her immediate concerns were relieved as she noted his sides slowly heaving in deep, rhythmic breathing that seemed much easier than his ragged, labored efforts before Aryn's arrival the night before. She smiled when she saw the archer, sound asleep, there on the floor of the cave, with his head resting against the wyvern's great chest.

They had argued the night before about which of them would take the bed, and which one would, and should, sleep close to the beast to monitor their patient during the night.

Which one of us is the physician? — Which one of us would know what to do, if there's an unexpected problem?

She experienced mixed emotions as she watched the archer bedding down next to *her* púca that night. It had galled her to admit that Aryn had been right... that Nightmare had needed *him*, more than he'd needed her. So soon after the surgery that got that poisonous, iron-tipped arrow out of him, surviving that first night was absolutely crucial to his continued survival. After she'd finally relented and snuggled down into the soft, warmth of Aryn's bed, she wrestled with emotions totally foreign to anything she'd ever experienced before.

Surprisingly, she'd actually enjoying frying up those slabs of bacon that she'd magically retrieved from her storage area in the otherworld. She hadn't really minded cooking for him... especially after all he'd just done to save Nightmare's life. Aryn certainly did his part to contribute to their late-night meal, bringing out wedges of cheese, a loaf of bread, fresh butter and real strawberry jam. She remembered her emotions churning in a totally unfamiliar way, as she'd watched the archer stuff strips of bacon, chunks of cheese and jam slathered bread into his dirty, scratched, stubble covered face. Kyla wasn't used to sharing a meal with anyone else, and was surprised to find herself enjoying his silent company.

The man was obviously exhausted, but he'd persevered until that horrid arrow was out, the wound slathered in a healing poultice, and bandaged securely. She was proud of her contribution to saving the púca's life, but she knew deep inside herself that without Aryn's expertise, the wyvern would not have lived to see the sun rise this morning. She owed him for that, but what might she offer him to show the depth of her gratitude?

Kyla had suddenly felt herself coloring and she had to turn away from those intense blue eyes, sparkling with good humor in the torchlight, lest her own eyes betray what she had been feeling at that moment.

Where in the world did that *thought come from?*

Deciding that she had slept enough, Kyla threw off the covers and tiptoed out into the bright sunlight, past the still sleeping archer. Kneeling down at the edge of the pool outside, she splashed the cold, spring fed water on her face.

The feeling was so invigorating, she decided that a bath was definitely in order, so she stripped off all of her clothes and waded naked into the icy water. Holding her breath, she plunged head first into the pool's icy depths, reveling in the shock it gave to her body. Underwater, Kyla suddenly noticed that she wasn't alone down there. A couple of sexy water nymphs grinned at her, imploring her to come play with them.

Humpf... no wonder that archer likes living alone here.

She immediately felt ashamed of her knee-jerk indictment of Aryn's motives. Admittedly, the fae are highly sexual, promiscuous creatures by nature, needing little encouragement to enthusiastically engage in the bawdiest acts imaginable. She had never questioned Aryn's friendship with Rhoslyn, nor ever wondered whether the pixie had ever expanded to full human size and copulated with the archer in that soft, warm bed of his. Aryn was one-quarter fae himself, and so, considerably more randy than was considered normal for the mortals inhabiting this island. It was highly probable that Aryn and Rhoslyn were fucking like minks, every time the opportunity arose.

That never mattered before... so why is the thought bothering me now?

Jealousy was unknown amongst the fae, but the gods of the Tuatha Dé Danann had developed the concept into an art. Kyla was half fae, and half goddess. She'd always envied her mother's freedom to openly display her naturally flirtatious nature... and her the ability to satiate herself regularly, rutting her father to exhaustion.

Kyla had certainly had her share of suitors among her father's people, oh yes. Considered an exotic, her virginity was considered the ultimate conquest and competition for it had been fierce among the males of the Daoine Sidhe...

until she found out there was wagering among her suitors. It had crushed her to learn that none of them had ever really cared about her, as a person — that she was just a prize to be won, boasted of... and just as quickly discarded. And so, she had withdrawn into the forest among the fae, virginity intact, religiously avoiding the Daoine Sidhe commonly guesting in her father's underground palace.

Only the iron will of her Tuatha Dé Danann side could tame the wanton desire for sex she'd inherited from her mother. She'd been at war with her own body since puberty. Admittedly, she had occasionally flirted with the idea of taking a big, hairy, Celtae warrior to bed when the itch became especially bad, but she never did — most of them neglected bathing for far too long and thus, were exceedingly dirty... a horrid assault on her sensitive nostrils.

At least Aryn bathes regularly.

~

Underground
3232 A.D.

THE DWARVES WERE GRUMBLING under their breath at the miner's universal desire to walk on their own, rather than suffer the embarrassment of being carried further, like babies, by the diminutive creatures. Yes, the miners understood that getting to the surface would take longer, but as long as they had plenty of torches, food, water and fresh air, they didn't care.

"That dwarf said there are people, living on the surface of this planet."

Brian Steele looked forlornly at big Dan Weaver, who walked beside him.

"You know that's not possible."

Weaver snorted. "Neither is all this fresh air... or being drug out of the mine by dwarves. Use your eyes, man! — These guys are just as real as we are."

"It's much more likely that we're hallucinating all of this from oxygen deprivation. We're probably all still lying in the bottom of that mine, dying right now... if we haven't died already."

"Do you really think we're all having exactly the same hallucination, at exactly the same time? — What are the odds against *that* happening?"

"Better than the odds against intelligent life evolving the past few months, on a barren planet having no breathable atmosphere."

"So, what is this we're all breathing right now, then?"

"Are we really breathing, right now? — Or, do we only think we're breathing?"

Weaver sighed, shook his head... and then punched Steele in the solar plexus with a massive right fist.

"*Oof!*"

The blow knocked all of the breath out of him, and Brian Steele bent over, gagging... unable to take another breath. His diaphragm was in spasm, paralyzed by the ferocity of Weaver's blow. Agonizing seconds ticked by, during which, Brian began to fear that Weaver had killed him... that he'd never be able to draw another breath.

Just as the world began graying out, an enormous final effort to inhale produced a tiny squeak of air, flowing into his lungs... followed by another, slightly better one. After what seemed like hours to the air-starved man, he finally managed to take a full, ragged breath, his first since Weaver launched his unprovoked attack.

"Jesus, Dan..." Brian croaked. "What the fuck did you do *that* for?"

"Why you stop?" yelled the dwarf closest to them. "You wanted to walk... walk!"

"Just proving to my friend here, that he was breathing... and that you guys really exist," Weaver said cheerfully.

The dwarf looked at the two miners as though they had lost their damned minds, and turned to walk away, shaking his great head and muttering to himself.

"Come on," Weaver said. "We'd better get moving before they insist on carrying us again."

"You planning on hitting me again?

"You plan on talking complete nonsense again?"

Steele shook his head, rubbed his sore stomach and started walking again... walking with a slight wobble, but walking.

"He also said those people living on the surface called themselves *Celtae*... just like the people in your story."

"I don't want to talk about that, right now."

"Why not? It passes the time."

"I don't want you to punch me again."

~

Aryn's Cave
Mid-August, 81 A.D.

A FLY ALIGHTED on the side of Aryn's nose and he drowsily swatted it away. Being a particularly pesky sort, the fly returned repetitively to alight on his face, nose and lips, whenever he swatted at it. Eventually, Aryn cracked open an eye and squinted into the sun, low enough in the sky to flood the entire entrance to his cave in brilliant afternoon light. He purposely laid his ear against the wyvern's great chest, satisfying himself that the púka's heartbeat was strong and its breathing was deep, regular and clear of any gurgling that would indicate fluid building up in the lungs.

Aryn got to his feet haltingly, stiff from lying on a bedroll spread on the bare rock of the cave entrance. He glanced toward the bed, noting that Kyla was no longer there.

I wonder where she got off to?

Satisfied the púka was in no immediate danger, he saw to Frisky's needs before his own, as was his habit. He filled the horse's feed troughs with oats and hay, and grabbed the bucket that Kyla had banged her head against the evening before, and then headed towards the pool outside, to fill it with water.

As usual, he'd awakened with a case of morning wood and had to piss, so he decided to relieve himself before filling Frisky's water trough. He fumbled to untie his trousers left-handed, his right arm still hanging in the sling that Rhoslyn had helped him fashion the day before. He turned parallel to the edge of the pool when he finally managed to drop his trousers and small clothes to free his stiffened member, so he did not foul the pool water.

Just as his piss stream commenced with an audible sigh of relief, a very naked Kyla suddenly burst up, breaking the surface of the icy pool, not a spear-length from where he stood with his erection in his hand, urinating lustily, like horse just before a race. Aryn instinctively turned quickly away, so she wasn't subjected to witnessing him finish pissing.

But, before turning away, Aryn *had* seen the beautiful demi-goddess in all her naked glory... and the sight of her magnificent body was absolutely staggering. He closed his eyes as he finished peeing, so nothing hindered him burning every detail of his momentary full-frontal view of Kyla's delicious, naked body, forever into his mind — her small, conical breasts with their incredible rose-pink nipples, and the dark thatch covering her inviting pubis, that disappeared mysteriously into the depths of that treasure trove between her legs.

Well, this is certainly awkward. — Perhaps with all that water in her eyes, she never saw my stiff dick.

Aryn never had the slightest thought about how his abrupt turning away to hide his dick, would offer Kyla an excellent view of his naked ass.

KYLA LUXURIATED in the depths of the pool, warming a bit as her body acclimated to the icy cold water. The two water nymphs were absolutely delighted this direct family member of the old gods who'd created them deigned to frolic with them in the pool, darting about on all sides of her, like minnows playing in the shallows.

Although the demi-goddess could have held her breath longer, she felt her body beginning to turn blue with cold, so she turned and glided along the bottom of the pool, as it rose toward the edge. When the depth of the water shallowed to about knee-deep, she pulled her knees under her and burst out of the water suddenly, into the brilliant sunlight. She was just beginning to suck in a fresh breath of the warm, clean air, when her lungs locked up.

The demi-goddess possessed superior eyesight and had no difficulty seeing clearly through the river of water pouring off her head. There at the edge of the pool stood Aryn, sporting the largest erection she'd ever seen... at least on a man. She'd witnessed Frisky impregnating some of her father's brood mares some years back, so while Aryn's dick wasn't nearly on that scale, it appeared absolutely huge to a horny demi-goddess. The sheer unexpectedness of the sight caused a lightning bolt of raw desire to shoot through her loins.

She found herself slightly disappointed when Aryn suddenly turned away, to finish his piss with his back to her.

Damn... nice ass!

"Ah... sorry about that," Aryn stammered. "I, ah... didn't know you were bathing in the pool. — I just came out to get a bucket of water for Frisky, and had some... er... *other business* I needed to attend to first."

"Don't let me stop you."

"If I kick the bucket towards the water, can you fill it for me and set it at the edge of the pool where I don't have to turn around to retrieve it?"

Kyla snickered. "You can turn around anytime you want. I'm not overly modest."

Aryn finished peeing and shook it out... milked it down and shook it out again, to ensure there was no residual urine remaining inside that might inadvertently dribble into his small clothes when he put it away.

"Maybe not, but maybe I am."

Aryn bent over to retrieve his trousers that lay bunched around his ankles, giving Kyla an even better view of his naked derrière. He found that he had to slip his right arm out of the sling, as tying the strings on one's small clothes and trousers was an impossible task to complete one-handed.

"You want some help with that?"

"No! — No... thank you. I'll get it."

"Oh, quit being silly, and let me help you."

Kyla waded to the edge of the pool and bent down to pull Aryn's small clothes up over his sexy ass, but misjudged how much room she needed to allow in the front, accidentally touching his now semi-flaccid penis with the back of her hand.

"Oops... like you said, 'sorry about that.' It's bigger than I thought."

She thought she'd embarrass him, with such a direct comment regarding the size of his manhood, but he didn't flush at all.

"Never had any complaints."

Kyla suddenly found herself very glad that Aryn had his back to her, as he'd somehow totally turned the tables on her — glad he couldn't see how her entire body flushed bright red at his vivid reminder that here she stood, a virgin, stark naked, in close proximity to a fertile, sexually experienced male... and a damned attractive sexually experienced male, at that.

Kyla finally got the ties to Aryn's small clothes tied, and then hoisted his trousers up to his hips, being extra careful to avoid his groin area, this time. She tied his trousers off, grabbed the bucket, filled it and placed the rope handle in his hand.

"If you're sure you don't want to sneak a peek at a naked goddess, go water Frisky and then get your ass back out here... I'm not the only one that needs a bath."

Aryn stood stoically with his back still turned to Kyla's enticing nakedness. "Tease."

"Damn it, Aryn... I am *not* teasing you!"

"What would you call it, then? — The minute I responded with any kind of desire for you sexually, you'd probably fry me with one of those blue lightning bolts, flying out of your coochie!"

"I wasn't teasing... I was... um... *offering.*"

Why? Aryn didn't say it, but he certainly thought it. *Why would a goddess be making sexual overtures to me? She doesn't even like me!*

"Let me go water Frisky, and then I'll grab some scented soap that my mother gave me and I'll come back out and take you up on that bath."

"You have real scented soap? — Really?"

"Yup... you'll have to settle for lavender though, it's my mother's favorite."

Kyla smiled and squeezed his arm gently.

"Mine too.... she has good taste. Something tells me I'd very much like to meet your mother."

KYLA WAS SUBMERGED in the pool up to her neck when Aryn came back with his mother's lavender soap in hand. He tossed her the soap with a grin and began removing his clothes in preparation for his goddess recommended bath. He didn't even look up to see if she was watching him as he disrobed.

He turned his back to her, just prior to dropping his small clothes, so he could surreptitiously stroke his flaccid manhood out to something approaching "normal" length, knowing it was going to shrink to near invisibility when that icy cold water came into contact with his genitals. He turned to face her, naked as the day of his birth, and waded into the water.

And look, she did. Kyla gave him a sly smile, and a wink that told him she wasn't disappointed at what she'd just seen of him.

Before the water reached his genitals, Aryn suddenly dropped into the water, completely submerging himself. With his head underwater, even across the pool he had no difficulty at all discerning every interesting asset of her body through the crystal-clear water. He noted she spread her legs slightly, as if to purposely afford him a slightly better view of her luxurious vulva. He wondered if she might have forgotten about the magically enhanced vision that her father's incantation had provided him all those years ago, so that he could see targets over a mile away.

When she again spread her legs a little further apart, Aryn couldn't help himself. He "zoomed in" with his magical vision until the slit of her womanhood appeared as close as though his nose was less than a hand width from her sex. So enrapturing was that heavenly vision before him, he almost extended his tongue to taste that nectar of the gods that truly was yards away, not directly at hand, as it appeared. Feeling foolish, Aryn snapped his vision back to normal and launched himself to the surface, purposely away from that unachievable treasure.

He turned his back to Kyla and scooped up a handful of clean sand and began scrubbing his body with it.

"Don't you want to share your mother's soap?"

Ashamed of what he'd just done, Aryn paused to clear his throat... mostly to eliminate any trace of guilt remained in his voice, of his recent visual violation of her most secret places.

"You go ahead. I'll scrub the dried blood, sweat and grime off with sand first, and then borrow the soap back from you, after you get done with it."

Minutes later, Kyla handed Aryn the soap as she went by him, teeth chattering.

"Your teeth are chattering. You were in this cold pool for much too long. You need to get warmed up quickly, by more than just a towel."

Kyla stepped out of the water and retrieved a towel from her magical storage area in the otherworld. Her left eyebrow arose at his last comment, wondering exactly what he might have meant by that.

"Oh?"

"Don't get dressed just yet... You'll see."

Kyla's eyebrow rose even higher at that comment.

Interesting... whatever it is he has in mind, he wants me naked for it.

Aryn did a quick once over with the scented soap, pausing only at his armpits and hair for extra attention. He then rinsed off again and traipsed out of the pool, heading past her, but strangely, not making eye contact with her as he went by.

"Follow me."

Kyla did a quick snort... she thought it comical that Aryn's genitals were so shrunken by the cold water, yet there still remained enough dangling between his legs to at least make a decent attempt at bouncing as he went by her at a trot. She followed along behind him, admiring the bounce of his naked ass cheeks, as he loped along ahead of her.

Aryn stopped inside the entrance just long enough to place his head against Nightmare's chest to ensure all was still right with the púka. He then grabbed a torch as he went by one, and yelled back to Kyla for her to bring along the stand. Aryn trotted past his living area, heading deeper into the depths of the cave, where Kyla had never been.

"Where are we going?"

"You'll see," Aryn called back over his shoulder to her. "Don't worry... you're really going to enjoy this!"

Kyla almost laughed out loud, at Aryn's cocksure attitude.

Yeah... I know you're a lot more sexually experienced that I am, but you're awfully damned sure of yourself, buddy.

The two of them padded naked, deeper into the cave for about a quarter mile when Kyla finally stopped looking at Aryn's naked ass long enough to admire the ripple of muscle outlining his broad back. Aryn hadn't put his sling back on after bathing, and was holding his damaged right arm against his barrel chest.

"How much deeper are you planning to take me?"

"Only about another quarter mile deeper than we are now. Believe me, it'll be worth it once we get where we're going."

It better be!

The coarseness of the rock they were walking on was slowly rubbing away the softened callus from off the bottoms of her feet, and they were already beginning to get tender. She began wondering what it was that Aryn had in mind, that they both had to remain naked for. Before she could ask 'how much farther' again, Aryn suddenly pulled up and raised his torch high... and she saw it.

A hot spring!

There, about a half-mile deep in the unused portions of this cave was a mineral spring. Wisps of steaming water vapor misted lazily above the pool, heat rising from the depths below.

"Careful... this mineral pool is quite hot. Lower yourself slowly down into the water, so your body has a chance to acclimate to it. Once you can finally get in over your shoulders, it will be heaven on earth."

Aryn was right. The steaming water in the pool was quite hot, but as she inched her way in, her body acclimated to it faster than she could have possibly believed. Once her shoulders were finally submerged, it was indeed, heaven on earth.

"Ah... you were right. This hot spring is absolute heaven! — When I think of all the time I spent in this cave, and never knew this was down here... Hope you don't mind me dropping by a lot more often from now on."

Aryn merely grinned at her, as he followed her down into the water, positioning himself well away from where she sat with her back to the rear wall.

"How long will it be before Nightmare wakes up?"

"I'm not exactly sure... that concoction we used to put him to sleep will normally keep a man my size out for one-to-three days. I estimated the púka's weight at about two, to two and a half times my own weight, and adjusted the formula accordingly. He might wake up late this evening, or it might be another eight-to-ten days. — I just don't know."

"But he *will* wake up, right?"

Aryn looked at the beautiful demi-goddess and saw the expectation in her beautiful violet eyes. She wanted him to reassure her that her beloved púka was going to all right. The look on her beautiful face told him she was silently imploring him to reassure her that Nightmare was going to recover. He desperately wanted to give her that reassurance, but he wouldn't lie to her.

"I think so," he finally said softly.

"You *think* so?"

"Kyla, there is always a risk when putting a man under. A very few never wake up... and Nightmare isn't a man. There are a thousand things that could go wrong. — I did the very best that I could to estimate the differences in weight and calculate the adjustments I needed to make to the dosage, but no one has ever tried to put a púka under before."

Kyla's voice quivered a bit, as she whispered her next question. "Are you sure that your initial weight estimation was correct? — Nightmare is a lot larger in wyvern form, than he is in horse form, you know."

"I know, but all flying creatures have hollow bones. I figured that Nightmare must have too, whenever he's in a flying form... he couldn't possibly get all that extra weight off the ground, if he didn't. While his size is much larger in wyvern form, his total weight has to be the same, or possibly a bit less."

"Birds have hollow bones? I didn't know that."

CHAPTER TWENTY-FOUR

Between lovers, a little confession is a dangerous thing.
-- Helen Rowland

Deep inside Aryn's Cave
Mid-August, 81 A.D.

As Kyla sat luxuriating in the hot mineral spring, she was puzzled. She'd already spent an entire afternoon with this man, stark naked. For most of it, they'd both been naked... yet here she sat, virginity still intact.

Although she was half fae, she had never been wanton. She'd told herself that she was saving her virginity for her future husband, yet she had rejected all of those potential political marriages her father had tried to arrange for her... something else her father had never fully forgiven her for.

But to Kyla, her virginity represented something utterly precious — very deep and personal... something she could only give away to someone very, very special, someone she truly loved and loved her in return, because it could only be given one time in her entire life. From the depths of her being, she knew, without doubt, none of the males among her father's people were worthy of her virginity... they were all too arrogant, narcissistic, and emotionally shallow.

That's exactly what Aryn once accused me of.

That sudden revelation shook her to her core. — Introspection wasn't normally a strong suit among the gods and goddesses of the Tuatha Dé Danann. But with her body so incredibly relaxed, soaking in the steaming, hot mineral water, she paused within herself... to reflect on her life and her motivations. It didn't take her long to discover that she hadn't always been the best possible manager over her life.

She'd always known that she wasn't happy, but she'd always blamed her loneliness and misery on never being fully accepted by her father, nor his people. So how had she reacted to all that?

I withdrew from everyone and everything, into an angry sulk.

She discovered that in the process of hating all the arrogance and haughtiness she so detested in the Daoine Sidhe, she had become just like them. She looked down on everyone who wasn't in a position to look down on her.

Even her own mother wasn't exempt from her contempt. She had always considered her mother a mere faerie, yet she'd always envied her mother the sweet disposition that had so attracted her father. Most of all, she had always been horribly jealous of the loving, intimate relationship her mother shared with her father.

This incredible self-realization opened like a spring flower within her. Loneliness and jealousy had consumed her entire life like acid. Tears streamed down Kyla's face as she choked back sobs.

Oh, Momma... I'm so incredibly sorry!

Kyla cracked one eye to see if Aryn had noticed the quaking of her body, but he was still sitting clear across the pool from her, head resting on the rock ledge behind him with his eyes closed.

Why have I been throwing myself at this man all day, anyway?

Truth be known, Nightmare was the only creature in the whole world she could safely love without being hurt, and she just couldn't bear the thought of losing him. She had been so incredibly thankful to Aryn for saving Nightmare's life, she'd desperately wanted to truly thank him, yet knew of nothing else she might offer him, other than her precious virginity.

And he doesn't even want me.

She'd even coming right out and offered to have sex with him and yet... he didn't seem interested.

What's wrong with me?

Sex between members of the same gender was totally unknown among the fae, although she'd heard rumors that some among the Tuatha Dé Danann observed the practice. Most were bi-sexual, but some were that way exclusively. Was it possible that Aryn might be one of *those*? That might certainly explain his peculiar lack of interest in her.

Pfft... wouldn't that be just my luck?

"Aryn, do you ever get lonely... I mean, living like a hermit, all alone out here in the forest?"

Without opening his eyes, he answered her. "Terribly... like wolves, man is a pack animal. We're always happiest among others of our own kind."

Kyla snorted. "Maybe that's my problem... there are no others like me."

Aryn opened his eyes and bore holes through her with the intensity of his gaze.

"Me neither. — Maybe there's no one *exactly* like you, but some are reasonably close... if only you weren't so preoccupied reveling in your own inherent superiority to see it."

Ouch!

Kyla sighed. "Look, Aryn... I'm really sorry about ridiculing your fae heritage that day. I was angry with my father and..."

"Angry with him because he commanded you to nursemaid me, after he almost destroyed my eyes with that magical incantation of his."

"Yes... I'm sorry about that too. I was acting like a real bitch, but I'd like to make it up to you, right here, right now, if I can."

"Not *that* way."

"Not what way?"

Aryn turned his eyes toward the cave ceiling and shook his head.

"Is it because you prefer sex with little boys?"

"WHAT?"

Aryn and Kyla sat staring across the pool at each other for a long moment, until Aryn raised his head back and roared with quaking laughter. Massive guffaws shook his entire body, until tears ran down both cheeks. It took him some time to regain his composure, but he finally got his breath back and shook his head with an enigmatic grin on his face.

"Ah, gods! — *That* has got to be one of the absolute funniest things I've ever heard."

Kyla had a puzzled look on her face. "You mean... uh... you're not..."

"No... I'm not. — I like girls, Kyla."

"Then why... I mean... why didn't you...?"

"Why didn't I jump your bones, when you first offered me the chance?"

Kyla's face flashed red, and she extended her lower lip into a pout.

"Um... well, yes... I'd really like to know."

"We both know you didn't mean it when you offered to have sex with me earlier. I really have no idea where that came sex thing came from, but if it had anything to do with gratitude for my help in getting that Roman arrow out of Nightmare, don't worry about it. Just consider us even for your having to wipe my ass while I was still out of it after that magical *whatever* your father did to me."

Kyla continued her pout, and whispered, "You still didn't answer my question... why didn't you want me?"

Aryn just sighed and shook his head.

"Two reasons, actually. — I normally don't like talking about deeply personal things... never had anyone I could talk to about them with.

"I was betrothed once, just before I was called away into the high king's army when I was sixteen. She didn't wait... betrayed me."

"Did you love her?"

"Desperately. — You see... my parents are divorced."

Kyla was shocked by that revelation. Divorce is totally unheard of among the Tuatha Dé Danann, and exceedingly rare in Celtae society.

"My father betrayed my mother... divorced her, tore our family apart. He later married a barmaid he liked better.

"I was an only child, so I never really had much of a family life growing up, after that. I was really looking forward to building a family of my own with Máire, so when I gave her my heart, I held nothing back."

Kyla could see the pain in Aryn's eyes remained fresh... resurrected as he tore the scabs off of those old emotional wounds.

She also felt Aryn's story tearing something within herself. She felt a flare of pure rage surge within her that wanted to throw lightning bolts at the bitch who betrayed Aryn's love. Yet, although she'd never had much of a mothering instinct, she also wanted to hold and comfort that sad little boy he'd once been.

"Máire's betrayal left me feeling numb inside. Unfortunately, that numbness didn't extend to my physical parts. Being around women evoked an intense sexual tension that tended to make me act stupid around them, like a dog near a bitch in heat.

"Oh, I certainly had my share of totally meaningless sex... mostly with fat, ugly barmaids, considerably older than me. While that knocked the edge off for a little while, it wasn't fulfilling emotionally. So after I was discharged from the army, I came out here to live alone in the forest."

"You became a hermit... to avoid women... because you couldn't find love?"

"Umm... that would pretty much be it... yeah."

"So you didn't want to have sex with me, because there would be no love involved?"

"Exactly! — That... and the potential for blue lightning bolts flying out of your coochie, if I somehow managed to do an especially good job of it."

Kyla barked out a laugh at that unexpected witticism, coming right in the midst of this deep, emotional discussion.

He uses humor as a shield, to deflect away potential pain whenever the discussion gets too close to the tender areas inside him.

"You said there were two reasons. What's the other

one?"

"Ah, well... that. — That one is even more personal... and also deeply embarrassing."

Kyla's left eyebrow rose at that tantalizing bit of information.

"Go on..."

Aryn shot her a disgusted look and shook his head at her. "You're not willing to allow me to retain the slightest shred of personal dignity, are you?"

The only thing in the universe more inquisitive than a cat is a woman... and the only thing more inquisitive than a woman is a female faerie. Kyla was both, so she certainly wasn't about to allow Aryn to get out of this pool of marvelously hot, steaming water without telling her his juiciest dark secret.

"Kyla, you are, without doubt, the most beautiful... desirable... and thoroughly aggravating woman, I have ever met in my entire life!"

Kyla's mouth dropped open, as she stared at Aryn like he had three heads.

"If you *must* know, the main reason I didn't jump your bones when you first offered is because... I CAN'T! — There, are you satisfied, now?"

Confusion raced across Kyla's features. "What do you mean, you *can't?*"

"Something happened after that magical *whatever* your father did to me several years ago."

"Something... such as?"

"Such as, parts of my plumbing don't work like they used to anymore... refuses to rise to the occasion, so to speak."

Kyla was stunned.

Is it possible my father purposely unmanned him, while

working that magical incantation to enable him to use that magic bow? — Could my father have possibly been that jealous of a mere mortal, just because my mother chose him as her champion, when the Romans came?

Yes, undoubtedly... that would be so very like him.

"But... you had an erection just this afternoon... I saw it!"

"*Pfft...* that was just what we call a 'piss-hard.' Most men wake up with one of those every morning, but it goes away right after we take a leak."

"And you haven't been able to get an erection any other time?"

"Nope... hadn't really thought much about it, though... until today."

My family has deprived this man of ever having a normal life... a wife, children. He gave his heart away and had it thrown back at him, shattered. He has known pain... and loneliness... as have I.

What more could any woman possibly want in a man, that Aryn is not? We are both fae. He is a healer... I am a warrior. What better compliment to one another could there be? Is it possible that I met the true love of my life years ago, but was just too blind and arrogant to see it?

Am I falling in love with Aryn? Or, have I already fallen for him and just never realized it... until today?

She decided.

Kyla rose up from where she'd been sitting in the pool, slowly walking toward Aryn like a lioness stalking prey.

Aryn's eyes bulged at the sudden sight of her magnificent nude body, hot water running off in steaming sheets. Her skin glowed pink from where the heat of the water had brought so much blood to the surface. Her rosebud nipples glistened wetly in the torchlight, fiery red and inviting. His jaw dropped open, as if in anticipation of suckling her small, but majestic conical breasts.

"My father's magic robbed you of your manhood. I intend to give it back."

"But..."

"My mother is queen of the faeries... the most sensual and sexual creature on this entire island. Magic is the very essence of her entire being. What my father's magic took, my mother's magic can restore."

"But..."

"*Shhh...* only believe... I am my mother's daughter."

Kyla brought both of his hands up to cup her heaving breasts. She then spread her legs and straddled him, thrusting an erect nipple into his mouth. She then reached down between her legs and stroked him, kneading his unresponsive member with tender determination.

The added heat from Kyla's soft, gentle hand set Aryn's body aflame.

She suddenly thrust back from Aryn's ravenous lips suckling at her breast and kissed him... a thoroughly toe-curling kiss, with dueling tongues exploring every nuance of the depths of each other's mouths. Although Aryn's breathing was deepening with passion matching her own, his manhood remained unresponsive to her continued ministrations.

Aryn was right. I know the feel of my father's magic... fighting me, trying to keep Aryn's cock flaccid.

Aryn chose just the right moment to remove his left hand from where it had been fondling her breast, to reach down between Kyla's legs, where his finger landed expertly atop that most tender nub... just above the entrance to her love hole.

Ahh... ahh... oh, my! — By all that's holy... that feels

incredibly good!

Kyla lurched away from their impassioned kiss to draw breath, and moan with guttural, animalistic sounds she'd only ever heard once before... coming from her parent's bedroom.

Father, I know your weakness. Mother told me once what you like best in the bedroom!

With that, lest Aryn's ministrations to her clit drive her beyond all rational thought, Kyla pushed back off of Aryn's lap. She took a monstrously deep breath, dived under the steaming water, and took Aryn's flaccid manhood into her mouth.

Oh, Father... if only you knew what your sweet little daughter is doing right now... and with a mortal you detest, no less!

Aryn's breath caught at the unexpected feel of Kyla's tongue suddenly caressing his dick, as she sucked it into the depths of her mouth and out again. Never in his life had he ever imagined anything feeling this good! The feel of her mouth enclosing him added even more heat than her hand had, drawing more and more blood into his cock. As wonderful as it felt, Kyla had been working her magic on his man-parts underwater for so long that Aryn began getting concerned she might drown.

Then... slowly... they both felt it. — The dead was beginning to rise.

∼

The Planet Eerie
3232 A.D.

CAPTAIN ALLAN JOHANSSON, of the interstellar transport S.S. *Pegasus*, was fuming. Subsequent analysis of the continuous recordings made of the mining station's VLF beacon in their archives showed that Ensign Pyrx Nata's assertion they were digging in the wrong place was correct... the beacon was moving. Johansson had been forced to cease the dig and allow the majority of his groundside crew to stand down and rest, while all of their available shuttles resumed conducting sweeps, enabling them to acquire mountains of new positioning data on that wayward beacon.

Knowing his schedules were already shot to hell, Johansson gave his shuttle pilots free rein to also take additional holos documenting all of the impossible shit happening on this crazy planet... as long as they still managed to acquire triangulation data on the station beacon. All of this information was uploaded directly to the ship, in geosynchronous orbit above the island, which was then retransmitted it down to the ground crews, so they could monitor what the shuttles were seeing, almost in real time.

It appeared that a couple of large groups of indigenous peoples were hacking away at one another with spears and massive two-handed swords in one area, while another group, tentatively identified as an ancient Roman legion, was marching towards a large, stone-walled city on the northeast coast. Johansson knew that these holographic recordings were going to create a sensation among the scientific community, as they added visual evidence to the earlier recordings they'd made that documented Eerie's inexplicable change in orbits. The laws of physics were apparently taking a vacation here... and they might just make some money from it, if they played their cards right.

One of the important deliveries that *Pegasus* had been tasked to deliver to the mining station was a finished geologic report, including a complete analysis of geological surveys taken earlier that mapped out Eerie's underground features from measurements taken earlier of variations in the planet's magnetic and gravitational pull. Subtle changes in the planet's magnetic and gravity fields can indicate where underground faults are located, so this report was intended to enable the miners to refine their estimates of the region's seismic hazard.

Johansson assigned members of his bridge crew to cross-referencing that geologic underground map, to the noted positional changes of the station's VLF beacon. He wanted to see if they could possibly find a clue about what those miners underground might be thinking, and why.

The captain's personal communicator chirped. "Johansson here."

"Captain, this is Sánchez... I've overlaid our track of the VLF beacon onto the subterranean survey map, as ordered. The beacon has definitely deviated from its previous position and is now tracking along a geologic fault. They appear to be trying to utilize that fault line as an easier path to dig their way back to the surface."

"Can you give me an estimation for new dig coordinates, so we might hurry the process by intersecting their dig route, and rendezvousing with them underground?"

"Already plotted, sir... if they maintain their current projected path along that fault, new coordinates for a dig site and requisite angle of deflection should now be in your in-box."

"Very well, Sánchez. Good work. Hopefully this info is exactly what we need to finally get those miners dug out and above ground, so we can get off this crazy planet!"

CHAPTER TWENTY-FIVE

If poetry is like an orgasm, an academic can be likened to someone who studies the passion stains on the bed sheets.
-- Irving Layton

Deep inside Aryn's Cave
Mid-August, 81 A.D.

"WHY DIDN'T YOU TELL ME YOU WERE A VIRGIN?" ARYN whispered softly, as he kissed the top of Kyla's head, where she snuggled against him, nestled in the crook of his damaged right arm.

Things had gotten out of hand pretty quickly after Kyla's *magic* finally broke through all the barriers her father had cursed Aryn with. When he was finally ready, she burst out of the steaming water and leaped into his lap, impaling herself upon him. She'd screamed with the initial shock of her maidenhead giving way, asking Aryn to wait a moment, before she slowly began to move upon him.

It didn't take them too long to regain the heights of passion they'd reached previously, finishing with a thunderous, simultaneous orgasm. Resting between bouts, they made love multiple times that evening, in almost every position imaginable — a regular two-person orgy... they're both having fae blood giving them a ridiculous advantage over mere mortals and animals.

"Would it have made a difference to you?"

Aryn snorted. "No, probably not... Watching a lithe goddess traipsing around buck-naked all afternoon had me as horny as a three-peckered billy goat."

Kyla giggled, "All the better to seduce you with, my dear."

"About that... why me? — I mean... a few days ago, you didn't even like me."

Kyla looked up at him and grinned. "Ah, Aryn... how little you know about woman and demi-goddesses. So tell me, how did it feel to deflower a princess of the Daoine Sidhe?"

"It felt incredible! — Weren't you there?"

Kyla laughed again and said, "Oh, yeah... You were doing such an exceptionally fine job of it, you had me convinced that blue lightning might be actually flying out of my coochie, for real."

Aryn shot her an ear-to-ear grin. "You sure know how to stroke a man's ego... as well as other sensitive parts of his anatomy."

They remained quiet for several minutes, basking in the sexual afterglow before he roused her from her drowsing dreamily in the steaming hot spring.

"I am kinda worried about one thing though... what do you think your father will do when he finds out about this?"

Kyla remained snuggled against Aryn's side, and with eyes still closed, murmured, "He'll probably kill you."

"Kill me? — I thought that your people were a lot more open minded about sex than that."

"The fae are... the Tuatha Dé Danann are not. You really might want to begin thinking about how much more of this you might want to enjoy with me in the future."

"The future... as in before, or after your father kills me?"

"Seriously, are you really worried about my father killing you?"

"A little bit... I told you that was sex to die for, but I didn't realize it would come attached to a blood feud."

"Sorry we did it?"

"No, if your father came for me right now, I'd die a happy man."

"Mmm... there just might be a way we could indefinitely postpone your imminent demise — if you're interested, that is?"

"Really?"

"Yup, but it would require some pretty drastic measures on your part though."

"As drastic as death?"

"You might think so afterwards."

"Can you give me a little hint?"

"Well... my father seems to think I need a husband."

~

The Planet Eerie
Deep in the Planetary Core
Present Day

HUMAN ORGASMS WERE A TOTALLY overwhelming experience to the millions of adolescent *We* females enraptured by the alien thought patterns emanating from the planetary surface, far above. Sex among the *We* was infrequent and only mildly pleasurable, compared to the staggering intensity of what they experienced alongside the male and female as they coupled. Initially it affected the *We* females like a highly addictive drug, as they constantly replayed those vivid experiences with perfect recall, over and over again.

A few decided to experiment, sharing those experiences with adolescent *We* males during actual physical coupling. This, in turn, caused adolescent *We* males by the millions to begin actively seeking sex with any willing *We* female and the phenomenon spread like a virulent, sexually transmitted pandemic.

Sexual promiscuity among the young was not totally unheard of among the *We*, but was rare and generally confined to the overly curious. But now, it exploded with the power of a tsunami sweeping through *We* society. So powerful were these billions of artificially enhanced sexual liaisons, they drew the attention of adult *We*. Aghast, they in turn, informed the slow, but deep thinking, *We* elders.

∽

Deep inside Aryn's Cave
Mid-August, 81 A.D.

ARYN ONLY ALLOWED them another hour, soaking in that marvelously hot pool, and the sexual afterglow before he needed to check on Nightmare again. He also suggested that she dress fully, down there near the pool. She could reach into her magical storage area in the otherworld from anywhere, so it didn't make any sense for her to walk all the way back the half-mile to the entrance of the cave, naked and barefoot. Walking along behind Aryn fully dressed, while he was still stark-naked seemed more awkward than all the time they'd spent together completely nude.

Aryn hadn't really responded to her implication that he might avoid her father's wrath by marrying her... other than an incoherent sputter. She began worrying that she might have misjudged his reactions to the new semblance of rapport they seemed to establish as they worked together to get that cursed arrow out of Nightmare's chest.

Did I come on too strong, or has he truly not forgiven me for my arrogance toward him earlier?

Aryn worked his damaged shoulder as he walked, even testing it by occasionally swinging his arm in a circle.

"Shoulder feeling better?"

Aryn turned his head to speak to her over his bad shoulder, "Yes, much... and it shouldn't be. Any chance that pool might have some kind of magical healing properties that I'm unaware of?"

"It's possible. My father called this place the *Cave of Dian Cécht,* and told me it contained residual healing magic when he commanded me to bring you here after your eyes were hurt in that magical incantation he put you through."

"The degree of relief I'm feeling in my shoulder is a great deal more than just residual healing magic. Are there any legends among your people of some kind of magical healing pool of any kind?"

"Dian Cécht was a great physician among the ancient Tuatha Dé Danann. It is said that he had the ability to restore life to the mortally wounded in battle by throwing them into a magic well, and pulling them out alive."

"So, do you think this pool could have anything to do with that magic well?"

"Legend has it that the Tuatha Dé Danann last used that magic healing well when they were engaged in a great war against the Fomóraig... gods of night, death and cold. It is said to be lost when the Fomóraig filled it with rocks, to prevent the Tuatha Dé Danann from resurrecting their casualties."

"Hmm... interesting."

They walked in silence the rest of the way, with Kyla trying to not admire the sexy sway of Aryn's naked ass — but, not really trying all that hard, if truth be known.

Aryn walked directly to check on the púka, listening to his heart, and changing the poultice and re-bandaging the wound... all before donning a stitch of clothes.

Kyla was surprised to find the clothes she'd taken off at the edge of the pool were now clean, folded and laid on the end of Aryn's now made-up bed.

"I think there are a pack of brownies living in this cave, somewhere," Aryn said, in response to her unvoiced question. "I usually leave them bits of biscuit, or morsels of cornbread, along with some honey and milk, as payment for their housekeeping services."

Aryn then surprised Kyla again by feeding and watering Frisky, and rubbing him down with a towel before dressing himself.

"You take care of your animals, before doing for yourself?"

"Something my grandfather taught me, when I was a child. It's just habitual now."

Kyla smiled in approval. "I think I'd like to meet him, too."

Both pitched in to prepare an evening meal. Kyla fried them both more of that bacon she never seemed to run out of, while Aryn boiled them some vegetables and wild onions, and then pan-fried some cornbread, which he served with butter and blackberry jam.

As Kyla ate, she smiled and said, "You live very well out here, all by yourself, Mr. Hermit. I can see why you didn't seem to think much of my idea that we get married."

Aryn choked on the piece of cornbread he'd been chewing, and had to quickly grab for his cup of water to get finally it down.

"I didn't think you were serious... I mean, who am I to think I could ever be worthy of marriage to a goddess?"

"Are you being facetious again?"

"No... I mean it. — I'm just a socially challenged mortal, having almost no fae blood, and even less to offer in material goods to someone of your rank and stature. The whole idea is preposterous! Why would you even consider it?"

"You might be surprised, archer. I did give you my virginity, after all."

"Yes, and I still haven't figured that part out. Why in the world did you pick me?"

"We have a lot more in common than either of us realized, at first glance. We both love this land, and we've both defended it against invaders. We're both part fae. We've both been rejected and hurt. We're both lonely. So, why not share our loneliness together?"

"Ah, so we should get married because it's logical?"

"That... and because I'm pretty sure that I've fallen in love with you, you big ignoramus!"

Aryn's eyes widened at Kyla's surprising admission.

"And demi-goddesses always get what they want?"

Kyla grinned at him. "Yeah... pretty much."

"So, which comes first — we finish killing Romans, or the wedding?"

"The wedding... can't have my father finding out you've been diddling his daughter and violating the treaty by coming up here to kill the groom, now can we? Those Romans will still be here when we get back."

~

Deblin
Late-August, 81 A.D.

A COURIER from the Roman base camp on the Drumanagh peninsula pulled his well-lathered horse up in front of the Roman governor of Britannia's command tent and shouted to the guards stationed just outside. One advanced to take the man's leather satchel, while the other announced the courier's arrival to those inside. General Gnaeus Julius Agricola emerged from the dark recesses of the tent, squinting against the bright, late morning sunlight.

The ninth legion of the Roman army arrived outside the walled Hibernian city of Deblin, late the previous afternoon. Horns blared out a warning to the city's inhabitants and the massive city gates were hurriedly closed and barred against the invader, long before the lead elements approached. Agricola ordered General Servius Marius Paterculus, legate of *Legio IX Hispana,* to take the legion's second, third, and fourth cohorts and surround the city on the other two landward approaches to the west and south, while Agricola himself remained with the first and fifth cohorts to the north. Gaps between the cohorts were filled with the legion's auxiliaries, made up of native troops from throughout the Roman Empire. This left only the seaward approach to the east open... for now.

Agricola stepped to his map table and began breaking the seals on the dispatch scrolls, scanning each one quickly until he found the one he'd been waiting for. A big smile spread over the Roman governor's face when he read that a multitude of supply ships from Britannia had arrived, bringing him a plethora of items needed to quickly take a large, walled city. Disassembled siege towers, catapults and battering rams, and a contingent of Roman naval galleys, equipped with catapults for sealing the city from the sea, awaited his orders at the Drumanagh peninsula.

Agricola sat and began issuing written orders for the flotilla commander to bring his naval galleys and initiate a blockade of Deblin harbor. He also wrote orders for the transport galleys to deliver the siege equipment to a sandy beach area about seven miles north of the city. A small contingent of his surviving Roman cavalrymen had found an area having a difficult, but usable path up the cliff to reach the coast road. Fifth cohort would take all of their wagons, emptied of baggage, to rendezvous with the transports. They were also instructed to light a fire at the top of the cliff, to signal the transports where to drop their loads.

First cohort stood rotating watches to sound the alarm, in case the barbarians sallied out from behind their stonewalls to launch annoyance attacks. Off duty legionnaires ate, repaired their armor, sharpened swords, or just napped if all of those tasks were complete.

When his written orders were complete, Agricola called for a fresh courier to take them back to his base camp at the

Drumanagh peninsula. Only after those dispatches were finally on their way, did he pour himself a cup of wine and sit down to read the remainder of those incoming dispatches more completely. Other than more routine logistical reports, the only thing of note was a dispatch from that Hibernian prince, Túathal Techtmar.

In it was a glowing report indicating that his force of 600 Hibernian allies and the 827 Brigantes he'd recruited from Britannia, had defeated just over a thousand warriors and killed High King Elim mac Conrach in battle at the hill of Achall, near Tara, the traditional seat of the Hibernian high king. A subsequent dispatch told of how Techtmar was currently engaged in a march to eliminate the other three local kings who had allied themselves with Elim to overthrow Techtmar's father, Fíacha Finnolach.

Agricola found these reports most gratifying... and hoped this rare piece good news might signal a change in the local Hibernian god's previous antiphony towards his army.

CHAPTER TWENTY-SIX

When you are doing something neat, and you're doing it with
neat people, and there is that convergence, something
amazing will happen.
-- Rony Abovitz

Aryn's Cave
Late-August, 81 A.D.

IN THE LATE MORNING, KYLA SUDDENLY GLANCED UP
with her ear cocked to one side, as if listening intently at a
far-off sound. Several minutes later, Aryn also heard something... a grunting sound, and heavy breathing. They both
dropped what they were doing and went outside to see what
was approaching. Aryn grabbed his hunting bow and a
quiver of hunting arrows, while Kyla pulled her short-sword
from its sheath.

There on the path the dyad and wood-nymphs had
cleared through the storm-snarled forest for Aryn days

before, walked the largest and most rarely seen of all fae creatures: an *ogre*. Fully twenty feet tall, the beast had greenish skin, rippling muscles... and was stark naked. An intimidating phallus, the length of an axe handle, bobbed obscenely between its enormous legs. The hideous face was dominated by six-inch fangs that protruded from beneath the lower lip, but it had relatively tiny eyes and ears.

In its right hand the creature carried a massive club... a rock larger than Aryn's head, tied with leather straps to a five-foot tree branch, nearly the size of Aryn's thigh. In the crook of its left arm sat a twelve-foot pixie.

"Rhoslyn!" Aryn started to step towards his oversized pixie friend, but Kyla grabbed his arm.

"Careful, Aryn," Kyla cautioned. "Ogres are totally unpredictable... even I can't control one."

Aryn nodded and stepped back, as they watched the creature approach.

"I can't imagine how Rhoslyn managed to have an ogre carry her here," Kyla continued.

POP!

"Oh, that would be my doing."

Aryn and Kyla both jumped, startled by the unexpected appearance of Kyla's mother, Queen Úna, popping into existence right behind them.

"Mother!" Kyla ran to embrace her mother. "What are you doing here?"

"Wilmonia, the lilac faerie that hid Rhoslyn within a ring of massive lilac bushes, popped into our castle beneath *Cnoc Meadha* to tell me that Rhoslyn and Aryn had both been injured during the fighting against the Roman invaders. I popped to where Rhoslyn was, ascertained her problem, and decided she needed to be brought here. So I summoned the only fae creature large enough to carry a twelve-foot pixie."

"Nightmare was also shot by a poisonous, Roman, iron-headed arrow that somehow managed to find its way between two of his chest scales, while in wyvern form."

Úna looked stricken at this news, but was relieved when Kyla told her how Aryn had used his physician skills to save the púka's life.

"Don't let her fool you, your majesty," Aryn interjected. "Kyla was the one who actually dug that arrowhead out of him. My damaged shoulder wouldn't allow me to do it, so she had to."

Úna raised an eyebrow at that, seeming to see her daughter in a new light. "And how is your shoulder now, archer?"

"Better than it should be. There is a hot, mineral spring fed pool deep in this cave that appears to have rather astounding healing properties."

"Aryn thinks it might somehow be related to the magical healing well of Dian Cécht, lost during the ancient war against the Fomóraig."

Úna laughed and clapped her hands. "Oh, my... that is absolutely marvelous! — Aryn's rediscovery of the *Well of Dian Cécht* is so momentous, your father will be forced to give his blessing to your marriage."

Aryn and Kyla were both thunderstruck.

"But... how...?" Kyla sputtered.

Úna laughed again at the incredulous looks on their faces and replied, "Oh, daughter... I knew from the first moment I saw the two of you together that you'd finally met your match — and your soul mate, in Aryn. Besides, I *am* the queen of the faeries, you know. There is very little that happens anywhere in my kingdom that I am unaware of."

"Can you have that ogre carry Rhoslyn to that pool, deep inside this cave?" Aryn asked. "Perhaps the brain bruise she suffered that is blocking her magical abilities might be cured by the healing magic of the pool."

"Good idea," said Úna.

Immediately she flew to the still approaching ogre, and spoke to it in hushed tones. The ogre's clouded eyes seemed to clear for a moment, and it nodded its massive head, seemingly in understanding. The beast turned toward the cave, pausing when it saw the unconscious wyvern laying just inside the entrance. The ogre cocked its head oddly, as if considering something... then dropped the huge club it was carrying, and picked the sixteen-foot wyvern up under its right arm, before ducking its head to proceed deeper within the cave.

"NO!" Kyla cried. "Not Nightmare. — Mother, stop it from..."

"Hush, darling... Ogres are more intelligent than is generally known. Perhaps it perceives that your púka could benefit from some time in Aryn's healing pool, as well."

~

Deep inside Aryn's Cave
Mid-August, 81 A.D.

MID-AUGUST, 81 A.D Aryn and Kyla both grabbed torches, which Kyla lit with a small blue arc from her finger. Then, they and Úna followed the hulking ogre as it walked stooped over beneath the cave's eighteen-foot ceiling, maneuvering deftly among the stalactites that hung periodically from above. The stalagmites normally rising from the floor had been ground flush in some ancient time, leaving only small lumps, from more recent drippings, protruding to give their walkway to the pool a slightly uneven appearance.

"Where are we going?" asked Rhoslyn, the twelve-foot pixie.

"You'll see when we get there," Aryn said.

"I should have hit you harder," replied Rhoslyn, miffed that no one would explain why they were traveling so far underground.

"I'm afraid that you'll have to ask Kyla's permission before hitting Aryn again, anytime in the future," said Úna. "He is her betrothed now."

Rhoslyn blinked in astonishment. "So when did *this* all happen?" When none deigned to answer her, she retreated into a sulk.

When they reached the healing pool, Aryn and Kyla placed their torches into bronze sconces attached to the cave walls on opposite sides of the pool. The ogre gently lowered Rhoslyn to sit at the edge of the pool and then stepped into the hot, steaming water, with no apparent reaction to the heat.

Aryn quickly stripped off all of his clothes and gingerly lowered himself down into the pool, grabbing the wyvern's head, to hold it out of the water, as the ogre lowered the rest of the massive beast into the pool.

"Mother, Rhoslyn... you both have to try this. It's absolutely heavenly!"

Kyla then stripped off all of her clothes and slowly lowered herself into the steaming water. She then moved to where she could help Aryn hold Nightmare's massive wyvern head.

Without hesitation, Úna began removing her garments.

When Aryn realized that Úna was about to get nude, he gave Kyla and exaggerated head jerk, indicating he wanted her to move slightly, so he could keep his back directly to his soon-to-be-naked future mother-in-law.

"Take off the bandage, so the water can get direct access to the chest wound."

Kyla nodded, releasing Nightmare's head to begin untying the bandage knots that held it in place.

Rhoslyn hesitated... pixies absolutely detest getting wet, so she merely extended one toe towards the steaming water. At first contact, she hissed and jerked her foot away. "Great gods, that's HOT!"

"Get in, Rhoslyn," Aryn said. "This healing pool can't do you any good, if you don't get into the water."

"Umm... no thanks. I'll just sit here at the edge and breathe in the steam."

"Rhoslyn, stop acting like a baby," Kyla said. "If you take it slowly, your body will acclimate to the temperature and it will begin to feel very good."

Still Rhoslyn hesitated, until Úna said, "Consider it a command, Rhoslyn. Get in."

Rhoslyn pouted, but could not refuse a direct order from her queen. She again extended her toe, but allowed it to acclimate before inching her entire foot into the steaming water.

"You're stalling, Rhoslyn," said Kyla.

Sighing, Rhoslyn finally acquiesced, slipping fully into the water.

"You need to dunk your head fully under," said Aryn.

"But..."

"Your injuries are to your head... the water must come into contact with the affected area to do any good."

Rhoslyn appeared about to cry, but did as Aryn

instructed... slipping all the way under and disappearing from view.

Aryn relaxed, allowing the healing waters to again sooth his recently damaged shoulder. But he suddenly stiffened, as he felt the faerie queen's nipples burrowing into his back. Her breasts seemed eminently hotter than the water and Aryn felt his manhood responding again. Just as he finally relaxed enough to breathe again, Úna inserted a finger into his butt crack and reached around with her other hand to stroke his now raging member.

Oh gods... I can't believe she's doing this, right in front of Kyla!

Aryn's sudden intake of breath drew Kyla's attention and her eyebrows narrowed as she recognized what must be causing that unusual ripple in the water near Aryn's middle.

"MOTHER! — Just what in the world do you think you're doing?"

Úna laughed as she withdrew her hands from Aryn's nether regions and said, "I was just checking to see whether I needed to personally break your father's prohibitive magic... magic that would have put a serious kink in your marriage, sweetheart. — I must say, I'm impressed. That was no feeble spell that you managed to break.

"I'm also rather impressed by what Aryn will be bringing with him to your marriage bed."

Aryn and Kyla both turned beet-red at Úna's blatant reference... which delighted the faerie queen to no end.

"You needn't worry about that," Kyla snapped. "Father's magic is broken, so I'd very much appreciate it if, in the future, you kept your enchanted fingers off of *my* man!"

Úna laughed, but moved away from Aryn. First she checked on Rhoslyn, placing her hands on the submerged pixie's head and closed her eyes. Satisfied, she then moved to the púka, where she probed his wound with her fingers. Again she closed her eyes and tilted her head back.

When she finally opened them again, Úna seemed to collapse within herself, in sheer exhaustion.

"What was that, you just did?" asked Kyla.

"Aryn was right. This pool is fed by the same magical spring that originally fed the *Well of Dian Cécht,* but all of those earthquakes we experienced several months back created tiny cracks that has allowed a trickle of natural mineral water to dilute the pool's magical properties. While it still retains very powerful healing properties, I'm afraid there won't be any more resurrecting of the dead.

"I imparted a portion of my own essence into Rhoslyn and Nightmare... a *royal* essence, if you will, to give them both a bit of a boost in their bodies abilities to respond the magical healing properties of this pool."

"Are you alright?"

"I'm just tired. — I'll just go sit and rest over here near the edge of the pool for a while, so that Aryn won't have to try so hard not to look at me."

Aryn's relief was almost palpable, but merely inquired, "Is Rhoslyn okay? She's been underwater without taking a breath for an awfully long time."

After Úna got situated out of Aryn's line of sight, she answered, "She's fine. All faeries breathe, but not all out of necessity. Her life essence is based on magic... not natural means of respiration. Pixies are distantly related to water sprites, so technically, Rhoslyn doesn't really need to breathe at all."

"And Nightmare?"

"Oh... he needs to breathe, so it's good that you two are holding his head out of the water."

~

Deep inside Aryn's Cave
Mid-August, 81 A.D.

ABOUT TWO HOURS LATER, a waterlogged three-inch pixie popped into the air above the pool, hissing and spitting like a half-drowned cat. Rhoslyn's abrupt appearance startled three of the four occupants of the pool, who had all been drowsing in the hot, relaxing water. Nightmare remained in his semi-comatose condition, but appeared to be breathing easier, and more deeply than before.

"Rhoslyn... you've got your powers back!" Aryn exclaimed in delight.

Rhoslyn presented a comical figure, her hair hanging straight down as water streamed off her head.

"Where'd that big ogre go? — I need him to wring me out like a rag."

All turned to look toward where the ogre had been seated on the path next to the pool, after gently placing Nightmare into the pool... empty now.

"Evidently, it thought it had completed its mission and left while we were all drowsing," said Kyla.

"Gods... I HATE BEING WET!" wailed Rhoslyn.

Aryn turned to give Kyla a sly look. "She's complaining, so I guess she's back to normal."

"*Pfft*... just see if I try to catch you the next time you fall out of a tree!"

"Rhoslyn, you knocked me out of that tree, if you'll remember,"

The pixie ignored the jibe. Turning to where Úna still

lounged at the far end of the pool, "Your, majesty... if you will excuse me, I need to go dry out."

"Go, my child... go with my thanks for your helping Kyla when Nightmare was injured."

"See there, Aryn! — Queen Úna just thanked me for knocking you out of that tree."

And with that, Rhoslyn disappeared with a muffled pop, that squished a bit more than usual.

"Too bad this pool couldn't do a better job of healing Rhoslyn's attitude," Aryn groused.

"Well... Mother said not to expect *miracles* out of this pool, anymore."

Aryn snorted, but before he could answer Kyla, Úna spoke again.

"Kyla, darling... lounging in this hot pool has been absolutely wonderful, but be a dear and help me dress. I need to check on a few things... like what those Romans are up to... and then get back to prepare your father's supper. You know how cranky he gets when his supper isn't ready when he wants it."

Kyla gave over holding Nightmare's wyvern head out of the water to Aryn, and climbed out to help her mother.

"As Nightmare is still out, how are we going to get him out of this pool, without that ogre to lift him?"

Aryn sighed. "Oh, gods. I hadn't thought of that. We may have to set up camp here, until he rouses on his own."

~

Underground
3232 A.D.

THE MINERS REQUIRED many more rest stops in their march towards the surface than would have been necessary, had they just allowed the dwarves to carry them. More rest periods meant more torches, water, meals, and sleep periods, all of which required much more work for the dwarves to fetch these supplies from wherever they were getting them. This of course, led to much more dwarvish grumbling at the miner's slow rate of progress.

"Contrary critters, all these tall ones," groused one black haired and bearded dwarf to his brown-haired marching companion.

"Aye, arrogant... like elves, they be."

Elves?

This elicited a chuckle from the surrounding dwarves, lightening the festering mood a bit. The miners, sensing growing discontent among their rescuers, remained quiet for the most part, not wanting to draw unwarranted attention to themselves. The sheer distance they'd already traveled starkly revealed the fact that they would have never been able to dig their way out themselves, before succumbing to the choking dust. Without this inexplicable rescue, by even more inexplicable creatures, they would all be inarguably dead by now... and the miners all knew it.

With few and minor exceptions, the smooth-walled tunnel they were traversing had been as straight as a plumb line, until it suddenly veered off at an uncharacteristic right angle, just in front of them. After negotiating that hard turn, the environment changed abruptly — gone were the monotonous smooth walls of the tunnel they'd been traversing for so long, and they found themselves surrounded by stalactites hanging from the ceiling and stalagmites rising from the floor of a natural cave.

"About seventeen of your miles to surface from here,"

said the red-haired dwarf, who had carried Brian Steele out of the mine.

Dan Weaver glanced over at Brian with an unspoken question on his face:

How could they possibly know how long one of our miles is?

CHAPTER TWENTY-SEVEN

An orgy looks particularly alluring seen through the mists of righteous indignation.
-- Malcolm Muggeridge

The Planet Eerie
3232 A.D.

SHUTTLE-3 DEVIATED FROM ITS SEARCH GRID PATTERN to record something the pilots thought would be of definite interest to the captain. Along the Northeast coast of the island was a natural harbor, having a rather large, walled city above it... that appeared to be surrounded by an entire legion of Roman soldiers. The shuttle circled to get holos recorded of the city from all angles, occasionally dropping lower to fully document the events unfolding on the ground. Catapults ringing the city hurled rocks the size of a human head at the formidable stone walls, chipping away bits with every impact.

But the primary assault came from three battering rams, pounding away at massive wooden doors on the city's north, west and south sides. Attacking from three sides simultaneously deliberately spread the defenders thin, but the defenders on the walls above still managed to rain rocks and tip massive iron cauldrons of boiling oil down on the battering rams below — but this tactic was largely negated by the Roman's incorporation of a metal roof in the design of their rams, to protect the legionaries working the rams from just such inconveniences.

With all of those massive rocks from the catapults flying around, the shuttle dare not go low enough to actually monitor the ram's progress at battering down the doors to the city. But from the thousands of Roman soldiers formed up behind them, it was evident that someone in command believed a breakthrough was imminent.

Some of the legionnaires waiting behind as the rams did their work, and several defenders atop the city walls looked upwards and began pointing upwards towards the shuttle. The shuttle crew knew, at altitude their small ship would resemble a star shining in the heavens through the bright blue sky, but as low as they had descended to video the events below, those on the ground might begin to make out details of the shuttle's exterior.

All eyes were on the shuttle's view ports, as the spectacle of a Roman army battering down the doors of a stone, walled city wasn't a sight one could afford to miss in the thirty-third century. Thus, the sudden appearance of an exotic, incredibly beautiful white-haired woman peering into the shuttle's interior through the view port window from the outside took them all by surprise.

They had slowed their forward momentum considerably from their normal in-atmosphere cruising speed, but they were still traveling at several dozen kilometers per hour. Yet, the woman outside paced them easily, her face not varying within the view port by more than a couple of inches... considering they were also several hundred feet in the air.

One of the female crew-members screamed, as the shuttle pilot yelled, "What the hell?"

Their violent reaction evidently startled the woman, as she backed away about eight feet... just far enough the shuttle crew could see her in total. She was full human-sized, but had double, transparent wings. Pointed elven ears protruded through her long, snow-white hair, and she wore a revealing, golden diaphanous gown, with the bodice split to her non-existent navel, exposing half of her magnificent bosom. The dress sparkled in silver flashes, but somehow did not blow in the wind. Strategically placed slits in the sheer material provided the shuttle crew with glimpses of creamy white skin and voluptuous, very feminine curves — to which their hormones responded instantly... even the women.

The woman outside gave them a mischievous smile and then returned to peering through the port at close range again. She slowly extended her long pink tongue and did a lazy swirl, moistening her full, glistening lips. This elicited soft groans from most of the shuttle's crew, as hands unconsciously reached for openings in their flight suits. She then closed her magnificent violet eyes and her forehead wrinkled, as if in deep concentration.

Suddenly a bright purple glow penetrated the hull of the shuttle, coming right through the shielding as if it wasn't there. This glowing energy passed right through the shuttle crew as well, causing them to all gasp, as their eyes glazed over. Hands began ripping their flight suits open, flinging them carelessly aside as they dived upon one another in a sexual frenzy.

Men upon women, men upon men, women upon women... mouths sought genitals, regardless of their natural orientation. Everything they were and had been doing was totally forgotten, as they ravenously sought sexual gratification from whoever was closest at hand. Grunts and groans and the sounds of heavy breathing were everywhere, as the unmistakable odors of frantic sex filled the cabin.

The shuttle, flying in manual mode so close to the ground, flew straight and level for a couple of minutes, even without the guidance of a pilot until a sudden wind gust tipped one wing, causing the entire shuttle to roll and the nose lowered towards the ground. This sudden rolling motion caused the elevating shuttle wing to strike the woman outside in the ankle, and with a squawk of pain she disappeared.

The few of shuttle crew regained their senses just a couple of seconds before impact.

∽

Underground
3232 A.D.

WHILE THE TUNNEL the miners had trudged through was uniformly monotonous is its sameness, this natural cave they seemed to have entered into was anything but. The path forward the cave offered meandered like a drunken snake. Water seemed to drip from everywhere... creating stalactites and stalagmites, producing a maze the miners had to negotiate to follow the "open" path before them. While most were the standard white-tan color of natural limestone, several contained other impurities that produced an incredible riot of gorgeous rainbow colors in the flickering torchlight.

In places, magnificent vaulted ceilings gave the impression of being in a massive cathedral, while at others, they literally had to squeeze themselves through some extremely tight areas.

"I'd like to know how the hell those dwarves managed to get that 800 lb. battery pack, powering the VLF beacon, through some of these tight spots, without breaking off some of these stalagmites," said Brian.

"Just add it to the long-lost impossible things we're seen recently," answered Weaver.

At one point, they passed what looked like a waterfall of snow-white sparkling crystals. It seemed that every bend produced yet another reason for the miners to *ooh* and *ahh* at nature's wondrous beauty.

"Are you still in denial, thinking that we're all lying dead from asphyxiation, down in the mine?"

Brian Steele looked wearily at big Dan Weaver, who trudged alongside of him, step-for-step.

"No... my feet hurt too damned bad to believe this is all merely a delusion — unless, of course, we really are dead, and we're all just marching in endless circles in some strange form of perdition."

Weaver barked a laugh and said, "I hear ya. My second-shift group leader desk-job certainly never prepared me for this kind of walking. Besides, don't you think our rescuers are a little short, for demons in disguise?"

"I am a little worried about one thing though. You still acknowledge that there's no air at the surface, don't ya?"

Weaver sighed. "Brian, I really don't know what to think. Logically, my brain tells me there's no air on the surface, but it also tells me all these little hairy guys can't be real either. I'm just going with the flow... waiting to see what happens when we get to where we're going."

"I never really thought about it, until we entered what appears to be a naturally occurring cave."

"So, what's to think about?"

"Most caves have an opening at the surface. If that's the case, what's keeping all of this air inside?"

"There are underground caverns that are sealed at both ends, but that just brings us back to the question of where all of this air we're breathing came from in the first place. Face it, amigo... we've all got a hell of a lot more questions, than we have believable answers for."

"I keep thinking we're going to turn a corner and whoosh... all the air suddenly goes rushing out."

"No, that might happen in a vacuum, but this planet has an atmosphere, just not one that's breathable. More likely, the CO_2 levels would begin creeping up and we'd all just fall asleep on our feet from oxy starvation, never even noticing we were asphyxiating."

"That thought doesn't trouble you?"

"Nope... I figure whoever, or whatever, engineered this rescue must have some kind of plan for keeping us alive somehow. If they wanted us dead, they could have just left us down in that mine."

$\sim$

Deep inside Aryn's Cave
Mid-August, 81 A.D.

KYLA PUT out a psychic call and soon dozens of fae creatures responded to help with holding Nightmare's head out of the water, so she and Aryn could finally take a break and climb out of that hot pool. Aryn tramped the mile back to the cave entrance, dressed, and then loaded Frisky down with provisions and bedding they'd need for an extended stay down near the pool. No sooner had he returned with the horse when Queen Úna unexpectedly popped back into the depths of the cavern near the pool.

"Agh!" Úna screamed, and she immediately floated up to get her weight off of her ankle.

"Mother! — What's wrong?" shouted Kyla, as she rushed to her mother's side.

"My foot..."

"Aryn! — Get over here... Mother's been hurt!"

Aryn was struggling to hold onto Frisky's rein, who had shied from Úna's noisy and unexpected entrance. "Easy boy, it's all right..." Aryn coo'd, as he gently stroked the horse's jaw to help quiet him. "Stay."

Frisky then snuffled the carrot that Aryn retrieved from the saddlebag, munching contentedly on the treat. "Good boy..."

"Aryn... today!"

Aryn dropped Frisky's reins on the ground, which also told the horse to stay, as he turned and hurried to Úna's side.

Úna grimaced in pain, as Aryn gently probed her extended foot with his fingers.

"What happened?" Kyla asked her mother.

"The Romans are besieging Deblin, throwing rocks

with catapults and using battering rams on the gates," Úna said, clenching her jaw against the pain.

"Were you hit by flying rock, then?" Aryn asked her.

"No... I was much too high to be in any danger of that."

"So, how did you get hurt?" Kyla asked in exasperation.

"Agh!" Úna screamed, as Aryn twisted on her ankle a bit.

"Sorry..." Aryn said. "I think her ankle is broken. Perhaps one or two of the small bones in the side of her foot, which lead down to the toes may be broken as well. There was a chip broken off in your ankle that was out of place, but that little twist I gave it seems to have gotten it back in place, where it should heal properly. Into the healing pool with you... your majesty."

"But, I need to get home to fix Finvarra's supper!"

"Pfft..." Kyla snorted. "It's not like you actually cook his meals yourself. Father has plenty of servants who normally prepare victuals for you both. Father didn't marry you for your culinary skills, you know."

Úna looked stricken by Kyla's damning words for a moment, but then smiled and stuck out her tongue at her smart-aleck daughter.

"Normally I'd apply a splint of wood or brass rods to immobilize the joint for an injury like this, but I don't think that will be necessary in your case. As long as you don't move your ankle, a few hours soaking in this healing pool should set you arights in no time," Aryn said.

Kyla then helped her mother remove her dress, as Aryn belatedly remembered that Úna wore no undergarments, and hurriedly turned his back. He then retrieved his bedroll from behind his saddle and backed towards the two women, holding it extended behind him.

"Once you get her settled into to pool, you can put this behind her head as a pillow."

"My, what a considerate young man," Úna said. "That's a very rare trait among the barbaric Celtae. Daughter, you might want to consider hanging on to this one... and fucking his brains out, every chance you get."

"MOTHER!" Kyla instantly turned a violent shade of crimson, and was glad that Aryn's back was turned where he couldn't see her embarrassment... but she knew he had to be grinning like the village idiot after that remark.

With Úna's ability to float, it took no time at all for Kyla to get her mother submerged and settled into the pool, with Aryn's bedroll cushioning her head.

"You said you were watching the Roman attack on Deblin, but were too high to be hit by the rocks their catapults were throwing... so how was it you managed to break your ankle in mid-air?" Kyla asked.

~

The Planet Eerie
3232 A.D.

CAPTAIN ALLAN JOHANSSON'S communicator chirped. "Johansson here."

"Captain, this is Sánchez... Shuttle-3 has disappeared from off of our scanners and is not answering our hails. I have directed all but one of our remaining shuttles to rendezvous at their last known coordinates and begin a search. Shuttle-2 is currently en-route to pick you up, as I knew you'd want to take charge of the search personally."

"Good thinking, Sánchez... there may be hope that someday, you'll develop into a decent ship's officer yet."

Shuttle-2 grounded about ten minutes later and departed again just as soon as the captain came aboard.

"Any further news about Shuttle-3?"

"No, Captain. I doubt the other shuttles have had time to arrive at those coordinates yet," answered the shuttle's communications officer.

"Very well. Have the other shuttles break out their anti-radiation suits, just in case Shuttle-3 went down hard and there's a reactor breach."

The pilot and co-pilot of Shuttle-2 glanced at one another fearfully, upon hearing that. A reactor breach was one of the feared events that could possibly overtake a spacer... especially if a crewman took too many rads and had to take those nasty-ass anti-radiation pills that left a person deathly ill for over a week.

Better than dying though, if only barely.

~

Deblin
Late-August, 81 A.D.

A COURIER KNOCKED on the tent pole of the Roman governor of Britannia's command tent. Soon, General Gnaeus Julius Agricola emerged from the dark recesses of the tent, squinting as he usually did against the bright, early afternoon sunlight.

"Yes?"

The courier snapped to attention with his right fist over

his heart in salute. "My lord... Tribune Calix Quintus Falco, of the third cohort, send his regards and begs to inform the governor that one of those mysterious day-stars we saw in the sky earlier in the week appears to have come to earth a short distance from the west gate of the city."

Agricola's eyes widened at this unexpected news, regardless of the brilliant sunlight.

"He has ordered fifteen of our remaining cavalry to investigate," the courier continued.

Agricola cringed inside, fearful of whatever mysterious powers lay behind those flying whatever-they-were, but as leader of a Roman army, he dare not let his discomfiture show.

The fat's in the fire now... I just hope that tribune's curiosity doesn't get his men killed.

"That is well. Tell Tribune Falco to also dispatch a full century of infantry to support those cavalry, in case there is something nasty awaiting them."

"At once, my lord!"

≈

Deep inside Aryn's Cave
Mid-August, 81 A.D.

ABOUT MID-AFTERNOON, Nightmare finally showed signs of rousing. Aryn breathed a massive sigh of relief that his educated guesswork involving the strength of the anesthetic he'd had Kyla administer to the great beast had been sufficient to put him under, yet not send him into a death coma.

"Aryn! — He's awakening," Kyla marveled, as she immediately jumped to the side of the water sprite holding the púka's head out of the nearly scalding water.

Aryn jumped up, but instead of going straight to Nightmare, he headed towards Frisky.

"It should be another couple of hours before he completely shakes off the effect," Aryn said. "He'll be as ravenous as a bear when he comes out of it, so I'd better go kill some game for him to eat."

"But, he eats grass and hay in his normal form," Kyla said, confused.

"He's not in his normal form... and I don't want him transforming again until after I can confirm his wound has totally healed. In the meantime, wyverns eat meat, so I'd better get him some down here, lest he begins eyeballing Frisky as a tasty snack."

"Nightmare has been around him since Frisky was just a colt. He would never eat Frisky."

"Kyla, you may know fae creatures, but I know animals. Wyvern's are predators and he'll be out of his mind with hunger, so just humor me on this, will ya?"

Kyla initially started to continue the argument, but suddenly thought better of it and her mouth snapped closed, allowing Aryn to have the last word.

Aryn mounted Frisky, bending low over the horse's neck to avoid hitting his head of the cave ceiling.

"I'll be back as soon as I have enough meat to at least take the edge off his hunger," Aryn called over his shoulder, as he swung the horse around and began heading back toward the cave entrance at a trot.

Kyla shook her head and turned back towards her mother, who was still soaking her broken ankle in the pool... slowly noticing the growing smirk on her mother's face.

"What?"

Úna merely grinned at her and said, "You're learning, Daughter. You're learning."

∾

West of Deblin
Late-August, 81 A.D.

FIFTEEN HORSEMEN of the Roman cavalry stopped their horses and dismounted before they reached the wreckage. They tied their horses to bushes within the forest and proceeded on foot toward the strange sight before them.

That *something* had fallen from the sky... was obvious. Trees all around the site were broken and bent. In the midst lay some kind of large metallic box with stubby wings — its nose embedded in the ground. Wisps of whitish smoke, or other kind of vapor, rose lazily from unseen recesses. An unusual acrid odor made the legionaries wrinkle their noses in disgust as the centurion who led them stepped closer.

"By the gods, what is that incredible stench?" griped one of the cavalrymen.

"Quiet, you!" hissed the centurion. "Keep your eyes open and your mouths closed. Let me know if you see anything unusual."

"Everything about this, *whatever-it-is*, looks rather unusual to me," quipped another.

"Quintus, one more unnecessary word out of you and I'll shove my foot so far up your ass, you'll be choking on my sandal laces."

Chastened, the legionaries quietly spread out to

examine the site from all sides, but none, other than the centurion, wanted to venture too close to the foul-smelling thing. Strange popping noises occurred at irregular intervals, which further unnerved them all a bit. The men whispered among themselves, but only the centurion ventured close enough to actually touch the thing.

"Smooth and surprisingly cool to the touch," said the centurion, after reaching out with his hand. He knocked on the thing with his knuckle to see it were hollow, but heard only a dull thud in return. As he loitered, still touching the side of the thing, he considered what little he'd ascertained about it so far, an odd vertigo swept over him and he wobbled a bit on his feet.

"Whoa... feeling a might woozy there," the centurion said — just before he toppled over onto his face.

"The centurion's down! Must be those infernal vapors that got him. You men closest to him, hold your breath and then go grab his foot and drag him away from that thing!"

Those closest to the prone centurion did exactly that, and they then checked him over once they'd moved him a sufficient distance.

"Is he still breathing?"

"Yes, but shallow... and his eyes are huge."

A strange whining sound suddenly came from somewhere above them and the legionaries panicked.

"Get him up on his horse and let's all get away from here. Pluto's minions only know what other nasty surprises still lurk near this infernal thing."

~

Deep inside Aryn's Cave
Mid-August, 81 A.D.

ARYN RETURNED to the healing pool just as the púka began regaining full consciousness. The smell of fresh blood caused him to rouse himself, and he turned to look toward the two fresh deer carcasses that Aryn had across Frisky's back. Smoke rolled from Nightmare's nostrils as he snuffled the scent, eager to begin his feast.

Aryn drug the first deer over near the edge of the pool, where the púka could reach it without leaving the water. The wyvern's head suddenly shot directly towards Aryn, causing him to dive away from the wyvern's gaping jaws that greedily enclosed the carcass.

Kyla screamed Aryn's name and rushed to ensure he was okay.

"Are you all right?" Tears formed in the corners of Kyla's eyes, as she realized just how close she'd just come to losing him. "I've never seen Nightmare lunge like that... never. — I thought for sure he had you."

Aryn wiped away a tear that threatened to roll down Kyla's cheek and said, "I told you he'd be ravenous when he awakened fully." Aryn turned to watch the púka rip a haunch from his meal. "It's not Nightmare's fault really... wyvern's aren't exactly known for having the most delicate table manners."

~

The Planet Eerie
3232 A.D.

THE RADIO CRACKLED to life inside Shuttle-2 as a disembodied voice announced, "Shuttle-1 to all *Pegasus* units. We are at the Shuttle-3 crash site. Be advised the shuttle housing is relatively intact. We're detecting elevated levels of radiation, but we do not believe that a full reactor breach has occurred. Also, there are some toxic vapors escaping the wreckage. All personnel near the crash site are therefore required by regulation to wear full anti-rad gear and a full ventilator package.

"Condition of the crew is unknown at this time, as the manual release mechanisms for the hatches are all non-functional. We are attempting to power them open with hydraulics at this time."

Captain Allan Johansson leaped out of Shuttle-2's airlock as soon as it grounded and the hatch swung open. Running was difficult wearing a full rad-suit and ventilator, but run he did, directly toward the crash site about 200 yards distant, just inside a forest.

"Report!" Johansson yelled, as he arrived at the crash scene... doubled over from exertion and completely out of breath.

I'm getting too old for this kind of shit.

"Captain, the impact warped the frame, so our portable hydraulic units have failed," a nearby crewman responded. "We're currently attempting to use laser torches to cut our way inside."

"Captain, we're seeing alarming respiration and blood pressure levels on your bio-monitor readouts," the ship's doctor said over the private comm channel in his suit. "Are you feeling alright?"

"Nothing that getting off this crazy planet and knocking back a few beers on a beach somewhere won't cure, Doc," Johansson wheezed weakly.

"After we heard they were having trouble getting the hatches open and then to see these readings, I could have sworn that you were huffing and puffing and trying to blow them open like the Big, Bad Wolf."

"Very funny, Doc. How do your bio-monitors on the crew of Shuttle-3 look?"

"Unknown. We lost bio-telemetry on the crew when the shuttle went down, so you'll have to tell us, once you get inside."

Johansson sighed. "Understood. You'll know something just as soon as we do. Johansson out."

It took another forty-five minutes for the industrial grade laser torches to finally cut the balky personnel hatch away from its warped frame enclosure. He'd been as antsy as a teenager's father, awaiting his only daughter's return from her very first date during the whole ordeal. But the delay gave Johansson the time he needed to fully recuperate from his run and get his respiration and blood pressure back down within nominal levels.

He leapt right behind the cutters when they announced they were almost through, fully intending to be the first one to go inside the stricken shuttle. The moment the hatch door finally fell away, Johansson immediately stuck his head inside. He'd thought he'd prepared himself for the worst imaginable scenario... but not this. What the captain discovered inside the shuttle defied imagination.

In complete defiance of a multitude of regulations and anything resembling common sense, it was obvious that none of the crew-members had been buckled in on impact... and they were all naked. It took Johansson a moment to assimilate that from the positions of the bodies, the entire crew had to have been indulging in a sexual orgy for the ages, just prior to the crash. No other possible explanation could account for what he saw inside that shuttle. Bile rose up in the captain's throat, as his mind refused to accept what his eyes were telling him.

"Captain, are you going in?" asked a crewman who'd been manning the laser.

"No... and neither is anyone else. I'm declaring a Class-1 biohazard emergency. Get everyone well away from this open hatch. Someone call the ship and get Doctor Littleton down here on the first available shuttle. Have her bring a full medical team wearing airtight biohazard suits... and also have her bring down a shit-load of airtight body bags with her, when she comes."

CHAPTER TWENTY-EIGHT

*Man is a creature who walks in two worlds and traces upon
the walls of his cave the wonders and the nightmare
experiences of his spiritual pilgrimage.*
-- Morris West

Underground
3232 A.D.

BIG DAN WEAVER LOOKED OVER AT HIS OFF-WORLD
friend Brian Steele in wonder, and no little bit of worry.
Steele was utilizing the vast majority of his time devoted to
sleep periods and rest stops to banging away on the
keyboard on that antiquated computer he used for writing
his Celtic fantasy book. He seemed a man possessed by
some dire need to finish that book, regardless to the toll it
was taking on his body... as though continually hacking dust
from their lungs and walking seemingly endless miles every
day were no more than an inconvenience.

From eating the simple, but nourishing meals provided

by the dwarves and all exercise their trek was providing, most of the mining crew grew stronger each day, while Steele continually grew weaker from sheer exhaustion. Weaver sometimes wondered how much of what Brian was writing even made sense, fueled by little more than delirium brought on by unending physical exertion and chronic lack of sleep. Steele was definitely burning his candle at both ends, his creative fire growing brighter as his physical body visibly wasted away. At least he'd finally acquiesced to allowing the red-haired dwarf who'd rescued him from the mine to carry him during their walk periods, which Brian slept through like a baby cradled in his mother's arms... instead of a massive, hairy creature that couldn't possibly be here.

Weaver inwardly shared Brian's apprehensions about their miraculous rescue, and their seeming continued existence underground, on what they all knew was barren planet having no breathable atmosphere... but he never shared them. Survival was highly dependent upon state of mind, so Weaver wasn't about to throw around any doubts upon whatever hope the individual minors could still muster.

Just before nodding off on this, hopefully, last sleep period before finally reaching the surface, Weaver vaguely thought he heard the dwarves whispering amongst themselves... something about hearing voices up ahead.

∾

Deep inside Aryn's Cave
Mid-August, 81 A.D.

AFTER FINISHING off the two deer Aryn had brought him, Nightmare licked his chops and looked around expectantly for more. When he realized that no more deer carcasses were immediately forthcoming, Nightmare gave a disgusted snort, causing smoke to roll out both nostrils. With a last reproachful look to all of the cave's other inhabitants, the wyvern crawled out of the pool and curled up on the ledge above and closed his eyes.

This gave Aryn an opportunity to finally examine the wound caused by that Roman arrow, and Kyla's subsequent surgery to remove it that saved Nightmare's life. The mysterious properties of the pool had done a marvelous job of speeding up the natural healing process. The wound appeared closed and had a nice residual rosy color to the new flesh that had overgrown the hole. The beginnings of a new scale that would eventually cover the entire area was also evident.

Satisfied with the púka's progress, Aryn again examined Úna's ankle, which she obligingly lifted from the water. Knowing that both Úna and Kyla were watching his every move, Aryn employed an iron will to force his eyes to remain solely on that delicate ankle... and not stray towards the bubbling water which was all there was between him and a deliciously naked faerie queen. *Damn it, Aryn... you're a physician... act like one!*

"Ooh! — That one spot is still a little tender," Úna gasped, as Aryn's fingers gently probed her ankle.

"The in-line bones in your foot appear to have completely healed, but joints as flexible as an ankle always take a little longer," Aryn told his future mother-in-law. "Another few hours of soaking in this pool and you should be completely back to normal."

Aryn then excused himself and left them to go hunting again. Those two deer carcasses certainly hadn't satiated the wyvern's hunger, but merely bought them some time for him to gather more.

"Interesting man you've chosen for yourself, Daughter. Not once did his eyes stray to anything besides my ankle. He was totally professional, although we both know he was most surely tempted to peek elsewhere. But, he didn't steal so much as a fleeting glance... amazing, really."

"He loves me... even if he doesn't fully know it himself yet."

"I wonder what the presence of those people I saw inside that flying ship portend for our island?"

"A flying ship suggests a level of magic rivaling that of the Tuatha Dé Danann at the height of their power."

"I don't think so. I detected no hint of magic about it, but I did get the distinct impression it was powered by inert, yet incomprehensible physical laws and forces the Daoine Sidhe have little knowledge of."

"Father prophesied the coming of the Romans. Has he ever indicated any foreknowledge of beings like the ones you saw inside the flying ships that look so much like daystars from a distance?"

"No, but then your father never shares much of what he discusses with the Daoine Sidhe with me. From what he sees on the outside, he evidently believes it's not possible I might be intelligent enough to understand any of it. I sometimes act rather flighty, allowing him to continue believe that fiction, because it makes him so much easier for me to manipulate."

Kyla laughed out loud at that, and then she and her mother went on to have one of the longest and deepest conversations about love, life, magic and men they'd ever shared with each other.

∾

Deblin
Late-August, 81 A.D.

GENERAL GNAEUS JULIUS AGRICOLA, Roman governor of Britannia, sat brooding in the dark recesses of his command tent, just outside the north gate of the Hibernian city of Deblin. *The only city on this entire accursed island, even worthy of the name.* He was troubled by the confusing reports he'd received back from the cavalry detachment that Tribune Calix Quintus Falco had sent out to investigate that flying daystar that had evidently lost control and crashed just west of the city. The centurion leading that small cavalry detachment had been overcome by some kind of noxious vapors seeping from the wreckage, and didn't revive until long after he'd been brought back, face down across his saddle.

Agricola had personally interviewed every trooper in that detachment, and received fifteen different versions of a story that shared little in common. Even disciplined Roman legionaries can become unnerved when confronted by events totally outside of their understanding. Fears, vivid imagination and wild conjecture colored every report and Agricola despaired of ever truly understanding what really went on out there. Of course, he gave more weight to the testimony he'd received from the centurion leading the cavalry after he finally regained consciousness, as he'd been the only one to actually touch the strange contraption.

He'd also interviewed the centurion in charge of the century of infantry he'd ordered dispatched to reinforce that small cavalry detachment. He was a grizzled old battle-hardened veteran of dozens of campaigns who had not been impressed by the body draped over the saddle, nor the fantastic tales told by the cavalrymen of their experiences in the forest when they'd met the cavalry returning at a gallop.

He'd been ordered to support the cavalry in their inves-tigation of that mysterious daystar that came down and he saw no reason to deviate from carrying them out... even if the cavalry was no longer investigating. Just before arriving at the edge of the forest, two more of those flying stars had approached them at high speed. He'd had his men sprint the final yards to the forest and get under cover as quickly as possible.

They watched intently as those two daystars performed a fully controlled soft landing on the open ground just outside the forest. Doors in the sides of those strange flying vehicles opened, discharging ten man-shaped creatures wearing silver suits that gave off blindingly brilliant reflec-tions in the sunlight. Those suits covered the creature's entire heads and had some kind of strange tube-like appa-ratus that ran between a protrusion on their chests to the area where the mouth and nose would be on a human being... suggesting these creatures could not breath the air here, which required them to bring something else, from somewhere else, with them in order to breath.

Boxes and crates of various sizes were unloaded and carried by eight of those creatures, which had donned strange metallic exoskeletons that whined as they moved. These seemed to function as some kind of artificial muscles, giving the creatures the strength of an ant, which allowed them to manipulate tremendous loads.

When those creatures turned and started toward the Romans at a slow trot, the centurion ordered his men to spread out, hiding behind trees with a warning for absolute silence... and a stern admonition that anyone drawing the attention of those creatures would never see Italy again with their balls still attached. Discipline held and the creatures somehow passed through the midst of a hundred Roman infantrymen, in their banging and clanking armor, without detecting them.

After the creatures passed by, the grizzled old centurion selected ten of his best men, had them quickly remove their armor, and follow him to see what those odd-looking creatures were up to. The Romans watched intently as one of the creatures climbed up to where the door had been on the daystars they arrived in and yanked and pulled on what they assumed must be some kind of recessed door handle.

When that failed, the other creatures got immediately to work opening those crates and extracting exotic looking tools. They assembled something that looked like another box that connected to strange metal jaws through things that resembled ropes. Soon the box began emitting a loud roaring sound and one of the creatures handed the metal jaw part up to the one nearest the door, who applied it to the door itself. The tone of the roar coming from the box deepened noticeably, but still the door did not open.

Other crates were opened and another tool was assembled, resembling the first, but without jaws on the end of the part they handed up to the creature nearest the door. The noise from first box stopped and the box part of this second tool soon began emitting a strange warbling buzz and a bright red light about a finger in length was applied to the balky door. Sparks of flame shot in all directions from the door, so the Romans assumed this tool must be some kind of cutting device.

It was obvious that this was some kind of rescue operation they were observing. From the level of cooperation between them, it was obvious the creatures had to be communicating among themselves somehow, yet they emitted no sound, nor did they appear to be using hand signals. Except for the noise generated by their tools, the creatures were eerily silent.

A legionary they had left behind them with the rest of the century soon arrived, minus his armor as he'd seen the others do earlier. He reported that a third daystar had just landed and that a single creature looking like all the others had exited and was heading their way at a dead run. Alerted that this single creature was coming from behind them, the Romans successfully hid themselves as it passed by. They continued to watch as the cutter tool slowly made a complete fiery circuit around the entire circumference of the door. In less than an hour, the door finally fell away, but it was the last creature to arrive that stuck its head inside.

Although the door now stood open, none of the silver garbed creatures went inside the wrecked daystar, but backed away into the fringes of the undamaged forest, causing the Romans to hastily retreat further back to avoid being spotted. The creatures milled about aimlessly, as if waiting for something... or someone. It was obvious this rescue operation had not gone as the creatures might have hoped. Removal of the dead was something all Roman soldiers understood thoroughly, but why were the creatures waiting? They had hoped to possibly get a glimpse of the creature's true forms when the bodies were brought out, but it now appeared that wasn't going to happen.

Sure enough, about an hour later another messenger from the century watching behind them arrived, sans armor, to warn them that two more daystars had just landed, discharging another twenty of the creatures. These new arrivals did not wear the same silver garb as the others, but similar looking bright shiny green outfits, with interlocking symbols resembling bright red moon-slivers on them.

This news caused a near panic among the Romans, as there was only one condition they were familiar with where the dead required special handling... plague.

~

Deep inside Aryn's Cave
Mid-August, 81 A.D.

ARYN RETURNED about six hours later with three more deer carcasses, a couple of plump rabbits and a squirrel. He also brought back some fresh mushrooms he'd found, a fist-full of wild onions and a melon. He cut away one deer haunch, while Nightmare was busy scarfing down the next two, and then started a fire with pre-chopped wood from his living quarters at the cave entrance. After getting a couple of fires started, Aryn gutted and skinned the rabbits and the squirrel, de-boned them and cut them up into chunks. He seasoned the meat with a few herbs and spices and then dunked about half them in flour, ready for Kyla's bronze frying pan. The rest of the meat chunks he added to the chopped mushrooms and onions simmering over the second fire in a boiling bag, hung from a tripod frame he'd retrieved from his saddlebags.

Úna raised an eyebrow at Kyla, as they watched Aryn diligently preparing, and then cooking them all a long overdue meal.

Kyla merely shrugged, as she added bits of shredded bacon to the cooking bag, from her magical storage place in the *Otherworld.*

"He's a better cook, than I am."

Úna smiled at her daughter. "Perhaps you should have him teach you some of those skills, if you're to be married. — He can't do *everything*, now can he?"

Kyla started to snap back at her mother's implied criticism, but caught herself.

She's right... I'm not a faerie queen who can get away with being good for little more than a sex toy for a husband.

"Perhaps you're right, Mother."

That surprising comment made Úna raised the other eyebrow in total astonishment.

With that, Kyla stood and went to Aryn, grabbing the fork he was using to stir the frying meat chunks from his hand.

"Let me do that, and you go rest for a while. You've been out playing manly hunter-gatherer all day, while Mother and I have done little more than lounge in this marvelous pool of yours."

Aryn gave her a puzzled look, then nodded. But instead of resting, he then proceeded to fully unload Frisky, feed and water him, and then wipe him down with a rag.

"Aryn always takes care of his animals, before doing the slightest thing for himself," Kyla said, in way of an explanation for her astonished mother.

"First he takes care to provide supper for us, and then he provides for his horse before doing anything for himself. Incredible. Your father could stand to spend some time around this fae-mortal of yours... even *he* might learn a few things!"

Kyla and Úna blinked at each other after that remark, then they both burst out laughing.

"NOT!"

∾

Underground
3232 A.D.

BIG DAN WEAVER nudged his friend Brian Steele awake with the toe of his boot. He was glad to see Steele finally getting some rest, instead of using up his rest period writing. He'd have probably done it again, but the antique computer he used was low on power and needed recharging from the huge 800 lb. battery pack the dwarves were bringing along to power the VLF beacon.

"Wha?" Steele responded groggily.

"Hate to wake you, but your computer is fully charged again and the dwarves are eager to move out."

"God, I'd kill for a cup of coffee, right now," Steele said, as he rolled unsteadily to his feet with a groan.

"You, and me both, brother. Unfortunately, our dwarven friends don't appear to have discovered the joys of coffee yet, so it's not included on their menu."

"Did I sleep through breakfast?"

"No, the dwarves say we should be reaching the surface today, so they are foregoing the morning meal so they can be rid of us just as soon as they can."

"But..."

"I know, 'what awaits us, once we get there?' No one has a clue, but they didn't rescue us and bring us this far just to let us all die now, right?"

Steele took a swig from Weaver's water skin he offered and set off to follow his big friend as the dwarves set a brisk pace in their eagerness to finish their gods-given task, and get back to whatever it was that dwarves normally did with their time.

CHAPTER TWENTY-NINE

Last night the secrets of the universe were revealed to me,
and they had nipples.
-- Jarod Kintz

Deep inside Aryn's Cave
Mid-August, 81 A.D.

ARYN WAS STILL SLEEPING WHEN THEIR ENTIRE WORLD changed. Kyla was munching on crisps of bacon and pan-fried cornbread with slathers of some of Aryn's grape jam as her breakfast. Úna munched on some of the mushrooms and wild onions from their supper the night before. She also snarfed down several slices of the cornbread and jam Kyla offered.

"Your cooking has certainly improved, since you started spending so much time around Aryn," Úna said, with a sly smile. "Your attitude also seems to have mellowed somewhat as well. I don't think virginity suited you very well... it made you cranky."

"MOTHER!" Kyla blushed furiously.

Nightmare suddenly raised his head from the remaining deer carcass he'd been disemboweling, on full alert, looking further down the tunnel... giving off a loud, smoke-filled snort.

Voices from deeper within the cave soon became audible, coming closer by the minute.

Kyla rushed to rouse Aryn, shaking his shoulder.

"Wha?"

"Shh... listen."

Aryn propped himself up on one elbow, and nodded to acknowledge he'd heard the strange voices coming from deeper in the earth.

"Has there ever...?"

Aryn shook his head and got to his feet, as even Frisky was beginning to become agitated at whatever was disturbing the púka. He walked down the tunnel a few steps and cupped his hand to his ear.

"This beacon thing is getting mighty damned heavy, I don't mind telling ya," came a guttural voice from below.

Nightmare rose up on his haunches and bunny-hopped on his massive hind legs to beside Aryn, virtually shouldering him aside as he inhaled a tremendous breath... and shot a colossal column of flame down the tunnel toward the intruders.

"Nightmare... NO!"

There was complete silence from the tunnel for a full second after the púka's flame finally subsided.

"A great snarkin', gods-damned lizard just singed me beard, it did!"

"It didn't do yer eyebrows a heapin' lot of good neither," a second voice snorted in obvious amusement.

"Don't just be standing there laughing. Make yerself useful for once, and go up there and smack that beastie upside the head with that wee hammer o'yers."

"WHO'S DOWN THERE?" Aryn yelled, through hands cupped around his mouth to further project his voice.

"We all be down here... that's who. And just who might *you* be? — Attacking peaceful folk, just out for a stroll, with no warning and all."

"I've lived in this cave for many years and never has anyone come out of it from the depths... how did you get down there and how many of you are there?"

"Well, as to the first, that's a wee bit of a story. And the second... a couple o'hundred, as best ah kin reckon. If'n ya will jes rein in that fire-lizard of yours fer a spell, we'd surely lak to get our charges out of this hole, without git'n anything else singed off us. We'll be out of yer hair drekly."

"Two hundred?" Kyla stammered, as she walked to Aryn's side. "Nightmare... down boy, it's all right."

The wyvern gave his mistress a dubious look, but turned away with a snort, indicating he didn't necessarily agree his protection wasn't going to be needed further.

"Come ahead, then," Aryn called. "The púka won't trouble you any further."

Aryn and Kyla urged the wyvern back to the pool area, where there was sufficient room for people to maneuver.

A gaggle of mixed voices came from below, mostly questioning what a púka was, and continued snickering about a singed conquer beard. A couple minutes later, the queerest looking creatures that any of them had ever seen came stomping up the passageway, carrying a huge box-like contraption. Squat, thick beings about three feet tall, having long, bushy beards of various colors... except for the one in the lead, whose reddish beard was blackened and half burnt away. That one did present a rather comical sight — especially the venomous look he shot at the wyvern as he tramped by, continuing to head for the surface.

"Wait!" cried Aryn. "Who are you... and for that matter, what are you?"

The two carrying the big, heavy boxy-looking thing continued on, but another paused and turned aside out of the pathway the others were taking.

"What be we? — Who be ye, who doesn't know a dwarf when he sees one?"

"Dwarves?" Kyla asked. "I have heard tales of such. The Tuatha Dé Danann have ancient legends that speak of dwarves, but they are not native to Éire."

"What be an Éire, elf girl?"

"I'm not an elf!"

"Tall... thin body... pointy ears... look like elf to me... except dress funny. Elvin females wear long gowns."

"Éire is where you are... it's an island to the west of Britannia," Aryn interjected.

"Dunno, no isle of Éire. We live heart of mountain."

"How did you get into the depths of my cave?"

"Kleidmar... our chieftain... he say follow earth elemental into depths. Bring beings we find out to surface."

"What beings?" Kyla asked.

"They follow... some hurt."

The three turned to watch the slow parade of dwarves continuing their trek past the pool, headed on toward the surface. Not long after came dwarves carrying several humans lying on litters. Some had crude splints applied to their legs, or arms tied up in slings tied around their necks.

"Wait!" cried Aryn. "Let me ensure those broken bones are set properly, and then put the injured into this pool."

"Bah... dirty and smell bad — but no time for bath," said the dwarf.

Úna floated up and out of the water, hovering above of the pool with all of her naked charms on public display... immediately freezing all of the dwarves in their tracks, with eyes as large as meat pies.

"Aryn is a talented physician and this pool has magical healing properties," Úna said. "Do as he says!"

"Holy Mary, mother of God and all the twelve apostles!" screamed Benny Lopatka, who had just stepped into view of the magnificently naked faerie queen.

This outburst cause a minor stampede from those behind, including Brian Steele and Dan Weaver, who broke into a trot to see what was going on. They too, pulled up short, wide-eyed at the unexpected sight that transfixed them like a deer frozen in a spotlight.

"MOTHER!" gasped Kyla, scandalized at her mother's wanton behavior. "Would you please put some clothes on?"

"No need ta bother on our account," a dwarf quipped softly... unconsciously speaking for all the males in their entire mixed party.

That elicited a mischievous smile from the faerie queen, who meekly said, "Very well, Daughter, if you insist I must... but I think our new guests may be quite unhappy with you for spoiling their enjoyment."

Virtually every head bobbed in complete agreement — even the two women from the mining facility, far below.

∿

S.S. Pegasus

In Orbit Above the Planet Eerie
3232 A.D.

"NOTHING?"

Doctor Jennifer Littleton was exhausted. She had just completed her preliminary autopsy reports on the six shuttle crew-members, and delivered her synopsis to Captain Allan Johansson in his ready-room.

"Nothing that is documented in my med-computer, at any rate."

"God damn it! — Something must have happened to have caused that... that..."

"Orgy?"

"Yes... orgy!"

Johansson took a deep breath to calm himself, and ran his hand through his thinning hair. "A highly trained shuttle crew doesn't just suddenly decide to strip down and jump each other's bones in the middle of a God damned mission... especially when they're flying on manual, only a couple of hundred feet in the air!"

"Agreed."

"So, *something* had to have caused such totally irrational behavior, but now you're telling me you can't find the cause?"

Doctor Littleton pinched the skin between her eyes, just above her nose... a nervous habit she'd had since childhood and never quite broken when under stress.

Look, Captain... I'm only a general practitioner, not a pathologist, or diagnostician. Anything beyond the realm of broken bones, a burst appendix and runny noses, I'm at the mercy of what the med-computer can tell me. There are a thousand things that might cause an individual to lose touch with reality and display irrational behavior, but nothing that would come on that suddenly, and certainly nothing that would affect multiple people in exactly the same way. It's more than just losing their sexual inhibitions. It's more like their sex drives just suddenly shorted out, and produced a totally irresistible level of uninhibited sexual lust. There's nothing remotely similar to such an occurrence that's ever been documented in human history."

"Do you think there's any danger of whatever happened to the shuttle crew happening to the rest of us?"

Littleton sighed, and not just from exhaustion. She knew the captain was gravely frightened by the sheer inexplicability of whatever event caused the shuttle crew to literally fuck themselves to death. Oh, it was the injuries they sustained in the crash that actually killed them, but had they been strapped in at their posts and not entangled together doing the nasty on the deck during impact, they all would have probably survived the crash itself. She also knew the captain desperately wanted her to reassure him that the phenomenon that killed the shuttle crew would not be repeated... that they were all safe from such an occurrence ever happening again.

"Captain, I truly wish to God I could tell you it won't, but my crystal ball has a software glitch. How can I say for sure that it won't, when I have absolutely no idea what caused it? All I can say is that we took every biologic hazard precaution in the book. If whatever caused the shuttle crew to suddenly lose their minds was some kind of airborne pathogen, then we should all be safe. We followed every isolation and decontamination protocol there is."

"And if it's not an airborne pathogen?"

"Who the hell knows? We're taking every precaution

against bodily fluid contamination among the remaining crew, but who really knows how well *that's* going to work?"

Johansson could see in Littleton's pained expression that she was just as frustrated as he was.

"I don't suppose that there's any way to keep this orgy thing from getting out to the rest of the crew, is there?"

"I threatened the wrath of God coming down on the entire med-team that took the videos and bagged the bodies, if one word of the details of this case were to leak out, but with human nature being what it is... no, probably not."

CHAPTER THIRTY

*People, in my long experience, want to talk. They may
believe they wish to keep secrets, and they may believe that
they are capable of doing so. But the truth is that secrets exist
to be revealed; and it is usually very easy to find the
combination of words that will cause them to emerge.*
-- J. Robert Lennon

Deep inside Aryn's Cave
Mid-August, 81 A.D.

ALL OF THE MINERS AND DWARVES WATCHED IN SLACK-
jawed fascination, as Kyla helped her mother dress. Aryn
kept his back turned away from the peep show going on
behind him, and went to check on the injured miners — one
lying on a litter complained vehemently when Aryn's body
inadvertently blocked his view of Úna. It was obvious when
the memorizing effect of the faerie queen's nudity was
finally broken, by the sudden clarity returning to everyone's
eyes.

"Úna, Aryn and Kyla," Dan Weaver whispered to Brian Steele. "Aren't those the names of your char..."

"Shh... don't go there — don't even think it!" Steele hissed back.

"All right, ye slaggards!" the dwarf declared. "It's not far to the surface now, so be off with ya."

"Wait!" Aryn called out. "Put these four men into the healing pool first," as he pointed to those most severely injured. "We'll walk them out after they're healed sufficiently."

The dwarves shrugged, but did as Aryn instructed. Brian Steele and Dan Weaver glanced at each other fearfully, but neither spoke as they both turned to follow along towards the surface.

"You!" Úna yelled and everyone froze, turning back to see who the faerie queen was calling to. Úna flew over to where Brian Steele stood, and eyed him up and down suspiciously. "You are different from all the others. The entire land of Éire literally rings with your magical essence. How is it you are so intimately connected to our island?"

Steele recognized Úna, Aryn, Kyla, Frisky and Nightmare immediately upon first seeing them. They all appeared exactly as they always had in his mind's eye, as he wrote their story... but he couldn't bring himself to believe these physical beings before him were actually his characters, somehow made flesh.

"I... ugh... I'm not exactly sure what you mean," Steele stammered.

Úna gave Steele a dubious look, but then her features softened. "I think you do — but you may not realize it. Still, my powers tell me that you are inexorably linked to the very soul of Éire. I've never experienced anything quite like it, for anyone other than the fae."

"What did you mean when you said something about 'his magical essence' earlier?" Weaver asked the faerie queen, while jerking his thumb toward Steele.

Úna scowled at the big miner standing beside Steele, as if his presence and his question were both minor irritants. "You are mortal, so it's no wonder you're oblivious to the incredibly powerful magic that flows within this man. When he reaches the surface, all the fae on Éire will instantly know that a new god has arrived in their midst."

Weaver startled the faerie queen when he suddenly burst into unrestrained, full-throated laughter.

"Did I say something you found humorous?"

When Weaver regained control, he said, "You don't know this guy like I do, your majesty... but you may be more right than you know."

"Dan... don't go there... please," Brian pleaded.

But he did.

∾

Deblin
Late-August, 81 A.D.

GENERAL GNAEUS JULIUS AGRICOLA, Roman governor of Britannia, once again sat brooding at his field desk in the dark recesses of his command tent, just outside the north gate of the city of Deblin. The Roman catapults and battering rams continued their assault on the walls and gates of the besieged Hibernian city. When either one first produced a breach offering his legion entry, there was little doubt the city would fall. But Agricola wasn't worried about that.

Plague.

The very word sent shivers of trepidation down the governor's spine.

I'd rather face an army of 30,000 Hibernian barbarians, than face another plague.

A massive Hibernian army was something his men were trained to deal with. That was something they understood and knew how to defeat. There was nothing understandable about a plague... especially an alien plague. Oh, he'd already taken all of the standard precautions. He'd ordered General Servius Marius Paterculus to quarantine the century of legionaries and the fifteen cavalrymen who'd investigated that fallen daystar — which was reported to be some kind of mysterious flying metal box.

What kind of wizardry could possibly make a huge metal box fly like that?

He was dealing with a complete unknown here. Would their standard procedures for quarantining those potentially exposed even be effective against an alien plague? None of those men had developed any notable symptoms as yet, but what kind of symptoms would an alien plague display... if any at all? Perhaps it might just cause men to suddenly keel over dead, without any warning. Who knew?

The detailed reports he's received from Paterculus indicated the "crew" of the daystar that landed at the edge of the forest wore silvery metallic suits of some kind. — Suits that covered their entire bodies without breaks, even appearing to include some kind of filter apparatus on the chest the creatures apparently breathed through. It wasn't armor, as the Romans understood it, as those suits appeared totally flexible... like a second skin. The shiny green suits worn by the next creatures to arrive were similar, except these included pellet-shaped tanks of some kind, worn on the back, which apparently fed "air," or whatever else those creature might breathe, into the helmet section through flexible hoses.

Obviously, these creatures saw the need to totally isolate themselves from anything to do with this accursed island. Jupiter only knows if I should just abandon this expedition and flee from this place of magical creatures, flying boxes and alien plagues.

A knock sounded on the tent pole, so Agricola raised his head from his hands and said, "Come."

A legionary from Agricola's personal guard stuck his head inside the tent flap and said, "My lord, the battering ram on north gate reports it is failing rapidly. Do you wish to lead the assault on the city personally?"

～

S.S. *Pegasus*
In Orbit Above the Planet Eerie
3232 A.D.

"CAPTAIN, I am receiving an incoming Priority-1 message from shuttle six," called Ensign Pyrx Nata, communications officer of the S.S. *Pegasus*.

Captain Allan Johansson's medical monitor registered an immediate spike in his heart rate, blood pressure and respiration. Priority-1 communications were reserved strictly for emergencies. They superseded all other transmissions, requiring all other transmitters on the net to shut the hell up, until after the emergency had been dealt with. Rarely was a Pri-1 call anything but the direst news imaginable, so Johansson's mind immediately snapped to the six bodies lying in the medical quarantine area of the ship's sick bay.

"Route that call to my station, Pyrx."

The little alien touched a couple of electronic pads on her communications console and said, "The call is transferred to your station, Captain... go ahead."

"This is Captain Johansson. State the nature of your emergency, Six,

"Good news, Captain! – We've just captured holo of what appears to be survivors from the mining station exiting onto the surface from a cave... and they're being escorted out by dwarves."

Before Johansson could reprimand the officer making that report for such an insensitive remark, his holographic monitor tank illuminated with images being uploaded from Shuttle-6 in real-time. Sure enough, a line of people exiting the cave did indeed appear to be the buried miners they'd been desperately trying to rescue. But the beings escorting them out weren't at all what the current politically correct crowd insisted calling "little people," but real, honest-to-God dwarves from right out of a fantasy tale. About half the height of the people, but twice as wide, they were squat, massively built and very hairy... except for one whose long beard was half burnt away from some subterranean mishap.

"How close to that cave can you find a place to safely set down?" Johansson inquired.

'Not very... the forest is extremely dense anywhere close and appears to have suffered extreme storm damage. No clear areas within six miles, but there is a narrow trail of some kind that appears to have been deliberately cleared between that cave and a road running along the east coast of the island."

"Good work," Johansson said... implying the crew was forgiven for using the emergency priority to get their message through to him immediately. "Send us the coordinates for that open area closest to that trail you spotted, and then hover just above treetop level to see if that's close enough to hail those miners below. See if you can get a message through to them. Let them know we've located them, and we'll be soon dropping supplies down to them. Also tell them to just sit tight right where they're at, and that we're mounting a rescue effort."

$\approx$

Deep inside Aryn's Cave
Mid-August, 81 A.D.

BRIAN STEELE LOOKED at his feet... at the stalactites hanging from the ceiling, and the injured men par-broiling in the healing pool. He looked everywhere except anywhere near Dan Weaver, as he spun his ridiculous notions about some inexplicable connection between his book and the living, breathing beings before him. Aryn and Kyla stole dubious glances toward the thoroughly embarrassed author. Úna also shot Steele an occasional look as Weaver told his tale, but hers were more considered... as if the faerie queen wasn't completely dismissing the idea as totally absurd.

"So, you think I'm nothing more than a character in some grand epic tale your friend is making up from his imagination, huh?" Aryn said derisively.

"*Pfft...*" Kyla snorted. "So, what do you think would happen if I fried your friend over there with a lightning bolt, right now? Would we all just cease to exist?"

"Kyla, NO!" Úna commanded. "These men have done you no harm, nor are they avowed enemies of any of our peoples."

"Possibly," said Weaver.

"Dan... just drop it... please!" Brian pleaded.

"Possibly, what?" asked Aryn.

"Damn it, Dan! Stop provoking these people. What can it possibly accomplish?"

"All right," Weaver said. "But answer me this...what is right outside this cave we're in?"

"Éire!" exclaimed all three natives.

"No... I mean specifically. Birds, trees grass... air?"

"Of course," answered Aryn.

"What would you say if I told you that eight months ago, there was no life at all anywhere on this planet... not even breathable air?"

Kyla and Aryn both looked incredulous, but Úna looked grave.

"That's ridiculous!" snapped Aryn. "My memories go back much farther than that. I have an entire lifetime of memories." Aryn started to step towards the big miner, but Kyla threw out a restraining hand.

"Careful, my love. This fellow is obviously soft in the head. He might snap if provoked, so don't get between him and my lightning bolts."

Weaver continued on, as though totally unimpressed by the demi-goddess' implied threat of frying him with a lightning bolt... if it even registered with him at all.

"Do you, really? – I'm sure you distinctly remember your trading expedition to the village of Loughshinny, the day you first spotted those Roman galleys landing troops on the Drumanagh peninsula... the same day you first started killing Romans from the top of a wind-whipped tree."

Aryn's brows narrowed suspiciously. "How did you know about that?"

"I read about it in Brian's book."

"Don't start that shite again!"

"So tell me, what was it that you sold to the merchants in Loughshinny... exactly?"

"I... ugh... don't remember exactly. Herbs and herbal medicines that I'd concocted from whatever I'd managed to find in the forest. That was a long time ago."

"Or, maybe your memories are fuzzy because Brian didn't specify exactly what you sold them in his book."

Aryn rolled his eyes, but before he could respond further, Weaver continued on.

"And another thing... exactly what language are we all using to communicate with each other right now?"

"Gaelic" — "Dwarvish" — "English..." came the responses from the members of the various races conversing next to the healing pool.

Úna interrupted.

"Actually, the big man's conjecture may not be quite as far-fetched as it first sounds."

Kyla turned to her mother, aghast. "Mother... really?"

Úna smiled at her daughter in the way of all mothers, whose child just doesn't understand.

"Kyla, I'm your mother, right?"

"Of course... what are you getting at?"

"So why is it that I no memory at all, of your birth? I'm also your father's wife, but somehow I cannot remember anything about our wedding. Those are two of the most important events in any female's life, so how is it possible that I have no absolutely no recollection of any of the details of either those most momentous of occasions?"

"You really don't remember giving birth to me?" Kyla asked, stricken.

"Kyla, I don't even have memories of ever being pregnant. I know I must have been, for I distinctly perceive the parental bond between us. All of the fae and the *Daoine Sidhe* acknowledge our kinship, so I know it's true... so why can't I remember actually being there, experiencing those events first hand?

"Even to having sex with your father. — I mean... I remember having done so, but no memories of actually doing it. Does that make sense?"

CHAPTER THIRTY-ONE

I sometimes think that the universe is a machine designed for
the perpetual astonishment of astronomers.
-- Arthur C. Clarke

The Planet Eerie

BRIAN STEELE AND DAN WEAVER BOTH SQUINTED
against the blinding glare of the mid-morning sun,
streaming through the mouth of the cave they were finally
about to exit. Steele glanced away from the brightness and
was unsurprised to see Aryn's home exactly as he'd always
envisioned it while writing his novel. Even recognizing
Aryn, Kyla and Úna at first sight, as surprising as that had
been, hadn't fully convinced him that his fantasy novel had
somehow magically come to life on this lifeless planet
having a carbon dioxide atmosphere.

He'd merely listened as Weaver debated the merits of
his unbelievable argument with the three natives, and

marveled when Úna began offering unexpected support for the ridiculous idea. Why Weaver became such a true believer in his fanciful delusions Brian would never know, but Steele was much too grounded in the laws of physics that governed physical reality for him to even begin to accept the utter impossibility of Dan's wild theory, until...

Rhoslyn, the three-inch pixie, suddenly popped into existence in their midst, and interrupted the debate when she loudly announced, "Nightmare... you're all better now!"

Aryn's forehead wrinkled in surprise, and he turned away from the miners to check on the púka's condition. "Kyla, have Nightmare step out of the pool, please."

Kyla whistled and slapped her leg in a hand signal, calling the púka to her side.

From what had originally appeared to the miners as a merely a hunk of rock sticking up in the far corner of the pool, a pair of gigantic blood-red eyes suddenly opened, and a geyser of water snorted from its nostrils. The injured miners lying in the healing pool yelled in alarm, trying to put distance between themselves and the massive beast, slowly rising from the pool with wings outstretched, flinging hot, steaming water into their faces. As the sixteen-foot wyvern reared to its full height, it began walking on its massive hind legs toward where Kyla stood on the bank above the edge. The miners in its path between them screamed and scrambled clear out of the pool, in their efforts to get clear of the monster about to crush them beneath it huge claws.

Aryn's eyebrows rose when he saw such badly injured men moving so quickly, and he stopped to reexamine some of them.

"Amazing... their broken bones have somehow knit

themselves back together, if only minimally, after such a short time in the healing pool."

"Perhaps the healing magic of the pool effects these men at a more highly accelerated rate, as they are not native to our world," said Úna.

Aryn could only shake his head in stark disbelief at how quickly their injuries had healed. "Apparently."

Kyla held her hand out flat and lowered it slowly. In response to her hand gesture, Nightmare scrunched himself down to a level where Aryn could examine the damaged plate on his chest, where they'd had to remove one to get that poisonous Roman iron-tipped arrowhead out of him.

"A new scale has begun forming over the wound," Aryn announced. "It wouldn't have done that if the wound beneath wasn't healed completely. While it's not complete yet, I think it's far enough along to where he can safely transform again."

Kyla smiled at Aryn's pronouncement and said, *"Trom-laighe… cruth-atharrachadh pwca."*

The big wyvern immediately began melting, reshaping itself back into its more common horse-like appearance. Within a couple of minutes, the wyvern was gone and in its place stood a huge black stallion with a snow white main and tail, blazing red eyes and yellow-orange flames licking up it lower legs from its hooves.

Brian Steele watched the transformation with huge, unbelieving eyes as the huge creature manipulated its own mass, and rearranged itself into a totally different creature entirely.

"Well, I'll be damned," said Weaver. Turning towards Brian, the big miner said, "I read about shape-shifters in your book, but never thought I'd ever actually get to see one in action."

"Me neither," Steele admitted softly.

Aryn then examined all of the injured miners and proclaimed them fit enough to walk to the surface, even if a couple of them had to do so with a noticeable limp.

As their remaining torches were slowly dying Úna summoned several glowing will-o-the wisps to illuminate the cave for them. She then winked out with a soft *pop*, saying she needed to go apologize to her husband for not being there to prepare his supper the night before.

Kyla and Aryn escorted all of the miners out, with Aryn leading Frisky by the reins attached to his halter. Nightmare brought up the rear as Rhoslyn continually darted about Brian Steele's head, looking at him strangely.

"There is an incredible amount of high magic surrounding you. Are you some kind of new god?" she finally asked shyly.

"NO!" Steele thundered.

Rhoslyn flitted away quickly, hiding behind Aryn to escape the strange god's wrath.

Big Dan Weaver laughed and said, "Don't worry, little one. He won't hurt you. He's your creator."

Rhoslyn peeked out from behind Aryn's shoulder where she'd taken refuge. "But, all of our legends say the Tuatha Dé Danann created the fae ages ago, just before they retreated into their underground burrows."

Weaver grinned at the tiny pixie and said, "Ah, but who was it that created the Tuatha Dé Danann... hmm?"

Rhoslyn look startled, as though *that* particular thought had never crossed her mind.

Weaver looked towards where his friend Brian Steele walked beside him and asked, "Are you still in denial of what your own eyes are telling you?"

Steele shook his head. "I honestly don't know what to think anymore, Dan... I really don't."

They walked in silence until finally turning a corner and wincing at the harsh glare streaming into the mouth of the cave. They all held up hands to shield their eyes, until they could adjust to the dramatic increase in light level. When they finally exited the cave, Dan Weaver looked about, seeing the pool right outside, and marveled at the tangle of battered trees in the surrounding forest. Brian Steele couldn't help but look up, directly into the blazing sun for just a moment, before glancing away from that intense brightness.

Benny Lopatka, from the tool crib, ran up to Weaver excitedly, when he saw them finally emerge from the cave. "Dan, can you believe all this? We're actually outside on the surface of the planet, but there's birds and trees... and air out here!"

Weaver looked about, noting that many of the surviving miners appeared to be tearing open packages of emergency rations. He nodded towards them and asked, "Where did those all those rations come from?"

"The dwarves carrying that VLF transmitter, and its big-ass battery, placed it on that ledge, just above the mouth of the cave. Within minutes, a shuttle from that supply ship we were expecting appeared right overhead. They used their PA system to tell us to stay put, and that a rescue party was on its way. Within an hour, a second shuttle came over and dropped those emergency rations and water down to us."

"Speaking of the dwarves, I don't see any of them about. Where are they?"

"Ah, now that's a damned good question, Dan. After they got that beacon located above the cave entrance, without a word, they all just started sashaying off towards the forest."

"So, you're saying they just walked off into the forest?"

Benny got a confused look on his face, and said, "No, before they even got to the edge of the forest, they all just started fading away."

"What do you mean, they faded away?"

"Honest-to-God, Dan. I ain't shitting ya. One minute they was walking away from us, and the next, they just started getting all transparent... like smoke. That red-haired dwarf who carried Brian out of the mine, turned back for a moment and waved to us, but then he too just faded from sight without ever making it into the woods."

∽

The Planet Éerie
Deep in the Planetary Core

THE SINGLE ADULT *We* who finally investigated the raging sexual promiscuity spreading throughout their adolescent population was horrified by this uncharacteristically wanton behavior in their young. She immediately began broadcasting her alarm throughout the adult population. It took some time for her to garner enough interest among the primarily self-absorbed adults, and was thoroughly exasperated by the number who insisted on investigating this "alien" thought pattern for themselves.

Like their adolescents, most were initially overwhelmed by the sheer impact of vivid alien sex— reliving those intense experiences of incredible human orgasms among themselves over and over again. Some even emulated their offspring, combining actual physical sex with those the alien memories... and for most, it was the first time they had physically coupled in thousands of eons.

Eventually enough adults tore themselves free from the influence of those alien thought patterns to argue amongst themselves about what should be done. These alien thoughts even provided a name for the incredibly intense cravings these sexual experiences produced in the *We*... addiction.

It was completely outside anything known to their race, and none could even begin to formulate an answer to the problem. They finally decided their only logical choice was to violate one of the most basic of tenants of civilized behavior among their people... by attempting to petition the ancient conclave of *We* elders for guidance. They initially hoped it might take only a few millennia to get an elder's attention, but were astounded when one of the most ancient of their entire race answered their call almost immediately.

Those only a few hundreds of millions of years old could never understand the irritating bouts of near lucidity that often plagued the true elders, billions upon billions of years old. One of the oldest-of-the-old was merely drowsing when the mental call by nearly half the entire adult population of the *We* thundered through his mind, rousing him to full wakefulness. At first he thought to just ignore it, but then he wondered what could possibly cause so many of the youngsters to purposely breach established protocol, by infringing upon an elder's mental privacy.

Curiosity prevailed, and thus, an incredibly ancient *We* elder, surfing the outer fringes of the singular adolescent female's thoughts, was present in Brian Steele's mind when he first stepped out of the cave and glanced upward at the sun.

HOME!

Few others still surviving would have recognized that brightly glowing yellow orb in the sky, nor truly understood its unique significance to the *We* people. This elder had only been a few millennia old, hardly old enough to even be considered an adolescent, when he and his immediate family had been trapped within irresistible centrifugal forces, as their rapidly spinning stellar home was sloughing off mass from its outer reaches into the cold void of space. But he remembered... and experienced a completely foreign emotion the alien thoughts also had a name for — anticipation!

CHAPTER THIRTY-TWO

Writing a novel is a huge adventure... when it's going well, it's more fun than fun. When it stutters to a halt, put it aside. Go for a swim, go for a walk, take a week off. Don't panic or be afraid — you and your characters are in it together. Trust them to come to your rescue.
-- Deborah Moggach

S.S. Pegasus
In Orbit Above the Planet Eerie
3232 A.D.

"THIS IS THE SITUATION WE'RE FACING," JOHANSSON began as he addressed the five members of the crew gathered in the conference room. "We don't know what caused the planet to suddenly plunge into the Goldilocks Zone, form an atmosphere with breathable air, produce a small sea, suddenly sprout vegetation and create what appears to be first-century Romans and Celts. But what we do know is that we have roughly two hundred miners and support crew down there on the surface and I want to get them off that planet before it decides to do something else equally impossible.

"But my concern is this," the Captain continued. "We still don't know what caused Shuttle-3 to malfunction and crash."

"A hormonal imbalance in the control stalk," Sanchez quipped without considering his commanding officer's mood. Johansson waited out the few chuckles in response to his astrogator's joke which quickly died out as those assembled caught the look on their Captain's face.

"I see," Johansson replied, remarkably calm, considering his reputation. He wasn't surprised that word of the orgy-in-progress on the doomed shuttle had gotten out. But he was going to put an end to any more joking about it here and now. "Need I remind you, Lieutenant, that six of our fellow officers died in that crash and that is far from a laughing matter. Or would you prefer to spend the flight back to Cælius inside a spacesuit and tied off to tow line attached to the stern of the Pegasus?"

"No, sir," Sanchez said softly in the suddenly quiet room.

"Good," Johansson barked. "Because this is the last time I want to hear anything like that about the crash, from anyone on board this ship. Have I made myself clear?"

Five heads bobbed up and down in assent.

"Very good," Johansson replied, order restored. "Now then, Doctor Littleton, do we know yet what affected the crew of Shuttle-3?"

"No, Captain, we don't. Whatever triggered their... activity at the end, it left no trace behind on or in the bodies or even inside the shuttle itself. All we can say for sure is that whatever it was, it is down there on the planet below, though how it got through to the shuttle cabin is also unknown."

"And we are about to bring aboard over two hundred people who could have been exposed to whatever killed our crew," Johansson pointed out. "Not to mention exposing the crews of the shuttles we're going to have to use to ferry those people up from the surface. How do we ensure that we don't bring something aboard and wind up flying the Pegasus straight into the nearest star?"

"We'll need to examine them on the surface before they board the shuttles," Littleton replied. "And to play it safe, we'll need to quarantine them, along with the pilots and any crew on the shuttles and on the surface until we are certain they're all clear. I recommend the bridge be sealed during the evacuation and remain sealed until I can medically clear everyone."

"So ordered," Johansson said. "As far as how we're going to handle having ten times as many people aboard this ship than we normally do, we're going to double up in the cabins and everywhere else we can fit a body. We'll have to convert some cargo space into temporary living quarters until we can get back to Cælius. It isn't going to be a pleasure cruise by any stretch of the imagination, but it's doable. Start making the arrangements."

"Sir, if I may make a recommendation on the actual evacuation?" Gatta asked.

"Go ahead."

"We have five serviceable shuttles remaining" Gatta began. "But perhaps we should only use three to evac. With only two crew in the pilots' seats we can probably fit six evacuees in each shuttle meaning each shuttle will make a dozen trips each and we can complete the evac in about sixteen hours if we can keep the rotation going smoothly."

"Why not use all five and get it done faster?" Littleton asked.

"Using three shuttles we only expose six crewmen instead of ten," Johansson answered, figuring out what Gatta had in mind. "That's four fewer crew risking exposure and four more crewmen who could help out on the bridge or the engine room if needed instead of being quarantined. I like it. Set up the schedule Gatta and I want you overseeing the operation from the bridge."

"Aye, sir," Gatta replied. "Where will you be?"

"On the first shuttle going down," Johansson replied grimly. "Someone down there knows what the hell has been going on in this system and I want to talk to that person as soon as possible. I want some goddamned answers even if I have to dig up every square inch of that miserable little ball by hand to get them. Doctor, I want you up here checking the evacuees as they come aboard. I want someone able to run medical scans in the field to report to Shuttle-1 in fifteen minutes along with two pilots. I plan on departing on Shuttle-1 in twenty minutes."

~

Deblin
August, 81 A.D.

GENERAL GNAEUS JULIUS AGRICOLA, Roman governor of Britannia sat astride his white mount in full battle gear, surrounded by his personal guard just outside the walled city. The battering ram continued to hammer away at the splintering North Gate and it was clear to see that it was only a matter of minutes before the gate would give way and the assault on the city would begin. A thick grayish-white mist, no doubt blown in from the nearby sea, was gathering beyond and above the wall.

"In cannot withstand many more blows, my lord," one of his legionary called out.

"Indeed not," he agreed offhandedly. The gate would fall, of that there was no doubt. But of more concern to him was the lack of response from those on the other side of the wall. There were many possible responses from defenders of a besieged city: arrows, boiling oil, return fire from catapults, these were all expected options. But complete ominous silence, like that coming from the other side of the wall, was not among them.

The defenders had chosen instead to dismiss their attackers in complete disdain. They had slammed the gates shut when his forces had approached and apparently gone on about their business as if all was well. That they were all still within the walls he did not doubt. The naval blockade had ensured the city hadn't been evacuated in that direction, nor had he received any reports of a breakout along the wall.

Either the King along with his army's commander were insane or, Agricola thought as a cold chill shot down his spine, the plague that had brought down those in the fallen daystar had struck the city. His forces could be attacking a city of the already dead or damned and if plague was running rampant he and his legions could be marching directly to their deaths at the hands of an enemy they could not fight.

This gathering fog would not help in determining what lay beyond the wall once the gate fell either, Agricola thought bitterly. But there was nothing more to be done now than attack the breach and let Pluto decide what fate lay ahead for them all. Suddenly, a great splintering crack came from the gate as the battering ram smashed once again into the sturdy wood and this time kept on going through.

"The gate has fallen!" came a loud cry from the men manning the ram, followed by the celebratory roar of all of the legions. Agricola spurred his horse forward a few paces, then turned to face his legions.

"Soldiers of Rome," he called out in a booming voice. "Ride with me to glory and tonight we will dine at the tables of our fallen enemies as victors. Those among you who fall in battle today rejoice! For you will dine with honor in Elysium!"

"For the glory of Rome!" he called out as he turned back to face the wall and began riding toward the breach, his legions falling in behind them to charge into the breach, already under assault by the legionnaires who'd just created the hole.

Hiding behind the Roman lines, safely camouflaged in a thick green tree, Rhoslyn observed the fall of the North Gate and the charge of the Romans into the besieged city. The mist that had gathered before the breach puzzled her. She had never before seen it's like and doubted any Fae creature had summoned it. If this fog had been of magical creation, surely it would have enveloped the invaders and not the city itself.

But the mystery of the fog quickly became of secondary concern as Rhoslyn watched the first line of Romans begin to fade away into nothingness before they reached the fog, even before they reached the breached wall itself. Nor did any of their companions seem to take notice as those ahead faded into nothingness. They simply continued to march forward until they too faded and disappeared.

Terrified, Rhoslyn popped out – before whatever magic that had just claimed the invaders could reach out and ensnare her too – and fled back to Aryn's cave to report on the impossible event that she had just witnessed.

~

Outside Aryn's Cave
August, 81 A.D.

"HEY," Benny Lopatka shouted suddenly. "Here comes another shuttle!"

Over two hundred sets of eyes followed Lopatka's raised arm and locked onto the approaching shuttle. In the time that had passed since the departure of the previous shuttle, the survivors had eaten from the ration packs and started wondering exactly how they were going to be lifted off of this impossible planet. They were, at least so they hoped, moments away from finding out. The shuttle glided to a stop just overhead, hovering about twenty feet above the tallest tree.

"Attention below," a voice boomed out from the shuttle's external PA system. "This is Captain Johansson of the S.S. Pegasus. We are prepared to transport all of you aboard the ship and get you all back home but we cannot land here. The closest open area where we can land is six miles from here. Follow the trail from here to the coastal road to the east and that road will lead you south to the clearing where we will be waiting. If you understand and can make it there, start waving your arms."

Almost immediately, every arm below waved vigorously.

"Very well," Johansson said. "Get moving as quickly as possible. We'll see you there."

The shuttle flew off in the direction of the clearing, leaving the survivors to start getting organized and on their way to the evac point.

"Well if that isn't the best damned news I've heard in a long time," Dan Weaver exclaimed. "Alright people, let's start getting our shit together. We're fresh out of dwarves so if you can't carry it and walk quickly, leave it behind. We're going home."

The camp of miners exploded with activity. Aside from food and water no one had anything they cared to haul on their backs for six miles on foot, with one notable exception. Brian Steele slipped his laptop into a pack along with as many rations as he could fit inside next to it. Aryn had given him a full waterskin, made from what he supposed were rabbit hides, which he slipped on along with the more modern pack so he could judge the total weight he would be carrying on the hike.

"It'll probably takes us a good three or four hours depending on the terrain," Weaver said, sizing up his own pack. "I suppose there's no way in hell you consider just taking the hard drive out of that thing? It would make for a lighter load."

"Not a chance," Steele replied. "It's safer contained inside the case than it would be outside of it. If I have to crawl to get it there, I'll do it."

"I guess I'm not surprised," Weaver said with a chuckle. "You figured out how you're going to finish it after all of this?"

"Not a clue."

Weaver nodded then started making his way around the camp to make sure everyone was ready and able to start their march toward rescue. Aryn and Kyla looked on as the men and women made their preparations.

"We could help lead them to the clearing," Aryn said quietly.

"What of the Romans?" Kyla asked, surprised by the suggestion.

"The Romans will still be there," Aryn replied as he walked toward where Weaver and Steele were now standing only a few yards away. "Let's see these folk home first, then we'll rid our home of the invaders."

"That task may have already been completed for you, Aryn," Rhoslyn said as she popped into existence a few inches in front of Aryn.

"What do you mean, Rhoslyn?" Kyla demanded.

"I was watching the Romans attacking the gate at Deblin," she explained as Weaver and Steele also listened. "The battering ram finally knocked down the gate and the Romans started to march toward it. The city was already shrouded in a type of mist I've never before seen and as the Romans approached they just faded away and vanished. After the last one disappeared everything was a silence, even from the city itself. I feared I would disappear too so I left and came here to tell you what I saw."

"You mean they vanished into the mist?" Aryn asked.

"No," Rhoslyn said firmly, angered by the implication that she would not know the difference. "They started fading and had completely disappeared well before they ever got close to the mist."

"Like the dwarves that hauled us up to the surface," Weaver remarked. "When they left here they simply faded and vanished."

"That doesn't make sense," Kyla replied. "Why would the Romans just disappear?"

"Because their part of the story is either finished or it hasn't been written yet," Weaver answered with a sideways look in Steele's direction, who by now had completely given up producing any vocal protests over Weaver's theory that Steele had invented all of this in his mind. The logical portion of Steele's brain desperately clung to the thought that, even if he actually had imagined all of this in his head, there was no way he could possibly have caused it all to manifest itself. The problem he was running into was the logical part of his brain was growing quieter with each passing impossibility that presented itself for inspection.

"There appears to be some truth in the big one's words," Finvarra's voice boomed out as both he and Úna popped into the area near the mouth of the cave. "There is much happening here that can only be explained one way. Powerful magic is at work and the one called Brian Steele is very much at the heart of it."

Neither Steele nor Weaver needed to be introduced to the latest arrival. The High King of the *Daoine Sidhe* was even more impressive in person than he was within the pages of Steele's story on his computer screen. Somewhere deep inside, Steele heard what was left of his logic center declaring it had more than enough of this shit, was packing up its bags and departing for good.

"Then the Tuatha Dé Danann had nothing to do with what happened at Deblin today?" Rhoslyn asked.

"What has happened at Deblin?" Úna asked.

The King and Queen listened in shock as Rhoslyn repeated her tale of the mist-enshrouded city, the breached gate and the Romans who simply faded away as they approached the breach they'd worked so hard to open.

Finvarra was moved to utter an ancient curse in a tongue so old whatever magic was enabling them to understand one another failed to translate it.

"None of the Tuatha Dé Danann did this," Finvarra said when he finally recovered his voice. "I know of no magic capable of it."

"Then who the hell is responsible for everything we've seen here?" Aryn asked, the thought of something even more powerful than the Tuatha Dé Danann at work allowed a hint of fear to creep into his voice. Everyone, human, Celt or Fae all turned to gaze at Steele, who stared right back in denial and opened his mouth to vocalize his innocence. But when he opened his mouth, one last impossibility occurred: A booming voice that caused the ground itself to rumble and shake sounded out.

"*We!*" and the voice seemed to vibrate through any solid object within a one-mile radius. "The *We.* have caused all of this to pass."

The last thing Steele recalled was seeing a pile of rocks seemingly forming out of the ground into the rough shape of a head, torso, arms and legs. A pair of glowing green eyes stared out at the assembled people. A roughly shaped mouth split open just below the eyes.

"And the *We* have done so because of the one called Brian Steele."

All Steele saw after that was black and Weaver was hard pressed to catch the man before he collapsed to the ground and prevent his friend from striking his head on one of the smaller non-moving rocks.

CHAPTER THIRTY-THREE

*Can you feel it? Things are changing, can you see it? Watch
as the worlds collide into themselves.*
-- 30 seconds to Mars

The Planet Éerie
Coastal Road Clearing

SHUTTLE-1 GENTLY SETTLED ONTO THE GRASSY
clearing, well away from the road that ran along the rocky
coastline but easily in sight the instant the miners rounded
the bend on the road at the opening of the clearing.
Johansson led his three-man crew down the ramp and
quickly mapped out where he wanted the equipment set
up. The four men quickly offloaded the crates they'd
brought down and set up the med station where each miner
would be scanned and checked thoroughly before boarding
a shuttle up to the ship.

With Littleton setting up the quarantine up on the ship,

she had sent down the best-trained medic on the ship, Ensign Mishiki Kamata, to handle the pre-screening on the surface below. In less than an hour, the med station was fully setup, food and water rations were stacked and ready to be distributed and there was nothing left for them to do but sit and wait for the evacuees to arrive.

"It'll be another two or three hours at the earliest before they get here. You two go get some rest while you can," Johansson ordered the two pilots. "Once those miners get here it's going to be a very long day with no chance to take a break."

"Aye, sir," the two men answered crisply and hustled into the shuttle. With the deaths of the Shuttle-3 crew still fresh on his mind, Johansson fought down the impulse to order the two men to sleep at opposite ends of the shuttle. But, by god, he silently swore that if he saw that shuttle start rocking even in the slightest he was going to go in there shooting.

～

The Planet Éerie
Aryn's Cave

SOMETIMES THE OLDER METHODS ARE THE best ones. So when a considerable amount of cold water from the pool made contact with Steele's face it immediately roused the unconscious man.

"Oh, no you don't, buddy," Weaver said, not unkindly, when Steele caught sight of the living rock and tried to check out once again. He lifted the stricken writer to his feet and helped steady him. "I think we've clearly estab-lished this is your mess to clean up and you need to be awake to do it."

"What are you?" Steele asked the pile of rock, already knowing the answer but needing to say something.

"An earth elemental," Finvarra answered. "But we've not seen their like in ages."

"Do you have a name?" Aryn asked it.

"*We.*"

"Is that what you call your...people..," Úna asked, "or is that your own name?"

"Yes."

"Where did you come from to get here?" Kyla ventured.

"Below."

"Let me see what he thinks of my lightning bolts," Kyla muttered angrily as she started to raise her hands. The rock creature seemed unconcerned.

"Kyla," Úna admonished, the universal talent of all mothers to rein in their child by merely speaking their given name. No lightning bolts flew at the creature as Kyla lowered her hands, but she decided to glare at the annoying pile of rocks instead.

"You said your people have caused all that we have seen here on the surface," Weaver jumped into interrogation. "And that my friend here is also responsible. Do you know how?"

"Yes."

"Can you tell us?"

"Yes."

"Feel free to start anytime then," Weaver replied, getting exasperated with the creature's monosyllabic responses. "Right from the beginning if you don't mind."

"Eons ago," the *We* Elder said. "The *We* lived within

the Sun in this system. This planet you call Éerie was part of a molten mass ejected from the star. The *We* were trapped inside what was to become our new home.

"Time passed as our new home wandered far from the Sun," the *We* Elder continued. "The planet cooled and hardened and settled into an orbit in cold space far from our former home. For so very long nothing new ever happened and the *We* settled into the same pattern of watching in silent contemplation as millennia after millennia passed. Then something new happened. Strange creatures appeared on the surface and began digging into the ground above."

"That would be us," Weaver said.

"These new creatures stayed far above us," The Elder continued. "So the *We* paid them little notice. Until a new creature arrived to join the others, similar to those that came before, but so very different. This new one, the one called Brian Steele, caught the attention of the juveniles among us. His mind was nothing like the other mundane creatures that had come before."

"Geez, no offense taken there," Weaver groused.

"Dan, please shut up," Steele chided, suddenly caught up by the rock creature's story.

"The one called Brian Steele carried within him a strange new world unlike anything the *We* had experienced before and our juveniles desired to fully experience it all, especially this strange activity that your kind call 'sex'. It caused quite a reaction, especially among the youngest of us and they wanted to experience more of it along with all of the other aspects of the way your species lives. So they caused this barren world to move closer to its parent star and began to form that which was needed to bring this new world to like upon the surface of our old planet."

"The quakes," Weaver exclaimed. "That was from Éerie being shoved sunward into the Goldilocks' Zone and all so you could create the conditions needed to make all of this?"

Weaver spread his arms about to indicate the surrounding forest.

"Yes."

"We lost nineteen people," Weaver exclaimed hotly. "And you damned near killed the rest of us too and all so you could create this?"

"The younger ones among us did not realize your life-forms were so fragile," The *We* Elder explained. "They were eager to create the conditions so they could bring the creatures of Brian Steele's world to life and did not stop and fully consider their actions. Once the Elders became aware of what had happened, we caused the Dwarves to come and bring you up to the surface. None among us ever wished you harm, those below the surface or those in the flying ship."

"What flying ship?" Steele asked.

"Six of your kind were in a flying ship that crashed after it collided with the one called Úna."

"I was struck by their ship and injured my ankle," Úna confirmed. "But it was still flying after I left it."

"It flew on for a short time," The Elder said. "Then it fell to the ground. None inside survived."

"It must have been a shuttle from the rescue ship that was out looking for us," Weaver said.

"Hold on," Kyla interrupted, a thought suddenly striking her about an earlier comment by the earth elemental. "What 'creatures' are you talking about bringing to life, Elemental? You don't mean us do you?"

"That's what I've been trying to tell you," Weaver said.

"Dan...." Steele started, then gave up on stopping his

friend as he struggled with the horror of the growing thought inside that over twenty people may have died because of his story.

"Yes." The *We* Elder replied simply.

"I'm real," Kyla stated loudly. "Aryn is real. My parents are all real!"

"No." Was all the *We* Elder said in reply.

"Let's see how 'real' you think I am after this," Kyla exclaimed, quickly firing blue lightning bolts at the rock creature. But the bolts simply faded away as they got near her target. Weaver chuckled out loud, drawing his own set of lightning bolts which also faded away harmlessly before reaching their target. Frustrated, Kyla aimed her next shot at a nearby tree, which obediently burst into flame when the bolts struck it. Kyla launched one more volley each at Weaver and the *We* Elder but once again, the bolts faded out before reaching their destinations.

"Your lightning bolts won't work on him, me or any of my miners," Weaver said gently, taking some of the sting out of any possible insult. "We're real, living creatures. Your magic will only work on you and the creations made strictly for this little corner of the world, and only because they are supposed to work on you."

"Father," she called out to Finvarra, who'd been very quiet during the exchange. "Tell them they are wrong. Tell them we are real. Father?"

But the king merely shook his head sadly and exchanged a look with his wife. After a moment, Úna nodded her head.

"If it were in my power to make their words all a lie," Finvarra said as he returned his gaze to his daughter. "I would do so if but for your sake alone, my child. But the truth is undeniable, even though everything within me tells me I am as real as I perceive all around me to believe, everything within me also tells me otherwise as well."

"Deblin, Tallamore, the forest, the sea, all of the Romans I killed," Aryn asked bleakly. "None of it exists?"

"None." The *We* Elder answered.

"It was all for nothing then?" Aryn asked.

"It was all created to tell the story of Brian Steele so that our young could fully experience all of it firsthand."

"What happens to us now?" Kyla asked.

"The story has come to an end," The *We* Elder replied. "It is time for us to go home again. When Brian Steele departs this planet, this world created on the surface will fade and be no more."

"Why can't he remain here?" Úna asked. "We all could share this world in peace."

Steele opened his mouth to protest that he actually had a life back at his own home world that he very much wanted to get back to. But the *We* Elder beat him to the punch.

"You do not understand. When the *We* return to our original home, this entire planet will go with us back into the star. I do not think any of you would survive very long upon the surface."

"When we leave this place," Finvarra asked. "Or when Steele leaves this world, we will simply fade away?"

"Yes."

"What happens to us after?" Kyla asked, having only just found the love of her young life she was not so willing to just let if fade quietly into nothingness. "Do we just die and that is the end? Is there some afterlife, even for the unreal?"

"The answer to that question," The *We* Elder replied sagely, "can only be discovered by each being and only after it has ceased to exist."

"That's not very comforting, even for a cold unfeeling rock," Kyla replied.

"How long before Éerie is sent into the Sun?" Weaver asked.

"We will wait until your kind has left the surface," The *We* Elder said. "But do not take too long. Our young have already become eager to journey home and their desire has caught on among the older ones among us. As you have already seen, they do not hesitate too long to act on their desires."

"Well, boys and girls," Weaver exclaimed. "It looks like we'd better get going. Unless you all want to find out what it's like to be a side of beef at a barbecue."

The miners began gathering up their packs for the journey to the evac point. Finvarra reached out for his wife's hand in a surprising gesture of tenderness.

"I do not know what fate awaits us my wife," the King said. "But I will gladly face it with you at my side."

"And I, with you, my husband," Úna said, taking his hand in hers. "Shall we return to Cnoc Meadha?"

"If either it, or the castle remains? Of course. I can think of no better place to face the end. Kyla, Aryn, are you coming?"

"I want to soar in the sky with Nightmare one last time," Kyla said, turning to Aryn. "There is room for two aboard him."

"Let me turn Frisky loose and then one last journey together," Aryn agreed as he headed into the cave to free Frisky. Kyla followed him in to lead Nightmare out as well.

"Rhoslyn?" Úna asked the fairy.

"I will travel with you."

"Then let us depart," Finvarra said, sparing a final look

at Steele. "Farewell, my creator, and thank you for this life you granted us however short it has turned out to be."

Instead of popping out as they usually did, Finvarra, Úna and Rhoslyn simply faded away. Aryn led Frisky out of the cave and pointed him toward the forest

"Goodbye, old friend," Aryn said, slapping the horse hard on the rump. Frisky bolted into the forest, fading away before he raced out of sight. Kyla led Nightmare out and quickly mounted him. Aryn scrambled up behind her, locking his left arm around her midsection.

"I can think of worse ways to go," Aryn whispered in her ear, earning himself a sad smile and a quick kiss before Kyla urged Nightmare to take flight. On the ground below, Steele, Weaver and the miners watched the great beast soar into the clear blue sky...and it and its two riders faded into nothingness.

Steele looked away from the sky and over to the *We* Elder just in time to see the rock creature melting back into the ground without saying so much as goodbye.

"Well," Weaver said. "Looks like we'd better get a move on unless we want to get broiled. Benny, get 'em started down that path. C'mon, Brian, there's nothing more to see here."

Still somewhat shell-shocked by the revelations of the past few minutes, Steele numbly followed his friend and the rest of the miners down the path.

∾

The Planet Éerie
Costal Road Clearing

"WHAT THE HELL IS KEEPING THEM?" Johansson growled as he checked his watch for the tenth time in the past ten minutes. "They should have been here an hour ago."

"The terrain is uneven," Ensign Kamata said. "Depending on the extent of any injuries, it will slow them down."

"Is that your expert medical opinion, Doctor?" Johansson quipped.

"Aye, sir," Kamata answered, having been briefed by Littleton on the best way to handle the Captain when he was in one of his moods: Stand your ground. Johansson shot the Ensign a withering look before flipping on the communication station and calling his ship. "Pegasus, are you still tracking them?"

"Aye, Captain," Gatta replied. "They've stopped a couple of times for rest breaks, but they're moving now and should be coming into view in a quarter of an hour at most if they keep up the current pace."

"Very well," Johansson acknowledged. "Have Shuttle-2 ready to launch as soon as we start loading up down here."

"Understood."

"Johansson out." He said as he snapped off the unit and resumed staring at the point where the evacuees should finally come into view. He stood there like a marble statue until the first miner appeared around the corner twelve minutes later.

"Kamata," Johansson called out. "Go wake up the others and tell them it's time to get to work."

Over two hundred weary men and women slowly trudged into the clearing, making their way over as directed by the two pilots to Kamata's medical station. After getting the miners settled, the two pilots quickly distributed food and water, while Kamata tended to any injuries and began screening for any sign of what had affected the Shuttle-3 crew so as to ensure whatever it was didn't make it aboard the Pegasus. While his men went about their business, Johansson went looking for answers of his own.

"Which of you is in charge here?" Johansson called out to the group.

"I suppose that would be me, Captain," Weaver said, standing up.

"Good," Johansson said as he walked up to Weaver. "Maybe you can tell me exactly what the hell has been happening on this screwy planet?"

"I can," Weaver said. "But I doubt you're going to like what you're about to hear."

"Try me," Johansson shot back.

So Weaver laid it all out for the Captain, the *We*, how they had latched onto Steele's story and decided to create real world conditions, including shoving the planet millions of miles into a new orbit, and form an atmosphere, a sea and a living world for the Celtae, the Fae and the Romans to roam and play out Steele's story for them to experience. Weaver closed his story with the *We* Elder's warning that Éerie was soon to rejoin the star that had given birth to it eons ago and there was a dire need to get the hell off this planet before that happened. Johansson heard Weaver out quietly, never once interrupting the miner until the man had finished completely. Then the Captain tore him a new one.

"That has to be the biggest pile of horseshit anyone has ever tried to lay off on me," Johansson erupted. "Fairies, talking rocks, Romans? And all because some writer cooked up a story on a laptop? I've got six dead crew on a shuttle who literally fucked themselves to death while they were crashing and now you're telling me all of this nonsense?

"No, sir, I'm not buying any of it," Johansson raged on. "I'll tell you what is going on here. There is something in the air on this planet, or maybe there's some strange effect throughout the system that is making people do and see crazy things. No one gets aboard my ship until we figure out what it is!"

"What happened to the shuttle crew?" Weaver asked.

"Shuttle-3 crashed," Johansson repeated. "And when we finally cracked open the hatch at the crash site we found all six of them naked, out of their seats and obviously in the middle of a goddam orgy at the time of impact. Obviously there is something in the air here that makes people go insane."

"Úna," Weaver said, looking down at Steele, both men remembering the effect the Queen had on everyone when they'd seen her stark naked in the cave pool.

"What is an Úna?" Johansson demanded.

"Not a what, Captain," Steele said, finally joining the conversation as he stared at a point just over the Captain's shoulder. "A who. She is, was, a Fairy Queen who could have quite a powerful effect on anyone not prepared to deal with it. Your shuttle crew came into contact with her. The 'orgy' you saw was just the effect of their coming into contact with her. If it's any comfort, I doubt they even knew what hit them, both with her or when they hit the ground."

"You two honestly expect me to believe a single word of this shit?"

"Yes, Captain, we do," Weaver said. "And you had better believe us when we tell you we all need to get the hell off planet and fast. There is not a plague, or an airborne virus, here that we will take back up with us to your ship."

"It's going to take a lot more than just your assurances, gentlemen," Johansson barked. "I'm ready to run tests on everyone here from now until doomsday until I find out what is going on down here."

"If you won't believe us," Steele said, pointing behind the incredulous Captain. "How about that?"

Johansson turned to see what Steele was pointing at and immediately reached for his sidearm. Weaver clamped a strong hand over the Captain's, preventing him from pulling the weapon clear of its holster.

"Steady down, Captain," Weaver said calmly. "It's friendly."

"What the hell is that," Johansson asked, trying to comprehend how a pile of stacked rocks, with glowing green eyes could be walking toward him. Then it produced a mouth to open and begin speaking with.

"You must hurry," the *We* Elder said. "Our young are eager to return to our home and we cannot contain them much longer."

"We're leaving now," Weaver assured. "We just need a few more hours, right, Captain? Right, Captain?"

"Yes, right," Johansson said, finally forcing his mouth to work past the shock. "We'll have everyone off planet in eight hours."

"That will be sufficient," the *We* Elder said, pleased. "Farewell, Brian Steele. Thank you for sharing your story with the *We* and inspiring us to find our way back home. We will never forget you or the experiences you gave us."

With that, the pile of rocks seemed to sink back into the ground and was gone.

"Captain," Weaver said to the Captain who seemed frozen in place. "With all due respect, we need to get our asses in gear."

"Right," Johansson said, tearing his gaze away from the spot where the rocks had disappeared. "Kamata, shut down the quarantine protocols. Chandler, Unguwe, get at least eight people on board your shuttle. Get up to the ship, get'em offloaded and get back down here ASAP.

"Pegasus, this is the Johansson," The Captain barked as he activated the communications panel.

"Pegasus here, Captain."

"Gatta, there is no bio-hazard down here. I don't have time to explain, just shut down quarantine protocols and get all of the shuttles up and running. We need to get everyone off planet and we don't have a lot of time to get it done."

"But, Captain..."

"Stop arguing with me and do it, Gatta. I'll explain later but if we don't get moving we're all going to be fried to a crisp. So get moving, goddammit!"

The Captain snapped off the unit as his crew hustled eight miners aboard Shuttle-1. The craft quickly lifted off and headed up for the Pegasus, they watched it until it had flown far enough that they could no longer see it. Then he turned back to Steele and Weaver.

"We are going to have one hell of a long discussion after we get back on board the ship," Johansson said. "Because I still have a lot of questions about what exactly happened down here. And I'm betting the people we work for are going to have enough questions of their own to fill a goddamned library."

Johansson stormed off to get ready for the next shuttle arrival, leaving Weaver and Steele alone by themselves.

"None of this is your fault, Brian," Weaver said, divining his silent friend's thoughts.

"Isn't it? If I hadn't come here none of this would have happened."

"Yeah," Weaver said. "And if none of us had ever come here to begin with, you'd never have had to come out here, so maybe it's our fault and not yours? That's bullshit thinking and you know it. No one had any way of knowing what was here, or how it would react to us being here. And you certainly didn't intend for this to happen, did you?"

"Of course not. But Twenty-five people are dead because..."

"Because the universe is a dangerous place, no matter what part of it you happen to be in," Weaver interrupted. "Shit happens and people die. That's just the way it works, buddy."

"And what about the others?" Steele asked. "Aryn, Kayla, Rhoslyn, Finvarra, Úna and the rest. They thought they were living beings and then they just blink out of existence as it they never mattered."

"They mattered to you," Weaver said. "They mattered to the *We*."

"That's not much comfort," Steele said bitterly.

"Then make them matter," Weaver said, pointing at Steele's computer, "this time to everyone. Finish the story."

"You think it will work?"

"It can't hurt to try, can it?"

Steele stared long and hard at the laptop before reaching out and grabbing it. He headed for a now abandoned table and chair and fired up the unit.

"Hey, boss," Benny called out. "They want everyone to start gathering in groups of eight to get everyone loaded up faster."

"Go ahead and get in line," Weaver called back without looking away from the screen as Steele began typing. "We'll catch the last shuttle out. I wouldn't miss this for the world."

CHAPTER THIRTY-FOUR

We chase after ghosts and spirits and are left holding only memories and dreams. It's not that we want what we can't have; it's that we've held all we could want and then had to watch it slip away.
-- Charles De Lint

The Planet Éerie
Coastal Road Clearing

Brian Steele bent over his keyboard, focusing every ounce of concentration on the task at hand, zoning out everything else around him – Dan, the miners, the Captain constantly shouting orders, the roar of the sea beyond the cliff and the constantly blowing wind. He had little time to accomplish what he had in mind and, something in the back of his mind seemed eager to see how the story would end, the only way to find out would be available only as long as he remained planetside.

Even though they had never really existed, and whatever he did next would not survive beyond his departure, he felt an overwhelming compulsion to give these people he'd created here a proper ending to their story. To do that, he would need to go back to the point before he and the miners encountered Aryn, Kyla and Úna in the caves. With the basic outline laid out in his head, Steele started typing...

∽

Deblin
August, 81 A.D.

GENERAL GNAEUS JULIUS AGRICOLA, Roman governor of Britannia, once again sat brooding at his field desk in the dark recesses of his command tent, just outside the north gate of the city of Deblin. The Roman catapults and battering rams continued their assault on the walls and gates of the besieged Hibernian city. When either one first produced a breach offering his legion entry, there was little doubt the city would fall. But Agricola wasn't worried about that.

Plague.

The very word sent shivers of trepidation down the governor's spine.

I'd rather face an army of 30,000 Hibernian barbarians, than face another plague.

A massive Hibernian army was something his men were trained to deal with. That was something they understood and knew how to defeat. There was nothing understandable about a plague... especially an alien plague. Oh, he'd already taken all of the standard precautions. He'd ordered General Servius Marius Paterculus to quarantine the century of legionaries and the fifteen cavalrymen who'd investigated that fallen daystar — which was reported to be some kind of mysterious flying metal box.

What kind of wizardry could possibly make a huge metal box fly like that?

He was dealing with a complete unknown here. Would their standard procedures for quarantining those potentially exposed even be effective against an alien plague? None of those men had developed any notable symptoms as yet, but what kind of symptoms would an alien plague display... if any at all? Perhaps it might just cause men to suddenly keel over dead, without any warning. Who knew?

The detailed reports he's received from Paterculus indicated the "crew" of the daystar that landed at the edge of the forest wore silvery metallic suits of some kind. — Suits that covered their entire bodies without breaks, even appearing to include some kind of filter apparatus on the chest the creatures apparently breathed through. It wasn't armor, as the Romans understood it, as those suits appeared totally flexible... like a second skin. The shiny green suits worn by the next creatures to arrive were similar, except these included pellet-shaped tanks of some kind, worn on the back, which apparently fed "air," or whatever else those creature might breathe, into the helmet section through flexible hoses.

Obviously, these creatures saw the need to totally isolate themselves from anything to do with this accursed island. Jupiter only knows if I should just abandon this expedition and flee from this place of magical creatures, flying boxes and alien plagues.

A knock sounded on the tent pole, so Agricola raised his head from his hands and said, "Come."

A legionary from Agricola's personal guard stuck his head inside the tent flap and said, "My lord, a messenger has arrived with urgent news from Northern Caledonia."

"Bring him in," Agricola commanded, a slight feeling of dread seeping into his brain as he awaited the messenger.

"My lord," the man looked like he'd run the length of this accursed island, perhaps even across the sea from Caledonia itself judging from the ragged look of him. "The Highlanders have staged an uprising in Northern Caledonia, the frontier is in jeopardy. You are requested to retire from this place and come address this new threat."

Dread became shock. Should this uprising succeed the barbarians from the Highlands could sweep down the entire length of Caledonia. Britania itself could then be threatened. On the doorstep of Deblin, with control of this entire island within his grasp, Agricola knew he had no other choice. If they lost Caledonia and then Britania, then Hibernia would be of no use to Rome.

"See to it this man gets food and water," Agricola commanded as he scratched out a set of orders. "Send this to the flotilla commander blockading the harbor and then get the men preparing to break camp at first light."

"My Lord?" his aide asked, confused.

"We are withdrawing all of our legions from Hibernia," Agricola explained. "We will board our ships and sail immediately for Caledonia to relieve our legions there and put down this uprising."

"And the Hibernian campaign, my Lord?"

"Is postponed until further notice, we have no other choice under the circumstances."

"And Techtmar?"

"Send our Hibernian guides to him. I will send him a note explaining the situation in Caledonia and the High-landers. He will have to make do with his own troops and the Brigantes. If Jupiter is smiling upon us, he will be able to continue the campaign during our brief absence."

When the first sliver of light appeared in the eastern sky, Agricola and his legions were already marching to the rendezvous point south of the harbor. By the time the sun reached its zenith, they were aboard the ships and sailing away.

Sentries along the Deblin wall watched in disbelief as the Romans abandoned the siege and left Eire. As word spread throughout the city, the people cheered and a cele-bration to end all celebrations began. In the tallest tree in the area, Rhoslyn watched the Romans withdrawal in equal astonishment. When the last gallery sailed beyond the horizon she popped out to tell Aryn the incredibly unbeliev-able news.

∼

Just Outside the Village of Tallamore
August, 81 A.D.

TECHTMAR RECEIVED the news of the Roman with-drawal well, at least while any spying eyes that could report back to Rome were around. Once alone in his tent with his two most trusted aides-de-camp he let loose.

"Damn those thrice accursed Roman *Cúl Tóna!*" he raged. "Only a Roman could be such *cladhaire a bhuail-*

feadh buille feall ar iontaoibh ort as to snatch complete defeat from the clutches of absolute victory."

Having just called the top representative of Rome an asshole and a backstabbing coward in short order, Techtmar's aides were glad their leader had waited until less forgiving ears had departed to launch into his tirade. Now that Techtmar had gotten that tantrum out of his system, it was time to decide how to proceed with just 1,400 men under his command without a single Roman legionnaire for support.

"Under the circumstances, m'lord," one aide ventured. "Should we hold our position and suspend the campaign until we have a better idea of how long the Romans will be in Caledonia?"

"And allow the rest of the island to gather their forces together against us the minute they learn of the Romans' departure?" Techtmar thundered, incredulous at the thought of even pausing the campaign to avenge his father for a single moment much less halting it. "No. At first light we march on Tallamore and then onward to Deblin. We will finish what Agricola would not. And when that Roman *Cúl Tóna!* Returns to Eire he will be the one asking me for aid."

～

Aryn's Cave
August, 81 A.D.

ARYN WAS STILL SLEEPING when their entire world changed. Kyla was munching on crisps of bacon and pan-fried cornbread with slathers of some of Aryn's grape jam as her breakfast. Úna munched on some of the mushrooms and wild onions from their supper the night before. She also snarfed down several slices of the cornbread and jam Kyla offered.

"Your cooking has certainly improved, since you started spending so much time around Aryn," Úna said, with a sly smile. "Your attitude also seems to have mellowed somewhat as well. I don't think virginity suited you very well... it made you cranky."

"MOTHER!" Kyla blushed furiously.

Nightmare suddenly raised his head from the remaining deer carcass he'd been disemboweling, on full alert, looking further down the tunnel... giving off a loud, smoke-filled snort as Rhoslyn popped in. Seeing the fairy, he returned to his meal.

"Aryn," Rhoslyn exclaimed, in her excitement failing to register either Úna or Kyla's presence in the cave. "I have the most wonderful news!"

"What is it?" Aryn asked calmly, knowing that with some fairies what counted as important news oftentimes was anything but.

"The Romans have left the island."

"What?!" three voices roared as one, sending Rhoslyn scurrying behind an outcropping in fear.

"Rhoslyn," Úna ordered. "Come out here and explain yourself. Are you certain of what you saw?"

"Yes, my lady," Rhoslyn squeaked, her head barely peering above the rock she had taken refuge behind. "One of them ran into the camp and was taken straight into their leader's tent. Moments later the whole camp was in an uproar as they began taking down their tents and loading their carts and horses. No sooner had the sun began to shine than they were riding for the coast. The ships blockading the harbor at Deblin sailed to meet them and as soon as they got every man and beast aboard, off they sailed!"

"Was there some kind of counterattack from Deblin?" Aryn asked, puzzled by the Romans' behavior.

"No," Rhoslyn answered, rising a little further out from her hiding place. "It was all quiet from the city while Romans kept smashing away at the gate. Then, just when it seemed they were close to breaking it down, they left."

"But it makes no sense," Kyla remarked.

"No, it does not," Úna agreed. "I will return home to the castle and inform your father of the news of the Romans departure. Is Nightmare healed enough to carry you to Deblin?"

"I think he is," Kyla replied after giving him one last looking over.

"Then the two of you should make haste for Deblin and confirm what has happened," Úna said and without further ado, or even so much as a by your leave, popped out to head for her castle below.

"We'd better get going," Aryn said. "Rhoslyn, perhaps you should let the other Fae know what has occurred and see what else they can find out."

As they fairy popped out, Aryn followed Kyla and Nightmare outside. He hated leaving Frisky behind, but haste was needed here and Nightmare could reach Deblin much sooner.

"Can it really be true?" Kyla asked as Aryn climbed aboard behind her and the beast launched itself into the sky.

"I certainly hope so," Aryn answered, praying to whatever gods were listening that it was so.

～

The Village of Tallamore
August, 81 A.D.

SEAMUS FINNEGAN WAS GETTING FAR TOO old for this. When nearly fifteen hundred armed men gathered in an attack formation just beyond Tallamore, the village elders asked him and two other former soldiers to ride out and treat with the leader of the arrayed forces. When the small army had been spotted approaching the village the day before an urgent plea for help went out to Deblin and any other village that could send help in time. Fearing the worst, the women and girl-children along with the only boy under the age of three had been sent into hiding during the night. Every other man from four to one hundred years of age had formed a meager defensive line behind the negotiators.

Until some response was received, all the people of Tallamore could do was play for time and hope aid would come. With the flag of truce attached to a short pole in his hand, Finnegan led his small party of three out toward the leader. They had ridden three-quarters of the way out when the leader suddenly raised his hand and then quickly lowered in back down in a swift chopping motion. The air grew thick with arrows and the army surged forward, breaking into a full-throated charge.

Despite the shock of being dishonorably attacked while under a flag of truce, Finnegan whirled his mount around and tried to return to the line. But his horse had managed but two leaps toward safety when the arrows struck home, three of them impaling the old man in the back with such force that all three arrowheads penetrated out of his chest. The old man tumbled to the ground, long dead before his body struck the green grass. Grass now being watered with the blood of one its children.

The charging army trampled over Finnegan's body, as well as those of the other two negotiators, who fared little better than he had, and charged straight into the line of defenders. To their everlasting credit, the men and boys of Tallamore bravely stood their ground – and died almost as quickly as Finnegan had.

~

Deblin
August, 81 A.D.

ALL OF DEBLIN was still celebrating when Aryn and Kyle arrived. They'd flown over the area and found no trace of the Roman invaders aside from the tracks of a large army marching toward the sea. Clearly, Rhoslyn had reported exactly what she had seen.

"But why would they suddenly leave," Aryn asked as they inspected the heavily damaged gate below. "Only a few more blows with their battering ram and they would have broken through. This makes no sense."

"As long as they are truly gone," Kyla answered, "it little matters why. Perhaps King Doimthech can explain what has happened here."

Bringing Nightmare into a swooping dive, the beast settled in for a soft landing near where the King and his court were leading their people in celebration.

"Hail and welcome," the King greeted them. "It is truly

a great day. The vile Romans have fled the field and scurried home like frightened rabbits to their warrens."

"A great day indeed, sire," Aryn replied, only just keeping a dubious tone out of his voice. "How did this great victory come about? Were they driven off?"

"Hah," Doimthech scoffed. "They huffed and puffed at our gates until they exhausted themselves and gave up when they saw it was fruitless to continue."

Aryn and Kyla exchanged a look that spoke fully of their doubts of the King's boasts even as the people roared in approval of them.

"They have returned back to Rome no doubt," Doimthech continued. "We'll never see them back here again, I'll wager. The threat to our great city, and our island, is over."

"Have all of the Romans and their armies departed?" Aryn asked when the latest round of cheering subsided. "There were more than just Romans among their ranks."

"Bah," Doimthech scoffed. "A handful of rabble-rousers following Techtmar at most. If that lot shows their face around here we'll give them a good thrashing. Let them roam around bothering the villages until they all grow old and gray."

"What do mean 'bothering the villages'? Are they attacking defenseless people out there?"

"Making themselves nuisances at worst. Last we heard they were conquering the great 'city' of Tallamore," Doimthech scoffed. "They'll likely get defeated by the old women of that village long before they dare try Deblin."

"My grandparents are in Tallamore," Aryn said quietly, his face stricken with worry, as another round of loud cheering erupted. Without a word, Kyla urged Nightmare back into flight, leaving behind the celebration and hoping they were not too late to help save Tallamore.

~

The remains of what had once been the Village of Tallamore
August, 81 A.D.

LONG BEFORE THEY could make out the village itself, they saw the smoke rising from where the village should be and then they saw Techtmar and his army leaving behind the charred remains of what had been a peaceful village. Kyla could feel the rage burning within Aryn, felt her own rage growing and what had to have been a slaughter and knew that Aryn's response would be her own. She produced the dragon war bow even as Aryn opened his mouth to ask for it.

Without a word he took the bow, closed his eyes and unleashed his rage in the form of a never-ending supply of arrows that never once failed to take the life of a murderous enemy. Kyla fired her own arsenal at any target she could locate as Nightmare swooped back and forth over the terrified army below.

Techtmar's men scrambled about wildly in disorganized terror as no hiding place could be found to spare them from arrows that seemed to turn corners and change direction in mid-flight. Those fortunate not to fall to an arrow suffered incineration from blue fire than rained down mercilessly from the sky.

As fate would have it, Techtmar was the last to remain

alive and he suffered the double blow of both arrow and fire. Aryn's last arrow impaled him against a young oak tree just as Kyla's final bolt struck, setting the tree ablaze in a gruesome funeral pyre for the would-be conqueror of Eire who had failed after all in his quest to avenge his father.

Aryn reached back for another arrow, but found none waiting for his hand to grasp. It was if the quiver itself knew that no more enemies remained to be slain. He'd fallen into that same trance as before, only this time it hadn't taken a twelve-foot pixie to bring him out of it. As reality returned, he became aware of Kyla's lips upon his and she was staring at him intently. Seeing sanity had returned in his eyes, she broke off the kiss and leaned back.

"It's over, Aryn," she said as she took the bow and quiver from him and sent them back to where they belonged. "They are all dead."

He nodded his head, then looked over at the burning village. His enhanced eyesight scanning the ruins until he found who he was looking for just outside the village. His grandmother, kneeling over a horribly battered body, tears flowing down her cheeks. He did not need to look at the body to know who it had been, the only person it could be: His grandfather.

Pointing to where she was so Kyla could direct Nightmare, they flew down and Aryn leapt off as soon as it touched down and approached his grandmother.

"Aryn," she said around her sobs. "Oh, Aryn..."

He took his grandmother into his arms and just held her. It was all he could do for her right now. Kyla produced a blanket of fine silk and laid it across the old man's body. He had already avenged his grandfather by slaying his killer. All he could do for the old man now would be to bury him properly...and fulfill one final promise.

~

The mouth of the River Erne, near Ballyshannon
August, 81 A.D.

THEY HAD SEEN to the burial of his grandfather, and all of the men who had died valiantly trying to defend their homes at Tallamore. The surviving women and young children – all but one maid – had decided to stay on and rebuild, with a single exception. Aryn's grandmother.

Taking possession of two of Techtmar's surviving horses and a small wagon, Aryn had driven his grandmother to Ballyshannon. But first he had sent Rhoslyn off on an errand with instructions to retrieve a certain box and then bring it to him at the mouth of the River Erne. Kyla had ridden along on Nightmare, who had transformed into a much less frightening steed.

Rhoslyn popped in just as Aryn pulled up to a halt and helped his grandmother down from the wagon.

"But why are we here, Aryn?" The old woman asked, mystified by her grandson's refusal to say anything more than it was a surprise from her late husband.

"Because many years ago," Aryn finally explained as he walked her to the riverbank, "Grandfather asked me to do one thing after he died."

"Bring me to a river miles from home?"

"No," Aryn said as he took possession of the box from Rhoslyn. "To bring you home."

"Home? Here? Have you gone mad, child?"

Aryn merely opened the box and took out the red, feathered cap and cloak, the *cohuleen druith*, and placed them into her hands. The old woman's eyes went wide as she first caught sight of them as if a long-forgotten memory had suddenly made itself known once again. As her hands touched the cap and cloak, her eyes lit up brightly and she quickly donned the items.

In just moments she began to transform from an old crone and into a woman of great beauty. She was once again a mulrruhgach and Aryn could see why his grandfather had fallen so helplessly in love with her, even had he not heard her sing.

"Aryn, I remember now," Clydie exclaimed.

"Grandfather said he wanted you to be able to go home again once he was no longer alive."

"Home," she repeated, looking out at the sea where she had once roamed free. After a long minute, she tore her gaze away from the shinning water to say goodbye to her grandson. "I did love him, you must know that, even though he took me away from my home."

"I do," Aryn said. "So did he. He loved you, Grandmother, and hated that to love you he had to deny you your home."

"I have to go now, Aryn," she said, looking back quickly at the sea. "And I'll likely never see you again. Take good care of yourself, grandson. And love her as much as your grandfather loved me."

"I will. Goodbye, Grandmother."

With a final kiss on the cheek, she turned and sprinted toward the sea. As she reached the water's edge she leapt up into the air to dive into the water. In midair her legs began to fuse together and just before her fingertips touched the surface of the water they had formed into a long tail. She dove full into the water and never resurfaced.

"She's home and happy now," Rhoslyn said then popped out without another word.

"We should all be so lucky," Aryn said. "It has been so long, battling invaders, I'm not sure what is home anymore ."

"We'll find out together," Kyla replied. "But first, we have one piece of unfinished business to attend to."

"What's that?"

"Not what, my love," Kyla said. "Where and with whom."

~

Deblin
August, 81 A.D.

THE KING OF DEBLIN, Dáire Doimthech, was still leading the celebration two days later when his world came to an abrupt end.

Without warning Nightmare swooped in on a fast-landing right in front of the King, flicking one foreleg out just enough to send him painfully bouncing along on his royal posterior. Seeing their King so unceremoniously abused brought an immediate halt to the festivities. Before any of the royal guard could come to their fallen King's aid, a thunderous popping sound all but flattened everyone in the vicinity as Finvarra, Úna and Rhoslyn popped in near Nightmare. Úna and Rhoslyn were their normal sizes while Finvarra had arrived standing fully ten feet in height and growing in height with each passing second.

Grabbing the downed King in one hand, while relieving

the man of his crown with the other, Finvarra shot all the way up to forty feet in height, towering over the city with a look of anger upon his face that would frighten away all of the other gods themselves.

"Your father got your message, dear," Úna said by way of explanation to Kyla, who only favored Aryn with a mysterious smile when he asked what the hell was going on.

"Dáire Doimthech," Finvarra's voice boomed out, and surely was heard in every corner of the island. "When the Roman invaders first landed upon Eire, you were informed of their presence. What did you do?

"Nothing!" Finvarra continued without letting the dangling King respond. "You hid behind these walls like a coward. How many died while you hid in safety rather than drive off the invaders when fate had given you a perfect chance to do so? You are unworthy of your crown and unfit to tread the grass and soil of this island!"

With that pronouncement the giant Finvarra mightily flung Doimthech far to the west, well out into the ocean. None assembled in Deblin witnessed the landing, but at the speed, distance and height the former King had traveled, the water would be harder than granite itself. Some fortunate sea life had a royal feast that night. After dispatching the former King, Finvarra shrunk back down to a less fearsome height of eight feet, tall enough to still have to reach down to place the crown upon Aryn's head.

"Your cowardly King is dead," Finvarra pronounced as he lowered the crown into place. "You need a King who has fought for Eire, fought the invaders and destroyed those that dared stayed behind and came to the defense of those your former King abandoned. Aryn is such a man and is truly worthy of leading, not only this great city, but all of Eire itself. All hail, Aryn, King of Eireland!"

"All hail the King," the crowd cried out, mostly in fear of the giant god glowering at them, but a few in real appreciation of the accomplishments of their new King.

"There is one thing your new King is lacking however," Finvarra said slyly, holding his hand toward his wife and daughter. Úna gently shoved Kyla forward and Finvarra led his daughter's hand to Aryn's. "A queen."

The people cheered again as Finvarra leaned forward to whisper in Aryn's ear.

"The least you can do is make an honest woman out of her, my boy," he jibed, enjoying the slight look of panic on Aryn's face as he worked out what Finvarra's remark implied. The fairy King laughed aloud, letting his son-in-law off the hook. "One bit of advice when it comes to dealing with a wife, lad. Always let them think they've manipulated you into doing what you had planned on doing all along. It makes it so much easier to get them into bed."

With one final chuckle and a slap on the back that would have flattened a forest, Finvarra led one more cheer for the new King and Queen and then got out of the way so that the royal couple could be congratulated by their Court.

"Will their reign be a happy one, I wonder?" Úna asked aloud as she looked on.

"It will be," Finvarra said.

"You've seen this?"

"I see a long life for them both," Finvarra said. "The Romans will be tied up with the Highlanders for much longer than they think and by the time the next Roman galley sets anchor in Eire waters, they will come looking to trade and not to invade. Theirs will be a time of peace and happiness."

CHAPTER THIRTY-FIVE

"I've come to accept the voices in my head... I just wish they didn't spit when they talk."
-- Michael Gibson

The Planet Eerie
3232 A.D.

"THE END." WEAVER SAID ALOUD, HAVING READ OVER Steele's shoulder the entire time he'd been writing the final chapters of the story. "That's damn good work, Brian."

"I hope so," Steele said as he saved it, he felt exhausted mentally and physically. "I just wish they actually were aware of how their story ended."

"The last shuttle is coming in, gentlemen," Johansson called out. "Get aboard or get left behind."

Aside from the three of them, only Kamata was still on the surface and that only in case of an unexpected medical emergency occurring before the last evacuee departed. As soon as Shuttle-5 landed and opened its hatch, Kamata, Weaver and Steele – holding onto his computer – scrambled aboard and strapped in. Johansson looked around one last time, just to make sure some idiot hadn't wandered off and was about to be left behind. Once assured that no human being was left in the area, the Captain boarded the shuttle and sealed the hatch behind him.

"Hey, look at that!" the pilot called out, pointing out the window.

All six men looked out to see the *We* Elder standing a few yards away, his arm up and waving farewell. Standing next to him were a handful of similar looking rock creatures of various sizes. Without knowing how he knew it, Steele understood that these were some of the adult and juvenile *We* – the ones that had started all of this when they'd tapped into his subconscious – that had come to bid him farewell.

"Let's get going," Johansson said, having taken the co-pilot's seat.

"Pegasus to Shuttle-5," Gatta's voice came over the com.

"Go ahead Pegasus," Johansson replied, as the shuttle lifted off the ground.

"Captain," Gatta said excitedly. "We've had long-range camera's monitoring the area. The outlying forest and seas are starting to fade out. There's some kind of massive celebration at the big city we located and it too is fading from view."

"Hey," the pilot suddenly exclaimed. "Look at that fleet of ancient ships out there."

Turning their attention out the starboard windows, they could see dozens of old wooden ships sailing to the East, away from the island.

"It's a flotilla of Roman galleys," Steele said to no one in particular. *Agricola's flotilla taking him back to Scotland, what the Romans called Caledonia.* Weaver made the connection and gave his friend a big smile.

"I think they got to live out the story after all," Weaver said.

Steele could only nod his head in relief.

"Captain," Gatta reported. "It looks like the atmosphere is fading along with everything else and the planet is starting to move again toward the sun."

As they looked on, the galleys below faded out, followed by the sea they had been sailing on. The forest and everything else on the island below quickly followed suit.

"Holy shit, what is that?" The pilot exclaimed.

Éerie was once again a barren world, but on the surface they could now see millions of rocky creatures, all with green glowing eyes, and all with their arms stretching out toward the sun.

"Gatta," Johansson ordered. "As soon as the shuttle has docked and is secured, break orbit. Don't wait for me to get to the bridge, just get as much distance between us and that planet as fast as you can. I don't want to get caught in that star's gravity well."

"Aye, sir."

Shuttle-5 turned away from the surface and made top speed back to the Pegasus, which welcomed the last of its crew and the evacuees and then hauled ass away for Éerie.

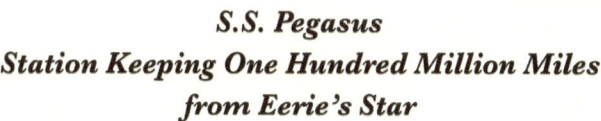

S.S. *Pegasus*
Station Keeping One Hundred Million Miles
from Eerie's Star

3232 A.D.

BY THE TIME Johansson reclaimed his command chair, the Pegasus was well away from the dangerous pull of the star's gravity. Weaver and Steele had been invited to join Johansson on the bridge so they could witness something never-before-seen: A planet plunging back into the star that had borne it.

"Are we recording this?" The Captain asked as he stepped onto the bridge.

"Have been ever since the planet started moving again, sir," Sanchez replied. "Figured it was the only way anyone would believe us."

"Good thinking," Johansson replied, without the slightest trace of irony in his voice given his reaction to Sanchez's initial report of a wandering planet.

They all watched silently as the mysterious planet picked up speed and drove straight into the fiery star.

~

The Planet Eerie
3232 A.D.

AS THE FIRES of the outer edges of the star claimed Eerie, billions of *We* voices cried out in joyous unison:

HOME!

And trillions upon trillions more *We* voices cried out

from the depths of the star in reply:
WELCOME HOME!

~

S.S. Pegasus
The Eerie System
3232 A.D.

"WOW." Weaver said quietly, his comment carrying clearly across the silent bridge as Eerie disappeared in fire.

"I guess that's as good as any other way to describe it," Johansson said. "Mr. Sanchez, lay in a course to Cælius. Let's get these folks on their way home."

"Aye, sir," Sanchez replied. "Course laid in and ready to execute."

"Make the jump, Ensign," Johansson ordered. "Gatta, please escort Mr. Steele and Mr. Weaver to my quarters. They can bunk in there. I'll probably be spending my time off the bridge in my office anyway, trying to figure out how the hell I'm going to report this insanity."

"Aye, Captain," Gatta replied. "Gentlemen, if you'll follow me."

"Mr. Steele," Johansson called out before they left the bridge.

"Yes, Captain?"

"The next time you're going to come out in space to do a job..."

"Sir?"

"Leave your damned computer at home, please?"

Johansson finished, smiling to take any sting out of the remark.

"Count on it, Sir." Steele answered, turning back around to follow Gatta to the Captain's quarters.

"Mr. Sanchez," they heard Johansson say. "When we get to Cælius, and if you should happen to discover it isn't there, just keep it to yourself. I honestly won't want to know."

Gatta showed the tired men into the cabin and left them to get some rest. Steele fired up his computer and quickly typed out a message to his editor, attaching the finished story to it before sending it on its way. He leaned back in the comfortable chair while he waited for confirmation that the message had been sent.

"Well," Weaver said. "Looks like we'll have to flip for who gets the nice cozy bed and who gets..."

He trailed off as he looked at his friend, sound asleep in the chair. A message sent window was flashing on the screen. Weaver shut down the unit and then pulled a blanket off the bed.

"Looks like that's settled," Weaver said as he draped the blanket over his friend and dimmed the lights before crawling into the bed. "Good night buddy. Better get some rest now, you're going to have to work your ass off to come up with your next story if you want it to top this one."

The S.S. Pegasus soared through the dark night of space and when it arrived at the point among the stars where Cælius was supposed to be, much to the relief of everyone aboard the ship, Cælius was actually there.

AFTERWORD

This is the fourth book written by Gibson Michaels. It will also be the final book written by Gibson Michaels. There is no sadder sentence in the history of all mankind than the one I just typed before this one.

I'd known Gibson Michaels, who was actually born Michael Gibson and took some good-natured ribbing from me over the long hard search he embarked upon to create his pen name by the way, for thirteen years and considered him not only a good friend, but the older brother I'd never had since I was the eldest child of my family.

Thanks to the wonders of the Internet Age, we had never met in person, nor had we so much as spoken over the phone. Yet good friends we were since the days we both haunted the same fantasy football website. Mike's screen name was Rebel (we always called him General or Reb or some combination of both) and mine was Scribe (okay, so neither one of us went into extreme mental gymnastics when we cooked up our *nom de plumes*).

Over the past few years, when we both decided it was time to get serious about our fiction writing, we both encouraged each other, read each other's works, rejoiced at each other's successes and commiserated over each other's setbacks.

In March of 2017 I was supposed to travel to Houston and meet Mike in person for the first time as well as meet the writer's group he had founded. But a mere few hours before departure I got very sick and was unable to travel. On September 14th Mike was heading out to nearby Santa Barbara and I would drive up and meet him there.

Only fate had other plans. Seven days before that meeting, Mike passed away suddenly. Months later, as I write this, I still choke up when I think of that day and what we all lost. I was not the only person who had counted Mike as a great friend. Many others who both Mike and I had known from the old fantasy football website felt the same sense of loss as I and to this day still feel heartsick that he is no longer with us.

I can think of no better epitaph for any man than to have this said of him by someone who'd also only known him from afar over the Internet: "I loved that old man." Our friend Larry, who we'd known as Guido, a man my age who like myself unashamedly wept like a baby for weeks after that day – like I am right now as I write this.

And if Mike's friends are feeling this loss this way, you can only imagine how his wife and family have felt.

He was a great friend, one any of us would happily have gone to war for if so called and he will be missed.

He wrote a great military science fiction trilogy, the final book earning Dragon Award Finalist in the inaugural

Dragon Awards in 2016. He lost to the legendary David Weber but was very satisfied to have been a finalist.

He began working on *Éerie* in late 2016 and I had the pleasure of reading the first 30,000 words when he asked me if I thought it was worth finishing. I read it and told him if he didn't I'd fly out to Houston and kick his butt.

He was working on it when he passed and when his wife had mentioned that he was close to being done, I asked if someone in his writing group who'd been reading each chapter as he finished it, was going to try to take it up and complete it.

"Actually," she messaged back to me. "We were thinking of asking you to finish it."

If you had the over on .000001 seconds as for how long it took me to say yes, you lost your money.

Because if there was anything I could do for my friend as one last thing to do on his behalf, it was to see that his final book was completed so it could be published and read. And there was no way in hell I was not going to pick up Reb's banner and carry it on to the finish.

So you can imagine, when I got the manuscript and the notes from the critique group spread out on my desk and after I had spoken with his wife and son about what he had in mind for the rest of the book (because a certain coffee-lovin' writer didn't use notes or outlines), the first thing I did was – if I may be allowed to shamelessly steal James Garner's line from *Space Cowboys* – was recite The Shepard's Prayer. Alan Shepard's Prayer as he sat on the launch pad prior to the first manned Mercury launch back in the 1960s:

"Dear Lord, please don't let me fuck this up!"

Hopefully, if I have done my job, only those few people who have actually read the manuscript up to the point where Mike left off will be able to tell where I picked up the story. (And really, if you think you know, don't send me a note with your guess, just let me carry on in blissful ignorance.)

I know there is no way I could write exactly what he would have word for word. But I'd like to think I came pretty damned close and at least matched it in spirit.

So thank you, dear reader, for coming along on this final adventure of Mike's creation. And thank you to his family for entrusting it into my care. I am honored, and humbled, that you chose me for this task and I very much hope I lived up to that trust. And thank you Dawn Greenfield Ireland for editing this final work of Mike's to make it the very best sendoff it could possibly be for our dear friend.

As for Mike, I suppose when that day comes when I fade from this world he'll likely be there to let me know how I did. He'll hand me a Dr. Pepper (he knows I take my caffeine ice cold) and give me a hug if I got it right.

And if I didn't, he'll hand me a Dr. Pepper, give me a hug and lead me off to the woodshed saying, "Now, Scribe, how the hell did you ever come up with that ending, boy?"

-- *Richard Paolinelli*

ABOUT THE AUTHOR

Gibson Michaels was born in Beech Grove, Indiana as Michael Gibson. As an only child, he began spinning tales while walking the family farm. After returning from Vietnam as an electronics specialist in the US Navy, he worked as a field engineer for IBM, a supervisor in a Naval Defense plant, and technical instructor at ABC Network. The oil and gas industry brought Gibson to Houston, where he continued his writing craft working on technical manuals for companies such as Hydril, and Toshiba.

Retiring in 2008, Gibson began to pursue his passion, writing science fiction. His first project, The Sentience Trilogy went on to become Amazon best sellers, and gained him his first nomination as a Dragon Award finalist.

Gibson was a member of several Houston area writing guilds as well as Science Fiction and Fantasy Writers of America.This is Gibson's fourth book.

www.ingramcontent.com/pod-product-compliance
Lightning Source LLC
Chambersburg PA
CBHW020930020726
47495CB00002B/424